MW00322955

THE RED SERPENT

ROBERT LOW

CANELO

First published in the United Kingdom in 2019 by Canelo

This edition published in the United Kingdom in 2020 by

Canelo Digital Publishing Limited
Third Floor, 20 Mortimer Street
London W1T 3JW
United Kingdom

A CIP catalogue record for this book is available from the British Library.

Print ISBN 978 1 78863 768 8
Ebook ISBN 978 1 78863 503 5

Look for more great books at www.canelo.co

Printed and bound in Great Britain by Clays Ltd, Elcograf S.p.A.

Chapter One

In the second year of Marcus Aurelius Severus Alexander Augustus

His chest was tight, his mouth was dry and that was all irony because his bowels were loose as water and everywhere else was slick with sweat. Inside, panic built like a fire and drove sick up into Drust's throat.

Not for the first time, he cursed the place, the goddess Fortuna and the assurances he'd been given that the Parthians were all done with, falling apart with every robed turban-head fighting with his neighbour.

It will be easy, he had been told, to get to Dura-Europos these days along a solid, dependable caravan route leading to the western end of the Silk Road.

Across from him, Drust saw Quintus like a comforter, a solid, warming sight with the sour-milk light falling on his dirt-etched face. He still wore his thick cloak, draped against the night chill – but the night was going and the rising heat, added to the danger, made faces wet-slick with sweat.

Dying for a drink. It was such a trite phrase, dropped in so frequently to every conversation that it had long since lost meaning – save for here and now. They crouched behind rough stone walls no higher than their knees if they had been standing, but if they had been standing, Jabal Tayy slingers, out there in the yellow gritted dunes, would have smacked them down.

The tribesmen had enough ammunition to do it, Drust knew, and the only mercy in them was that they had left the camels alone – they wanted them alive and only people needed to die; more than a few were now stink and flies.

There was another low wall ahead and to the left and a crouch of sweated men behind it, head-coverings gone, faces grim and set; they were luminous in the bad dawn light, even allowing for the blood and filth on their white robes. Not a star shone and the palms round the oasis stood like wild-haired harridan shadows against the black vault of the night – then something cracked like a whip near Drust's head.

A figure slithered in with a shower of grit, making Drust curse and choke.

'If Manius were here with his bow,' Sib said, breathing heavily, 'those stone-hurlers would be screaming.'

Manius wasn't here. Manius had supposedly been dead for years but Sib had never believed it, the same sure way he had once believed Manius to be a *jnoun*, some sort of demon. For six years since they had come back from exile in the far south of Africa, Drust and the Brothers had filtered slowly up and down the desert lands, from Tingis to Alexandria, dealing in grain and animals and sand for the amphitheatres. They had word that Manius had been sent to the mines and that Dog had freed him because he was in favour, his golden boy Elagabalus now Emperor and his golden ma equally raised.

Then had come the fall of them both, two years ago, and the rise of their cousin Alexander. Drust was sure Dog and Manius were dead – he had heard of them both being killed in the purges and the Brothers had had a mourn, spilled salt and wine to their memories.

It had come as a stun, like a sharp blow to the temple, when Drust had the message, sent from deep in the heart of Parthian darkness. Manius and Dog were alive and in need of help.

Kag called out, almost sounding cheerful. He was laying out his *gladius* and a curved knife, but they were for the final moments, when the tribesmen rushed in with their own blades. For now the surrounding goat-fuckers skulked and shot – Drust could see them, leaping up, whirling their slings, then dropping down again. Not that they were in any danger – no one in the caravan had anything to return fire with.

He worked his sweaty fist on the hilt of the sword, an old friend from the *harena*, worn dangerously smooth in the grip; stone splinters flew up near Kag's head and Drust wanted to call out for him to watch it before he realised what a stupid shout that was. Gripping the sword, he squinted into the harsh dawn glare and heard someone shifting closer to him; there was a sound like wet mud thrown against a wall, a sharp grunt, and a body crashed down behind him.

'Hard to see the little bastards, ain't it?'

The voice was surprisingly gentle and Drust knew it at once, half turned to see Praeclarum crawling over the fallen corpse of one of the camel-herders. It was still twitching, but she noticed only long enough to confirm that he was not going to recover.

'Time those bastards from the fort got here,' Drust said and Praeclarum admitted she had considered the possibility they might not.

'They are all around, these rag-arses,' she pointed out. 'When they think we are weakened enough, they will rush us. The fort might not get here before that.'

'No, listen, be pragmatic,' Drust said witheringly. 'Don't try and offer cheer, or the love of Fortuna.'

She made a moue. 'Well, we could make a run for it, but they will wait for us to pass where they lie among the scrub. Then it's a knife in the back and left for the women. Even I don't want that and I have no fruits for them to cut off.'

Drust made a small shivery noise in his throat, then scrambled round in panic as a dark shape slid up to them.

'Authentēs,' said a familiar voice and Drust's hoarse voice cursed him.

'I almost gave you iron,' he said bitterly and Kisa's eyes gleamed in the sheen of his dark face.

'That would be a hard thing for us both, I am thinking.'

'One less idiot *mavro* in the world,' Praeclarum said moodily, turning back to peer out.

Kisa Shem-Tov made a non-committal head bob. 'The honourable lady knows best,' he answered, with a smile like the delivery of venom.

'Can you get us out, Kisa? Possible, d'you think?'

The man sucked his teeth as he thought. Then he nodded brightly to Drust. 'No.'

Praeclarum laughed, soft as rotten aloes. Kisa scuttled into cover while the dawn flickered over the oasis. A little way to the north of it, Drust knew, was Dura-Europos where the fort was. He had sent Stercorinus two days ago, before the Jabal Tayy had fully closed in, but he wasn't sure if the man had got clear. Wasn't sure, if he was honest, if the man was reliable. Stercorinus was a whip-thin length of leg and arm the colour of baked mud and naked save for a loincloth and a double-handed curved blade used by Palmyrans. He claimed to be Palmyran but Drust was sure that was a lie. Most of Stercorinus was a lie.

'You put too much faith in that goat-fucker,' Praeclarum grumbled and Drust did not know whether she spoke of Kisa Shem-Tov or Stercorinus. Not that it mattered, he thought.

4

They'd got Stercorinus a few months back, from a School in Antioch which was falling apart and selling off stock – he had been cheap, even as a 'bonded *harena* fighter' because, the *lanista* reliably informed everyone, he was as shrieking mad as a bag of burning harpies.

Kisa Shem-Tov was a Jew, a freedman from some mountain sect round the Dark Sea and an expert with camels, thievery and procuring. Just what this band needed, as Kag had said at the time. He had come to them with the message, sent by some tribal leader, a friend of Rome in Dura.

Praeclarum was once billed as the Queen of the Amazons and had fought in the *harena* with a curved knife and a lasso. When old Emperor Septimius Servillius had banned women from being gladiators, she had been sold on and on and on, too homely to be a whore, too unlearned to be a house slave and too snarling to be trusted. She had run at least once and had the neck-brand that told of it – Quintus, smiling like a curve of the Euphrates, had bought her for 'nothing' in Emesa two months before and if he'd had designs there, quickly revised them and pretended otherwise.

Now they were all Brothers of the Sand even if one was a sister. Procuratores, a wry name for a collective of people who said little but thought rich – the term applied properly to the *procuratores dromii*, those luckless who had to dart out into he crashed wreckage of splintered chariots and ruin to clean up the mess before the next circuit of the Circus. They had cleaned up the mess of their patron, Servillius Structus, for years until his death.

The shadows slanted and the sky lightened; the shooting slackened but no one was eager to move. Drust had discarded his head-covering, which had protected his neck and had a veil to draw over the face. He was sorry he had now and was looking round for it when he heard the li-li-li-li-li from out beyond the drift of dunes, a high, shrill call that chilled the sweat to cold soup. For a moment the fetid air hung, panic weighing duty, fear battling the code that said gladiators never run. Why? Because the *harena* is a circle – what's the point? You only die tired and back where you began.

Others heard it too and dealt with the fear in their own way – a voice bawled out: 'Who are we?'

'Fortuna's fucked,' a voice roared back. 'The sand is our country.'

Drust blessed Quintus – and Ugo, who was clearly starting to snort and work his shoulders round his big axe. Drust wiped his lips with the sweated back of his sword-hand, tasting the salt. Praeclarum turned her chap-cheeked face and grinned at him; she had a mouth of teeth that made it look as if she was trying to eat cobbed corn through a fence.

'That skinny rat Stercorinus might have footed it to the dunes he came from,' she said. 'He can pass for one of them better than any of us save the Jew, or maybe Sib. Shouldn't be surprised if he is out there with a knife of his own and looking to commit unspeakables.'

Drust did not want to think that of Stercorinus but the Palmyran was wily and had some unshakeable belief that he knew when he would die, come to him in a vision from Bel-Shamun, the god of the Palmyrans. He never said what it was and Drust wondered if the prophecy involved a desert oasis and screaming tribals.

Yet they were all bound together by the sand and the blood.

'They are coming,' Drust said dully, though it was hardly necessary – the tide of tribesmen, turbaned and robed, washed up over the sand with their chilling, high-pitched li-li-li-li-li cries.

6

He heard Kag roaring his way to his feet and then a man came at him, a snarl with a beard and a curved dagger raised above his head, so that Drust had to meet him on the rise with the *gladius*. Watched the dagger hit and slide sideways along the sword, and when the tribal, unable to stop moving, lumbered past, Drust back-stroked him. Felt the jar, heard the crack of his backbone and the scream, but didn't turn to look because there were more.

The grip jolted in his fist, his head buzzed with his own roaring and he heard Ugo bawling and cursing somewhere close. Quintus flickered at the edge of his vision, dancing and weaving and slicing.

The man in front of him dropped a spear, clutched his flushed-red robes round his belly as if to seal the lipless wound, to stop his insides spilling out. Wouldn't work, Drust thought dully as he elbowed the man to one side and took another.

Too many. It was shriek and ringing metal, blood, sand, drool, and no more planning, just wild panic, stumbling from one fight to another, working on old, ingrained training and desperate reactions.

A man loomed up, curved knife and snarl, same as all the others. Drust was too late to duck or dive, or do anything other than go over backwards when the man collided with him. They rolled in a whirl of blinding, gritty sand and when Drust tried to spring back up he found he'd made it only to his hands and knees. The warrior, his veil flapping loose, showed bad teeth in a worse grin; the knife went up and Drust tried to move, tried to blink the sand away, spit it out of a sered mouth and knelt like a sacrifice-ox waiting for the priest.

The knife-man suddenly flew backwards as if he had been dragged; the weight of his body knocked Drust over and he

7

rolled on his back, staring up in bewilderment at a man on a camel. How had he got here?

The man wore a *keffiyeh* round his face and helmet, white as driven snow. Beneath it was a dusty white tunic that showed he had another beneath it, this one of metal lappets. He had a cloak, bright as fresh blood, and his legs were a flutter of Parthian trousers touching the sides of a great, dust-coloured grumble of camel. He pulled a fresh throwing spear from a quiver behind his right leg while the knife-man curled and writhed round the first one he had thrown.

'Dromedarii!'

Someone bellowed it out with delight, a roar of relief.

The blood-cloaked men loped their beasts round the little fortress of low walls while the tribesmen fled screaming, showered with javelins, skewered with arrows. Ugo, his hair and beard matted with sweat and dust, raised his terrifying axe in the air and gave a shout of recognition which all the others picked up, herders, loaders, watermen, everyone. The water in the oasis flushed pink.

And while they did it, Stercorinus acknowledged it as if it was for him alone, perched on his own camel, grinning his gaps and gums and waving, while a shrill voice called out who had saved them.

'The Red Men.'

Drust crawled wearily to his knees until his eyeline found a hand; when he looked up he saw Quintus's lopsided grin.

'Tell me again why we are here?'

'Because of fucking Dog and fucking Manius,' Kag growled, overhearing this. He wanted to spit but had no water left in his mouth. 'I don't know why we bother – the pair of them are dead. I know – I offered a spill of good drink to the gods in their memory.'

Because they were also Brothers of the Sand, Drust thought. Because of a message, which said to speak to Uranius of the 20th in Dura. Drust had no idea who Uranius was and he would have ignored the message entirely save for two reasons. One was that it was written in Latin, on decent paper with good ink and not just a scratched tablet. The other was that it came from men who could neither read nor write even when they had been alive.

—

Dura-Europos was a grimace on the lip of the world. Hard, like someone facing a relentless wind, smart-mouthing sideways and unable to shut up even at the edge of the grave. If it could speak, it would talk in an accent you could use to build its many towers, and it lolled along a bluff above the Euphrates like a drunken whore on a dais.

It was veiled with the tattered remnants of faded Parthian finery, Jewish geegaws, Roman pomposity and even Christian icons – the walls had been built so long ago no one remembered and it had been held by the Trousered, the Persians, for years, until Rome finally wrenched it from them in the time of the Divine Aurelius. Rome had held it ever since, studding it with towers and citadels.

It was important for only two reasons, as the military commander explained to Drust and Kag and the others – as a standard to wave at the Parthians and to control the western end of a rich trade route that ran east to the gods knew where.

The military commander was Virius Genadius Attalus, a *laticlavius*, a *vir militaris* and Lord of the River, all titles he smacked Drust and Kag with when they stood on his tessellated floor, looking out of the arches to a terrace through which a soft breeze blew, bringing the scent of river mud, sewage rot

9

and the sweet headiness of roses. A boat glided gently. There were tamarisks and palms.

'What brought you here?' Attalus, the *vir miliaris*, *eques*, *laticlavius*, wanted to know.

'A long dusty road,' Drust said.

'Camels,' Kag added.

Attalus scowled. He had a full beard, carefully curled because it was the fashion, and he endured the hot itch that went with it because of that. He wore his broad-striped tunic and toga, the full fig, because – like with the titles – he was trying to beat these new upstarts into submission.

'Do not fuck with me,' he said and the crudeness of that from the mouth of the nobleman of the Palatine Hill almost made Drust smile. Almost.

'You came here for what purpose?'

'Trade. This is the hub of it, after all. We bring barley, full-grown pigs, suckling pigs, decent wine, dates, oil, *garum*.'

All things soldiers would buy and carefully chosen for that reason even if Drust had wished the pigs and their offspring a rapid and broiling death on more than one occasion.

'And ourselves,' he finished, which made Attalus stare, wondering if he was being given more impudence.

'We are of the *harena*,' Kag added swiftly, before the matter boiled up. 'Formerly of a School in Rome until given the wooden sword. Now we are freedmen and citizens but offer exhibition bouts for the discerning.'

'Gladiators?' Attalus asked incredulously. 'Former slaves?'

No one answered him and he paced, stopped and stared at them with disbelief.

'You took a caravan all the dangerous way here for fish sauce and barley and some gladiator contests?'

'And pigs,' Kag offered mildly. 'Don't forget the pigs.'

Attalus scowled. 'I have never met them, yet I feel sorry for the beasts already, having to travel in your company, you scoundrels.'

He was looking them up and down and Drust knew what he saw – tough, lean men burned by sun and strange winds, a long way from the flush of youth but not yet into the final frosts. We are on the cusp of our lives, Drust thought, have seen and done a great deal – but we do not look like fighters of the *harena*, I will grant him that. We were never much when in our prime…

'We were told the way was clear,' Kag said, spreading his hands apologetically. 'The Parthians are too busy fighting themselves, it was said.'

Attalus paced behind an ornate desk which, apart from a chair and some other recliners, marked the only furniture.

'It is so,' he admitted. 'Some disturbance around Fars has resulted in the death of the Parthian king Artaban at the hands of some rebel called Ardashir and his son, Shapur. That has not, as you have discovered, solved many problems. Lack of Parthian control has allowed the local tribes out – the ones you met, the Jabal Tayy, are but one. Why did you ask for Uranius?'

'A name I had from back west,' Drust lied. 'I was told he was the man for camels in Dura-Europos.'

'Your messenger seemed insistent on talking to him. Came up to the gates shouting his name.'

It must have been a facer for the guards, Drust thought – a tall, rangy *mavro* with a huge curved sword and a loincloth looming out of the desert on the back of a scabby camel and yelling for a Roman by name. It would do nothing for Uranius's social standing.

'I can see why it would be upsetting,' he added. 'I simply told my messenger to convey a certain urgency in our situation – I thought using the name might help him get taken seriously.'

'Did too,' Kag added, smiling beatifically. 'After all – Uranius sent his camel-warriors to the rescue.'

'I sent the *dromedarii*,' Attalus countered sourly. 'Uranius was not among them – you do not know Decurio Uranius?'

'Never met him,' Drust said firmly, which was true enough and Attalus's frown told Drust he had asked Uranius the same question. He wondered why all the interest and that nagged him. Dog and Manius, he thought bitterly – they have pissed off someone important, as usual.

Then the man's coiffed beard split in a smile. 'Gladiators,' he said and Drust was immediately wary.

'We have a new amphitheatre here,' Attalus went on, 'built only last year for the garrison. In a few days it will be the Rose Festival of the Standards and I am sure the men would appreciate the sight of real gladiators in their amphitheatre.'

Drust did not want it and Kag picked up on it as soon as Drust mentioned the cost, which would have choked a senator. Attalus frowned.

'Let me consult,' he said and Drust's heart sank. He would go to the centurions and get them to use the legionary bank – which meant the soldiers would pay.

'No deaths,' he said, hoping that would kill it. Attalus merely smiled and indicated they could go.

–

The place teemed with Roman tunics, Greek cloaks, pointed Scythian hats, the baggy trousers of Persians, the long robes of Arabs and Jews, and the fat turbans of Pandyan silk traders from Tamilakam.

Drust's train had been trailed through the city to the 17th Tower, a compound that encompassed their caravan but which had a bathhouse attached, so that Drust could not work out if he had been snubbed by isolation from other *caravanserai* or favoured. The main lots for parking caravans from east or west lay outside the walls – only the truly favoured were permitted a billet inside. Drust did not like to dwell on why they were truly favoured.

They took time off in the shade to braid themselves together and consider what was best, while Kisa Shem-Tov organised the caravan into some order; he was good at that, even if he stole a little.

'I don't care for a performance here,' Kag muttered. 'I heard the sum you mentioned and did not see Attalus blink. He's the sort of well-born arse who will pay for deaths.'

'Then we won't do it,' Drust soothed. 'We are freedmen after all, not slaves dedicated to the old oath.'

'We follow it anyway,' Sib pointed out.

Ugo sat with both hands on his tall axe and looked mournful.

'I hate fighting without the axe,' he said and Quintus snorted derision at him.

'Not a weapon for the *harena*, is it? You need to be a decent *hoplomachus*, not some bull-fucker barbarian from the Germanies. Besides – you don't even like that axe and have said so.'

Ugo nodded sadly. 'My best axe I left in the head of a great beast in the north,' he admitted. 'This one is not the same.'

'So find another,' Kag spat irritatedly. 'Or, better yet, something more civilised.'

'You did not find it uncivilised when I cut down those goat-fuckers at the oasis,' Ugo pointed out bitterly and there was too much truth in that for anyone to argue.

'I could fight with Stercorinus's sword,' Ugo added hopefully, but had no response from the man, who leaned against the wall like a windblown palm, cradling his great curved sword.

'Where did you get such a weapon?' Quintus prompted and Stercorinus turned his black, dreaming eyes.

'From god,' he said. 'When he told me the manner of my death and that I am the bearer of this sword. It was carried by Simon, known as Cephas and the defender of the Christ. He cut the ear from a high priest when those people came to arrest his master.'

'How did you come by it?' Ugo asked.

'I have a destiny. That is why I have this sword and why I have stayed – Drust and god will tell me my destiny.'

They had heard it all before but hoped each time to find something new in it, but the sword and the god had no names, it appeared, and Stercorinus would not tell of the manner of his death.

'You stay,' Praeclarum pointed out, 'because you were bought and freed and bound to a contract to pay off what you owe, which is as good as the slavery you had before. As I was.'

Stercorinus merely looked, in such a way that said: believe what you like, the truth is different.

'Anyway,' Kag added morosely, seeing nothing new was coming, 'that bent knife might be bigger than others we have seen, but it is still no weapon for the *harena*. Lacks *dignitas*. Like women fighters.'

'If they let me,' Praeclarum answered, unfazed by Kag's scathe.

'In Rome it's forbidden as a perversion,' Kag answered, 'but here it is an acceptable one. That's the East for you.'

'Of course,' Sib added viciously, 'if you can't dance the steps and make a cow's hole mess of it, they will howl and mark you down for a six just the same as any man.'

It was the traditional way of registering a gladiator death, scrawling 6 against their name, and Drust was determined that wasn't going to happen. He said so and no one spoke for a long time.

Then Quintus said, 'What about this Uranius?'

Drust had no idea. It was clear they were being kept apart from everyone else and especially Uranius and he didn't know why. It was what made this amphitheatre affair uneasy.

'You think they will try and kill us all?' Sib demanded, alarmed, and Quintus laughed his big, easy laugh, mouth as wide as an open drain.

'That's what they do out here,' he answered. 'Dog would know better.'

People fell silent at the name. Dog had been one of them, a man with a face ink-marked to make it look as if it was inside out; he had gone with the Imperial Julias of the family who had clustered round the boy-emperor Elagabalus. Drust and the others took sensible and hidden exile far to the south of the Africas and no one had heard from Dog since Elagabalus and his mother Julia had been purged in favour of a cousin, the new boy-emperor Alexander. By both the matriarch of the family, yet another Julia and the mother of Alexander, yet one more Julia.

Every female in the Severan dynasty was a Julia, it appeared – Elagabalus had married two Julias, the second a scandal because she had been a Vestal – and it was worth remembering that, Drust thought. They are the deadliest power in the Empire and Dog had practically worshipped at the feet of Elagabalus's mother, dragged off in bloody chains with her son.

They'd all thought Dog was dead and Manius with him – yet here they were, alive and asking for help from the only family they knew, the only people they could trust. Drust told the others that was why the message was short on detail – the lost pair did not want to let anyone know.

'It will be women,' Quintus said with his big grin.

'A pile of gold,' Kag muttered moodily, 'whose shine is all in his death's head.'

They gathered themselves together in this fortress city, which was a trembling nerve end that thrummed the whole body of Rome, perched like a raw wound at the edge of the Empire, facing an ancient enemy which seemed to be changing into something no one could recognise or understand.

Kisa Shem-Tov knew the city, though, so that when he came back, every head turned to look. He was small, dark, fringe-bearded round the jaw of a broad face with an open smile which was mostly lie. He had overseen the parking of the caravan camels in two facing rows and the gurgle and grunt of them were now muffled with a muzzle of feedbags. All the cargo was laid out in neat piles on ground cloth, covered with oiled cloth and tied down as best as was possible on the hard-packed ground. He handed over the train bell, worn by the last camel in the line when they were on the move, and managed to make it look like an offering to a god.

'What's being said of us?' Drust asked and the little Jew bobbed, looked sideways at Stercorinus, now folded on the ground like some huge spider with his great scimitar cradled like a beloved child, then at Sib. He did not like nor trust these desert-dwellers, but he had his task…

'That you are fighters from Rome,' he said. 'The caravan guard commanders are wondering how good you are, since you are few and every caravan needs at least a hundred guards.'

Quintus snorted. 'I have seen these guards. You can dump all their arses in the dust with a small bladder on a large stick.'

'The city is fretted,' Kisa Shem-Tov continued. 'The trade with the East is not yet broken, but it is being interrupted – these usurpers seem to have wrecked the old Empire and not yet replaced it with anything of their own. The desert sands are boiling.'

Then he smiled. 'Next year, who knows? It has always been thus in this part of the world. People fighting over it, from your honour's glorious warriors to dogs from the sands.'

It was worth fighting over too, Drust thought, for trade made it rich even if it did not look much. The whole city could be ridden across in twenty minutes if you could find a good horse and a straight street – yet those streets were golden with possibilities.

'You might find the first,' Kisa Shem-Tov answered when Drust voiced this, 'but never the second.'

He knew this, he told everyone who would listen, because this was like his birth-city as to be a sister and that was why sensible folk appointed him as guide in these lands. He knew this city and beyond and it would be good knowledge to have. He had said much the same at Antioch when he had brought the message that had dragged them all here.

Drust listened with half an ear. The little Jewish man had made his presence felt the moment they had appeared in Antioch, and they had learned since that the Jew was an overfull cup when it came to lore, but not all of it was useful or made sense.

Drust was wondering – not for the first time – if he was worth listening to. He did not trust Kisa Shem-Tov further than he could throw Ugo with an eyelash, but he did not say that, just listened and watched the festered huddle of flat-roofed

17

mud-brick houses, the bloom of tents and the heat haze from a rumbled gurgling of contented camels.

It felt good to be smelling woodsmoke and new-baked bread and hot onions, even if he had to filter them through the stink of camels and unwashed people; if he closed his eyes, he could imagine the roofs were taller and closer together, that the narrow streets were in Subura, Rome's teeming heart. But this place was as far removed from that as the chances of avoiding a fight in the new amphitheatre.

'There are many folk such as myself,' Kisa was saying, 'Jews, though we call ourselves Karaite and follow the teachings of our own since Hillel and Shammai argued. Some say we came from Chufut Kale, but no one likes to hear that, since the legend speaks of Karaites being slaves of the Grass Sea animals beyond the mountains.'

'I hate this midden,' Kag declared, scowling into Kisa's broad smile. 'I hate the heat and the strangeness and do not give the smell off my balls for your Karaite Jews. All I need to know is where the road is that will carry us from here. That and what brought us here in the first place.'

'If your nethers smell,' Kisa answered politely, his smile only a little wavering, 'I can find a place for you to bathe. The people here bathe regularly, as do we Jews – except for new fathers, who are not allowed to wash or write for forty-nine days after the birth of their child. The Arabs also bathe, but not as often. The traders from the eastern deserts seldom bathe…'

'Enough bathing,' Ugo growled. 'You sound like a stream in flood. I am washed clean in it.'

'I am sure your honour has the correctness of it,' Kisa said, inclining his head. Then he turned and moved closer to Drust, close enough for him to smell vinegar sweat, unwashed linen and the faint incongruous perfume of roses.

'There was a man,' he said softly, his breath brushing the hairs around Drust's ears, 'who whispered to this one, saying to seek the house of Shayk Amjot in the Street of Cheap Iron. There you will meet the Red Man.'

'A man?' Drust demanded. 'What man? And why tell you? And why do you only tell me all this now?'

He said it in a loud growl which made Kisa Shem-Tov draw back and look from side to side as if searching for an exit. Instead he found Kag.

'Calm yourself, Jew. First law of the *harena* – take a deep breath and if you are going to piss yourself, squat and pretend to be rubbing sand into your palms.'

'I am not of your profession,' Kisa Shem-Tov replied with vehement relief. 'I was told this suddenly – I did not solicit it. This man was a shadow who said these words and vanished. They mean little to me…'

'Well – you have told me,' Drust said and Kag looked briefly at him, seeing how he had let go of the neck of the rat but not why. He grinned, feral as a wet cat, and Kisa trembled.

'Do you know this Street of Cheap Iron?' Drust demanded and Kisa inclined his head obsequiously.

'I believe I might find a way to it.'

Drust said nothing more and, gradually, Kisa realised he was to go. He tried to move away with dignity but broke after a few steps and scuttled.

'You are right not to trust him.'

Praeclarum's voice was soft yet it came as a startle from a shadow in the dark; Kag recovered first and managed a chuckle.

'As if we need this advice – but you have our thanks.'

'He smells of roses,' she went on and Drust exchanged a look with Kag which confirmed it.

'They are everywhere in the town up by the Palmyra Gate and beyond,' she went on. 'Every house seems to have a balcony or a roof growing roses.'

'They garland the standards with them in memory of the dead,' Drust said, 'every year.'

'Good earner for people,' Kag pointed out, 'so they will grow hundreds of them for this very moment.'

'He did not meet anyone on the way here,' Praeclarum added, squatting carelessly so that the dark mystery of her fork pointed accusingly at Kag, who tried not to look. 'He must have gone back, which means…'

'Which means he knew to meet someone,' Drust finished. Kag stroked his beard and squinted.

'Who? This Shayk? This Red Man?'

'The Red Man will be Uranius,' Quintus said, sliding in and grinning whitely at Praeclarum. 'Remember Kag shouting that out at the oasis? Those camel-riding Romans are the Red Men, from the cloaks they wear.'

'Not me who shouted,' Kag said. 'I thought it was you.'

'It was Kisa Shem-Tov,' Praeclarum said. 'He clearly knows these *dromedarii* well.'

'Take him with us to this Shayk,' Kag said and Quintus nodded.

'Take us all. Strange city, strange people.'

'Let me think,' Drust said and moved away, looking for air and space. He found Praeclarum smiling at him.

'You have two wives there,' she said and he looked sideways at her.

'Don't let any of them hear you calling them old women.'

'Take me,' she said.

'Why? Do you want to be a third wife so much?'

She didn't answer and the silence lengthened until he stood and stretched, feeling the weariness; somewhere goat was frying and he wanted simply to eat and sleep.

She looked at him and trembled a smile. 'Slaves cannot marry.'

'You are not a slave now,' he answered and she acknowledged it with a slight neck bow.

'I am whatever your contract-bond says I am,' she answered, 'until I run away and decide otherwise.'

He knew she was joking – at least, he hoped she was joking – so he smiled. 'What would keep you from that terrible fate?' he asked lightly.

She leaned forward a little, hands behind her back as slaves always did. 'Take me with you.'

He did not answer as he moved to the smell of food, but he felt her eyes on him.

Chapter Two

They ate goat and flatbread, dozed a little until the heat left the day, then Drust stirred Kag and Kisa – and Praeclarum. Kisa did not like a woman coming with them and said so.

'It is not a good matter. These Persians and Arabs have a different way of thinking about women, which does not include them as warriors or in the conversations of men.'

'Then tell them not to fight or talk to her,' Kag said.

Drust was surprised that Kag had no objections and seemed to be making a case for Praeclarum to come along. He did not say a word on it, just indicated for Kisa to lead the way. Praeclarum stayed silent too, but for all his attempts, Drust could not keep from at least one look and, when he did, he saw her smiling back.

Dura-Europos, though it sat at the fat end of a rich trade trail, was firstly a soldier's town, and the legionaries with permissions were out looking for drink or whores, or stuff from the bazaar that would make their lot a little better. They also promenaded, because the fact of them being out with only legionary tunics and boots and a cloak against the night chill meant they were favoured, not because they were best, but because they were cunning and tough, which is what the army wanted.

They were mostly vexallations, detachments of legionaries who were five years into their twenty; and those five years had taught them a lot, Drust knew. Exercises after muster and paired boxing after that, to keep everyone on their toes. Breakfast out in the desert was always *suci* – last night's stale bread soaked in *posca* laced with the many spices you could buy here. It came in a pail and was scooped up with the *rutabulo*, the ladle which hung on a hook above a bunk. They sucked it down quickly while making a packet of bedclothes and tunics and equipment into a just-so neatness that kept the Seniors happy and let you know where everything was, even in the dark.

They had learned to love eating *puls*, so virulently green with leeks it looked dangerous. They had learned marching, for marching was the legion. Long trudges with heavy yokes of equipment and, at the end of it, hurling javelins with a steady, unerring hand. Digging roads, making bricks, carpentering, all for a laughable pay before deductions.

Drust could have commiserated with any one of them on their lot because it was little different from what his own had been as a gladiator and a slave. Yet they would sneer at him and consider themselves several cuts above, those young-old men with rank still to gain.

Drust was now the wrong side of their age, still lean and hard though bits ached in the night chill. When he looked in any reflective surface he was no longer shocked at the lines and the furrows and the silvered fret around the slightly popped eyes, hardly ever experienced that pang when he remembered how the fan-girls had called him 'handsome' and how most of that had been replaced by a raw, scraped chisel to the jaw and cheekbone.

Kag had the same look, but his was sauced with the desert stare, a hooded and dark way of looking; folk didn't like him because he looked sly, but most of that was sun and wind and a natural caution about what walked on their trail. If you are leaving tracks, Kag said, you are being followed. That was one of his many bits of lore…

Yet he was, in the very essence of himself, exactly the same as all the other Brothers of the Sand, even the newest, such as Stercorinus and Praeclarum. They had already shared their privations and the nag when their poverty permitted them to think on something other than survival. They did not often think of anything other than survival and now was no exception.

'You think this Shayk Amjot will help us?' Kag asked quietly, looking round as they moved, always watching, watching. 'We have to get decorated.'

He had no argument from Drust; getting 'decorated' was an Army term they'd picked up, used for a fine art comprising work, cunning and theft. Do anything to make sure of a swallow of wine, a few coins and a complete kit; such theft was ignored by Seniors until someone was caught, and the punishment was equally ignored by the Tribunes. The Seniors staked the offender out on the mess table with a crucifixion nail through each palm. Then they took the bloody-palmed victim to the infirmary – and put him on punishment for being 'culpably physically unfit'.

Shayk Amjot was, on the face of it, not the man for decorating two Roman men, especially rough-arsed ex-gladiators and former slaves. He was head of the Ouled Janir, one of the most bloodthirty of the tribes, had once led *ghazzu* – raids – of thousands against rivals, explored far to the east, forged surrounding tribes to his will by force or alliance, and even cowed the desert raiders who operated a protection racket over caravan traffic out along the Silk.

He had decided, when age crept on him, that he was safer with the Romans than anyone else and so had come to settle in this fortress city, where he made himself invaluable to the smooth running of a place whose walls were scrawled with obscenities in Greek, Latin, Aramaic, Hebrew, Syriac, Hatrian, Palmyrene, Parthian, Safaitic and Parsik.

He was now, as Kag growled, a bigger rogue than Kisa Shem-Tov – but he was a Roman-friendly rogue along the disputed Euphrates. Still, he added, soft and morose, Shayk Amjot is not the man to decorate us lightly. Nor was Dura-Europos the place for it, but it was all they had.

The locals treated the Army with fear, contempt and scorn, yet their miserable town had grown up because of the Army. There were fashionable streets – or ones that tried to be – but they were not for the likes of the Army. There were other, much less fashionable streets and they were assuredly not a place for legionaries, even less so for strangers trying not to look like them.

Kisa wisely stuck them to the labyrinth of small courts and streets where the Jews and Arabs lived. They went through dark and treacherous alleys of hovels, pooled with weak lights from shops offering Sweat, a drink made from dates, or where the wine was ludicrously cheap and made from grapes which had already been pressed two or three times.

They slid into these dark places, wrapping it round them like a warm *keffiyeh*, the desert scarf they wore looped round their necks – or, in Praeclarum's case, round her face to hide that she was a woman.

In a place of planes and shadows, at a table pooled in a feeble spotlight, they stopped to waste some time, not planning to be too early. They ate tough pancakes with honey while Kisa got his bearings. Drust had an idea the little man wanted to make an excuse to slide off on his own, but made it clear he wouldn't permit that.

25

The *taberna*, though it barely warranted the name, looked on eating-knives as accursed implements of the demons of the desert or the Romans, so they ate with fingers. The old man who served them still recognised them as Romans.

Kag laughed, but Drust was affronted; they wore tan robes and the baggy Persian trousers with once-white linen over-robes. They had curved knives shoved in their belts and Drust thought they looked like fierce camel-bothering desert pirates and should have been as anonymous as dust in that place.

'You can't fool an old stager like that,' Kag said. 'He has seen too many of us. Besides – if you add a throwing stick or two and a red cloak, we look like those *dromedarii* lads.'

It was true enough, but there was no balm on Drust, who drank the bad wine with pointed disgust until the lanterns were refilled to make the flame higher, allowing the insects to sizzle and the stolid-faced grizzlers to continue playing some game involving slapping counters hard on the board and yelling.

Then Kisa said it was the hour appointed and they got up and clattered the last of their few coins on the table; the old man appeared like a *jnoun* to sweep them up.

'The house of Shayk Amjot,' Drust said in Arabic and the old man squinted up at him and sucked missing teeth. Kisa scowled because he knew Drust was checking to see they were close to it, as Kisa claimed, and had not been led up some dark alley full of blades.

'I would not go there. Your disguise is good, but perhaps not that good, *authentēs*. That is not a quarter for folk such as you.'

'There are such places in every town,' Drust answered sourly. 'This holds nothing we do not already know about.'

The old man shrugged, rolling his head in that ambiguous gesture everyone knew meant anything from compliment and agreement to insult.

'As you say, *authentēs*, you are the boldest of warriors and will not be put off even with a woman at your side. So follow this street to the end, turn left, then right, then left.'

They went, nodding polite bows to him, hands on breast and then, almost without thinking, resting one on the hilts of their daggers. This quarter, Kisa said, was the home of every disease, every vice, every crime, pitch-dark and full of lurking shadows. He warned them to pick a careful way around the holes and the clotted rubbish and everyone knew he was doing it to ingratiate himself after being so doubted.

One or two streets were lit with wan fish-lamps from square windows, but so narrow Drust could have stretched his arms and touched either side with his fingertips. He would have found miserable, low houses, half in ruins, a dim tunnel garlanded with shrieks and songs, wails and laughter.

Braziers glowed like rat's eyes and women crouched round them against a chill night. A negress, glowing like ebony and almost totally naked, lay on a blanket beside a firepan and, almost wearily, waved at them to come into the hut behind her.

There were others – a woman with a face furrowed with the ruin of her life called out to them in Arabic, and a girl, who might still have been a child, spat scorn at her and shook thin arms with copper bracelets that rang like a dull alarm-iron.

Through it all slid dark shapes. In daylight they would be the Jewish traders in their blue robes, or the ragged *mavro* who carried burdens mules would balk at, or the Persian stone-breakers or brick-makers. At night they were hunters.

There were shifts in the shadows, but Drust knew those who sidled and watched had weighed up the group, seen the dress, the daggers and the numbers and slid back into the dark to look for easier prey.

There was a glow and then a sudden bright flare of light which left an after-image on Drust's closed eyelids. The smell of hot iron reached each nose as they shouldered through the dark and the crowding shadows, the tang of it catching Drust's throat and banging memories into him with every blow of the hammer on the anvil.

The forge was a fat brick cone where a big man pounded red iron and idlers watched his skill, blood-dyed by fire; folk liked to see such hardness shaped into something new and different, even if the magic here only made nails and hinge brackets.

'The Street of Cheap Iron,' Kag said pointedly and Kisa beamed. He nudged Drust and pointed to where they should go. They came to a wall of ornate mud brick and crenellations and followed it to where the light pooled in front of a solid door. Kisa rapped on it and a shutter opened.

'Shayk Amjot,' Kisa said, and Drust expected an argument about what he wanted at this hour and who he was. Instead, the shutter snapped closed and the big, heavy door opened on to a lit courtyard; a huge silhouette filled the entrance, as effective as the closed door had been.

Then it stepped to one side and Drust ducked under the shadow of it, glancing sideways to see a striped robe, a pair of arms crossed on a massive chest, like two piglets suckling at a sow. The face above it was broad, black and gleaming, like a version of Ugo carved in jet.

He found himself in the courtyard of a neat Persian house, where dark shapes in white robes crouched on the ground offering nods and smiles.

The giant Nubian closed the door, the falling bar on it sounding sinister as a knell. Drust looked at Kag, who merely raised an eyebrow; Praeclarum kept the face-veil in place and Kisa looked like he had watery bowels and couldn't hold it in much longer. Then the Nubian led the way into a cloistered room where a brazier glowed. On the far side was a huge cloth hung from the wall, a great fantasy of gold embroidery on red and yellow in loops and swirls.

Men sat on mats, lounging in cushioned comfort, and the giant indicated for them all to sit – folk made room for them, shifting away with wary scorn. They were tribals, Drust saw, and armed to the teeth – which was fine if they kept to the house or the night. If they stepped outside in daylight with such weapons brazenly revealed they'd have the army to deal with, and he grinned ferally back into their fierce stares, letting them know how much he considered them wolves with drawn fangs here.

Yet there were a lot of them, and both men perched, aware that they were vulnerable as a clay cup under an elephant's foot.

'They are Tayy,' Kisa said quietly. 'The ones who attacked at the oasis.'

It might have been correct, but all Drust saw were hard-eyed, hook-nosed men with curved knives and blank stares.

They waited. At a respectful distance girls stood draped in veils and countless copper ornaments which rang when they moved. They sipped *sharbat* with elegant dignity out of tiny cups, which made Drust smile at the thought of them, like Roman matrons enjoying wine and gossip. Then he heard, with a shock like iced water, a soft chant:

'Sleep and dream while the Lares watch over you…'

It was in Latin, a soft, dreamy line from a lullaby, and when Drust turned he saw the folds of a cloak and the half-shrouded face of a woman with dark hair, skin like milk and eyes that were misted and blue. She had been beautiful once, he saw, but her life had wrecked it, and she sang with the happy smile of someone who was elsewhere, nodding like a sleeper and singing the same line over and over. Half remembered from a childhood long gone, Drust thought numbly and watched her as she squatted and drew the words in the thin dust of the floor. She can write, he realised dully. A slave who can read and write and speak Latin...

'*Papaver*,' Praeclarum whispered. Drust thought it probable – poppy seeds had always been popular and easy to get among slaves, and Manius had used a quid of some African leaves and worse when he could get it. Anything to ease the harshness of life as a slave. Or even just life... Drust wondered where Manius was now and if he had his leaf.

There was a sudden peremptory command in a tongue even Drust found hard to follow, a dialect so guttural it sounded like throat-clearing. The woman stopped crooning and scribbling and stood up at once; a silence fell so that they heard only the rasp of their own breathing and a soft shush as the woman let the thin cloak slide from her head, then all the way down to her hips.

A flute and a drum started, insidious as serpent coils. The chimes when she moved seemed like a carillon – she wore a collar of bells at her ankles and wrists and the same dreamlike expression as she raised her hands over her head then proudly threw it back. She was alabaster and still shapely; for all her face showed her age, her breasts and hips did not and she moved in bright colours and sweet, heady smells.

She swung and circled and posed, then suddenly seized the offered torch from an offered hand and swung it round her head in broad circles, the flames lighting her with a bloody glow so that, for a moment, the hissing torch and the swaying veil seemed interchanged; Drust held his breath, expecting a disaster of fire.

It did not come. She swung the torch free, sank to a panting heap and stubbed it out with a final hiss on the tiled floor. A low murmur of applause rolled out from the watching tribals and then a soft tinkling rain of silver coins. Drust's admiration changed to concern when he saw her try to get up and stagger; he moved swiftly and caught her arm before she fell.

'Steady, girl,' he said and she looked at him; just for a moment, the eyes cleared and she saw him – then Drust felt himself wrenched round by a powerful hand and stared into the twisted face of one of the tribals.

The man was squat, bent-nosed, pig-eyed with fury, and stank. He said something which Drust did not quite understand, though there was enough in it to make him break out in an angry flush, but it was the spit that did it and when it hit Drust's chin he did not think twice about the reply.

He drew back like a strutting cock and drove his forehead into the bent nose, which promptly exploded with scarlet as the man reeled back, bellowing. He caught a heel and went flying, legs waving like an upturned beetle. Kag laughed.

Then there was uproar, shouts and roars and the hiss of knives coming out of scabbards. The three of them fell into a familiar stance, shoulder to shoulder and backing up to find the nearest wall, while Kisa whimpered and tried to make a ball on the floor; a table went over with a clatter and smash. Praeclarum tore the veil from her face and, for the first time, the locals saw it was a woman; the cries got louder and uglier.

Then a voice cut through it like a whiplash and Drust saw the Nubian stride in to dominate the floor. There was a descent to muttering until even that ended and only the man with the bloody face kept on, cursing and snorting breath in through the blood. Kisa, who had recovered, was translating as fast as he could because it kept him from shrieking and running.

Bloody Nose was bellowing about how the Roman had insulted the Tormentor and Shayk Amjot since she was his woman. Kisa waited, hissing the Nubian's reply; since it was delivered in slow, insidious coils he had time.

'Is Shayk Amjot's voice raised?' the giant asked silkily. 'Is she his woman or yours? Is it his honour or yours? Are these his guests or yours?'

Bloody Nose had no answers save sullen anger and dabbing.

'What are you, then?' the giant demanded and he looked round them all when he said it. There was foot-shuffling now.

'You are beetles,' he answered the silence. 'You are the desert wind, which has no voice save sighs. You are nothing until Shayk Amjot tells you what you are.'

Drust saw that it did not sit well with these men and privately thought any one of them would cheerfully cut Shayk Amjot's throat – yet they were leashed, and he wondered what bound them, but the giant did not permit him to dwell on it. He held out an imperious curl of hand and said, 'Come.'

They went and, as they passed her, Drust saw the woman had been ripped out of her dreams with the shock; her O of a mouth and wide almond-shaped eyes, kohled and painted as they were, looked like a lost child.

'Thank you,' she whispered in heavily accented Latin as he passed, and he half turned in time to see the glass shutters come down behind her eyes and then, plaintive as whimpers: 'Sleep and dream while the Lares watch over you. I'll hold your hand, so when you wake in the morning I'll still be here.'

It tore him – them all, Drust saw, even Kisa, who knew the tune if not the words – with memories sharp as daggers. Drust doubted there was a child who had not heard that lullaby, which had been around since first there were Roman mothers.

The room beyond was dimly lit by ornate lanterns, pierced to allow soft shafts. There was a low table and cushions scattered round it; the man perched on one indicated for them to be seated and they folded into a worn familiarity.

A slipper of servants brought *sharbat*, and wine, cool and sharp; the brazier coals glowed and Drust saw the man – Shayk Amjot, he presumed – when he leaned across to peer myopically at them. He saw a wizened face whose grizzled, hennaed hair sprang out from under a round cap and whose beard was bright orange with it. There was dark skin, a withered neck, and a face slashed with age and venal cunning. Shayk Amjot had no marks about him that hinted at destiny or greatness – save for the eyes. They held a studied, controlled violence.

'You sent me a message, Shayk Amjot.'

Drust deliberately called him by name, omitting the many polite honorifics, and it did not go unnoticed; the little man shifted on his cushions and then made a gesture that caused the shadows to shift. They coalesced into a new shape and both men looked at it.

A man in knee-length breeks and a simple tunic, the collar wrecked by sweat – an Army tunic, belted and with a dangling knife scabbard, Drust noted. He wore nothing else but solid Army boots and his face was round and bland, the colour of old olives and split across the middle by a waxed line of moustache that crept into a neck beard; it served to highlight a mouth whose lips were thin and unsmiling. He had eyes like goat droppings on a dune and smelled of *nard*, the perfumed oil legionaries preferred.

'Thank you for coming,' he said in Latin, which threw Drust, but Kag had got to it at once.

33

'Uranius,' he said and the man inclined his head. Shayk Amjot laughed, a high cackling sound, and Uranius managed a thin smile.

'My apologies for the subterfuge,' Uranius said, 'but you have seen how my commander behaves. He does not trust me.'

He saw them looking round and smiled. 'Do not concern yourself looking for the doors. If murder was in this it would be done before now.'

'Explain,' Drust said simply and Uranius took a breath.

'I was not always as you see,' he began bitterly. 'Once, I was commander of the guards of the Emperor.'

'Which one?' Kag demanded and Shayk Amjot cackled again – it was as good a warning as any that he spoke Latin well enough and Drust hoped everyone had noted it.

'Antoninus,' Uranius answered, then waved a hand as if swatting a fly. 'Elagabalus as was.'

'You were purged,' Kag interrupted, grinning with a complete lack of sympathy. It was Kag's belief that if you fastened yourself to any star you only had yourself to blame when it hit the ground.

'We all were,' Uranius answered. 'Some more than others – I was blessed by Fortuna to only end up here, staring at the arses of camels.'

'Nothing wrong with camels,' Praeclarum said. 'In the desert.'

The Shayk leaned forward the better to look at her. 'What is her name?'

Drust told him, not liking the new steer of this conversation; the Shayk clasped his gnarled hands together and grinned. Then he repeated her name in his own tongue. 'Remarkable', Kisa translated, which was close enough.

'What do you want for this woman called Remarkable?'

34

Kag laughed and Drust thought it at least polite to tell him a sale was not offered and the woman was not a slave. The Shayk subsided sullenly, and Uranius looked at him then back to Drust.

'The Shayk collects exotica,' he said smoothly. 'You may have seen one outside.'

'The dancer,' Drust said and Uranius nodded.

'That was the spur for your being here,' Uranius went on. 'The message you have was carried by this woman – she is called Diwan.'

The Shayk chuckled. Drust knew *diwan* to be the name for a *kilne*, a Roman couch, but he said nothing; it was Praeclarum who said it, flat and blank.

'A piece of furniture you lie on.'

'Just so,' Uranius said warningly. 'However, that name is not the one she was born with. She knows Latin well enough to sing a lullaby – and write it down.'

'Meaning what?' Kag demanded.

Uranius shrugged, but Drust saw the man's eyes hood like a gloved hawk.

'Meaning Dog and Manius, who cannot read nor write, got her to pen their message and carry it a long way.'

No one answered, for it begged more answers, and they did what they always did and waited.

'There is a new dynasty, from the House of Sasan,' Uranius went on. 'When the camel-herders who have nibbled off pieces of the old Parthian kingdoms are dealt with, the Sasan will be a new power in the East. For now, Rome has respite. This will help us.'

Drust saw Shayk Amjot's narrow-eyed squint and thought that more of a true feeling for Rome than any of his bland smiles.

'Us?' Drust asked. Uranius nodded.

'You are Drust – Servillius Drusus. The one with you who looks as if he would bite is called Kag. I do not know the woman, but Kisa Shem-Tov is known to me.'

Kisa had no graces left, not even one which permitted him to look embarrassed or ashamed.

'You are sometime gladiators, though freedmen and citizens, I understand,' Uranius went on. 'The others of your little *familia* are Quintus, the *mavro* Sib, and the northerner, a barbarian from the Germanies called Ugo.'

'Kisa is indeed known far and wide,' Kag said, grinning viciously at the little man, who widened his eyes and spread his hands.

'I learned this not from Kisa but in conversations with others – mainly the one you know as Dog, though he was Crixus to me. He went around veiled, which was wise, for his face is a horror.'

This was so we know he has seen Dog, Drust thought. The clever ink marks of a skull had been worked onto his face so that it looked like his head was inside out. Once seen, never forgotten. His heart was pounding with this confirmation that both of them were alive, but he tried to show nothing.

'So you know Dog. And Manius?'

'Manius is tall, with part of his face and an ear melted. No hair grows on that side.'

Drust nodded. That's what Roman Fire does if you get too close, he thought, but mostly he was filled with the savage exultation that both of them were still in the world. Take that up the arse, Dis Pater…

'Shayk Amjot informed me,' Uranius went on, 'that the woman came down from the north with a party of traders – the Silk Road is not one trail but many. She came from the

36

place your friends went to, bringing their message for the Shayk – and, ultimately, you.'

Drust stirred. 'Then we must speak with her…'

'Her mind is gone,' Uranius replied and then looked bitterly at Shayk Amjot. 'She is now dependent on the mercy of the Shayk.'

'If she has knowledge of Dog,' Kag said viciously, 'it might be better if the Shayk gave her to us.'

Uranius scowled. 'Dog and Manius are as dependent on the Shayk. Some time before, a caravan came down the same route, from Hyrcania they claimed. They dealt in beasts and had one in a cage – a huge cat with fangs and claws.'

'Tiger,' Kag said with awe. 'A Hyrcanian tiger.'

'They are long gone,' Kisa declared loftily and Drust laughed him into frowns.

'The Shayk bought the beast,' Uranius said. 'We both saw the worth in it and so did the Emperor Antoninus – Elagabalus – when he came here from Emesa. The Shayk gifted it, but the Emperor asked me to organise a caravan to go and find more of them. That was the year before…'

'Before Elagabalus was ousted in favour of his cousin,' Shayk Amjot interjected in a high, slightly cracked flute of a voice, the Latin only slightly accented. Drust and the others could only stare until Praeclarum cleared her throat.

'Why would you want strange cats?'

There was a moment of bewilderment, then the Shayk cackled and Uranius smiled thinly.

'I want this woman,' the Shayk said. 'She is delicious.'

'Touch one of your little rat claws on me,' Praeclarum declared firmly, 'and I will gut you like a fish.'

There was a moment of shocked silence and then the Shayk laughed and clapped his hands with delight. Uranius stepped into the coiling tension.

'Such a beast is a rarity,' he began, but Kag growled across him.

'Such a cat is much more than that. It is a prize worth its own weight in gold – and it weighs a great deal.'

Praeclarum radiated a flush of embarrassment. 'Does it have six legs? Wings?'

'Stripes,' Drust told her, watching Kag's glaucous eyes, glazed with all the possibilities. 'Size of a small horse and thought to have been hunted out of the world.'

He fell silent, for he had seen one only in his lifetime and was glad he did not have to face such a thing in the *harena*. Even dead it had been a fearsome engine of muscle and claw and fang that sent a chill through him.

Uranius saw that he knew the beast and nodded. 'The Hyrcanian tiger has been hard to find for years – some said that there were no more, that the *harena* had devoured them all.'

'I saw one when I was a boy,' Drust answered dully. 'Never since.'

'The Shayk gifted this one to the Emperor Antoninus in honour of his name as the Sun God, Elagabalus, but in the way Syrians have it – *Ilāh hag-Gabal*, God of the Mountain. It died gloriously in the Flavian and the Emperor wanted more.'

Nicely fawned, Drust thought, flicking a glance at the impassive old man. Kag was less admiring.

'So now the new boy-emperor Alexander wants the same,' he said flatly and Uranius nodded.

'He wanted a new caravan to follow the old across the Wall of Alexander and into the lands of Hyrcania,' he said.

'You sent an expedition there. You sent Manius and Dog.'

Uranius nodded. 'Yes. Dog led it. Several score camels, packers, drivers, scouts, guards.'

Kag laughed aloud.

'You gave Dog a caravan,' Drust said dully. 'And sent them off. And are surprised you never heard from them again.'

'They probably went straight back to Antiochus and are now somewhere in Subura, enjoying the money they made from selling camels,' Kag added.

Shayk Amjot slapped his knee and cackled out his laugh, nodding appreciatively. 'So I said, so I said.'

That was when Drust looked sideways to catch Kag's eye; this old pirate would not have trusted Dog and Manius with such a camel train unless he was not the one ultimately paying for it. Someone else had stood surety, someone powerful enough for Shayk Amjot to obey.

It would take no less than an Emperor, Drust thought.

The Shayk leaned forward. 'We thought them dead and gone,' he said. 'Until the woman came with a message and we knew they were alive.'

Drust's ears roared for a moment and his vision blurred. When it cleared he found himself looking at Kisa Shem-Tov's hesitant smile.

'You knew. You had it sent on to us.'

'It was meant for you,' Uranius corrected. 'We made sure it reached you.'

Drust looked at Kisa Shem-Tov, who had stayed silent and shadowed and now blenched under the cold eyes. His smile was wavering thin.

'So,' Drust said, more to the Shayk than Uranius. 'Now you know why we are here. Why are you?'

'One camel for one man,' the Shayk said suddenly, and Uranius blinked, taken off balance. Kag, on the other hand, merely grinned back.

'Each one carries water in two *amphora quadrantal* – which should be covered – and as many *congius* waterskin as you can pile on it. They will always leak.'

'We took four hundred men and six hundred camels down from Alexandria into the lands of the Himyar and Saba,' he added. 'Half the camels died, killed by the goat-fuckers of the desert tribes, and the rest of starvation and thirst – never let it be said that camels don't need water. They need it to eat and if they don't eat and are worked on long marches, they die like flies.'

Uranius was stunned to silence, but Shayk Amjot chuckled and nodded, satisfied.

'These will do well, Uranius. You have told me true about them all save this Remarkable.'

Uranius shifted slightly. 'I do not know much of her, save that she was purchased as a slave following the death of the wife of a *lanista*.'

Even Drust had not known this and could see that Kag was wide-eyed with wanting to know more. He did not have to wait long.

'Something about a toothstick,' he added, puzzled. There was silence and then the Shayk's slightly amused voice cut it.

'You killed a woman over a toothstick?'

'Not mine,' Praeclarum answered flatly and now it was the Shayk's turn to be surprised; everyone else too – Drust and Kag stared open-mouthed, and Kisa crouched, his eyes glittering as he sucked in this new knowledge.

'She did not like me using her toothstick,' Praeclarum went on, trying to keep her voice level and seemingly unconcerned.

She even spread her hands. 'Some women are strange about such matters, it seems. We had shared intimacies in the times she demanded liaison – our mouths were on parts that… well, I need not become gross.'

Everyone stared; the Shayk licked his withered lips and Praeclarum smiled.

'Yet she objected to my using her toothstick and grew angry when I pointed out how ludicrous that was. Grew angrier still when I asked if she shared one with her husband. Grew unreasonable when I said I was more at risk than her, given the poor state of his teeth.'

She stopped and frowned. 'In retrospect, that was perhaps unwise. But I was angry.'

'You killed this… woman… over a toothstick?' Kag repeated disbelievingly.

Praeclarum spread apologetic arms. 'Not "this woman". Wife of the *lanista* – well, you are a slave, so you do as ordered. I did not kill her. She came at me with a silly little paring knife and I believe there was stored resentment regarding interests from certain other quarters – not encouraged by me, you understand – and this *lanista*'s wife did not care for it. Besides, it was the hot season, you understand, which makes everyone a little mad. I stepped aside and she went out the shutters, over the balcony, and fell into the street. Naked. Broke her neck. The *lanista* did not want to admit what had been going on, so it was hushed up as an accident – besides, female fighters were no longer of value, so I was put up for sale, to be bought by Quintus on behalf of this…'

She stopped, not knowing exactly what the group was, but it let Drust find some words.

'School,' he said dully. 'We are a School. Of gladiators.'

41

Shayk Amjot smiled his knowing smile, which Drust was growing to hate. '*Uri, vinciri, verberari, ferroque necari*. I will endure, to be burned, to be bound, to be beaten, and to be killed by the sword,' he said, but now no one was surprised by what this Persian knew.

'They are perfect,' he added to Uranius then turned to Drust. 'It is easier to find men who will volunteer to die than to find those who are willing to endure pain with patience, as your Caesar once said.'

Kag smiled, though it was cold. 'Best of all to find those who can do both – but the Divine Julius was never one to endure pain, for all his bold words. He had folk to put up his tent on campaign after all. The only pain he suffered was a dozen daggers in the bowel and it did not last long.'

The Shayk beamed, wisely not showing his gums, and it annoyed Drust on a visceral level that a raised-up desert-walker should be applauding their education in philosophy.

'You want us to go after this lost caravan,' he said brusquely, 'which seems to me to be pouring good money after bad. Besides, you have the Army here. Uranius has the best camels around – send him.'

Shayk Amjot nodded slowly, then laced his furze-root fingers as far as they would go and leaned forward a little.

'Two desert legions exist in Rome,' he said in his soft, high, accented Latin. 'One is the lie of bold fighting men and the women who flutter at the feet of these dashing, romantic warriors of the sands. The other is the truth – that they are the scum of the world, controlled only by the vine stick.'

Drust heard Uranius clear his throat meaningfully, but Kag laughed.

'No argument from us,' he answered as languidly as he could. 'Only the goat-fucking *mavro* of the desert are a match for their thieving and murder – and exceed all in treachery.'

Shayk Amjot growled and the room seemed to grow dark, as if the air had sucked the lamps low. Uranius cleared his throat warningly.

'I was the one who organised and financed the original caravan,' the Shayk declared, and Drust looked at Uranius then, saw in those eyes the lie of that.

'I am willing to do so again for these beasts are worth four times their weight – more – in gold,' the Shayk went on, and this time Uranius had veiled his stare so Drust could not be sure – but he smelled the lie in that too.

The Shayk suddenly paused and hauled out a coin, which he spun through the air. If he was hoping for them to fumble it to ring on the floor, he was disappointed – Drust flicked a hand and snatched it, then turned it over in his fingers.

It was an *aureus*, a new mint – not pure, because no coin was these days – but with a high enough gold content to be worth what it claimed. It had the Emperor's portrait on one side and the Flavian amphitheatre on the other.

'You see what it says?' Shayk Amjot demanded.

'P M TR P II COS PP,' Drust intoned. '*Pontifex Maximus Tribunicia Potestatis Bis Consul Pater Patriae*. A list of titles.'

'Priest of Rome, Consul of the People and the State,' the Shayk corrected, and Kag grunted assent.

'I hope for its brothers and in quantity,' he growled. The Shayk seemed to agree with a flap of one hand.

'You see the image of the Flavian?' he said and now he was talking to Drust, who nodded. 'What does it mean?'

'The Emperor likes his games,' he answered and the Shayk nodded.

'You only put images on coins which make a statement to the people who will see and use them,' he declared. 'This is a new coin, minted by a new Emperor. Young Alexander Severus has, rightly, put his portrait on the front, so he becomes known while his coins are used more and more because they are trusted. Thus, he is trusted – you see?'

Drust did, though he did not like to be lectured on the Imperium Romanum by a camel-herder, however rich. For all that, he was curious. 'And the Flavian?' he asked.

'Because that place has now become the focus of politics in Rome,' the Shayk answered simply. 'And thus the wider Empire. Feed the Flavian, you feed the people of the Empire with what they need, you feed the middle class and they feed the ones on the Palatine.'

'The Flavian was damaged by the whim of Vulcanus,' Uranius added meaningfully and Drust nodded; they'd all known of the fabric cracks that had closed the entire edifice down after the earth had shifted. It had reopened but had been littered with builder's mess for a long time after.

'Five years it took to repair,' Uranius confirmed flatly. 'Young Alexander Severus, all of fourteen in the year the Flavian was declared repaired, decided he needed that glory, being newly elevated over the bleeding body of his cousin. Or rather, his mother did. The growlers of the Army are paid in silver – but the important ones are paid in gold. So he has stamped his credentials all over the Flavian with this – look at me, who provides your entertainments.'

No one spoke for a moment, then Praeclarum cleared her throat.

'So the Emperor, this little boy, wants a fancy beast to show off in the Flavian he now claims as under his own special protection?'

'Get enough of them for one brilliant show,' Kag growled, 'and it will make his name ring. Hyrcanian tigers are the least of what the Flavian would eat – especially if it was a delicacy not seen for a generation.'

'We go all that way for beasts that will be slaughtered?' Praeclarum exclaimed. Now it was the turn of Kag and Drust to stare at her scornfully, these men who had scoured the lands for every exotic animal to feed the devourer that was the Flavian amphitheatre in Rome. What did it matter if you could no longer find Nubian lions or the Duba of Nandi? There were always new beasts… anyone in any village would confidently tell you about dog-headed people two hills over.

'These tigers are giants,' the Shayk said. 'Noted for their viciousness and the length of their claws.'

'Which brings us to the meat,' Uranius went on, sharp and bitter now. 'We were told Manius and Dog were dead – until now.'

Drust looked from Uranius to the blandly smiling, sly Shayk. There was a conflict here, he saw, which made the entire scheme even less attractive – they had had enough of such, and the last time they had accepted one it had driven them like a nail into bigger plots.

'We offer you a share in the wealth of whatever beasts you recover,' the Shayk added smoothly. 'Not to mention the opportunity to save your lost friends, so clearly alive and in need of rescue.'

Chapter Three

Back at the caravanserai, no one was even sure where Hyrcania was. Ugo was not even sure what it was – a mountain range, he thought. Kisa put them all right on it, of course.

'That is what Romans call it. It is Varkâna in Persian – land of wolves – though the Parthians call it Gurgān. It is a great land of peoples who threatened their neighbours to the south – so much so that a wall was built, some say by Alexander, some say by the old Persians. The Parthians certainly tried to man and repair it. They now call it the Red Serpent.'

'Now I know this from you,' Kag said sourly, 'I suspect everyone else does too.'

He turned to Drust. 'Cut this treacherer's throat and leave him in an alley – he went to this Uranius and told all he knew. We all heard it.'

Kisa shrank and looked wildly at Drust. 'I was sent to help your eminences...'

'You are a money-sucking liar in the pay of that dangerous old goat-fucker,' Kag fired back. Drust laid a soothing hand on his arm and drew him aside, out of earshot.

'Let him speak. We know he is whispering in the ear of Shayk Amjot, so keep him close. If we throw him out, there will only be another, whom we don't know.'

So they went back and smiled at Kisa Shem-Tov, who babbled more about what he had hoped to learn and what he had. He had been sent, he claimed, once the Shayk had

46

established who Drust and the others were and where they were likely to be.

'The Shayk had heard your names,' Kisa went on, 'I was to make sure the message was delivered and then make sure you found your way here safely.'

It came as no surprise to anyone that Kisa Shem-Tov was in the pay of the wizened old desert pirate – but it did not answer Drust's nagging fears about what the man wanted.

Kisa looked from one to the other. 'Provided you are of use to him, you have nothing to fear from Shayk Amjot – and you have every use to him. He is not a man to be crossed – remember, all those armed men you saw, delivered to the city in secret and against the Roman law, are from the Tayy, the same who attacked you.'

'And Uranius?'

Kisa nodded and frowned. 'Lucius Julius Aurelius Sulpicius Severus Uranius Antoninus was much more than a simple commander of camels in his day. Attalus believes he is a spy but is not sure for whom. It does not matter much – Attalus is aware that these new Persians, the Sasan, are not the benevolence Rome thought, but are likely to prove worse than the Parthians of old. He believes the Shayk is working with them.'

'Uranius – his name is longer than he is,' Ugo growled. 'And has a Severus in it, which is clue enough. Is he a spy for the new Emperor? I won't have any doings with spies.'

Kisa made an ambivalent hand gesture. 'He was an agent for Elagabalus – but who wants those same folk around when you have murdered your way to the purple? It might be that Uranius now serves Alexander Severus in the same way, or that he has wisely been sent here as a lowly commander of twenty camel-warriors by friends trying to keep him safe. Or that the

47

Shayk, who has friends everywhere, contrived to make him his man.'

Drust knew the little Jew was lying, mainly because his mouth moved but also because he prided himself on the skill of spotting such people, honed in long negotiations for fodder, for profit, for advantage. Yet he couldn't work out what the lie was and that annoyed him.

Sib cut the Gordian of it, all the same. He was working on the strap of some gear, but he looked up when Kisa fell silent. 'We must go to this Wall. There is Manius and there is Dog.'

'A wall,' Quintus mused and gave Drust a look that needed no words; they'd had no good dealing with walls along frontiers.

'Why is it called the Red Serpent?' Ugo wanted to know and Kisa put him right on it. It was built, he said, by Alexander – not the current boy-emperor, but the Divine one, the god-Alexander of the Greeks himself – or so folk claimed. Or by the old Persians of Cyrus. It was longer than both the Roman Walls of the north stuck together and made originally from no more than mud.

Since everyone here had seen such mud walls – sat behind them now, in fact – they were not drop-jawed with awe.

'The whole edifice has thirty fortresses,' Kisa went on. 'A canal runs the length of it, providing water for the garrisons and acting like a wet ditch. The Parthians wanted to rebuild it in stone, but there is none, nor enough trees – so they repaired and strengthened it using bricks, thousands and thousands of them, which are made red as blood in the firing and so it looks like a red serpent wriggling across the plain into the mountains. Even so, it is not finished and now may never be until the Persians stop fighting themselves.'

'Well, if we are to cross it,' Quintus offered up, 'a camel-sized hole would be handy.'

'More to the point,' Drust added drily, 'is where Manius and Dog will be on the far side. And how they managed it.'

'As to that,' Kisa said, 'it seems they planned to go to a river called Atarek, where it comes out of the mountains and runs across the plain to empty into the Hyrcanian Ocean. It is there they thought to find tigers. How they crossed the Serpent remains a mystery.'

Of course it did, Drust thought moodily. Everything involving Dog and Manius is a mystery because neither of them tell half of what they know even to those who should know it all. Yet there was a strange, alien feeling of understanding that it was the nature of folk like them to live and die cheaply in a world of broken promises, fine speeches and false truths, because they had been fed and watered on that for so long that the only reason they now understood had to be carried and a cartload of swords and spears and battered gladiator armour was the best conveyance.

He saw their faces, carved down by heat and strain, skin pulled tight over bone, eyes peering like wary animals from the perpetual shadows beneath bleached brows. They were the dirty, blooded, ragged remnant of what they had once been, a shrinking ring of a *familia* of the sands. They had few rules, if any, and there were times they would fight each other, as gladiators were taught to do – but even so, Drust would not leave two of them to die who had begged for help and he knew it was the same for the others.

Before all of that came the *harena*, the sands of the ring, as ever. Tomorrow would be the traditional feast, where no fighter with any sense ate or drank but simply endured because the Editor of the Games always put one on, introducing the fighters who would appear next day to the rich and powerful.

The Editor was Attalus, according to the sudden sprout of wall scrawlings advertising the affair, which meant the garrison had paid and, though the contract did not allow for deaths, Drust was uneasy. He would have refused it, but knew that Attalus held them all in his palm here; he was in this *caravanserai* because he could not get men nor beasts out of it without permission.

'You are right to be wary,' Kisa said. 'I think he means only to take the measure of you, to find out what Uranius and the Shayk are up to – but still.'

'I think he knows what Uranius and the Shayk are up to,' Praeclarum corrected flatly. 'I can see – anyone can see – that Attalus is frightened both of Rome and these new Persians. His fear will make him suspect anything and everyone.'

'Including this Shayk?' Kag countered.

'Especially him,' Drust pointed out. 'A friend to the Palatine who controls all the local tribes? He did not provide the coin for Dog and Manius – but someone bigger than him and big enough to frighten Attalus.'

'The Emperor,' Kag confirmed moodily and everyone chewed on that for a moment.

'There is no telling which way he will jump when the shit starts to fly,' Sib muttered.

Ugo scrubbed his head with irritated confusion. 'Why is it never a straight road where the likes of Dog is concerned? Here we are, it seems, set to travel across yet another Wall because of him. Does no one hear Jupiter laughing?'

'That's goats bleating,' Quintus offered helpfully.

'Jupiter Dolichenus,' Stercorinus corrected, and because this had a taint of Syrian Baal in it, folk stared, silent and moody, back at him. He shrugged.

'That god's laughter is more of blue-white sound. And the smell of sizzling.' Kag growled.

They laughed. There were murmurs and more questions and various answers, then Kag held up a *secutor* helmet ruefully. 'Well, we could let Fortuna, Blessed and Divine, fuck Dog and Manius up the arse – but we need a few decent coins here. Look at this – it will no longer take a polish and the dents cannot be fully beaten out.'

Quintus grinned, then threw a bundle of leather and straps to Praeclarum. 'There you go. Drust has you down to fight Kag as a *retiarius* – they don't care out here, it seems, for Imperial edicts banning women in the *harena*.'

She held it up, unravelling it to reveal a leather tunic, cut down and reworked to fit her better than the man it had been made for. It left the arms and legs bare from the thighs down, but she nodded her wary, slightly bewildered thanks to him.

Drust knew that the costume of women in the *harena* usually consisted of a loincloth. No helmet, so her face could be seen and drooled over if she died. Bare breasts for the same reason – but women fighters only died if they were supremely inept, for they fought the condemned and untrained.

No woman had ever fought a real gladiator in a serious bout and she would dance with Kag, who would be a *secutor*, the sacred of Vulcan. He would chase her round the *harena* while she fended him off with net and trident as the chosen of Poseidon. Fire and water… well, that was what it was supposed to be but any ideals in it had long since withered. If they played it well the growlers of the garrison would be happy enough.

They cleaned gear and practised, dancing with trident and net and sword and shield. Stercorinus was a novelty item, like Praeclarum, and Ugo would fight him as a *hoplomachus*, a big heavily armoured man with a small shield and a tiny little dagger. They went to it, mainly because Drust wanted to know if Stercorinus understood what was expected; the man was all whipcord speed with strong wrists and the blade hissed and sang as it flexed.

'Wish I knew what it was,' Ugo mourned sullenly, when he sat wiping the sweat away. 'I would like to have one.'

'You will never find one,' Kisa declared firmly. 'They are made for one purpose only – to execute the *noxii* of Palmyra. I believe Stercorinus came from Palmyra.'

'He's an executioner of criminals?' demanded Sib and made a warding sign. Kag laughed.

'If he was and stole it when he ran off, any Palmyrans he meets will take off his head with it.'

Stercorinus said nothing but did not need to. His name meant 'Little Shit' and was one given to the unwanted by-blows dumped in the garbage for the well-meaning to collect up. If they survived, they ended up slaves. If they died, they at least had a tombstone with a name on it. Stercorinus. Or Proiectus, which meant 'Exposed'. There were no names for girls; girls were never rescued, unless by Christians – and most thought they did that for their own foul rites involving babies.

Afterwards they sat in the singing twilight, eating bread, smelling woodsmoke and camels, and listening to the murmurs of the herders and packers, who had been appreciative of the free show.

'Six hundred camels,' Drust growled to Kag. 'You great liar. We never had more than what we have now – fifty – and we never went south of Petra. Maybe that time we went upriver from the City of Sharp-Nosed Fish looking for Nubian lions.'

'Now we go in the other direction,' Ugo rumbled, 'looking for tigers.'

'And a Dog,' Kag added.

The others laughed softly and Kag made a little side-to-side head movement. 'The Shayk was trying to see if we knew how to handle a big caravan. It is my belief he will provide more camels and supplies for us. Cages, too – I am not about to bring a Hyrcanian tiger back on a leash.'

'More than one,' Quintus pointed out.

'Are we doing this, then?'

It came from Stercorinus, his voice an astounding rasp from the shadows. Drust did not answer, but he knew they would. There was Manius and there was Dog – yet his sleep was the whimper and quiver of a dreaming pup.

-

When he woke into the blare and crash of a day of roses, Drust felt gritty and unwashed. Ugo had made his usual shrine, simply one stone on top of another and everyone was amazed and discomfited when they saw Drust spill his morning wine on it as a libation, something he had never done before.

The garrison vexallations paraded horns and cadenced stamping, the standards hidden by wreaths of roses, their path strewn with them. Drust and the others paraded in the forum in all their gear, wearing head-wreaths of plaited roses; they looked as splendid as they could and had a few of the better-looking herders and packers dressed in the extra finery to make it look as though they were a larger group.

There were others pretending too – half the beast suppliers had been persuaded to join in as actual *venatores* and hunt down the creatures they had captured and dragged here. Drust had wanted to find the traders who had brought the Hyrcanian tiger down to Dura-Europos, but it seemed they were long gone, headed east. They might be back, they might not, Kisa told them, spreading his hands apologetically.

Still, the crowd cheered well, the sacrifices and ceremony seemed to pass off smoothly and, Drust thought, we are off to a good start. Tomorrow would see…

In the evening, there was no disguising how few they were at the *cena libera*, held in Attalus's fine headquarters. It was much as all events were, Drust thought, a collection of fine-bred arses and their women, all trying to be dignified as they eyed up the fighters and picked at plates of olives, peahen eggs, mice rolled in honey and poppy seed, calf liver, and fish fresh from the river.

Attalus was dazzling in white and a broad-striped toga, smiling and waving, with his wife at his elbow. She was gilded and had never been a beauty, but the East destroyed some women, Drust thought, withered them up and sucked what little juice they possessed – this one's face looked like a smashed crab, as Kag whispered to him.

The fighters, for their part, ate nothing and drank less, but strutted and grinned and winked – even Praeclarum, to the delight of everyone, especially the plump wife of a Narrow-Stripe from the 3rd Cyrenaica. Earlier, Praeclarum had had to be ordered into a woman's *stola* and Kisa had made up her face – it did not surprise anyone that he had this art. The result did and everyone fell silent. She had scars and her head was shaved, but there was beauty in her kohled eyes and ochred lips – as long as she did not smile widely, as Kag noted.

'Did you give up using the toothstick after that incident?' Ugo demanded, and Praeclarum had glared at the laughter, which fell silent when folk saw something of the pain behind her eyes.

The men, officers and merchants mostly, affected a skill at assessment they did not have, questioned the fighters on how they would fight and discussed the relative merits of the *retiarius* against the *secutor* or the *murmillo*. Attalus particularly wanted to know how Drust would fight and started them all wagering with Shayk Amjot, invited for the sake of polite politics and his immense wealth. Drust, of course, lied. The contests were fixed anyway, but he did not want to help any of them.

He looked for Uranius at one point but did not see him, and Kag saw it and sidled up to say he had been doing the same, with no success.

'They have kept him away from us,' he growled and Drust could only agree – he was not surprised and that added to the ruffle he felt, like a cat with the wind blowing from the wrong quarter.

The women tried not to touch them, because these were – annoyingly – freedmen and not slaves who could be freely groped, but their *infamis* was affecting enough for one or two of the fine-born to leave damp patches on their ivory chairs when they rose to leave.

When Praeclarum offered her calloused hand to assist the plump wife off her couch, the woman's legs trembled so much Drust thought she would fall. It certainly made her lean closer and harder, and when Praeclarum smiled with her lips firmly together Drust thought the woman would faint entirely.

Attalus was the perfect host and drew Drust aside as everyone was leaving; Drust was not unduly concerned, since Attalus was presenting the Games and he expected some last-minute instructions or requests. When he realised they were alone and unseen in a small alcove, he grew more chilled.

'Hear me,' Attalus said and his voice made Drust's flesh ruche and hackle. 'I know you met with Uranius and Shayk Amjot. It would be beneficial to me – the State – if you revealed what passed between you.'

'An hour,' Drust replied, though his heart was thundering. 'Perhaps two.'

Attalus narrowed his eyes. 'This is a matter you are ill equipped to deal with,' he said. 'What do they want from you, that pair? And what do you want from them?'

Drust thought about it for a moment, then shrugged and pulled out the message, now folded so often that the creases had split. Attalus almost snatched it, read it and frowned, bewildered. Drust saw that he had noted the strange papyrus. It was a strip cut from a larger piece, no more than a finger wide and long. There were about a dozen words on it, no more; Drust thought there had been more, carefully cut off, and he saw that Attalus did as well, frowning as he turned the affair over in his fingers.

'What is this?'

'Two friends,' Drust declared. 'Sent east on an errand and believed lost. Now, it seems, they are not.'

'An errand? What errand?'

So Drust told him that too – the last act of a deranged Emperor. Attalus appeared confused and incredulous, yet Drust had the idea he had known all about that first expedition and who had ordered it.

'Am I to believe that you will go after these long-lost friends?' Attalus demanded. 'Out beyond the Red Serpent into the Land of No Return?'

'That is not the name we were given,' Drust admitted, 'nor does it have a friendly sound – but yes, that is what we will do. For them and for beasts.'

Attalus was silent, chewing on a hangnail. 'The Shayk and Uranius arranged this?'

Drust nodded, though the sweat was chill on him. He wants to know if the new Emperor is in this, he thought, and saw the moment the commander decided he wasn't.

Attalus glared, his face mottled like a wax mummer's mask left too long in the heat. 'You must refuse.'

Drust simply stared until Attalus spoke again.

'The lands of the Parthians are in turmoil thanks to these Sasan. They have forgotten us here, and the longer that remains, the better... I do not want some beast-stealers in the pay of a reprobate to kick up dust that leads to this gate.'

'A caravan,' Drust pointed out, 'one of the many travelling up and down the trade routes...'

Attalus made a hissing sound, like air being let out of a dead sheep. 'You are no fool. Five minutes after you quit the *caravanserai* the word will fly up the road ahead. Besides – the Shayk is full of plots.'

'Plots?' Drust repeated as if bemused, but it was only what he had already considered and he did not fool Attalus.

'You know it. He is head-to-head in secret with Uranius, a man toppled from favour along with the Emperor he served – toppled by the one he now serves on this frontier. You must see... implications.'

Drust had long since seen that, but he frowned and then spread his palms. 'I see you do not trust either of them – but I do not see why a line of camels and ourselves is a threat to the State.'

'No,' Attalus replied shortly. 'But I do. And in the unlikely event you come back with a few cages of rare beasts, what do you think these new Parthians, the Sasan, will do? They also know the worth of those beasts – and will not like Romans going back and forth through their Wall into the lands of their enemies. Would Rome, if you did it in Britannia?'

We did do exactly that and Rome had not liked it, Drust recalled; he wondered if Attalus knew of that history, but the man gave no sign of it, simply hitched his toga, the sweat sheening his florid features.

'You will refuse.'

Drust raised one eyebrow. Attalus leaned forward a little. 'Your camels and all your men are in my grip. When I release it, I must be assured you travel west, back the way you came.'

Attalus knew Drust could not make an answer and he smiled, a thin affair that never crawled further north than his lips. Drust felt he had fallen in a chilled bowl of wine.

'I mean you no harm,' Attalus soothed. 'Fulfil your contract here for the next three days, take the not unreasonable payment and go back to Antiochus and beyond. Or south, back where you came from – where was it? The City of Beaky Fishes?'

Drust's mouth went dry, mainly over the phrase, 'I mean you no harm', which rang like a cracked bell; the soft words made him more afraid than before. Attalus leaned in even closer, until Drust could smell the wine on his breath and the perfume of his hair oil.

'Be wise,' he said, then turned into the farewells and the thanks. Kag saw Drust's face and trooped after him, leading the rest out of the fetid light, creaking and clanking in their finery.

Outside in the cool dark, Kag blew out his cheeks. 'That was worse than the *harena*. Remind me never to do such a thing again.'

It was what he always said, but still there was laughter, low and soft because they knew something was wrong and waited for Drust to tell them. Instead he said nothing and worried at it all night, at what they had stepped in and how they could leap out of it.

While the camp slept – aware that it was now a prison – Drust sought out Kisa Shem-Tov and gave him some instructions. When the man slid into the shadows, Drust turned and saw the sweat-gleamed face of Sib, his eyes penetrating as nails.

–

The amphitheatre was mostly finished and the scaffolding on the bit that wasn't had been removed so as not to spoil the look. It was packed, mainly with legionaries in tunics and sandals and straw hats against the sun. Their tunics had originally been the colour of wine lees, but the sun had bleached them to a dusty pink and they formed a solid block of jeering and cheering.

There were others, the tan and stained-white robes and head-coverings of the traders and herders, packers and carters, but they were well outnumbered and segregated. This was an Army day; roses and their petals were everywhere and the solid ring of on-duty legionaries as crowd security all had garlands of the flowers.

Drust and the others formed up in the eastern part, where the Porta Libitina was still smelling of fresh wood and new stone. On the opposite side of the *harena*, the Gate of Death no doubt smelled the same, but that would not last long.

Drust and the others were last in the processional line, for all that they were the main event; in front were the musicians, the priests – and Attalus. Drust had seen other Exhibitors of the Games carried into the *harena* on chariots pulled by zebras or ostriches, on the backs of elephants and once, memorably, in a litter borne by young, naked girls – any silly outrage seemed acceptable when you were paying.

But Attalus was mounted and Drust elbowed through the throng to where the horse stood. Attalus looked down coldly.

'There is no need for threat,' Drust began and was instantly ashamed of how he sounded and stopped speaking even before

Attalus waved a silencing hand. Horns blared; the procession was moving.

'There is no threat. You will return west once this is done with and never return. Until then, you will remain under the protection of my garrison.'

'Yes,' Drust said – what else could he do? Attalus nodded and smiled, the horse edged nervously, and Drust put out a hand to fend it off, feeling the slick sweat of it.

'Fortuna attend you this day,' Attalus said and moved off, leaving Drust standing staring until the others caught up with him; Kag took him by the tunic and dragged him into the procession, then frowned.

'Problem?'

Drust shook his head, then thought better of the lie and nodded, sickness rising in him like the roil of a rotten drain.

'I think he may try and kill one of us. To make a point.'

Chapter Four

A hatch opens above, spilling light, bright as stars, to wash the ancient walls which are black with old blood. There is a flutter of shadows in it and the thump, the sickening crunch of bodies falling through.

A huge striped cat flops lifelessly on a man, a half-charred fox bounces and lolls – they had set fire to their tails and let them loose to run, crazed, through the wolves and bears and archers to add spice to the morning show.

The light flickers again, the hatch grinds and a horse is levered through, a heavy thump and clatter; dung sprays and the surgeon curses. The boy, dull with the stun of the place and the fatigue of trying to pull dead lions with his ten-year-old muscle, does not like the surgeon, who is a Greek. No one likes Greeks, who are altogether too superior – but Gennadios is in charge of the boy and so the boy is the slave of a slave. Is there any lower to go, the boy wonders?

A man thuds down and the light disappears, leaving it darker still. The boy hefts a cleaver and starts heaving one leg of the striped beast, but it is the biggest cat he has ever seen, he can't pull the weight away, so he will start chopping it up; the paw is as big as his head. The man under it groans.

'This one is alive,' the boy calls, and Gennadios moves to join him.

'Always one,' he says. The man is clearer to see in the Greek's torch, his dark hair matted and knotted, body slathered in blood. One arm is missing at the elbow; the boy looks, but there is no sign of it.

'Help…'

'What do we do?' asks the boy.

'… me.'

Gennadios hands the boy the torch and bends. A door cracks open somewhere, bringing the red glow of a new torch, and a voice hails them both.

'Ho – don't chop up that beast. Skin it first – that's a Hyrcanian tiger. You will find teeth on a hen before you find another – the pelts are valuable, even if they are a little damaged. The Flavian must help pay for itself.'

'Help… me,' groans the man, his voice a husk.

The newcomer is cloaked and masked as Dis, but when he pulls off the mask he is a sweat-gleaming old face, lined and weary, who clutches a hammer and peers at the man the Greek is fussing over.

'Ah, fuck – did I miss one? He must have been out cold when I smacked him – see, you can see the hammer mark on his skull. Never moved. Tough bastard to have survived that as well as everything else.'

'Can he be saved?' asks the boy, thinking about his mother and whether the Greek has powers to bring back the dead. The Greek frowns, then shakes his head.

'With expense and care,' he says and looks at the wizened old man. 'I doubt if anyone will bother if Hermes's Psychopompos here is any benchmark.'

The man, who does not like being given the Greek name, hawks and spits.

'Fucking truth, right there,' he says. 'That's Justus Felix, the Frisian Fox. Well, he ran out of lairs when he met that tiger and the handlers are furious – he put two arrows in their cat and killed it dead as old mutton just as it chewed his arm off. They're upset – they may never find another cat like it. They won't be helping Justus anytime soon.'

The Greek straightens, wipes his hands and takes back the torch.

'Well,' the old man says and solemnly draws down his mask with leaden finality, 'stand back and I will help him across the Styx.'

'No,' Gennadios says and the boy looks stricken. The Greek, who is no Greek but a Sardinian, sees the look and has sympathy with it – but he is put to the task and has to obey, same as everyone else. Servillius Structus has ordered this boy to be educated and so that's what will happen. Lesson one – the heart in the throat and how to find it…

'In the arena you may,' he says pointedly to Dis, 'but you missed this one.'

Dis Pater looks horned and blank, but the boy knows the old man is scowling beneath it.

'He is already dead,' Gennadios says to the boy. 'It remains only for you to remind him of it.'

The boy takes his knife; the one-armed man's eyes roll and he is aware of nothing much. The Greek nods to the boy and then at the groaning man whose chest labours to suck in life.

'Get it right this time,' he says. 'And do it slowly – I want to see the moment when your knife crosses him over.'

The boy has done this before and is still not ready for it. He puts the knife in the place allotted, the one the Greek calls the heart in the throat. Pushes, feeling that moment of resistance, then the sudden, slick slide. Blood pours and the man gasps and gugs; the boy pulls the knife out.

The Greek surgeon grunts with disappointment.

'Too little, yet again,' he says, taking the knife. 'You fear it too much, at the end. Be firm – here, like this.'

He guides the boy's hand and they push and slice. The man coughs, his heels kick and then he is gone. The Greek blows out his cheeks with exasperation.

'Missed it,' he says, as if he had lost sight of some rare bird.

The hatch grinds, the light floods, the bodies fall.

Drust follows the surgeon into the deep dark, trying to avoid the edges of the archways and failing – they smack him on the shoulder, time after time…

–

He woke at the slap on his shoulder, sat up so suddenly that his head spun and he had to blink a few times until the face coalesced into Praeclarum's broad concern.

'You were asleep,' she said. There was wonder and accusation in equal measure as she handed him water in a clay bowl; it was warm as soup but balm to a mouth dry and thick with mucus. She had not been enough of a ring fighter, he thought, but would learn how easy it is to sleep in a charnel house buzzing with noises. He glanced after her, marvelling at how she had slotted in to them after only two months – or perhaps it was just him who felt that.

Drust moved slowly; he wore his dusty gear still and was crusted with a dried paste of sand and sweat. Around them whirled the noise and stink of the undercroft – not as great as the Flavian, Drust thought, but enough to release the latch of memory. The lunchtimers stumbled through the gate in their costumes – the horn-blowing chicken, the flute-playing bear; it was the same everywhere, it was noon and the mummers and caperers were out, sweating in the heat to try and entertain a garrison of mostly men and whores, who only wanted blood and naked death.

The others were there, sitting quietly, working at some small task or, in Ugo's case, sitting with his hands on his knees, eyes closed, talking to his gods. They were all here, Drust saw, which is a blessing from that fickle cunt, Fortuna, blessings be upon her. Things had gone well and his own fight had been a decent enough dance, with just enough in it to make sure no one realised the rehearsals.

He was appalled at his own weakness, at how the heat and the exertion had made him nod off. The dream, he knew, was sent by Dis – the first time, the only one, he had seen a Hyrcanian tiger. The thought that it was a warning that he was too old for all of this came with a stab of fear; it was a thought he would never offer up to the others in any conversation.

Talk was muted and most of it was drowned by the babble of the *venatores*, who weren't anything like those professional beast-killers. They were hunters and trappers and hauliers who had brought animals for the Games and been made up for the day. Smeared with the excitement and dazzle of something they had never done and would never do again if they were sensible, they were loud as a barnyard of cockerels. They'd survived and now it was lunchtime, when the novelty acts went out – if there were any.

'Hares. More crucifixions,' Kag muttered. 'Attalus must be rounding up every suspect on a list. They only have crucifixions and hares and rustic farces from the local actors.'

'Hares?' demanded Ugo, frowning, and Drust recalled those animals had some meaning for the big man. Quintus squinted at the half-moon grill that let them look into the *harena* and jerked a thumb.

'Take a look. Hares and hounds and bad acting – that won't keep Army boots happy.'

The actors were aspirational Greeks who had expected to have the most of this new amphitheatre and put on the works of Terentius Afer or Plautus – if it had to be Roman – and Euripides, Philoctetes and the rest of the Greeks if they had their own way. If they had to sink to comedy, it would be Aristophanes or Susarion of Megara – not what they were

65

now doing, which was running around the *harena* waving giant phalluses and pretending to fuck the arse of a fat Parthian in a turban.

Judging from the jeers and the red-faced, food-pelted Greeks who staggered into the undercroft, it was not going well; but the hares were worse and everyone jumped with surprise, then laughed, when a small brown shape scrabbled through the grill squares and ran around among them, before it subsided, panting and frozen. The hound chasing it smashed off the grill in a welter of bloody saliva and mournful howls.

'Should have put Stercorinus out,' Quintus said, picking up the hare, which was too petrified to move or resist. He grinned his big wide grin and looked at the man for a reaction but had none; the skinny brown sliver, naked save for a cloth round his hips, just leaned against a pillar and cradled his big sword, his eyes lurking somewhere beneath a matted shock of hair and beard.

'At least look as if you are worried,' Kag told him, scowling.

Stercorinus split his beard in a small smile. 'Would it help?'

'This would have been my time once,' Praeclarum said. 'Killing tiros and the condemned and blindfolded dwarves.'

Kag slapped her on one leather shoulder. 'Would have been,' he said, 'but you are one of us now. And shush on that blindfold thing – don't give anyone ideas.'

Praeclarum said nothing, but when the others made the ring and thrust their hands into it, palms down and knuckles up, she stood apart and shook her head when Drust looked expectantly at her.

Later he drew her aside and she knew he was concerned. He was patriarch of this family, she had long since recognised, and it puzzled her why it was important to him. She had half an idea it was a bewilderment to him too.

'It has meaning to us,' he said, and she nodded, had already seen that.

He held up his hands, knuckles towards her, and she saw the inked marks, only slightly faded – E.S.S.S, one letter on all four fingers. Knew what they stood for too – *ego sum servus Servillius*. Every slave had one somewhere, the mark of their status, the brand that told how they were someone else's property. Even now that they were freedmen and citizens, it marked them as people apart from what was considered decent society.

'I am not… of you,' she said uneasily.

'You have been here two months, long enough to know better. You are free,' Drust said simply, 'to come and go as you please.'

Praeclarum knew this in her head, but her heart hadn't caught up with it yet and she could only nod.

'The big one who smiles, Quintus,' she said haltingly.

Drust knew Quintus was the one who had bought her for next to nothing and had brought her back, almost thrusting her into the midst of them and grinning as wide as a new-set trap.

'Say greeting to this one,' he had announced loudly. 'Her name is Remarkable. I have bought her and now I free her. Drust – you make it official, the writing and all, can't you?'

'Why did he do that?' she asked Drust, who spread his hands.

'He won at dice and spent it how he pleased,' he answered, then took pity on her. 'Because we are the Brothers of the Sand,' he added, 'who have all been slaves. I think he liked your mark.'

Her hand went to the side of her neck instinctively; for a time she had worn a kerchief round the seared old scars that read TMFQ but lately had stopped that and let people stare. *Tene me quia fugi* – arrest me I have fled. She glared back at those who stared, daring them to act – yet she was hovering on the edge of things here.

'I do not know anyone here,' she said. 'I am not part of you. Quintus made me free, but I owe him my price still.'

'Quintus,' Drust said, 'has been free longer than any of us. He has been everywhere and seen everything, or so he will claim. He likes money but will give it away for a kiss – yet, as you can see, he forces no woman to it.'

Praeclarum dropped her eyes a little. It had been a belly-clench of fear when the long-legged, smiling Quintus had bought her for the price of a dog, and that feeling had taken a long time to leave – she had slept with a dagger for several nights until she realised no one was creeping up on her. She still did not quite understand it – these were not the crew of the *Argo*, or the heroes of Troy, and she had heard enough to know that they were dark with old blood and rotten secrets. Yet Quintus had not raped her – or tried to, she corrected. No one would ever rape her again.

'Sib,' Drust went on, 'is no *harena* fighter. He is a *mavro*, a dark-skin, from south and west of Lepcis Magna. A desert dog who was a slave to the same Servillius who owned us all – and who freed us all, one by one, to serve him in different ways. Sib is a charioteer who raced for the Blues, or the Greens – whoever paid Servillius to have a good man at the reins. Won a few.'

Drust stopped and seemed to hesitate, then smiled. 'He is ridden by old fears and tribal tales. Believes in strange creatures from the desert. Believes that Manius is one – you have heard of Manius?'

She nodded. 'One of the two you seek. The other is called Dog.'

Drust's face went grim for a moment. 'Manius is a *mavro* also, but there is dark inside him too, as Sib will tell you. Sib once believed – perhaps still does – that Manius is a *jnoun*, which is some sort of desert horror from the depths of a sandy Dis. I think he tried to arrange for Manius to die once – now he is trying to atone for that.'

'And Dog?'

Drust was silent for a moment, then sighed. 'You will know Dog when you see him. His face is on inside out. Of us all, he is the true fighter, who fought in the Flavian and survived. He is… Dog.'

He sat for a moment, then stirred and grinned. 'Then there is Ugo, our giant from the Germanies. He believes he can move the world if you give him a lever and a place to stand – Kag told me that one, from some old clever Greek. Kag knows a great deal and that's what you should remember about him. He looks like shit that fell off someone's shoe, but there is gold in the man and, for all he curses them, he is like me and will traipse to the edge of the world to look Dog and Manius in the eye and call them arseholes for having put him to it.'

He stopped, then frowned at the curve of the leaning Stercorinus. 'That one is no slave. He was debt-bonded to a *lanista* we knew who wanted rid of him because he did not know what to do with the man. Stercorinus is not his name, nor is Palmyra his home, though he claims both. The sword, he says, belonged to a Christian, right hand of their crucified Jesus, but Kag says a man like that would carry a *gladius*, because it is shorter and more easy to conceal – you don't walk about with a displayed blade like that in Rome. Kisa says it is one an executioner would use. Stercorinus worships strange gods – or one at least – and does everything because he or they whisper to him.'

'He is debt-bonded to you now?' Praeclarum asked and Drust shook his head.

'We have no bonded fighters here. Some slaves among the paid men, for running things on a camel train – how else would the world turn? But not fighters. We are all Brothers of the Sand here. Even the sisters.'

She smiled, showing her lack of teeth. 'And you?'

There was pause, and for a moment the world teetered on the edge of revelation, so that Praeclarum, who had asked innocently, felt the coil of it and held her breath. Then, like a blast of hot fetid breath, Sib burst it.

'Drust – we have a problem.'

He had a round-faced man hovering apologetically at his back. They all recognised him as a local magistrate called Vespillo, which was his occupation – he was responsible for burying people too poor to afford a funeral. It was, perhaps, a joke by Attalus to promote him to *summa rudis*, the adjudicator of the fights, but he had done well enough. Now, seeing his sweating, stricken face, Drust felt a cold knife sliding into his belly.

'The Exhibitor has called for a special contest to start in the afternoon,' he stammered. 'A match between one of you and one of the garrison legionaries – for the honour of the Army.'

'Bastard,' Kag growled. 'Tell him to fuck off. We have a contract and there is nothing about this in it.'

'If you refuse,' Vespillo whined and looked back over his shoulder at where the low growling roar was like some prowling animal. 'Attalus suggests a *retiarius*,' Vespillo went on. 'Since the legionary will be in full kit.'

Of course he did, Drust thought dully. He knows Praeclarum fought as the *retiarius*. He thinks she will be untrained and weak and because she is a female *infamis* can be easily overcome, left begging for her life. Attalus sends us a message, Drust thought – but a ranker from the Army is no *harena* fighter, has no concept of the rules of it. He might make a mistake, or not wait to be told she had been let off.

'What have you been instructed?' he demanded, and Vespillo licked his lips, shame and desperation flowing from him like heat.

'Not to stand as *summa rudis*. It is not an official contest...'

'He means to humiliate us,' Quintus growled, and Ugo made a boar-grunting noise in the back of his throat.

'He will end up killing her,' Kag added.

Praeclarum laughed and Drust looked at her admiringly, for it sounded good.

'I have seen legionaries. Big men with small swords,' she answered.

'You might give him a shock at that,' Kag said slowly, 'but that will only make it worse. If you win, the Army lot will be appalled and hate you. Before that, your opponent will use every dirty trick to avoid being beaten by a woman, an *infamis*, a slave and a gladiator.'

'Four against one does seem unfair,' Quintus agreed, grinning; folk laughed. Quintus stopped stroking the hare long enough for it to finally stir, wriggle free from his loose grip and spring away, back through the grill into the *harena*.

'If it is your day to die,' Quintus said sadly, looking after it, 'then Dis will claim you.'

Drust simply turned and looked at Praeclarum. 'Strip,' he said.

–

Drust had no idea what face Attalus had on him, for the sun was on his own and the man was higher up and further back; he had an idea that it would be like a slapped arse, all the same, a scowl like a scar. Most of Drust's attention was taken with trying to squint sideways without moving his head, trying to see who he would face while both of them stood in the maelstrom of catcalls and howling, facing Attalus who had given up trying to be heard.

The legionary was young and well aware of all his mates. He was called, Drust had heard, Aurelios or Aurelio or somesuch, which was mainly Greek with a sauce of Syrian. He was from a vexallation of the 3rd Cyrenaica and was a big bastard, a long-termer about four years in, wearing full rig – bronze scale, helmet, a great curved rectangle of shield, and a *spatha*.

He was head-back bawling out his salute as if Attalus was the Emperor himself – this soldier swears that he will faithfully execute all that the Emperor commands and stands ready for any order. It would have been more impressive if apple cores hadn't been bouncing all round him and the bellows of his comrades hadn't drowned most of it out.

There was nothing left but to take a few steps back, turn and face one another, and when they did, the roaring increased so that it buzzed Drust's head like a struck bell. There was a pause that lasted a thousand years, long enough for Drust to see the set face and the grin, the knuckles flex on the hilt of the long *spatha*, the slight hunch as Aurelios settled himself behind that giant shield.

Drust felt naked – he was naked, and Praeclarum's padded harness, too tight in all the wrong places, did not hide much. He had a three-tined *fuscina* and a dagger, an arm guard and a tall shoulder piece attached to it, once ornate with dolphins and the head of Hercules and now battered. He had a weighted net and the feeling of an addled egg on a busy path.

'You should have taken the offer,' Aurelios said, and Drust realised he had been told to say that, a message from Attalus. Aurelios probably had no idea what was going on, but he had delivered the instruction and now there was only the bit he did understand; Drust saw him blow out his cheeks and make a little head movement to shake the sweat off his brow under the helmet.

Good, he thought viciously. Blind yourself, you cunt.

He really should have been expecting the sudden dart, fast even for a man with all that armour on him. It was a duel in the *harena* after all – what else would be happening? He was a trained fighter and had managed to make himself woefully unprepared – the blow struck the tines of the *fuscina*, a numbing force that almost ripped it from his sweat-greased fist. He went sideways, stumbling and flailing, the net trailing like a tail, and all thoughts of his first attack splintered away in the mad desire to get away, survive for one more eyeblink.

The noise of the crowd was thunder and Aurelios was made lightning by it. He bored in, swinging the long sword. Drust spun away, whipped the net round and heard the weights rattle off the shield before it slammed into his protected arm and sent him stumbling away yet again. Drust reeled and swung the *fuscina* like a scythe, a lucky blow that skimmed the rim of the shield and whicked dangerously close to Aurelios's nose, making the man jerk back and stop.

They circled, Drust slick with cold terror, Aurelios seemingly raised up to be Mars Ultor by his initial success and the great rolling waves of bellows from the crowd. He moved with a practised grace, the sword swinging slightly loose, making no overtly fancy moves – at least he is still worried about me, Drust thought.

They were all worried, he recalled. Praeclarum had been scowling when she had stripped off the leather and padded rig, claiming that this was not her first dance on the sand and that she was the *retiarius* after all. Kag and Quintus and the others had all offered advice, some of it no doubt useful but all of it, Drust saw, out of concern. Stercorinus continued to lounge against the stone, cradling the sword.

'At least try and look concerned for me,' Drust had spat at him, and Stercorinus came off the wall and took a breath. His voice was a rasp, not wounded or angry, just the sound of someone who did not use it too often.

'I will if it helps,' he said, then paused and added, 'he wears boots.'

Something flashed, making Drust blink, blinded – Aurelios had circled round so that the sun was now in Drust's eyes – the blow when it came was a sliver of arcing light that slammed into his left shoulder, shrieking on the metal guard. His own squeal almost drowned it out as he was driven sideways again and he slid a little, righted himself and risked a quick look for blood on the sand. Or even the arm...

He spat, gritted his teeth and lunged – if you are not attacking you are losing was one of Kag's many sage sayings, some of which were even true, like this one. He felt the *fuscina* slam the shield and grate off it, the momentum carrying him forward hard into the huge shield.

It was like shoulder-charging a wall. A husky, barley-fed legionary in a metal suit with a big shield? Aurelios did what he had been trained to do when he stood in the front rank, side by side with all his mates who were now howling him on. He shrugged and shoved Drust off, sending him backwards to land on his arse in a spray of grit.

Up, up, said a voice. Get up. Another whispered: Why? He will only knock you down again.

He rolled over and got up, pasted with a porridge of sweat and sand. Aurelios closed in, swinging left and right, and was surprised when Drust blocked and spun away and flicked out the net so that the weights thumped his leg just below the knee.

It made Aurelios pull up short, the thought of being wrapped in that coil and pulled off his feet. He had never fought like this, a man armed like this, but he had been warned and decided caution was best.

Everyone else had decided death was best and the chant got into rhythm, into cadence. That's good, Drust admitted grudgingly. Your average crowd couldn't manage to get that right in less than a thousand heartbeats – trust the Army to manage it quicker.

Kill him. Kill him. Kill him.

Aurelios heard it and Drust saw his eyes. No deaths in this contract, he thought bitterly and felt the wash of iced fear sluice him. No humiliation here – a straight-up kill and it might have been designed for the woman, but Aurelios did not know that. He had his instruction, like the message…

The legionary came on – one foot, drag the other, one foot, drag the other – in proper style, as if he was ranked with an entire cohort, all advancing in step.

Drust backed off, started circling the net above his head in slow, hissing loops; he saw Aurelios pause, eyeing it suspiciously, and when it suddenly fanned out like a flower in bloom, his eyes went wide.

It failed, missed by a hair – Aurelios tried to stamp on the edge as Drust whipped it back and flicked it a few times, shaking it back into the whip-tail. Aurelios heard the catcalls and jeers, and frowned – then he made a sudden rush.

Drust spun away from it, one of the moves he had used with other partners – but they had been rehearsed. No one had decided, in the mad flail of rushing past, to lash out with the hilt of a *spatha* and slam Drust in the ribs.

Pain blew in like a massive explosion of light. He found himself rolling in the grit, his whole body burning and his mouth tasting of old sick.

He came up to his hands and knees, saw nail-studded Army boots and the huge looming figure. Beyond were pale blobs with red gashes in them – the faces of those leaning out over the amphitheatre wall to try and not miss the ending.

Aurelios brought the edge of the shield down and it slammed the ground where Drust's head had been – the crowd bawled out disapproval and spurred Aurelios on to slashing and slamming the shield while Drust scrabbled away. He put out the *fuscina* to block a blow and heard the ping and crack as the *spatha* sheared off the lower third of it; the crowd's roars redoubled.

He crabbed backwards on his arse, trying to hold onto the *fuscina* and the net, but Aurelios's nailed boot came down and pinned the latter. A stroke, almost casual, then another and another, and Drust rolled away holding a useless net, almost cut in two.

Should have pulled, he thought, weaving to his feet. Should have pulled his big Army boots out from under him…

He wears boots.

Drust looked round. They had filled the amphitheatre with sand, to make it *harena*, but hadn't gone far for it – the desert was a spit away, so why would you import it? So what you had was grit, not the fine sand that the Flavian boasted, the silver-white stuff Drust and the others had brought in on grain wagons and ships as a priority. Fuck the grain dole – bring sand for the Flavian…

Here, they had skimped on it – all the contest would be in the centre, so that's where they had made it thickest. Out here, practically under the wall, it was a light sprinkling over the amphitheatre flags.

He wears boots.

'Aurelios.'

He had to yell it out to be heard above the crowd, but the man stopped, blinked at the sound of his name and stood uncertainly.

'I know your mother.'

The legionary was confused, sensing a trick, watching for it. Drust laughed.

'I was set to fuck her up the arse – but the donkey got in first and I couldn't be bothered waiting.'

There was a pause. Drust turned and ran, feeling the grit faintly on his calloused bare soles; no *harena* fighter ever wore anything on his feet in a fight save the feel of the sand; he blessed Stercorinus – the lanky streak of spit never said much, Drust thought, but when he does…

The crowd howled jeers at him and Aurelios spat out a curse and took off in pursuit; he was trained for this, to move swiftly in full rig. He could keep it up as long as this piece of gladiator scum…

His big hobnails came down, slid on the grains of grit like it was a slick of oil. He crashed down, feeling the ankle break, slamming the amphitheatre wall; he lost his grip on the shield and heard it clattering free. Dazed for a moment, he tried to get up and the pain made him howl, though no one could hear it for the roaring.

Then he looked up and saw the gladiator.

Drust batted the *spatha* away with the remains of his *fuscina*, did it again and again until Aurelios realised he wasn't getting anywhere. There was a sudden silence, even louder than the noise that had gone before, it seemed.

Aurelios climbed onto his one good foot and stood. His shield had skittered away, too far to recover. His *spatha* was still in one fist but he couldn't move forward to attack.

Drust stood, watching. Someone yelled '*missio*' and others took it up. Drust looked up and round at the crowd, then back at Aurelios, who had decided to forego a referee. He held the shattered *fuscina* just below the tines.

Then he stepped in suddenly, so close the long sword was useless, though Aurelios tried to flail a strike, rasping uselessly off the arm protector.

The *fuscina* went up under Aurelios's chin, the centre tine right up into his mouth, through his tongue, the force of the blow spearing it up behind his nose. The other two scored huge grooves in his cheeks – one, because it wasn't a perfect strike, cracked through the jawbone and went in under the eye.

Aurelios screamed and gugged. Drust gripped the last of the ruined shaft and turned, hauling Aurelios like a man trying to shoulder a sack of grain; the legionary burbled out bloody screams and fought to hobble on his good leg, trying to take some of the tearing weight off his face.

Drust dragged him right into the middle of the sand and flung him away like a useless bag; Aurelios fell and choked and gurgled and died, noisily and painfully. The crowd bellows started to sound ugly as Drust turned to where Attalus was sitting and raised one arm in salute and message. Even so, he felt veiled from it, as if he walked alone in the middle of shadows – until something grabbed his arm and started pulling him.

'Move yourself,' Kag spat, 'before they tear you to pieces.'

He didn't move. There was a dust cloud round him and all voices seemed to come from underwater – but he felt Kag drag him and then call out Ugo's name. The next second, Drust was floating until he vaguely realised he was being carried by the big German, grunting with the effort as if he hefted a bale of cloth.

There was a roaring and figures appeared – Drust saw Dis coming for him, but it was the *harena* one, who stopped and hesitantly looked round while his assistant, the one with the great cruel hook for dragging off the bodies, started to crouch and whimper. Shapes were dropping off the amphitheatre wall and Kag was screaming for Ugo to move his big fat arse...

They came in through the Gate of Life, crossing from blinding light to the balmed confusion of shadows and shapes running and shouting. Drust heard Quintus bawling for Sib to help him close the gates, and the heavy wooden batten slammed down a moment later.

There was a pinch on one cheek, a bee sting that made Drust raise a hand whose fingers seemed to belong to someone else. A second sting was sharper. The third was a clear slap that made him jerk away, and before the fourth arrived, he had caught Kag's wrist.

'You have sense now?'

Drust nodded. Now there were people running back and forth in the dim undercroft and Sib, his eyes white as eggs, thrust his face close.

'You fucking killed him – what did you do that for?'

It was the *harena*, you *Stupidus*, Drust tried to say. That's what we do... but his mouth wouldn't work and it was Quintus who slapped the back of Sib's head and told him exactly that. Kag gave a sour grunt.

'You might have poked him a bit, made him squeal or beg. His mates would have hated him for it almost as much as they hate you. But you stuck that fucking big fish-fork up his nose – do you hear how they feel about it?'

79

There was a mad hammering on the door and the thin threnody of a voice gone past fear into mad panic, demanding to be let in. It was Dis, or the one with the hook. The voices drowned in the hammering and howling.

'A *missio* was not an option,' Drust finally managed and no one argued with the look on his face.

'They will be in through the Gate of Death,' Stercorinus pointed out, looking warily at the dark that led in the inevitable circle back to where they were.

'We cannot stay here,' Praeclarum added and had a scathing look from Sib at this statement of the obvious.

'I have a way,' Kisa said.

'Of course you have, little man,' Quintus declared and slapped him hard on the shoulder, grinning that big white grin. 'Lead on.'

'You must remove all your gladiator armours,' Kisa warned, 'and wrap weapons in cloaks or tunics.'

They saw the sense in it, even though Kag cursed the loss of decent fighting gear, bawling out what he would do to any fuck who stole it while they were gone. Drust did not think anyone would be waiting around to do that – but these were trouser-wearing Persians, so anything was possible.

They followed Kisa, throwing aside panicked animal handlers and slaves until they reached a door, already flung open – a man dressed as the Atellan Manducus was forcing his way through the rest of his fellow actors, beating at them with his painted sword.

'The Actors' Gate,' Kisa explained, and Ugo grabbed Manducus by his tin armour and hauled him back out of the way like a terrier with a rat; they piled through.

Outside, people were scattering, others frantically gathering up the contents of shops and stalls and moving them to somewhere with a lock.

'This is the Street of Baths,' Ugo yelled out.

'You are correct,' Kisa replied, 'though it remains a mystery how you know. Keep close, do not linger.'

He led and they followed, dodging fleeing people, seeing the produce-laden dye seller and the spice merchant collide in a massive explosion of colours and then, astoundingly, simply get up and run off without argument or spilled goods. A speeding donkey, an ever-present threat in the streets of Dura, came rippling along at a fast trot, the rider swaying precariously. From somewhere close came the sound of shouts and breaking pottery.

'A riot,' Quintus said and grinned at Drust. 'You have started a riot in the city...'

They followed Kisa up a narrow alley between high, mud-wall houses to where an even taller wall loomed, with a single door in it. Kisa rapped loudly and the small grill in the centre flicked open, then closed; there was the sound of a locking bar sliding and the door opened for them to spill through.

They stopped short after two or three steps, gaping like yokels at what they saw – a square atrium with painted colonnades, open to the sky and with a tessellated floor, at the centre of which was a column statue of someone – something – with many breasts.

'Jupiter's hairy cock,' Kag swore, turning in circles.

'Jupiter never put it anywhere near here,' Quintus declared, not smiling for once. 'This is Artemis, whose priests are self-inflicted eunuchs.'

As if summoned, figures appeared, slippering softly over the tiled mosaic – a representation of Diana, Drust saw, hunting

81

with bow and arrow. The figures were in white and saffron silks and linens, turbans and heavy eye make-up – priests, they all thought, though they were not sure if there were women among them.

'Are they all cut slaves?' Ugo wanted to know in a too-loud voice. Kisa opened and closed his mouth once or twice, caught between his innate desire to show his knowledge and not wanting to offend the saffron-robed figures.

'Some are,' said a voice. 'All are slaves, women and men – the young men petition to join the rite of the Goddess once a year and most are granted. There they remove their own testicles with sharp knives.'

Uranius stepped from the shadows of the colonnade and crossed the tiles to them, while everyone looked at the priests with a new sense of awe and disgust; Sib hissed and made warding signs.

'Hecate,' Stercorinus growled, though it was hard to say whether it was approval or not. Uranius smiled and stretched his arms to encompass the place; for the first time Drust and the others saw a second statue, built into the wall under the columns, a great arch with a carving of a serene woman with long, rippling locks, surrounded by images of people offering her tribute. There was a pond of fat fish in front and somewhere a cote of doves fluted.

'The temple of Artemis Azzanathkona,' Uranius declared, as if he had personally built it. He wore bronzed lappet armour over a white tunic and the red cloak was flung over one shoulder. He wore breeks, padded on the inside thigh for riding.

'There is a wall cutting it off from the main barracks – the amphitheatre and the buildings beyond belong to the 20th Palmyran Cohort.'

'Wait – what?' Kag demanded and turned angrily to Kisa. 'You brought us into the legionary camp? Home of those who want to tear us to bits?'

'He brought you, at my bidding, into the headquarters of the 20th Palmyran,' Uranius answered levelly. 'The garrison of Dura-Europos. Every other Army clod here is a vexallation from somewhere else – the only garrison is us. We are auxiliaries. Worse than that, militia. You have nothing to fear from the 20th – they hate the Roman Army incomers more than they hate Persians.'

He turned, expecting them to follow and they did, whispering a way across the tiles on their calloused soles.

'My tribune has taken most of the 20th out into the streets to effect some order. You know we are all archers, a mixed unit of horse and foot?'

'And twenty camels,' Praeclarum added, which made Uranius smile as he reached another small door set in a wall.

'A *turma*, so there should be thirty-two. Illness, losses – no unit is ever full.'

He rapped on the door and it opened instantly – by someone waiting behind it for just such a task, Drust thought.

'The temple is cut off from the camp but open to the city. There are many worshippers here,' Uranius explained. 'The 20th are mostly Syrian and Azzanathkona is a huntress – the Greeks say she is Artemis in another guise. The Romans claim her as Diana the Huntress. Archers, you see – so the 20th venerate her.'

'We are safe here?' Drust asked and Uranius nodded.

'For now – but we must get you out of the city. There are provisions waiting at a spot beyond the Palmyra Gate.'

'Provisions?'

'Water and food enough for your journey.'

'Wait,' Kag growled. 'We have camels and herders for them. We have just thrown away all our fighting gear...'

'We will rescue all once the 20th has restored order,' Uranius declared, then looked grim. 'That will hopefully be before some drunken arsehole finds a slather of purple cloth and throws it over the head of Attalus or someone else.'

He looked round them all. 'That is what I am sent here to watch for. The garrisons here are sloppy and degraded, ripe for any foolishness, including declaring one of their own as a new Emperor.'

'Is Attalus a *Stupidus* then?' Praeclarum demanded. 'Enough to accept such a thing?'

'It is an honour few can refuse,' Uranius answered. 'If you accept, you are a traitor to Rome, and you all know how that ends. If you refuse, then the ones who offered it will be offended, and you all know how that ends.'

'I can hear it,' muttered Ugo, looking towards the faint sound of breaking. Uranius nodded.

'Attalus must be rescued before such a choice is offered – my tribune and the bulk of the 20th are doing just that.'

'*Authentēs*,' Kisa said warningly. 'Time.'

Uranius nodded; Drust realised, with a sudden shock, that Kisa was not working for the Shayk, but for Uranius.

'Kisa will take you to where you can find tunics and cloaks and helmets. You will each take a camel and ride out as men of the 20th. At the meeting point there will be camels provided by the Shayk. After that, you are on your own.'

He paused. 'When you return, contact me. No one else – the Shayk cannot be trusted and he offers this caravan with motives of his own. Also, do not trust the *Praeses Mesopotamiae*, who is no true friend to the Emperor.'

Drust had no idea who the assistant governor of Mesopotamia even was, and said so as he cautiously took Uranius's proffered arm in a wrist grip of farewell.

'Gaius Julius Verus Maximinus,' Uranius said as they filtered off, one by one, following Kisa. 'They call him Thrax because he was born there, a barbarian from Moesia. You will not miss him when you see him...'

The last slithered after Drust like an echo and was lost in the soft babble of the others arguing over too-short tunics and too-large helmets, while patient men of the 20th watched impassively, saying nothing, but listening to the sound of riot and wondering whether the world was indeed falling.

By the time they were out of the Palmyran Gate, urging dirty-white camels towards a distant, vague meeting, Drust's look back at the city only confirmed what appeared to be everyone's worst fears. Threads of smoke feathered the sky from where the rioters had started burning and the gate was choked with people fleeing with the detritus of their lives.

The world was falling.

Chapter Five

The country beyond Dura was as graceless as a dead lion, a
tawny slump where they rode between the ridges of its ribs,
shuffling up the powdered grit, scattering the little stones from
a well-worn trail. The ribs they moved over were striated, as
if by the claws of the *jnoun* which killed this great beast. They
had travelled other deserts, from Tingis to Palmyra and now
beyond, but all were agreed – this was a carrion land.

Drust did not know much of it for the first three days,
but he came to it at last, round the comfort of a camel-dung
fire with the soft gurgle of the beasts and the low murmur of
conversation. The only spoiling in it was Praeclarum, grinning
ruin down on his naked body.

She stopped smiling when she saw he was awake and the
others saw the change in her face.

'There you were,' Quintus said, grinning his wide, white
grin, as if to show Praeclarum's fault in a worse light, 'dreaming
of that Gaulish girl in Milo's and you get that.'

'Perhaps you can ease his hurts better than me,' Praeclarum
replied flatly, going on with the delicate touch of expert fingers.
Drust squinted down and saw the midnight colour of his side.

'Ahh,' he managed and Kag squatted by him, nodding
admiringly to Praeclarum.

'You carry on, girl, and ignore that long-legged lout. No
one knows the secret of bruise healing like you.'

'Unwashed wool, dipped into a mixture of pounded rue and fat,' she said, sponging gently. 'Plus prayers to Fortuna and Asclepius.'

'There's always a fucking Greek in it somewhere,' Sib murmured, turning something sizzling on a grill over coals; the smell made Drust's mouth water but he wanted more than food.

'What happened? Where are we?'

'Up Fortuna's arse, trying to duck Jupiter's fat cock,' Quintus replied sourly.

'Three days out of Dura,' Kag answered, throwing a quick scowl at Quintus. 'On the caravan trail to Singara, where we are to meet a man called Narseh. This is not a place you want to be if you have offended powerful deities.'

'Narseh-dux,' a voice corrected and Kisa thrust his smiling face into Drust's eyeline. 'He is one of the Shayk's men.'

'Like you,' Kag growled and Kisa's face closed like a stone clam. Not true, Drust wanted to say. He is the creature of Uranius, he wanted to say. But it all seemed such an effort, so he said nothing.

'No matter his name,' Sib said from beyond Drust's sight. 'Let's hope he can get us decorated. Our own camels and herders are gone. Our equipment is gone. We have only a dozen Army camels now. Just about enough water to reach the next oasis, which we would be in now except...'

He stopped and busied himself with the meat and the fire.

'Except,' Kag finished, looking at Drust, 'you kept threatening to fall off the camel and Praeclarum stopped us all before you did.'

'If not, it might have made matters worse,' Praeclarum interrupted; Kag acknowledged it with a flap of one hand.

'All well and good,' Sib argued, 'but the oasis will have other trains and their guards. We have already lost almost all we possess, and if anyone is on our trail, we will lose even more.'

'There will be folk on our trail,' Kag grunted in reply. 'If you are leaving tracks, someone always is – but we left riot behind us and that will gain us a few days.'

'If there is pursuit it won't be by the *dromedarii*,' Kisa soothed. What he did not add, Drust thought, trying to ease the throbbing ache of his ribs, was that Attalus wouldn't trust Uranius's camel-soldiers. He'd send riders, all the same.

Drust looked round as best he could without moving more than his head. Almost everyone had filched a red cloak and a tunic that, stained though it was, was better quality and cleaner than the ones they'd worn to fight in the *harena*. His thoughts were drowned out by arguments, the voices low and urgent growls; Praeclarum stopped sponging and got Stercorinus to help her raise Drust to sitting so she could bind him, a process of shrieking agony that slowly paled to a dull red glow of pain. The binding was tight and made it hurt to breathe deeply, but it let him stand on wobbling legs.

'He smacked you hard,' Kag said, breaking off from growling at the others. 'Still – that Army boy didn't deserve a trio of daggers in the face.'

'It is done,' Drust answered curtly, not wanting discussion or even thought on it, because he remembered what he had done, could watch himself doing it and did not like the wash of shame and revulsion he felt. Yet the man had been set to kill him…

'Done well,' Quintus put in. 'That greyback was set on sixing you for all that no deaths had been paid for.'

88

'Expensive all the same,' Sib spat back, 'considering that we have lost everything we owned and are now pursued into the desert.'

'Let's just wait until we reach Singara,' Ugo said, loud enough to drown everyone for a moment. They subsided, giving Drust a chance.

'This Narseh,' he began, and Kisa, squatting by the coals, looked up.

'Narseh-dux,' he corrected and Drust waved a dismissive hand.

'I am less interested in what he is called than in who he is and what he will do for us.'

Kisa explained it. The Shayk would, as promised, rescue the group's original camel train and the equipment they'd had to abandon in the amphitheatre – there were mutters about how that would be achieved, but Drust managed to silence them. Uranius had given them a dozen army camels, enough to get them to Singara, where this Narseh had been messaged to equip them with all they would need to get across the Red Serpent, meet with Manius and Dog and return with Hyrcanian tigers.

At the end of it, he grinned widely and clasped his hands, as if it was a deal already done. No one spoke for a moment. Sib doled out coal-fried lamb and passed round a bowl of *oenogarum* sauce for it, so that a long, peaceful moment was spent chewing and savouring. Praeclarum half turned from the rest to eat, since she could only cut small pieces and suck them soft enough to swallow; Drust knew her ruined mouth hurt constantly.

'You need cages,' Kag said eventually.

'Big ones,' Ugo added.

'Not something you can easily disguise,' Quintus pointed out, 'so that the guards on this Persian Wall can be fooled enough to let us pass.'

'We might build the cages there,' Kisa offered and Sib snorted his derision.

'There is no hiding a brace or more of those tigers on the way back,' he pointed out.

'Do these Persian guards care?' said Stercorinus. He was sitting half naked and cradling his sword, though one hand was feeding meat into the hole in his tangled beard where his mouth lurked. 'They let this Dog and Manius through and I am betting sure they had some carts with them.'

'The Persians on the Serpent care,' Kisa answered miserably. 'The land of Hyrcania smiles on the new Sasan dynasty. I would not be surprised if soon it came under the banner of these new Persians – but no matter what, the tigers are prized by all. I cannot see them allowing strangers – Romans among them – to walk away with a pair or more.'

'Ah well,' Stercorinus growled and he might have been grinning, but it was hard to tell. His voice did not sound overly concerned and Quintus squinted at him.

'Are you not worried at how we are to cross this Wall?' he demanded, and Stercorinus paused in licking his fingers.

'Would it help?' he asked.

No one had a reply to that, so they sat and ate and then slept, taking turns on watch.

In the morning, before it was fully light, they loaded up the groaning camels and moved on along the trail, east to Singara.

They fell in with a long train filtering westwards, preceded by wary scouts and protected by leather-clad scowlers with shields and spears and bows. The owner of the caravan was a Persian, though he feared them as much as Romans and nomads.

'They are all thieves,' he growled. 'It is good to know the road ahead is clear. The one in front of you is not – we saw horses and camels, from some desert goat-fuckers for sure, between here and Singara.'

'What of Roman patrols?' demanded Kisa and the caravan owner laughed.

'There are too few Romans around here for that. We came across the remains of four wagons which had once carried grain. There were dead mules, but no men.'

No one needed to be told what had happened – a supply train had been attacked and stripped. The men had probably been taken, to be sold on as slaves elsewhere, and the caravan owner clearly thought that this would be the fate of Drust and the others.

They moved on, with Sib kicking a grumbling camel away from the others until he was out of sight. He was a good scout, but this was a strange desert for him and Kag said as much.

'One sand-crawler is much like another,' Quintus growled back.

'I do not like the desert,' Ugo pointed out and ducked, only just managing to avoid the yellow-toothed snap of his mount. 'I hate this beast even more.'

'It hates you,' Kag said, grinning. 'Look at the way it stares.'

All camels stared the same way, Drust thought, a head tilted haughtily to look down the nose, but everyone seemed to think it was a revelation for that particular beast.

Praeclarum came to him each time they stopped and he stumbled off the kneeling beast that grumbled and groaned when he did. The others smiled and nudged each other – all but Stercorinus, who was always stolid as a post, stern and blank-faced as any acolyte of Zeno.

'You need a few days' rest,' she said to him. 'If you don't, the ribs may not heal properly.'

'Listen to your ma,' Kag said, grinning into Praeclarum's scowl. Drust, however, knew the balm of her touch and the potions she used, so he laid one hand on her whipcord forearm and patted it, smiling. He was surprised to see her eyes drop and turn away, the flush that bloomed on her face.

Sib rode in at the end of the day and everyone stopped when they saw him flogging the beast up in a welter of chewed foam. It came to a halt and stood, legs splayed, and the pelt on it spiked with sweat.

'There are men at the *caravanserai* ahead,' Sib said, accepting water gratefully; the camel moaned at the smell. 'They are Romans, maybe what is left of that wagon train, and surrounded by a great many goat-fuckers.'

'How great a many?' Quintus demanded.

'Enough for us to circle wide to the south,' Sib replied, dragging one hand across his mouth.

'There is water in that *caravanserai*,' Kag pointed out and held up the skin he had offered Sib. It hung like a wrinkled, accusing bollock and no one missed the point – they hadn't enough water to bypass here and reach Singara.

Drust indicated to Sib to get a fresh camel and lead the way; the only thing to do was take a look, as Kag said. The three of them loped off, shuffling up grit, which was already hissing in a rising wind.

It was no more than a long lurch away and they ground-reined the camels with stones in the lee of a dip, then crept almost to the lip, belly-crawling the last, which was an agony for Drust.

The place was typical – a square of blocky buildings, blank walls to the outside, entrances leading off a central courtyard. Stables, sleeping places, stores, all mud-brick and solid.

Drust saw the men inside and knew they were Army simply because they were out in the open; all the others, the herders and sometime-guards and owners, were cowering in cover against a spatter of fire arrows arcing over.

There was smoke and two fires where a dry midden and a wagon had been set alight, but fire was no danger to a place made of solid mud brick.

'Look there,' Kag said, and they saw the muster of men, gathering in a dry wadi out of sight of the defenders. There were men waving their arms and gesticulating and these, Drust knew, were the leaders. It was the only way to tell them apart, for they wore the same stained robes, wraparound head-coverings, carried the same weapons as everyone else. Bows and spears and little round shields, he saw. Ladders, crudely made out of rope with wood hook-frames, for scaling the wall.

Inside the *caravanserai* they were oblivious to this, though they had been attacked once already. Drust saw the harness draped carelessly over a heat-split, rickety fence, the smoke trickling from open fires, the chimneys in what was a kitchen. There was a man by the main gate, squatting with a sword across his knee, *keffiyeh* looped round his neck and his over-robe snowy, the wind snapping it open to reveal the ring mail beneath. He was eating flatbread from one hand and drinking from another; they had no fear of thirst or hunger here, but the attackers had, so they'd need to break in and swiftly, which was why they were massing.

He wondered how old the place was, this oasis. Three hundred years? Older? Caravans of wanderers had come here with their camel trains, taking freely everything that was here when it was no more than an oasis, because that was the way of the desert nomads. Then came the ones with stronger resolve and bigger ambitions, handsome men and women who built and grew and made children, stocked goats and camels and tough little horses.

That time was dead now, buried under the weight of sagging poverty and dulled will. The life that was here now, Drust thought, was charged with the sound of failure – and now, with these people, with the taint of death.

These were not the handsome men and women of old. They were the skin-and-bone people spreading mule meat to dry on canvas torn from some other hands, cooking on old fires, the women swaying gauds rather than the veiled flowers of the old Persians or the followers of Alexander.

Now there were also Romans of the Army, dusty and desperate – and one who was neither, as Sib pointed out.

'The size of him,' he breathed. 'He can give Ugo half a head.'

Drust had to admit that the man was big. He was dressed no differently from the others, but somehow he seemed like a leader, had that aura about him, emanating like heat.

'Well,' said Kag grimly, 'we need that water. We should wait until dark and sneak in.'

'You think a man like that will hand it out to us?' Sib sneered back. 'Should we even make it over the wall without the sentries skewering us?'

'We need to fight our way in,' Kag declared, then tugged at his cloak and grinned. 'We are Romans after all.'

Back at the others, he made the same point and had a look from Quintus that would have stripped the gilt off a god's statue.

'And out? With water freely given by the Army?'

'Quintus is right,' Ugo rumbled, frowning. 'We will have to attack these goat-botherers and drive them off.'

Now everyone cackled. 'With what legion do you suggest?' demanded Kag.

Drust held up one of the red cloaks, given the idea by Kag, who only now realised it. Quintus grinned and nodded.

'If we hit those leaders,' Kag added, stroking his beard, 'that might work.'

'There were at least a hundred of them,' Sib offered anxiously.

'Closer to fifty,' Kag soothed.

'Ah, that's all right then,' Stercorinus offered and Sib rounded on him.

'You might at least show concern,' he spat. 'A little sensible fear. It will be a hard fight.'

'Would it help?' Stercorinus countered.

They rode out, taking all their beasts and looking carefully at the sky, for they wanted it twilight, that time when the desert light goes flat as it heads down to a glorious blood-drop sun and then darkness. In that half-light they would look like what they were attempting and that bluff had to be all of this, the fake ankle turn that dropped you to one knee, the stumble, the bad strike that seemed to leave you open so your opponent would gloat and fall in the trap of it.

Still, it was crazed, as Kag whispered softly to Drust. They sat and waited in the lee of a nearby wadi, tensed and sweating about being discovered by those already setting up the yip-yip fox screams to unnerve the defenders of the *caravanserai*.

'Madness,' Drust agreed and then managed a rictus grin at Kag. 'Who'd have thought water could drive men mad?'

It was an old joke from another time, but it comforted like a fire on a cold night. They sat under a bowl of sky and a rim of stars in a place littered with rocks – a metaphor for us and the world, Drust thought. Living in the now, with the hot sky and an immensity that frightened folk with its vastness, dependent on one another, with the complete absence of a common sense that should have stopped them being there.

They were already shifting like a delicate mechanism, smoothing out back into the routine they had all perfected and would never be done with. They checked weapons with that old familiarity, felt the gritting rasp of dust in their mouths, bodies soaked with salted sweat under their red cloaks, camel-sticks held like javelins.

Drust blew out his cheeks. 'Everyone know the plan?' he called softly.

'Run in, kill everything, run out,' Ugo growled back and that got a few laughs.

'We stand ready,' Quintus added and that got a few more; it was the standard army response to any order, however bad it looked. It looked, Drust had to admit, quite bad.

There were a hundred – more – desert tribals crouched in a wadi not far from the wall of the mud-brick compound. They had ladders and bows, spears and blades, and for all that Drust had seen some big commander muster men in defence, they'd get over the wall and then numbers would do it.

On a nearby hill were about a dozen, perhaps more – the leadership of the tribals, overseeing the business next to the rope tethers of their camels and horses.

'Get in amongst them,' Drust had told them. 'Stercorinus – you have a blade long enough to be used from the back of a camel, so you slash free their mounts and scatter them. The rest of us will ride in like *dromedarii*, loud and proud and making it seem we are part of many.'

The cloaks would do it, Drust hoped. That and the surprise. Cut the head off the snake, wreck their transport, and if that didn't send all of them scattering, then run for the safety of the compound.

They came up at a shambling lope, Drust trying to kick the camel into running hard. There was a moment when the heads turned, staring in disbelief, which is when Kag bawled out, 'Roma invicta!' and Quintus went past, roaring with laughter at it.

Drust managed no more than a weary lollop, but saw Stercorinus come up alongside and pass him, heading for the tethered mounts. 'Cut the ropes,' he yelled, but had a mouthful of gritty dust and choked on anything else; he saw Stercorinus ignore the mounts and charge on past, heading for the huddle of men. They started to scatter and Stercorinus, both hands on the upraised sword, swept in, scything left, then right.

Cursing, Drust fought the camel to a staggering halt and then had to slither off, pain bursting all the way through him. He headed for the tethered line and struck, but it wasn't tight enough to be cut in one and he had to begin sawing; a horse tugged, making the affair bounce, while the camel on the other side eyed him bleakly and chewed sideways.

A shadow flicked and he reflex-ducked – the blade that would have slashed his face hissed over his head and he yelped, spinning away and wincing at the shriek of bruised muscles. His enemy had a face with a scar along it, an old white wound that tugged the side of his mouth up in a permanent lopsided grin. He had a baggy robe a size too large for him, thrown over baggier Persian trousers, yet the stance, the way he handled the *spatha* told Drust he was no tribal.

'You're no fucking camel-botherer from the 20th,' the man growled in Latin, and that confirmed it.

'You're no goat-fucker from the desert,' Drust answered, backing up and looking sideways for help. The man laughed, a dust-harsh sound.

'I knows who you is,' the man said. 'Dead man is who you is.'

'Come ahead if you have the balls for it,' Drust declared, then ducked under the tether rope and got among the mounts, which began to tug and mill. He slashed once at the rope and saw strands part; the scarred man scowled and sent a sweep of blade, easily dodged. It hit a camel in the face, which roared outrage and jerked away – the rope broke.

Drust was bumped and jostled – one horse's rear sent him spinning into the dust and the agony of the fall drove air and sense out of him; he was struggling to rise when he saw Scarface closing in, squinting and crouched as he came up, fending off the milling beasts.

He saw Drust and snarled. Or smiled – it was hard for Drust to tell with that scar, but it didn't matter. He bore in and slashed with the *spatha* blade; Drust had no time for finesse, did not use the flat of the *gladius* to catch it, but the edge and the force threw his arm out wide. Scarface launched a scythe that would have taken Drust in the face if he had not ducked. Then he stopped, grinning, which bewildered Drust.

He was getting to his feet when another beast hit him – camel, Drust thought as the hairy mountain of it knocked him off balance. He flailed his arms wildly for balance and felt a jarring as the *gladius* bit something; when he turned, a man was looking down it, his mouth wide and blood-wet, his eyes staring madly at the steel length that led from his throat all the way to Drust's fist.

Coming up behind me, Drust thought – sneaky bastard. Then he realised why Scarface had stopped and half turned to see the man now boring in, his backstab plan a failure. Drust gave a shriek and wrenched the blade to free it, so hard that it hissed out and round, with no control at all.

They both felt the tug of it and both fell over. Drust wrestled with the grit and shrouded air, scrambling back to his feet in time to hear a high, keening scream. By the time he was back on his feet and in a fighting crouch, one side of his body an answering shriek of agony, he saw the noise came from Scarface.

He was clutching his belly to keep the pale, blue-white coils in, and the shock of it had rendered him to whimpering for his ma. Drust spat dust and managed a lurching turn as shadows flitted in the murk; somewhere, above the screaming, someone seemed to be babbling for forgiveness.

'Not bad,' said a voice and Quintus came up, his face a paste of sweat and dust. He casually struck out with his own sword, a serpent-tongue flicker that took Scarface in the side of the neck and rendered him instantly silent. 'Shut up, you fuck. I have had horses die on me with less fuss.'

His grin was bright and wide and admiring. 'I saw that,' he said, nodding at the two corpses. 'A backhand in the throat, a slash to the belly – if I'd known you fought this well, I'd have paired you in the *harena* and we could have had some real fights.'

Drust said nothing, not even how glad he was to see him. They lumbered out of the settling dust to see beasts galloping everywhere, some of them mounted. Men were down and the babbling came from Stercorinus, who was kneeling and praying to his sword, which was driven into the ground; Drust did not understand the language but he understood the blood that slathered the man to his waist, clotting in the dust.

'Palmyran,' Quintus muttered. 'Or something. He is not right, that one.'

'He kills well,' Ugo growled, looming up and leaning on his axe. There was blood on his face and his sleeve, but it wasn't his. 'All these are his.'

A score or more were scattered, everyone with raggled necks and no heads. Kag and Praeclarum came up – still mounted, Drust noted – and Kag indicated some of the riders galloping to and fro.

'They are from the *caravanserai*,' he said. 'Not your usual Army horse neither.'

They were not. They were mailed, with crested helmets and white cloaks; Drust felt a belly-flip of unease at that, seeing that these were escort horses for some Stripe.

'Did we win?'

'They ran,' Praeclarum said, then frowned. 'Did you fall off? Are you hurt?'

Drust did not want to be embarrassed by any more grins from the others, so he flapped one hand to dismiss it, then stiffened as a group of mounted men rode up to them, skidding to a halt in a shower of dust. When it cleared, he saw through his squint that a giant had climbed off a horse which, big and black though it was, seemed relieved at losing the weight.

'20th Palmyra,' the giant said, cocking his head to one side. 'Timely and bravely done – how many are you?'

He didn't wait for an answer, but went to the lolled body of Scarface, his blood a scummed paste that the giant did not care to avoid. He will ruin those nice boots, Drust thought. Expensive wine-coloured leather with gold, the sort a serious Stripe would wear.

The giant bent and grunted, then came up with a small leather pouch, torn from Scarface's neck; Drust knew that there would be a *signaculum* in it, a small lead tablet that detailed the rank and unit of the legionary who wore it. It would be the last thing even a deserter would throw away.

'Alexandros,' the giant said after a cursory glance. 'Legionary of the 3rd Parthica. Fucker.'

He turned and stared at Drust, who tried not to blink and failed. It was not the size, though, that was impressive – even Ugo was not as broad or tall – it was the face, which seemed carved from a block of rough stone, the nose broad and flattened, the chin solid as a farmhouse. Most of it was a browline that was all one long awning above eyes that might have been kind once, but were now glaring from under this hood. It was a club, that face, and the owner used it to beat anyone he stared at into the ground.

Drust did not allow himself to be beaten, but he was suddenly conscious of what the giant was seeing – a broken-nosed face, broad and full-lipped, framed with a cropped beard and close-cropped hair. Eyes slightly liquid, a little popped, with that fret at the corners which told those who understood how many distant horizons they had stared at.

The giant studied him, then stretched out one hand, placing the flat of it on Drust's breast; it practically covered it like a breastplate, and even lightly done gave off a strength Drust wanted to recoil from.

'No *signaculum*,' he grunted, while Drust's bowels fought against turning to water.

'Not on a patrol such as this, yer honour,' he managed to croak.

'Maximinus,' the giant said. 'Praeses Mesopotamiae.'

Assistant governor of the province. Drust floundered, managed his name and an added 'yer honour', then his dry mouth clamped.

'Attalus send you out?' he demanded.

'Uranius,' Drust managed. 'Patrol. Singara. Roads clear…'

'Uranius,' Maximinus repeated thoughtfully, rolling the name round in his mouth as if chewing it to shreds. There is something there, Drust thought… but the giant had turned, was waving for a trooper to bring the horse.

'I heard there was rebellion in Dura. Legionary uprising.'

Drust managed to shake his head. 'Nah, your honour. Bit of a riot at some Games – one of their own decided to take on gladiators and lost. The 20th sorted it out.'

The giant levered himself onto the horse, which seemed to sink a little, then grinned as he took up the reins. Drust had never felt so sorry for a beast before.

'Good unit, the 20th. You will proceed with my grain wagons to Singara – Sempronius here will help you with food and water. I will mention your exemplary performance here to Attalus – and Uranius.'

Then he clattered off, dragging a trail of troopers and dust. The one left behind, presumably Sempronius, spat in the dust and blew out his cheeks.

'My men will help round up your beasts. That was timely, mark you.'

'Who was that?' Ugo demanded, and Drust could see he was measuring himself against the giant and coming up short. Sempronius saw it too and laughed.

'You have met the Thracian. Maximinus Thrax they call him, but not to his face. Assistant governor of Mesopotamia.'

'If he had been in the *harena*,' Quintus noted, 'he'd have been a big hit.'

'He's the one Uranius warned us to keep away from,' Praeclarum muttered in Drust's ear, and he remembered it as soon as her words were tumbled out. Well, too late now, he thought.

'Kag, Quintus – get Stercorinus cleaned up and quiet or we'll never get the camels back here.'

'You encountered Maximinus Thrax?' Narseh-dux said. 'He is riding the line, it appears.'

'Riding the line?'

'The defences,' Kisa interrupted. 'Mesopotamia has garrisons...'

He became aware of Narseh's glance and fell silent under it. The Persian took a date from the dish and popped it in his mouth, worrying the stone out of it as he chewed. He was a large man with a large beard and a matching laugh, who wore blue, sleeved robes over white and had thick fingers which bore the old, pale marks of rings which had been cut off when they grew too tight.

He spat a stone sideways and Drust waited, knowing it was always best to wait when questions crowded at your teeth. He sat on cushions on a woven hemp mat on the cooled floor of a dim room, listening to the banging of pots and bowls, the calls of street vendors, the bray of a donkey.

There were conversations, too muted to hear, and Drust knew this had been measured, so that the room, a square on top of a square on top of a square, had slat-shuttered windows for the breezes, but was too far above the courtyard for any conversations to be overheard.

It had been a long, hot journey, painful with every jolt of the grumbling camel. Praeclarum had done her best with her ointments, but too much had been done to him for it to be easily alleviated. Then there was Stercorinus; it had taken five bucket-sluices from the well to wash the blood from him and even then the garrison eyed him warily as he stood in a pink, muddy slush with his filthy loincloth and his sword.

They'd asked him what had happened. Drust told him he was supposed to have cut the animal tethers, not dashed off to lop off heads – and what had that been about anyway?

'Destiny,' Stercorinus said dully, and Kag grabbed the man's matted beard, snarling close to his face.

'You disobey again, you streak of ugly shit stain, and I will show you destiny…'

Drust had had the loincloth stripped off him and found him a tunic and Persian trousers. Stercorinus had put up no argument, but had balked when the shears came out for his beard and hair; they'd given up on it in the end.

Narseh-dux clapped his hands and Drust shifted a little to ease his blazing side, which made Kag glance over and question with his eyes. Drust shook his head, but closed his own eyes, trying to let the pain and weariness flow away from his tired limbs, trying to focus his mind. A camel bell's cracked clank and the harassing bark of dogs made him give up.

A slave appeared with a box, four fingers square all round and the length of a good arm, and handed it to Narseh-dux, who made a show of placing it on the low table, opening it and removing what looked like a scroll. Drust saw Kisa stiffen just a little, like a dog scenting rats, but it was nothing to do with the sudden strong waft of sandalwood.

'See here,' Narseh-dux declared, grinning brownly as he unrolled the affair and took two small polished stones, shiny black, out of the box to weigh down the edges. They all peered at a meticulously drawn map.

'This is the line,' Narseh-dux said, tracing an invisible one with a fat finger, joining up dots one by one. 'This is Singara – the Roman camps are a long spit from this *caravanserai* and contain the 1st and 3rd Parthica.'

He tapped the map. 'You would think that a great security, two legions of Rome, but it is not, for they are scattered in pieces all along the line, from fortress to fortress – here at Resaina, at Nisbis and elsewhere. Also, the garrison at Resaina killed the commander of the 3rd not more than a week ago, when he would not take the purple they offered him. Those who tried to rebel then fled. Some have joined the House of Ardashir of Sasan in his fight against the old order. Some have become bandits, joining with the desert tribes.'

Drust and Kag exchanged looks; this was quality news and a measure of the man who offered it. Drust caught that Kisa's eye did not miss the signal – here was a man who knew a great deal, and if he knew it, Shayk Amjot knew it.

'There are desertions everywhere,' Narseh-dux went on, 'which will help you – everyone is concentrating on watching his neighbour. Maximinus is galloping up and down cracking heads to put a stop to it all, but the same is happening all over – Flavia Firma, the Scythian, all the legions are unhappy, unpaid and unfed.

'This is the way you should go – out to Nisbis,' Narseh-dux said, then offered his grin to Kisa. 'This one will calculate how many camels it will take to reach the Red Serpent – but no one knows what you will find there.'

'Is it manned?' Kag demanded, and Narseh-dux shrugged, began rolling up the map. Drust saw Kisa's face grow cold, as if the sun had abandoned him.

'It has always been manned,' Narseh-dux replied, 'but now no one knows how well or where is weakest.'

'What lies beyond it?' Drust asked, and the fat merchant beamed and nodded.

'A good question. They are wolves – you know it as Hyrcania, but the true name is Verkana, land of wolves. The peoples there are grassland riders – Tschols and Saka and others. In the mountains further east they are horseless, but both use bows to great effect.'

'How do we cross this Wall?' Kag demanded, and the merchant shrugged and closed the box.

'That is your affair. I have instructions only to provide camels and herders and guards – and this.'

He drew a fat purse from inside his robes and dropped it heavily on the table, where it made a sound that brought Kag's lips up in a smile that showed teeth. Narseh-dux was grim.

'I did this once before – purse, camels, men – for those other two, the one with night in his eyes and the other – may the gods keep me safe – with the face of death. They have never been heard of again and so I think it will be with you.'

'It is not your money nor camels nor men, o wise one,' Kisa said, and Narseh-dux scowled.

'No, blessings be for that,' he declared, folding his fat hands over his massive belly. There was no chest that Drust could see, but he marvelled at the breasts, which seemed as plump as any woman's.

'One hundred and forty amphorae for three days,' he added. 'Eight hundred and forty-eight pints of wine.'

'Eight hundred and forty,' Kisa corrected quietly. 'It makes a total weight of 1561 librae. You can get all that on five camels. I have calculated, with fodder and food for herders and guards, for the packloads of trade goods – eighty-three camels. Eighty-five to be safe.'

'Trade goods?' Drust demanded and Kisa spread his hands.

'Wool, linen, glass, some tinware... the usual poor trade items along these roads. Rome's goods do not match the worth of silk and gems and spices, so we are also known for carrying coin, mostly gold.'

Kag chuckled. 'This is why you will come with us.'

Kisa's face went white and his eyes almost rolled up to match it. 'My part ends here,' he said hoarsely. 'I have no instruction or desire to go further.'

'You may believe so,' Drust said, and Kisa heard the tone, saw the faces, and everyone else saw him look for a way out.

'Do not run,' Narseh-dux said quietly to him. 'I am thinking it would not be an idea much liked, by them or the Shayk, my master.'

Then he smiled and clapped his hands for slaves to bring wine and food, beaming like some well-loved old uncle.

'The bandits are too weak to attack such a train as yours,' he said soothingly to Kisa. 'And the Sasan are too busy trying to take over the old Empire. You will have a pleasant walk to Hagmatāna, then north to the Red Snake, where your honours' glib tongues and bribes will see you through.'

Everyone agreed. Drust said nothing. Kisa trembled and ate little.

–

Drust said nothing for three days after they left Singara, then in the glimmering dim of a lamplit tent, after the camels had been bedded, meals eaten, guards posted, he called Kisa and Kag and the others.

He had no sandalwood box and no carefully notated map, just the gritted sand between mats, but he drew swiftly.

'We turn north tomorrow,' he said and Kag nodded, knowing why – if you are leaving tracks, you are being followed. Kisa opened and closed his mouth once or twice and Drust leaned closer to him.

'We head for the western shores of the Hyrcanian Ocean, leave the camels and take ship to the other side.'

'Sail round the Wall,' Ugo growled admiringly.

'Like every clever raider who ever came down from the north on Britannia,' Quintus added, grinning.

'Leave the camels?' Kisa managed. 'How will we get back?'

'Pick them up on our return. Or buy more.'

'And the trade goods?'

'Sell them. Buy a boat if we cannot find one to carry us.'

Kisa's face writhed with arguments, each one discarded when the flaw was seen. Drust did not give him time to find one that worked; he put his face closer still to Kisa, who drew back and then looked at the shadows of the others, which now seemed like a fence to him.

'From now,' Drust said grimly, 'we are all brothers in this. Whatever you were ordered to do, Kisa Shem-Tov, you had better forget it. It has taken me a time to get to it, but I saw your look when Narseh-dux unrolled that map and when he threatened you with the Shayk. You work for Uranius. You are supposed to go back to him and... what? Tell him which way we took? Steal that map?'

Kisa seemed to tilt a little, like a bag of grain that had spilled. He passed a hand over his face as if cobwebs had fallen on him.

'Narseh-dux is not clever enough to have made such a map. Shayk Amjot made it and probably has more, all handed out to his agents who will update them with new information when it becomes known. The Shayk probably knows as much about Rome's defences here as the Palatine does – this was Uranius's concern.'

'What of Maximinus Thrax?' Ugo wanted to know and they all knew he was obsessed with the man now. Not often a giant meets his like, Drust thought, but even so...

Kisa waved a dismissive hand. 'He is what he appears – a brutal man sent by the Emperor to keep weak and greedy people from being forced into taking the purple by the disaffected. Like the commander of the 3rd Parthica. Maximinus does not know who to trust and yet must keep forces sharp against the Persians – he has until these Sasan people clean out the old crew.'

'And Uranius?' demanded Kag.

Kisa sucked in a breath, then let it out. 'Is the Emperor's man. Some people do not care for family ties.'

They waited and Kisa eventually gave in. 'Lucius Julius Aurelius Sulpicius Severus Uranius Antoninus,' he said and stopped, waiting.

Praeclarum got to it first. 'Severus,' she said and Kisa nodded.

'He's kin to the Emperor?' Kag demanded furiously and Kisa nodded.

'Distant, but of the family. He is *sampsigeramus* – you know what that is?'

'A priest of the Sun God,' Stercorinus said blankly. 'Emesan.'

'Why would you work for Uranius?' Sib chimed in, though he was more curious than angry. 'You are a Jew, who are always stiff-necked about their religion. And you work for a priest of the Sun God?'

Kisa looked from one to the other and it seemed to Drust as if his face unlocked, then he fumbled round his neck, pulled out a bag and brought out the lead lozenge inside. Drust read it and looked at the little Jew.

'You are a *frumentarius*.'

Quintus flung up his hands. 'Jupiter's hairy arse – a spy for the Army. Spying on Uranius? On us?'

Kisa said nothing, but Drust filled in the blank of his face.

'On Uranius, because he is the current boy-Emperor's creature and a priest of Elagabalus – the god, not the strange boy who was Emperor until they dragged him off. He thinks you work for him, but you are a creature of the Hill. You spy on us because of Dog who is also a priest of Elagabalus the god of Emesa, if he is anything at all these days. Some folk do not care for that – they have had enough of pouring blood on a black stone in the Temple of Jupiter.'

'That's why Dog was chosen for this,' Quintus said, seeing it suddenly. He sat back, grinning. 'He always has a fat cock for boy-emperors of the Severan family. Gods above and below, that lot never ends – all the men are chanters at the Sun and all the women are called Julia. They are everywhere.'

'Chosen for what?' Drust demanded and everyone stopped speaking and stared. Kisa spread his hands.

'I do not know,' he said bitterly. 'Uranius does but he will not tell me, a mountain Jew, and besides, he thinks I am simply his paid man.'

He leaned forward meaningfully. 'But not tigers. Not that.'

Chapter Six

Ugo leaned on his big axe on the edge of a yellow mound of sandy soil, squinting at the bit of his axe and frowning. His face was a mask, painted with a sickly paste made from dust and sweat and blood; his beard was clotted.

Sib hawked up as much moisture as he could, then swilled it round and tried to spit out the dust in his mouth.

'This place is forsaken by every god known to man,' he growled and the others agreed – all save Kag, who passed a skin of water along the line of them.

'These dust trolls we have killed are the ones forsaken,' he pointed out, and they looked at the scatter of bodies, stripped clean of their robes, lolling naked and gutted – in case they had swallowed their wealth – and empty of everything of value. Darab, who liked to call himself a captain, was organising the caravan guards away from plundering and trying to distance himself from Stercorinus, who was praying to his driven sword.

Drust looked at the empty drifts of sand, the bare, dry stretches of scrub and wind-blasted terraces that marked the riverbed. Fourteen dead men littered it, waiting for the long slow spiral of the carrion-eating birds; it was no place to have died in, Drust was thinking. At least none were known to him.

Died for what – a long skein of ugly camels? Packed with… what? Even Drust did not know; the only man who knew was Kisa, who came up beaming and trailing the herders with more waterskins in his wake. He stepped with disgust through the clotted sand, waving at men to pass out the skins.

Darab looked biliously at him. 'Those beasts will think twice about coming down this far now. Fourteen of them slain – a great victory.'

'More could have been killed,' Drust pointed out laconically, 'if you and your men had spent less time worrying about those hump-backed cows you are driving. None of us are killed or badly hurt – my thanks for asking.'

Darab hauled off his helmet and scowled. 'We are paid to protect those hump-backed cows – and none of your men died. Two of mine did.'

Kag clapped him on the shoulder, hard enough to throw up dust. 'They are not your men – but my sorrow for your loss.'

Drust gave him a warning look that turned him away from further quarrel. 'We will make camp up ahead – in a few more days we reach a *caravanserai*. Water and food and probably women.'

Darab slouched off, calling for men to carry the bodies of his dead, and Drust watched their faces; most were lifted by the thought of water, food, women and drink, but when they grew tired of that it would all change and Drust was already looking for signs. Kag, it seemed, had found them.

'These folk are poor warriors,' he said, falling into step, and Drust had no quarrel with him on that – the ones who lay dead all around had been feared here. Brigands from further north who had grown bold, Drust was told, to have come down so far – but they had paid the price for it and Darab was right; the thieves and murderers would not be so eager from now on.

They had thought themselves no end of fine warriors, these brigands – until they had collided with real ones and tried to flee like chickens. Drust had to swallow the memory of them, just one more little horror among the many. They'd known the terror at once, like dogs who had pounced on some moving tail in the grass only to find out they had chewed down on a dragon. They ran screaming and were cut down with sixing strokes from behind by merciless men. Yet they had contrived to kill two of Darab's men with arrows and that bore scrutiny.

'You see this one?' Kag said, shifting a body with his foot; it lolled over, loose as a half empty grain sack. It seemed like any other, a bloodied corpse with a surprised look. When the man had risen that day, shaken the sand from his stained robes and battered boots and bagged trousers, he had not expected to die, but he looked like any other they had killed and Drust said so.

Kag tutted, which let Drust know he had missed something – then Kag pointed it out. Under the white over-robes was a tunic embroidered at collar and cuff, fastened with a blue cloth belt. Both were faded and the tunic patched, but this was not the usual undyed wool of the nomads.

'Loot?' Drust wondered and Kag waved Kisa over to see.

'Daylami,' Kisa said almost at once. 'They are the people of these mountains and allies of the Persians.'

'Which side?' Drust asked and Kisa's look told them why that did not matter; they left the body and moved on, thinking, until Kisa stopped and jerked his chin at the figure of Stercorinus. He was still kneeling before his sword, which had been thrust in the dirt, praying in that strange tongue no one knew.

'Something should be done,' Kisa muttered and Kag was forced to agree.

'He is scaring the camel-herders,' he admitted and Kisa scowled.

'He is scaring the camels.'

Drust moved up to where Stercorinus knelt and droned; it sounded like bees in a hive.

'To whom do you pray?' he asked and the droning stopped. Stercorinus opened one eye and squinted through the tangle of his greasy hair.

'God.'

'Which one?'

'The god.'

'From Palmyra,' Drust persisted, squatting next to him and feeling the twinge in his ribs, the last nip of his injury, or so he hoped. 'The temple there – weren't you a foundling?'

Stercorinus shifted a little, out of his kneeling and into an easier pose. He drew out the sword, then thrust it back in once or twice to clean the blood off in the sand, then fell to wiping it with the hem of his robe. Drust winced; it had taken a lot of stern to make Stercorinus wear the robe, partly to make him look a little better, mostly because he was scorching in the sun, but it was clear there was no fastidiousness in the man.

'I was a foundling,' Stercorinus said eventually, 'in the temple of Ba'al Šamem.'

Drust said nothing and, though this was not new, he anticipated revelation, so he waited.

'Jupiter of the Romans, Zeus of the Greeks, Mazda of the Persians and Amon of the Egyptians,' Stercorinus added. 'God of eagles and lightnings.'

He looked at Drust to make sure he had understood.

'I was named Stercorinus and became a slave. I served in the temple learning the work I would do forever.'

'Which was?' Drust prompted and Stercorinus stood up and cradled the curved blade.

'Blood,' Stercorinus said flatly. 'Every god needs blood.'

This was not news to Drust. 'Is that what you do now, provide blood for your god? If so, you need to provide less – people are afraid.'

Stercorinus gave a short laugh, a strange sound Drust was sure he had never heard before.

'The god who speaks to me now asks no blood – that comes when you fight. I have a destiny and if war is in it, then so be it.'

'You cut heads,' Drust pointed out.

'I was trained so. Bulls, rams and people. One strike. I was good at it. They gave me this sword.'

Drust levered himself up; he was no stranger to such deaths, in and out of the *harena*, but the way Stercorinus spoke made his flesh ruche as if a cold wind blew.

'What destiny is this?' Drust demanded and Stercorinus shook his shaggy head.

'It is no threat to you – just the opposite. And I fight the way I do because I know the mark and place of my death.'

Now Drust was chilled and annoyed at being so. 'You need to clean yourself up,' he said brusquely. 'Get the blood off and keep it off. Stop chanting. People are made uneasy by it. Otherwise you may go your own way and find destiny.'

The black eyes gleamed behind the tangled undergrowth of his hair, but Stercorinus nodded.

'Are you not concerned by what people think of you?' Drust demanded and Stercorinus shifted one hand away from the sword long enough to self-consciously part the tangle over his face. His eyes, Drust saw, were genuinely concerned.

'Would it help?'

Drust sighed, then made one last attempt.

'Your name,' he said desperately. 'Do you have another? We can't keep calling you Little Shit.'

The man shook his head. 'If I had such a thing, it was before I understood. I have been called Stercorinus for as long as my years – it is what they give to foundlings.'

Drust knew that already and gave up. The caravan groaned and grumbled back into staggered life and shuffled on up the trail, leaving the ragged, plundered bags that had once been men behind.

–

The camp that night was the same as they had made for far too many nights, each one carrying them further from what they knew – which was a problem.

'Darab has seen the sun,' Kag said and Drust nodded – the captain had spotted that they were headed more north than east and he did not like not having been consulted. When he and his men found out they were being paid off on the shores of the Hyrcanian Ocean, camels and goods all sold, there would be trouble. The herders would be easier to manage – money would salt that – but Darab and his men had expected to go all the way to Hyrcania and back and would think they were being done out of a share of the riches promised them.

'Is he speaking of it?' Drust asked and Kag nodded.

'Here and there. You wait – he and his men will draw apart from now, make a new fire.'

The land had turned from green to brown and worse, while the heat was bad during the day and the cold sharp when darkness fell; it never rained. The land was rising and falling too, undulating like a stormed sea, and ahead lay Arbela, which the Persians called Irbil; Darab would know it at once and know where he was.

They ate lamb cooked slowly in a sandpit, using flat stones as platters, but only after the camel-drovers had unloaded and taken care of their charges, tethered in two facing rows of rheumy gurgles and fitted with bags over their faces so they could eat. The cargo was laid carefully out and covered, fastened with ropes and staked to the earth.

The meal only began when Kisa had satisfied himself that all had been done properly and came up to the fires carrying the train bell.

Camels, most of the Brothers agreed, were vicious jests of creatures, who spat at you from either end and could not be ridden properly because of the hump. They had been working with camels for years and yet never took to them as they did to mules or horses; they spoke of them in the same way they spoke of the desert goat-fuckers who kept them.

As the men ate and talked quietly into the flaring sparks from the fires, Drust saw that Darab and his men had built their own and were sitting round it – he did not need Kag's knowing, mirthless grin to draw attention to it. He wondered what he would do when Darab worked out where they were.

He wondered what he was doing now, had half formed clouds in his head, swirling and shifting – sometimes it was clear what had to be done. Find Manius and Dog. Find what they wanted, what was so important that they'd summoned them halfway across the desert.

Other times it was simply the journey, the endless movement that they had been doing most of their lives, as if stopping would make the whole edifice of their existence start to creak and collapse. Drust could not summon up what he would do when he stared Dog in the face; they had been Brothers and enemies, and now he was not sure what they were, one to the other.

Then there was the promise of riches, faint as old dreams. Kag and Ugo and the others always looked at that sideways, with a raised, scathing eyebrow; they had never been rich and never thought to be, for all they chased it. Yet that was also in their quest to find Dog and Manius.

The thought of riches was what kept most of Darab's men moving and, somehow, Drust would have to salt them with silver.

That night the sky died hard in blood and morning rose in flames from the east as they moved on up the mountains, wary as cats. Sib flogged a camel out ahead at first light, while Quintus nudged Drust to notice Darab staring and frowning at the rising sun.

It was, in the end, all about Dog and Manius; the thought of them burned behind their eyes, night and day, awake or dreaming, left them grit-eyed and edgy as they hauled away towards the shore of the Hyrcanian Ocean.

Of course, the others had talked round it, as they always did, but it didn't matter much to Drust. Kag knew that turning north was not following the plan everyone else knew; they were leaving tracks, but anyone who followed would have a long ride in the wrong direction first.

'Why would anyone follow from Narseh-dux?' Quintus demanded. 'Why would he want to interfere with this enterprise?'

'A man will tell all when hot blades touch the skin,' Ugo replied with the air of someone who knew, from both sides of the blade. That made people frown and think and come up with any number of candidates hunting them down. Drust had them spread it among the herders and packers, and for a few days there was no grumbling about how hard and fast they moved, though the guards would not look them in the eye; Darab was barely civil.

On the day they came upon Arbela, it all came to a pus-filled head and it started with Praeclarum.

She had been distant and moody, saying little and eating less. Quintus had knowingly winked and hinted at women's troubles, but Sib got to it in the end.

'She has a bad tooth,' he said, coming up quietly to Drust as the train sorted itself out in the *caravanserai* compound. 'A real bad one. Bad as Martius – remember him?'

They all did – a willowy cart-driver like Sib, some Armenian blood mixed with the mongrel of the City and the whipcord skill all charioteers had – you did not speed-slide four powerful horses round a turn by strength.

None of it was of any use when his mouth ballooned and his breath stank. A doctor probed his mouth and they'd knocked him out with some potion or other, but when the offending tooth was pulled there was no end to the infection. Martius died a week later, what little flesh he had boiling off his bones, his muscle gone to string.

They came to her and told her she needed to have it seen to and she bridled, voice muffled with swelling as she told them to fuck off.

They went and huddled.

'We could thump her out,' Quintus suggested and Kag snorted.

'That how you woo your women?'

Quintus merely grinned his big grin and his own white teeth only added irony to the moment. 'It is not, as well you know. But if you think you can hold her down and keep her head still while someone probes her mouth, go ahead.'

Everyone thought of the wildcat that was Praeclarum and no one volunteered.

'I have tinsmith pincers,' Kag offered, 'but we will need to feed her some concoction to make her sleep.'

'Do we have some?' demanded Drust and it was clear they did not, nor knew anyone who did, though Sib slid off into the shadows between the flickering fires to see if there were others who might. He came back shaking his head.

'None of these have anything. Now if it were Manius…'

'What now?' Quintus demanded and it was clear he was one of the most concerned, possibly, because he had bought and freed her in the first place.

'I could thump her,' Ugo offered uneasily and Kag grunted scornfully.

'You will break her head open.'

'Perhaps we should ask Praeclarum,' Drust said finally, as they sat in gloomy silence in the small room which had been allotted to them as owners of the train.

'Ask her what?' Sib demanded. 'If she wants us to knock her out and rummage in her mouth?'

Said like that it did not sound much, but Stercorinus shifted in the dim, leaning forward a little to make his point and causing the sconce flames to make uncomfortable shadows on his face.

'Find a woman here,' he said.

'A woman?' Kag demanded, but Quintus was grinning and nodding as he rose to his feet.

'What does a woman have to do with this?' Sib demanded. 'Will Praeclarum permit a female to knock her out and rummage in her mouth?'

In a little while Quintus came back, grinning and presenting a square of linen cloth. 'Get some wine, spice it a little, soak this in it, and when Praeclarum comes in from sentry, get her to drink.'

'What is it?' Sib asked, sniffing it suspiciously; Quintus slapped him away.

'What women use,' he said and now Drust knew. *Papaver*-soaked cloths for their time of the month, to take the edge off cramp and all that went with it.

When Praeclarum sloped in, shrugging out of her leathers and helmet, she saw the sea of faces looking up and scowled back. It was worse, she thought, when they all started to smile at the same time.

'Here,' Drust said, offering her the cup. 'Take the chill off.'

'It is still hot enough to bake on the bare earth,' she countered.

'Well, I will fetch some bread,' Sib said, moving away and aware that Praeclarum was staring suspiciously. She drank all the same, while Quintus asked her about Darab and the guards. They were on duty as normal, it appeared, but she was sure something was happening. It did reach the part where she told them her suspicions all the same and, when she slumped silent, Kag let out his breath and brought out the snips.

'Fetch me some light. I don't want to pull the wrong tooth.'

Then he looked in her mouth and grimaced. 'I could pull any of these and it would help.'

'Pull them all,' Ugo suggested. 'She cannot use them anyway.'

'It would be good if we found the one which actually pains her most,' Drust pointed out and Quintus said that she held the right side of her jaw when she thought no one could see.

In the end it was a messy business of black stumps and blue splintered remnants. When it was done, Kag blew out his cheeks with relief, not only because Praeclarum had stayed unconscious throughout.

'I have seen less blood in an animal hunt,' Ugo said. 'She is not a big girl to have lost so much.'

'She is fine,' Kag said. 'No pus and the blood is all clean red, so if she keeps the wounds washed all will be well.'

He gathered up the ruins of teeth and buried them in a corner, offering a prayer to Asclepius, as was proper. Sib came back with bread and olives, all that was available because no one was cooking; he said the entire *caravanserai* was strangely quiet, everyone huddled in their own area. They ate and talked of nothing much, in low tones, all of them trying not to be seen watching the sleeping form.

She came awake like a whale breaching from a cold depth, whooping upright, wide-eyed and snarling out of dreams she had not wanted and did not care for. It took everyone by surprise, for they were half dozing, but it was Drust who spoke soothingly and Ugo who wrapped her until her weak struggles stopped.

'Dreams…' she muttered, shaking her head. 'Dreams… what have you done?'

They told her and Kag held out a new, evenly frayed tooth-stick. 'See if you can take care of the few you have left. It is a disgrace what I removed.'

Praeclarum trembled and that made everyone dumb and fixed to the spot, for they had never seen this before.

'The *lanista*,' she said and stopped, trembling on the brink of something which made everyone else want to walk away and hug her at the same time.

'The one whose woman ended up in the street?' Quintus prompted, and she shook her head, then flinched at the pain and worked her jaw a little.

'Yes,' she said, muffled by swelling. She spat blood and looked at it for a moment. 'He thought to break me – like a horse, he said. So he put a bit in my mouth and used the reins to haul on while he took me like a Greek boy. Bite down, he would say and laugh because the quarrel had all been about teeth. I bit so hard my teeth cracked. Every time...'

No one spoke. Quintus patted her arm and offered her more wine. 'This cup is normal though we can get more of the other if you are pained – it came from the blood-rags of a woman in the camp.'

Praeclarum's stare was jaundiced. 'Unused, I hope.'

They laughed and for a moment it seemed to Drust that the mud-hut room was soft with glow – then a great thunder of sound smashed it; dust trickled from the roof.

'One of your relatives is at the door,' Kag said laconically to Ugo. 'Go see which sister it is.'

Yet he had weapons up as a scowling Ugo crossed to the barred door and opened it, then stopped, staring. He stretched out a hand, laid it flat on a barrier and pushed.

'It's a cart,' he said. 'Someone has run a cart against the entrance.'

Drust felt his bowels leap up to his throat, then crash to the floor.

'Darab,' he said.

A voice hailed them and Quintus cautiously unshuttered the narrow window.

'You are blocked in,' the voice said and Kag came snarling up to the opening.

'Darab, you cock-rotted fuck.'

'I am here and you are there,' Darab answered, trying to sound mild but failing to keep the tension from his voice; that put some steady back into Drust.

'What do you want?'

'I want you to stay there,' Darab said, and Drust knew he was nervously eyeing the blocking cart, which was shifting under the efforts of Ugo's straining shoulder. Drust signalled the big man to leave off with it; he had worked out that Darab and his men could not set fire to the house, even if the other trains would let him.

'So we stay. What now?'

Darab, his face a gleam of sweat and shadow, nodded once or twice, as to convince himself that his plan was working.

'We are taking the train,' he said. 'All of my guards and most of the herders and packers – one or two have family in Dura, so they are headed back.'

'They fear the wrath of Shayk Amjot,' Sib offered up. 'As should you.'

'The Shayk sold us out,' Darab flung back savagely and then looked backwards as something smashed and voices bawled. The others here are not so amenable to his plan, Drust thought, but when he looked at Kag, he had a mournful headshake that let him know it was unlikely anything would be done. That was why the *caravanserai* was quiet; everyone else was keeping their heads down.

'The Shayk will hunt you down,' he reminded Darab, who spat derisively.

'He won't give a fuck. Not him is paying you for all this, nor was it last time. Romans are paying for this and who cares about them?'

'You should care. We will hunt you down,' Quintus added. 'Even if you know the way to the moon.'

'If you leave tracks,' Kag confirmed viciously, 'you will be followed.'

'You have money,' Darab said. 'Kisa told us of it. Hand it over and stay there with the woman until morning, then go back. It would be best – and if you don't, the Jew will get it.'

124

Praeclarum surged up to the shutter and spat bloody spray. 'You maggot fuck. When I get you I will slice off those little rat balls you have and use them as earrings.'

Drust stilled her with a hand to her arm. Kisa was out there and he looked at Kag, who scrubbed his head with confused annoyance; he had been thinking, Drust was sure, that the mountain Jew had gone over to Darab.

He drew Kag aside and told him what to do. Kag fetched his belt-purse and softly emptied it of fifteen iron links for ring mail and a solitary *as* – this was his decoy purse for thieves; the real one was fastened round his waist under his clothes and dangled as a third ball, which no one could get at that he wouldn't immediately feel.

He gently loaded the empty purse with a quarter of the coin they had and gave it to Drust, who hefted it so that Darab could hear the chink.

'Show me Kisa,' he said, and Darab barked an order that brought men from the shadows into the wan light of torches. The little Jew wobbled on his feet and his face looked strange and lumpen where they had beaten him.

'I am sorry,' he slurred. 'I do not like pain…'

'No one does,' Kag answered gently and then snarled like a rabid dog; Drust saw Darab draw back a little, then recover.

'Throw out the money. Stay in your hut until morning or it will be the worse for you, you Roman shits.'

Drust lobbed out the purse and saw it snatched up with a triumphant cry. Now he knew why no one had come to help – nor would they; they were all happy to see Romans robbed, would not piss on them if they were on fire.

He said as much while the noise of camels grumbling into movement knifed them all with the knowledge that they had lost almost everything else they possessed. Kisa lay on the other side of the wall beneath the window, huddled up and breathing hard.

'Fortuna needs a sacrifice,' Ugo growled.

'Fortuna needs a kick in the fork,' Kag responded bitterly, and Stercorinus finally shifted, clearing his throat as he did so – but it was only to put distance between Kag and himself, as if waiting for thunderbolts and eagles.

'Shall I open the door?' Ugo asked mildly. When the cart was manhandled far enough from the door, Darab and the train had gone into the dark and the *caravanserai* was alive with people complaining. The keeper, a short bustling man, tried to keep the peace between the outraged and men he could see were grim and well armed. He promised to send word of the theft to the garrison at Van, though he did not know who commanded there now, or even if there was one.

'Everything is in the air,' he declared, spreading apologetic hands.

'Your guards were not,' Drust pointed out. 'Where were they?'

'Not protecting this man,' Kag added, tilting Kisa's chin so the extent of the bruises could be seen; it was enough to make the keeper wince, and Kisa tried to protest but only blew air from between two strips of savaged liver which had once been his lips. One eye was closed in a blue–black sea and he seemed a leer with bruises.

The keeper spread more hand and, in the end, agreed to sell them a camel apiece and a spare for water at reasonable prices. By the time they had organised it and given a little to the uneasy herders and packers who were heading back to Dura, the purse had more wind than coin. Yet when they were out of sight of the *caravanserai*, Drust set up a small shrine of rocks, dedicated it with wine to Fortuna and left two more gold coins, one for each of her lovely eyes.

Kag grumbled at it and Stercorinus got off his knees from where he had been performing his own prayers, to the sky and the sand it seemed.

'It will be a good sacrifice the goddess will hear,' he said in his grit-rasp. 'A good sacrifice should hurt and that is clear from Kisa.'

There was laughter, little and not long — but it is a start, Drust thought.

Towards the end of the second day out, they came on the answer from the goddess and, as ever with those deities, it was cruel and oblique, marked by circling birds and those who flapped off the corpses, too full to fly.

They picked a way between the ruin, camels snorting the stink out of their noses; the dead had not been lying long, but even a few hours in the heat was enough, and Darab, when Drust found him, was blue-black already.

'Arrow-shot,' Sib said, moving cautiously round the lumped flesh of men and camels. 'Well mounted men on horses, not camels, did this.'

He swooped, rooted in the dust and came up with a prize. 'At least one attacker died,' he said, bringing it over so everyone could see. 'They took away his body, but missed this.'

It was a mask, gilded silver and tarnished here and there so that the bland face looked plagued; it had the remains of hinges at the top end where it had been torn free from the helmet.

'Parthian,' Stercorinus growled and spat. 'Not Daylami either, but real Persians who have metal armour and bows. Blades and long spears too, though they are fast horsemen, not the big oven-wearers.'

'They took the goods and the camels to carry them,' Sib said, and Quintus straightened from rifling the dead Darab, unconcerned by stink or rot. He grinned his big grin and hefted a familiar purse.

'They wanted only camels and water and what riches they could see,' he said, tossing the money to Drust. 'Poor raiders, these.'

'Raiders in a hurry,' Kag said, looking round and squinting, 'with no time to search bodies properly. We should fear what they feared.'

'Fortuna smiles,' Praeclarum lisped and spat; it was only faintly tinged with blood now, Drust saw.

'That would have been us,' Ugo added. He stretched out his arms, one hand holding the long-handled axe, and began chanting until Kag slapped his arm.

'Do it on the move, giant of the Germanies.'

They crawled on over the slashed land, which had once been a prouder mountain until the winds had beaten it down to a hunched old man whose breath was heavy with dust and sand.

Yet they were together, Drust thought, and Fortuna did smile, for not all her riches came as gold and the lopsided swollen smile from Praeclarum seemed as glowing.

Chapter Seven

The flame of that warmth has died to embers in this place, Drust thought miserably. Another mud-brick shithole beaten by a harsh sun on the shores of the Hyrcanian Ocean, it had a name, but no one could pronounce it and Kisa had given up trying to tell them. They needed a ship and some open water – even if they had to steal one, which statement filled Kisa with open dread.

This was, yet again, a place he knew well – he pointed vaguely to the west and declared that his mountain home lay there. In a day he had found a ship and announced it with as wide a grin as his battered face would allow.

'It is a good one, carrying trade stuff across to the other shore, the Varkana shore. The trade place there is called...' he broke off and considered it, then threw away the idea of trying to get them to say it. 'No matter. It is not much famous, save for a holy tree of the unbelievers, but slavers take shiploads of goods across to save time and losses.'

He stopped because so many words pained him, and for a man who had nothing but his wit and his tongue, the binding of his speech caused him more agony than his bruises and swellings.

'If it is a good one,' Kag replied morosely, 'then we almost certainly cannot pay for it.'

It was a truth that raked Drust, so he did not like to hear it. They had sold the camels and made no profit, stood in poor sandals and worse tunics and cloaks, armed with the remains of their old trade.

'Manius and Dog may not recognise us,' he admitted, and Quintus smiled.

'As long as we are Brothers with blades, we are war in the hand and they will know us.'

Praeclarum laughed at his bombast and others joined in, but it was a brief spark in a dying fire as far as Drust was concerned. They were sleeping at the harbour, as close to a smith's forge as decency would allow; it was as well, he thought, that the weather was dry and still warm save at night.

'Did Dog and Manius leave from here?' Ugo asked and Kag put him on the straight. Dog and Manius had probably gone across the Red Serpent if they had been daring and idiot or rich in bribes. Otherwise they had gone this way, but from some other shithole port.

Beyond the Red Serpent Wall. Across the Hyrcanian Ocean – Drust could scarcely believe he was about to do this. Once, a trader had come to them when they were in the City of Sharp-Nosed Fishes, south of Alexandria, bringing a single long blade which was not a *spatha* and not quite a Parthian sword. He wanted to sell it, without hilt or bindings, and asked such a ludicrous sum that Drust and the others had laughed aloud – but the smith who was brokering the deal had said it was the finest forged steel he had ever seen. The trader said it had been made from quality iron brought from a place called Stone Fort, all the way down the famed Silk Road.

We did not buy it, Drust recalled – yet I am about to sail across to a place a mere hawk and spit from Stone Fort, which the God Alexander knew as Marakanda.

'These people call it Samar-Qand,' Kisa confirmed when Drust brought up the memory.

'Well, we might pick up some decent blades,' Kag growled, squinting at the worn *gladius* and working at the loose hilt bindings. 'This rattles like Praeclarum's teeth.'

'You lie,' she fired back, grinning bare gums at him. 'You took them all.'

Later, when everyone slept, Kag and Drust sat staring at the dying coals, listening to Ugo snore. He had the mightiest night-noises of any man Drust had heard; his snores resonated, right up to the point he seemed to stop breathing entirely – and just when you feared he had died, he began again and you fervently prayed that he would.

The night was warm so they needed no shelter, but the banked glow of the forge fire was a comfort against the dark, so they kept close to it and sweated as they talked, soft and low. The smith slept with his family nearby and was glad of the protection.

'Darab was hunted down,' Kag said eventually and it matched cogs with Drust's own thinking.

'Persians. They were after us all – but how did they know where to look? Who sent them and why?'

'The Shayk,' Kag decided after a hard think.

Drust wondered why the man who had paid for the entire train had then made sure it was destroyed and everyone killed. Kag shrugged.

'He found out there were no Hyrcanian tigers at the end of it.'

That was possible, Drust thought, but since no one knew what was at the end of it, it still made little sense to destroy your own money in such a senseless act. The only certainty was that Dog and Manius were at the end of it – and that they had been sent in search of something other than big cats.

'Something the Shayk does not want us to find,' Kag mused. 'Or keep if we do. That and hubris – he does not strike me as a man who takes well to being duped.'

He has uncovered the truth of this affair, Drust thought, and it is something that does not sit well with him. What it might be remained a mystery – but it was clear that the Shayk had informed the Parthians, these new ones of the House of Sasan.

'It must be important,' Kag agreed, 'for him to reveal his true allegiance.'

'Only to us. We were meant to be dead with Darab and the others.'

'He will know no Romans were among those killed,' Kag added, 'so we are safe only for a little time.'

'Long enough to get away from here. He will want to make sure no one can speak of it.'

Like Kisa, Drust thought, glancing to where the little man slept, whimpering like a pup now and then. He had suffered a great deal and Drust felt a flicker of sympathy. Yet there was the nag that the Persians who had hunted them knew where they were headed – someone had left a trail like breadcrumbs and Kisa was the favourite in that contest.

'Everyone who hears of it marvels at us doing all this, travelling this far,' Kag said softly after a while. 'They cannot believe we would do this for Manius and Dog.'

'Don't you have a Greek with something to say on it?' Drust asked lightly. 'One of those philosophers you love so much?'

There was silence for a moment. 'We are men of the hot sand and the cold steel. Ignorant, stubborn, more god-hagged than any priest but only half religious. Suspicious of change and life beyond the horizon we can see, unlettered – mostly – but magnificent with an intelligence of our own world.'

He shifted and smiled. 'There is a philosopher – can't remember his name, but Greek as you suspect – who says that folk grow sour if they stay in the same place, that they never amount to as much as if they had moved, gone elsewhere. That does not apply to us. We know our place. Our country is the sands and it is harsh and demanding so that only the best stay alive. We are the best and staying alive is a greater triumph than going away and winning riches.'

He stopped, shook his head as if half ashamed. 'That is why we will go and rescue Dog and Manius.'

'Heya,' Drust echoed, soft and admiring.

He shifted his gaze to Praeclarum, swaddled in a cloak and sitting, head slumped forward. Her lips puffed out with every breath for her mouth was looser without teeth, but since they ate the fare they had always been used to she did not suffer hunger. A farro gruel of leeks and barley was no trouble to gums.

Her eyes flicked open suddenly and caught him staring. He dropped his own, pretending to be looking elsewhere, but he felt hers on his face like a heat.

–

He had bare arms on a big body with enough muscle left to show that, before age and good living, he had been as feared a sea-rover as he claimed. Well, for a Cadusian goat-kisser, Drust thought. He had silver rings on his arms and in his ears, and a fat, false smile plastered in the little clearing between all the red-gold hair where he hid his face.

He was called Atakan, which meant 'having ancestor's blood', according to Kisa, and if it were true, the man would have a lot of ancestor blood, all of it different. His name was Cadusian, a people once great but who had been faded even in the time of Divine Aurelius Augustus, who had fought them in their last blaze of glory. His dress was Arab, yet he wore a Persian fire-worshipper amulet and had ink-marked designs spiralling up his arms like a Scythian.

'That is the price,' Atakan declared with fake apology in his eyes. 'The Mazandaran Sea which you call the Hyrcanian Ocean is dangerous enough without having to give up cargo for people who take up more space and also eat and drink.'

He spoke bad Greek, which at least let Drust and the others understand him without having to go through Kisa, who frequently took the long road through a short speech.

'Perhaps I should give this sister-humper a club,' Ugo growled to Quintus in Greek. 'Then he can hit me and it will be a proper robbery.'

'Sister-humper?'

Kisa soothed the sea captain with pats on his arm.

'It is the way they talk to each other,' he explained hastily. 'They mean no harm by it.'

Atakan growled and peered truculently, then shifted his arm away from the close attention of Stercorinus, who was trying to trace the ink-marked spirals with a grimy finger.

'That is the price. Be it known that I do not haggle.'

'This may be because he also cannot sail,' Drust said in Greek to Kag, ignoring Atakan completely. 'Besides – his ship is a fat-belly. He says he went raiding with it, which may be, but this is a little sea and there is not much sailing in it, so that is not saying much.'

Atakan looked wildly from one to the other, while Kisa tried to fix his smile and soothe with more pats. 'Just the way they talk to each other,' he said through his grin.

'Raiding?' Kag answered scornfully. 'Only a dog's arse of a sailor thinks such a log is a raiding ship — he should be paying us to step aboard it.'

'Dog… dog's arse…'

'The way they talk,' Kisa interrupted desperately, but Atakan was glowering now and elbowed both Kisa and Stercorinus away with a curse.

'Little sea? You do not know it, that is clear,' he bellowed. 'Out there are raiders from the east and the west and elsewhere. Out there are monsters and worse…'

'A ship would need good fighting men to travel it,' Drust agreed blandly. 'Brave men not afraid to stand up to sea raiders and monsters.'

'Because such brave men *are* monsters, you hog's arse,' Ugo ended, grinning. 'You think you can get such men here? You think you can get such men to pay you while they fight?'

Atakan scowled and made a dismissive grunt, but he had been caught fairly and knew it, so he came up with less false in his smile and halved the price. There was spitting and hand-slapping and everyone went off happy.

'They look powerful,' Stercorinus muttered as they walked. 'Skin-marks of note.'

'Spell-bound,' Kag replied wryly, but Ugo shook his shaggy head, frowning.

'There were those back in my village who knew the way of it. If you make a mistake with them, you can turn a charm for a hard pizzle into something unmanly. Easily fixed if scratched on an amulet, or marked on a stone — but inked forever into your skin? You'd have to flay it off, or have a man-root that looked at your toes all its life.'

Praeclarum laughed, seeing Stercorinus worrying at that idea and deciding that, if Atakan had it done, he was clearly unaffected…

'How do you know he is unaffected? He looks like a bull, but under those fat breeks he wears…'

She broke off and wiggled her little finger suggestively; everyone laughed and moved away down the harbour, where slaves hauled bales of cloth and mysterious boxes and jars. A man with a red hat moved past them holding a basket of bread and calling for buyers; the woman with him had a baby wrapped in a shawl looped round to carry it in front of her. She smiled at Drust and held out her hand, pleading.

'Just as well he halved the price,' Quintus said, grinning at the baby, 'else we would be begging as well.'

'There may be work on the far shore – this Atakan will know, for he carries salt there and silk and spices back,' Kisa said, then stopped as he felt the stares on him.

'Hauling salt,' Kag repeated blackly and Ugo's smile was brief and twisted. Kisa shrank a little.

'I do not trust this Atakan,' Sib declared and Kisa nodded agreement.

'Wise. Atakan is like all his breed – he will trade when he can and rob when he thinks he can escape with it.'

'We are the skilled men in that,' Quintus pointed out. 'It may profit such a thief to know who he is dealing with before he makes a mistake.'

Kisa nodded and went off to spread that word to the sea captain. Drust heard excited voices and went to see what was causing such interest. The sun was dying in the sea, a harsh bloody glow spreading like a huge stain and rising higher and higher in the sky, spilling out left and right like wings.

'Bel,' Stercorinus declared, kneeling. 'Send your blessings with Aglibol and Yarhibol.'

'Ahura-Mazda,' Sib said, falling into the kicked-dog crouch he always did when faced with mysteries. He had seen Atakan's amulet, and Drust had to admit the effect looked much like it.

'What does it mean?' Quintus demanded and folk waited, knowing either Sib or Stercorinus would have an answer.

'There is blood in it,' Sib began, 'which is not a good thing...'

He got no further because Kag slapped the back of his head, hard enough to smack his scarred leather war hat off. He whipped round scowling until he saw who it was.

'Blood in it,' Kag scoffed. 'The sky is full of blood this time of evening – besides, if it is the fire-starer god who sends this sign, it isn't blood, only fire. If it is that skinny wolf's three gods, then, yes, there will be blood. Have you heard of a god who does not want such sacrifice?'

'It is no good sign to see in the sky,' Sib persisted and glared back at Kag. 'From Jupiter Best and Greatest.'

'You are after making me laugh,' Kag said mildly, 'for being worse than any old woman for bad signs you need to ward off. Yet you are clever to have seen it, you dog-bothering dirty sword – something dark *is* coming, brought by that sunset blood sign.'

He leaned forward, looking fearfully left and right and finally back into Sib's wide-eyed stare.

'It is called,' he said and paused ominously. 'Night.'

The laughter kept Sib growling sullenly for a long time, but eventually sleep took even him and they huddled where they were, wrapped in what tattered cloaks were left to them and, for all that the day had been hot, the night was chill enough to need them. Drust would not admit he was near to shivering and simply sat and waited, though he did not know what for.

He became aware of her slowly, like a warmth on one side, and when he turned she sat within reach, but looking straight out at the darkened, moon-glimmered sea. The firelight cat-licked her face, so that Drust could see the swelling had gone down.

'Your mouth looks better,' he said softly, and she turned to face him.

'I will not smile, all the same.'

'How many teeth are left to you?'

She shrugged. 'I can feel some at the back on both sides – at least my face will not cave in like an old woman's. The ones in front are mostly gone but so is the pain from them, so it's all good.'

He sat silent for a time until she laughed softly. 'Ask it.'

'Ask what?'

'How long it lasted. What happened in the end.'

He shifted towards her. 'How long did it last? And what happened in the end?'

'Too long. And when the owner saw my mouth and wanted to know why his goods were damaged, he had me sold before it got worse.'

'And the man who did it?' Drust asked. She hunched and stared at the ocean.

'Flavius Milo. He was dismissed as *lanista*, or so I heard.'

'I know of him. Good fighter in his day,' Drust replied, 'but vicious even then. His behaviour is no surprise.'

'One day,' she said, her swollen voice bitter with pain, 'I will find him.'

Drust reached out a hand, meaning only to pat her sooth-ingly, and encountered her own. For a moment there was unreasoning panic, but neither drew away, and they sat, fingers touching, breath stilled. Neither was ready for this, had never been.

You could leave life right now – let that determine what you do and say and think, Drust thought wildly.

The quayside had grown quiet. There were no friendly patrols to keep order, so night in this place was a hive of thieves and worse. In a while, Drust would kick someone to take his place and then sleep himself, but for now there was a night of moonlight and chill, save where they touched, which burned.

It was as well, Drust thought later, that she and I were the only ones awake, given the hag-fears of the others, to see the great red glow that spread on the night sky, raising the hackles on his neck. He felt her fingers tighten and turned to see her looking wide-eyed back – then they both stared. It was hard to see how close it was, though it was out to sea and made bloodier by the dark that lay that way.

It stayed that way for a long time as they watched, concerned and flesh-tightened by it – then in an eyeblink, there was a great, silent pillar of fire, shooting straight up to the sky, a bright flare that made the pair of them grunt. The darkness that followed was blacker still and their exchanged glances showed how pale it had made them. Yet they found they had to untangle their fingers when they started to speak.

'A sea dragon?' she asked after a pause to gather breath, but Drust did not know, could not speak and simply shook his head. He was blinking at the dark and wondering how far away it had been.

'Sometimes you can see them for a distance of two or more days' journey.'

The voice spun them round, Praeclarum's dagger whipping out of her boot; she cursed when she saw Kisa and Atakan.

'Such behaviour could lose you an eye,' she spat. 'Or worse.'

Atakan merely spread his hands in apology and squatted beside them, his eyes gleaming in the dark.

'Not dragons,' he declared, 'but worse. That fire comes from under the sea and if you are ignorant or unlucky, it will torch your ship and everyone in it as fast as...'

He snapped his fingers and Praeclarum grunted and nodded, which made Atakan's eyes narrow. He is disappointed, for he wanted us to think he was a great liar, then prove his point, he thought. He does not know we have seen worse things than fire that burns in the sea...

'We came because Atakan has a proposition,' Kisa interrupted, 'which begins with him offering us a safer sleeping place aboard his ship.'

'We have not agreed to pay the price to take his ship,' Praeclarum scowled back and Kisa spread his hands.

'As you say, honoured lady – but the price has diminished.'

'I want no coin,' Atakan put in, beaming. Now Drust looked at him calculatingly. A man who offers free what he haggled hard for at the start is one who is selling you nothing. One of Kag's many rules of life that Drust had sucked up over the years. Atakan saw it.

'There is a favour to be asked,' he admitted. Drust said nothing and watched the smile waver and crumble.

'A short sail from here,' he went on, 'is a small place called Bād-kube. It means...'

'Place of Winds,' Drust interrupted, just to let him know he knew enough Persian.

'The Place of Pounding Winds,' Kisa corrected, then withered under Drust's gaze. Atakan brought his smile back.

'A place of dirt and hovels, famous only for two matters. The first is, as you say, the winds that tear at the place and make sailing so bad few go there. I myself find it hard and I am the best sailor on this coast.'

He stopped as if waiting for applause and, when none came, cleared his throat and went on.

'The second is that about one *farsah* from it – to you, the distance you can walk in the first part of a morning – is a place where the rocks are always ablaze. Always, since the world was made. It is not the only such place. It stinks worse than the worst fart, which is how you know you are close to it if you are blind. That stink is also the way you can tell if you are sailing over another such place – the sea bubbles and froths, as if someone had broken wind in a bath. You do well to avoid it – that fiery pillar you saw comes from these places.'

Praeclarum was not sure if Atakan had ever been in a bath, as she said with a stone face, but Atakan only shrugged.

'It is a place of black pitch, the stuff the Great City of Rome pays a great deal to have sent to them,' he went on and glanced slyly from face to face. 'They use it to make their flowing flame, the Roman Fire.'

Now this Drust knew well enough, but the man who knew most about it was Quintus. Once, in the wilds of Britannia, he had shown them all what little clay balls filled with such Fire could do.

'Black pitch is only one ingredient,' Kisa Shem-Tov said, frowning. 'The way to make it is a great secret – but the Persians know it too.'

'They do,' Atakan declared, touching a finger to his nose in a knowing way. 'This is the eternal fire, the godfire, a sign from the Ahura-Mazda. This is the Persian god.'

'You wear his sign,' Drust answered, reaching to flick the winged amulet on Atakan's chest. The man grinned; Drust was beginning to think he was related to Quintus for the way he liked to show his teeth.

'I have many amulets. It helps when you trade with people if they believe you believe as they believe.'

Kisa growled something which might have been curse or prayer, then dragged matters back to the road.

'What has this to do with us?'

Atakan nodded. 'There is such a temple, on the eastern shore of this sea. It is said to be very old, very rich and very unguarded.'

Praeclarum squinted at Kisa, then at Atakan.

'This is your favour?' he scoffed. 'A fire-starers' temple which, if it is as old as you suggest and as unguarded as you say, has clearly been fired and emptied by raiders before now.'

'Tscha,' Atakan replied scornfully. 'This shows how little you know of these waters and how you should be grateful to me to the sum of three-fifths of all we gain.'

'Two-fifths of nothing,' Drust pointed out drily, 'is nothing.'

'This temple,' Atakan persisted, 'is called Bhagavan, which means "field of the fire gods". It is in a place called the Black Lake, a place fed by the Hyrcanian Ocean so that the water runs into it. It is separated from the main water by a narrow ridge of land and a shallow channel, through which the Hyrcanian flows. Too narrow for a boat – the temple lies on the far side of the lake, a half-day sail away. This is why no one has plundered it.'

'Not by landing further up and taking it from the landward side,' Praeclarum growled and Atakan shook his head excitedly.

'No, no – it is protected by cliffs and the land around the Black Lake is so salty nothing grows there – I know, I have been. I sometimes fetch salt from the folk along that coast.'

'So the only way in is to swim?'

Atakan laughed and slapped his fat-breeked thigh.

'If you are a fish – no, the only way in is to take a ship across that ridge, and you can throw a stone across it, from one water to the other. I have a crew of six – but with your men we could haul my *Emerald* out of the water and across to the Black Lake. Kisa says you are well travelled and have done all sorts.'

Drust looked at Kisa, who nodded excitedly.

'What have you told this dog-botherer?'

'Dog-botherer?' Atakan demanded.

Kisa patted him hurriedly and added, 'A way of talking – they all do it…'

Praeclarum rubbed her head where the hair was growing out and itching with life that should not have been there. She looked at Drust then back at Atakan.

'They have sailed in the great grain ships from Alexandria,' she admitted, 'but never had to get out and push. Yours is a heavy sow of a ship to be hauling over land.'

Atakan scowled at the description, but did not deny it. His was the biggest bellied of the trade ships and Drust could see that had always been the problem.

'My *Emerald* may be big and round,' Atakan declared, 'but that means she can carry more in that belly. I have six men sailing with me. You have as many – that is enough to drag it across a little sliver of land.'

'If nothing grows in this area, as you say,' Kisa put in, 'then we must carry logs with us, but they will be underneath when we haul, so the ship will be lighter. We also will be out, so it will be lighter still.'

'And coming back?' Drust pointed out laconically. 'Laden with these legendary riches?'

'Aha,' Atakan said, slapping his hands together. 'Your honour is a clever man. The riches are there and here is why they will be no burden.'

He paused and grinned, delighted with the squints and scowls he was getting. Then he laughed; Drust was starting to dislike him more and more.

'The rich prize is *lājavard*,' he declared and sat back, beaming.

'Now I know this,' Praeclarum answered curtly, 'and I know even less than before.'

'*Lājavard*,' Kisa said, 'is the Persian name. It is a stone, though that is like saying the sea is water, or a lion is a cat, for there never was such a stone. In Rome they call it Blue Stone, or the Stone of Venus. There are many types, but the best and most prized has flecks of gold in it. If powdered and sprinkled on fire, smoke of all different sorts appears, according to Apollonius of Tyana…'

'We are to travel all this way, drag a boat like a litter-full bitch across land and raid a temple – for a blue stone that makes many-coloured smoke?' Praeclarum interrupted, then put one finger to her nose and snorted derisively.

Put that way, Drust was thinking, it did not sound much and she had a point. Kisa, however, shook his head, eyes shining – Drust had never seen anyone so smeared with the fever of raiding. This is what happens to quiet folk when you let them off the leash – even a *frumentarius* spy for the Palatine. Perhaps that beating he'd had had forged something into him, or released something that had always been there.

'This stone is highly prized,' Kisa hissed, looking right and left as if to see ears sprout where none had been. 'The men of Rome believe this *lājavard* has… powers. Women of a certain type, the expensive kind, wear it round their neck for the same reason.'

He made an age-old gesture, crooking his arm at the elbow and Praeclarum laughed aloud, then hushed herself as someone stirred.

'It makes you hard?'

Atakan grinned. 'Like bar iron, lady. I would not know, for I do not need it – but those who do will pay for a mere chip of it and pay a great deal.'

Praeclarum sat back, one eye shut, thinking and looking from one to the other.

'Three-fifths to two?' she queried. 'When we do as much hauling and all the fighting?'

Drust almost clapped his hands with delight for her.

'What fighting?' Atakan answered scornfully. 'There is no one to fight – but you folk look better waving swords. They will piss their robes and flee, then all you have to do is dig out the eyes and be gone.'

'Eyes?' Drust asked and Atakan nodded.

'Did I not say? There is a likeness in this temple, a great head which may well be the face of Ahura-Mazda, who knows. It is hollowed out at the back – some say a priest stands in it and makes out that the head speaks, which may be true, but I have not seen it myself. The eyes of this statue are pieces of *lājavard*, big as your fist, the sort with gold flecks in it too, or so I have heard. There is an everlasting fire-flame behind it which makes the eyes glow as if it lived.'

Praeclarum looked at Drust, who stayed as grim as the stone head he had just heard about. He did not like it, did not like or trust this Atakan, but he knew the men needed something to hold in their palms, something that spoke of Fortuna's smile. Free passage and possible riches? It could hardly be turned down, so he nodded slowly and spat on his palm.

'I agree.'

145

Atakan slapped his hand and then rose up, cracking his knees and grinning. 'Bring your men to the ship,' he said as he went. 'I want to sail on the tide and it turns in the dark.'

He went off and Praeclarum shifted slightly, staring at Drust.

'If the others do not agree?'

'Why would they not?'

'It might seem foolish to some. And angering a god is never a good idea – ask Odysseus,' Kisa pointed out.

'I lead here. No one else.'

Kisa shrugged. 'If you tell it right,' he said pointedly, 'they will not resist.'

They woke the others and Drust told it, then listened to them worry at it like a dog on a bare bone until he reminded them there was a ship waiting. So they went, mumbling and growling as they walked.

In the end it came down to whether Kag thought this was a good idea. Drust felt the weight of his eyes but resisted the temptation to pay him or any of them any heed.

'We are not pirates,' Kag said thoughtfully and Quintus snorted scorn, which got laughter. Kag shrugged.

'My purse says it is a wonderful enterprise,' he grunted, 'though my bags say it is not.'

'Your bags?' Ugo demanded and Kag grabbed at the hem of his tunic and the baggy Persian trousers worn beneath.

'They are shrinking, drawing tight and making themselves small, though it is a difficult matter for such large affairs. They are hiding, lads, because they know something is wrong.'

'Jupiter's hairy arse,' Quintus declared with mock, grinning disgust, 'I am passing up riches because of the state of your balls?'

'Mine are bigger than his,' Praeclarum muttered and folk laughed aloud.

'What does Drust think?' Sib asked, and there it was, the bit that had always mattered and taken so long to get to.

Drust thought that it was as mad as a helmet full of frogs. There were mouth-frothers who would not undertake this, for if it had only been a matter of dragging his ship across a narrow neck and shouting loudly at some robes, then Atakan would have tried it before now. There must be muscled men for hire round here.

It stank, he wanted to say, worse than a three-day fish or an unwanted guest, and he should never have agreed to it.

'I have already made the deal,' he said mildly, 'so that's why I am thinking on it.'

He stretched and yawned as if it was all no matter, then pointed to the great bulked shape and the ramp that led up into it.

'There is the ship. Wake me when we get to this fire temple and when you run at these fire-starers I will be there. Right behind you.'

They laughed.

'I will buy new trousers,' Kag declared, ruefully examining the torn and stained remains of his once splendid Persian affairs. More laughter, and while the shadowed crew of the ship watched them warily they huddled together in the dark.

'Once this temple affair is done with,' Drust said, more confidently than he felt, 'we will be dropped at the mouth of a river where it meets the sea. If we keep following it inland, we will come across Manius and Dog and find out what this is all about.'

He looked at the dim figure of Kisa, who nodded.

'Said like that,' Stercorinus declared, 'it sounds easy.'

A little later they were woken by the slap of bare feet, the soft cries of the crew. Things rattled and flapped and the deck lurched; they were underway.

For a moment there was silence, then Kag thrust out his hand, palm down. One by one the knuckle-marked – and those who weren't, but knew the significance – added a hand to the splayed wheel of it. Praeclarum, half embarrassed but all determined, added her own and exchanged grins with Drust.

'Brothers of the sand, brothers of the ring,' Drust declared and everyone growled assent – then Sib stood up and moved urgently to the freeboard, peering back at the flickering lights of the quayside.

'Look there,' he said, so they all did. Drust saw men and horses, the firelight glinting blood on metal helmets and blades – and faces. Silvered faces. He heard shouting.

'That was proof Fortuna smiles anew,' Kag declared. 'I know those faces – I have one in my bundle.'

The Persians who had slaughtered Darab and the others, thinking we were in the mix, Drust thought, and the cold slid down him like iced rain at how narrow had been their escape. The others merely grinned; Ugo brought out a leather skin and poured wine into the sea, an offering to Fortuna and Neptune, for you can never have too many gods offering help.

But they didn't think on it for longer than it took to feel pleased they had escaped in time. They started curling up back to sleep to dream of riches, while Drust sat long into the dark, brooding on what lay ahead and what they had hopefully managed to avoid.

–

Running in any direction was an awkward business of stumble and roll, for the dark and the arid, uneven sprawl of ground, cut about by crevice and knoll, made movement difficult even at a walk. Drust was running all the same, as fast as weary legs and borrowed leather war gear would let him, and he could hear Sib muttering out his fear on one side and Kag grunting on the other. Behind was baying and not all of it from dogs; Drust wondered if the others had got back down the cliff to the ship.

He wondered if the ship was still there and the one thing he did not marvel at was how rotted the affair now was. If it was a game of *tali*, he thought, feeling his lungs burn, he would have flung his bones away and given in long since, for he was throwing nothing good in this game. Should have done that as soon as I found that the temple was on top of the cliff, not at the foot, he thought. How was it, then, that such an egg of a place had not been robbed from the landward side before? How was it that Atakan had said that it could not be reached because of the cliffs?

That revelation had come after a long sail and a muscle-cracking haul over the little ridge of land, which had proved rockier and wider than they had been told; Atakan had shrugged and said it had looked narrower to him when last he had been there. There were the marks of old firepits and Atakan said folk came here now and then, in the hope of being able to run the inflow, which vomited like an open gullet not far away, spilling the Hyrcanian Ocean into this Black Lake.

The sail across the inner lake had proved strange, not only because the winds were swirling but because it did not feel right to those who had sailed the Middle Sea. Atakan said it was the salt in it, coming up through the tunnels from other seas that let Poseidon swim the world. None of which made anyone easier.

They arrived at the far shore, a vast expanse of salt pan which had glowed in the dusk like a winding sheet. Atakan had turned the bulky ship, fat belly painted red and black and with eyes in the prow that looked at the sea. He had followed the curve of white coast towards a distant line which slowly grew to be high cliffs and only then revealed a collection of leather war gear, mouldy old chest-pieces and helmets and round shields, Greek stuff the men of Great Alexander would have recognised at once. In the gathering dusk Atakan had proudly shown them the fire temple, as if he had built it himself for their pleasure; it was a faint smudge on top of the grey-blue cliffs which fell sheer to the sea.

The only way up was a winding, narrow stairway, and Atakan argued that Drust had been mistaken when he'd thought it at the foot of the cliff.

'The land around it is barren and waterless,' he declared blandly, 'which is why you cannot approach it from that side. It has high walls and even if they are rank white-livers, a locked gate is a locked gate. Up the steps, however, there is no gate.'

'You could defend those steps with a pizzle-rotted old man and a stick,' Kag noted, but Atakan scoffed at them.

'It is night and we are unseen. A swift gallop up those steps and all the riches are yours.'

They looked at one another and everyone thought the same – there was no swift galloping up that, not if you wanted to keep your footing and not plunge off. If someone with a bow positioned himself just right he'd have all of us, Drust had thought, and it was small comfort that Atakan's men wanted to join in; Atakan was scowling at that but did not dare say anything about it, or the fact that Drust left Kisa and Stercorinus behind to make sure they had a ship to return to.

Drust led the way up the steps, a long, knee-ache of a climb, but no one opposed them even when they reached the top and passed under a crumbling brick archway.

Which was Fortuna's smile and Mars Ultor's hand, since everyone was sweating and bent, hands on knees, trying to suck in air. For all the night had been chill, the sweat was rolling from them and thigh muscles quivered like fly-bitten horses.

The temple had been a complex of structures big and small, and folk had fled, as Atakan had said they would. At the centre of a huge square of square buildings was another brick square, each wall an arch; it was easily found in the night because of the flame at the centre of it, a steady, strange flicker that went from red-gold to *murex* purple and back again.

Under one archway sat the head, just as Atakan had said, and it was true what he had told them of the light making the eyes glow – if you stood a certain way you could see it. The flame murmured softly out of an altar built round it, came right up out of a hole without so much as a single stick to feed it. That was as unsettling as the eyes.

Drust sent Sib and Ugo right and left to guard, while Kag and Quintus scrambled up the plinth to the bearded face, using their daggers to hook stones out.

'I do not care for this,' Praeclarum muttered. 'It does no good to offend gods, no matter that they are not your own.'

Kag laughed, dug the second eye out of its socket and stuffed it in a bag, which he handed to Drust to fasten to his belt. With a series of hissing cries, everyone was brought back together and set off back to the steps and the long descent. Drust felt the head behind him and turned to see the eyes now blazing blood-red, which was as unsettling as the shouts in the dark. Going down those steps, Sib moaned, was going to be worse than coming up, for it seemed the fire-starers were making a fist and would swing it at them.

It was more like two to Drust – a sudden flurry of little arrows and stones which clattered round them, and a rush of men out of the dark which caused a dog-pack of fighting, all snarl and confusion. Drust batted a shadow away with his old shield, slashed at another and ran on, the bag of stones dangling like a sheep bollock from under the face of his shield.

They were nothing much as fighters, these men, but they had courage and ferocity, numbers – and dogs. It was not long after that, stumbling and staggering, sweat and dust choking him, that Drust realised only Sib and Kag were there and they were all separated from the others.

Worse than that, they had missed the steps entirely. Drust was still wondering where they were when the ground went out from under his feet and he rolled in a whirl of black and stars and black again. A hand gripped him under one arm and hauled him up.

'Perhaps Praeclarum was right,' Kag said hoarsely, 'that stealing the eyes from a dead god's head was not worthy of us.'

'How is that working out for you?' Drust spat back angrily, shaking him off. 'The thinking? Hopefully it will get so good you will bring this up before we set off on such an enterprise.'

The baying was louder and now there were bobbing lights too.

'They really want their eyes,' Sib growled, and Kag spat dust and sweat.

'So do we,' Drust answered. 'Run.'

They ran, but only for a short distance before Drust slammed into the back of Sib, who squealed and grabbed hold of him. Kag skidded to a halt and the dust puffed up blue-grey in the moonlight – ahead was blackness, part of it sparkling with stars and part of it dancing with moonlight. Night sky and sea...

'Mars Ultor,' Kag panted, and the baying rose up mournfully. Drust saw with a sick lurch that they stood at the edge of a precipice.

'It is never good to run in the *harena*,' Kag snarled and his grin was feral. 'You only arrive back at the fighting.'

'I saw that show,' Sib responded, though he was round-eyed and darting glances right and left. 'The Ludus, back when I was a *tiro* – Christians did not fare well in it.'

'We are not Christians,' Drust spat back and threw the bag at Kag.

'I will stand guard while you get out of that leather and your boots. Do not let go of the bag when you jump.'

He stepped forward, ripped off his own helmet and gritted teeth at that too – Fortuna is a fickle cunt, he thought, who gives with one hand and steals with the other. It hadn't been much, but it and the leather and the shield were more than they'd had and a sign the goddess had been favouring them at last.

More fool us for believing that, Drust thought, starting to heel off a boot while keeping crouched, shield up, sword ready; behind, he heard Kag grunt, wriggling out of leather.

Sib, who had no leather, had had time to think and wail, running this way and that like a hen pursued by a rooster with intentions. He dragged off his own helmet and flung it away.

'Get over,' Drust roared, not turning round; he could see the torches and vague shapes between them.

'The sea might not be entirely beneath,' Sib shouted back.

'Jump far,' Kag snarled, hauling off his own boots.

'There may be rocks...'

'Jump farther.'

'I cannot swim.'

The last was a despairing whimper and Kag, sword in one hand and the bag in the other, whirled and booted Sib hard – his vanishing shriek was loud and pungent.

A dog burst out, howling, plunging forward to where Drust stood. It was a slew-hound, all nose and no fight, though it tried to bore in for the ankles, so he cracked the rim of his shield on its skull, then broke its back with the sword.

'This is how to lose all fear,' Kag bellowed, his voice high and crazed. 'Jump off a cliff.'

Drust was watching the second dog, cursing Kag to the banks of the Styx to get jumping; Kag laughed and stuffed the bag inside his stained tunic.

'I hope you can swim in leather,' he shouted and his grin was wolf-savage now. 'And I can hit water and not stone. If not, we will walk in Elysium.'

'Stop talking and jump,' Drust harshed back at him, and Kag flung back his head and bellowed for Mars Ultor to see this moment. His screaming was a descending note as he fell.

The second dog was a nasty lump of fur with a mouthful of blades which leaped on Drust, all froth and snarl. He took it on the shield, whirling it sideways, though the weight wrenched the shield away; the dog rolled over and over, only to get up and shake its head.

Drust heeled off his second boot and kicked it defiantly in the direction of the dog, which skittered sideways and then launched itself, baying in short, furious snarls; stones whicked past Drust's head and he turned, took a deep breath, then leaped, feeling the dog snap at his heels.

There was a moment when he hung like a crucifixion. Long enough to see his ma and wonder at it, at whether she watched constantly from the Other and only now, with his death, could he see her. Then he felt the first sickening tug of falling, heard the descending, mournful baying of the hound, falling with him in a frantic flurry of uselessly paddling legs.

Then he plunged into the blackness.

–

We stood there, Kag and I, reaching out to touch the fingers, shined from so many other times. Theogenes was the greatest of the harena, *though he never fought in it, for he was a Greek from the time before Socrates and Plato. He did the* pankration *and* pygmachia *served under the patronage of a cruel nobleman, a prince who took great delight in bloody spectacles. He had two victories at the games, won three times at the Pythian, once in the Isthmian and a thousand other times in lesser* munera.

He sat at the head of the Old Footpath on the Quirinal, a road into Rome which was venerable when the twins were suckling wolf teats. He was bronzed by Apollonius. Or Lysippos, no one was sure. Next to him stood a proud and haughty ruler – and everyone thought this was Theogenes and his cruel patron, but Kag knew different.

'Look,' he would say. 'Look where he sits. Look at his head.'

The pugilist sat on a stone, a man running hard into his middle years with a thick beard and a full head of curly hair. He had a broken nose and flattened gristle ears, the slanted, drooping brows that told of too many blows and a forehead furrowed with scars more than age.

He had big shoulders and Ugo pointed out the rest – his chest is thick and flat, without the bulging pectorals of those gymnasium lifters. His back and abdominal muscles are highly pronounced and he has, Ugo added admiringly, that greatest asset of all – good legs.

The man who sculpted it knew the subject well. The arms are large, particularly the forearms, which are reinforced with the leather wrappings of the caestus. *He has the* oxys, *those bands criss-crossing his forearms to give support to heavy blows. At the top is a band of fleece for wiping sweat and blood from his eyes.*

All lovingly rendered in bronze, save the blood, which is copper. He sits on a rock with his forearms balanced on his thighs and his head turned as if he were looking over his shoulder — as if someone had just whispered something to him.

Quintus knew better and pointed out the look on the bronze face — there is no trace of fear in the battered, broken-nosed, bloody stare. He looks ready to go, anxious not to cause a delay, to get on with it, even though he is weary to the bone and resigned to this time being the last. This time is the one he loses and gets beaten to bloody pulp.

This is no hero of the pankration. *Would he want to be behind the ox-plough, an obscure, reeking peasant? A slave cleaning the latrines? Would that be better?*

People come to meditate on the great, battered Theogenes — the ruler they ignore. Kag knows better. It is allegory, he declares, a work made by Greeks about Greeks. This is not Theogenes, it is one of the first boxers of them all, the ones great Theseus created to sit opposite one another on stones and fight with their fists until one fell off or died or both. His head is tilted because he hears his opponent arriving and the other statue, the unknown ruler, is brave Theseus of the supposedly civilised Greeks, who invented this bloody sport, and waits to watch.

We come here to polish his caestus-*wrapped fingers, for we are him and he is us.*

—

He launched from it, flailing. Hands found him, hauled him up. A dripping face like a wet mule shoved itself into his vision and grinned; the clap on his shoulder felt like being hit by a shield.

'You got out of that — well, all's good,' said Ugo and then waved to where Sib sat, hunched and hugging himself, his face a long, wet misery. 'So did he, though no one expected it.'

'Why is he yelling about Theogenes?'

Praeclarum's face was concerned, but she had no answer from those who saw no need to say.

'Jupiter's hairy balls, that was a moment,' Kag went on, beaming. 'I do not wish to go off a cliff ever again – but we have the riches and all are rescued. Well, save for one of the crew who clearly fucked off Fortuna. She tripped him on the steps down and he beat everyone to the foot. They found him at the bottom with his head cracked.'

Quintus grinned even more widely than usual. 'So you see, it was safer jumping – that is a good trick.'

'We have the stones,' Atakan boomed, while Drust struggled up, still wavering in a strange dreamlike mist where the weary beaten face of the boxer drifted. He is us and we are him, Drust thought, and struggled up onto uneasy feet.

The pinprick lights on the cliff – men with torches, coming down those steps – slapped the mist from his head. Drust looked around at the faces, all busy doing nothing at all.

'Why are we not sailing?'

'No wind worth a fart,' Stercorinus declared flatly. 'If it comes round a notch or two and starts blowing us west we may shift this fat sow of a ship, but not before.'

'Is this not a concern?' Drust spat back into his mildness and Stercorinus lifted his eyebrows slightly.

'Would it help?'

'Ha,' said Atakan, 'it does not matter. These fire trolls are not inclined to swim to us, are they?'

That much was true and Kag had organised folk to keep watch, so Drust lay back and tried not to be sick for a time, tried to order the wildness in his head. Praeclarum came with a cool, soaked cloth which she laid on his forehead.

'You knocked your wits about,' she said and he agreed.

'Who is Theogenes?' she asked again, and Drust waved a dismissive hand, closing his eyes.

'An old boxer,' Kag said. 'A Greek.'

It left her no wiser, but she dismissed all thought of it when one of Atakan's crew yelled out in his own tongue, bringing heads up. Under the moonlight, the dark water danced and black shapes slid.

'What is that there?' demanded Sib and Ugo got to it first, hawked and spat bitterly.

'The gods above and below are in a vicious mood this night. Those fire-staring little men have boats.'

There was a long moment of squint and point, then Atakan appeared, chivvying his own men back from the thwarts and into some work.

'Ha – they only have small boats and not many of them. They are no threat.'

The stone whicked out of the shadows and bounced off the freeboard, making everyone duck; an arrow clattered over the side, spun off a timber and vanished into the darkness.

'Shields up,' Quintus roared and Atakan began bellowing at his men to scoop up bilge water and soak the sail in the hope of getting wind to stick to it.

Drust sat while the *harena* dance foamed around him, thinking about little boats and not many of them. He felt as if his old helmet was back on his head, could feel the rim of it all round and the battered bit on one side which had never quite fitted properly. Left in Dura with everything else and, like the boxer on the Quirinal, he sat with his head tilted to one side, waiting for yet another opponent.

A chill kissed him on the cheek as the wind changed; there were cheers when the clumsy sow of a ship shifted and started to slide forward. More stones and arrows showered down and a crewman yelped. Another, halfway up the mast to soak the sail, seemed to jerk and then fell to the deck with a sickening crack – in the end, they had to put him overboard, for his head was broken open like a dropped egg.

There were faint cheers when the enemy saw this, darting about like shoals of small fish in narrow boats that seemed to glow out of the dark, then vanish. No more than a handful of oars and eight or ten men in them, Kag reported eventually, but with slings and bows.

'And we do not have Manius and his bow any longer,' Sib mourned.

'They will not dare come aboard to attack us,' Atakan soothed. 'And if we are careful, their stones and arrows will run out soon enough, together with their strength. They will give up and go away.'

'You wish it,' Drust said, staring at him. He blanched and Drust knew he had him on the mark.

'You knew these fire-starers had boats,' he went on and no one missed the tone of his voice. Kag looked warily at where the crew were and Quintus fell into a fighting crouch at his back, pairing as they did so often in the *harena*.

'You knew they had no weapons to speak of and only little boats and believed they could do you no harm – yet still you were afraid, for your men were not fighters. You knew all this because you had seen these fire-watchers before – and they know you, Atakan Fat-Liar, rich farmer of the seas.'

Kag growled and others, seeing the way of it, added low rumbles of their own.

'You traded for salt with them,' Drust went on, patching the cloak of it as he spoke. 'Always on the far side of that little ridge, coming ashore to make fires and leave… what? Food and drink, which they would need in a barren place like they have? Then you collect the cheap salt and everyone goes away content.'

Drust was prowling upright now and folk scattered away from Atakan, who began to swell up like a toad and opened his mouth to bluster. But the sight of all the other swords let it hiss out of him like air from a dead goat.

'Not you, though,' Drust said, stalking in a half-crouch like some beast. 'Not you, who sailed away fretting about blue eyes of stone and wanting them – until you found us, the poor idiot men you thought would gain you the riches. What was our reward after this, you fat lump of dung? Were you to fall on us in the dark, tip us over into the Black Lake or the Hyrcanian Ocean?

'No, no,' Atakan began, waving his hands in frantic dismissal. 'Two-fifths, as was said…' He looked desperately round at his own crew for help; Drust saw it and snarled like a wolf.

'No help from these,' he said. 'These are ship-handlers and haulers. Poor dogs who will not stand up to fire-starers, let alone fighting brothers like the ones at my back. Slit throats in the dark is their style – is that what you had planned? If you have not heard before how we are gladiators of Rome, fighters of beasts and men, then you have now.'

The men growled at that. Atakan scrambled back to the thwarts, felt the dig of them in the small of his back and wailed. For an eyeblink Drust thought he would find the courage of the trapped and launch himself – but there was a thump and a crack.

Atakan jerked forward, stumbled a few steps as if he charged at Drust – then he fell like a broken mast, crashing to the planks with blood spilling from the two arrows and the stone which had felled him. There was a moment of whirling-dog panic, but it did not last – there were no fighters in Atakan's crew and they cowered away while Kag sprang to the steering-oar.

'Work the ship,' Drust snarled at Atakan's men, 'if you want to live.'

There was a pause, then Ugo bellowed, incoherent and loud enough to buzz heads; they sprang to obey.

Stercorinus and Praeclarum pitched Atakan overboard and Stercorinus moaned out of the dark about how he would now never discover who had done the marvellous skin-marks.

'If they were for protection from his gods,' Ugo roared 'then you did not want them.'

All of Drust's focus was on the sound of the unseen boat enemy, cheering.

He had thought they might give up when they found Atakan rolling dead in the dark water, but he was wrong – when the first light crawled up over the horizon, the little stick boats were there, still rowing like frantic water beetles.

'They are tougher than those Greeks who fought in the Flavian,' Sib pointed out admiringly. 'Remember those? They stuck to their *hoplite* formation all day, like the Spartans at the Hot Gates. These Persians have rowed all night.'

They rowed most of that day too, while the wind held and drove the ship onward. They had, it seemed, run out of stones and arrows, but continued to keep pace. Still they wouldn't come close enough to be struck, which was frustrating to everyone.

'Water bugs,' Ugo scorned and spat, then stuck his neck out and howled across the water at them. 'Come ahead, you little dog-holes. I have an edge here for you.'

He waved his axe with frustration until Stercorinus, of all people, put a quietening hand on his massive forearm and brought him to silence. He seemed the only one not flustered by an enemy who did not want to fight but would not leave them alone. He should be mouth-frothing, Drust thought, or at least concerned, but he did not ask for he knew the answer he would get. Would it help?

'Why don't they shit or climb off the privy?' Quintus demanded of no one in particular.

They would not do either, Drust was thinking, and Kag agreed. They kept sailing until the little streak of black on the horizon grew into the ridge, and the ship faltered a little under the current flowing towards it from the inrush of the Hyrcanian Ocean. This, they all knew, was what the fire temple warriors had waited for.

They turned, heading to the narrow part where they had left the rolling logs, but Drust knew what they would find when they got there, was made certain of it by the smudge of smoke.

'They have made fires of our rolling logs,' Kag muttered, and the ship's crew began to argue and wail until snarled to silence. Drust plunged off the aft deck into the well of the hold, where there were bits of cargo that Atakan had found room for. No salt, but some hides and something Drust had spotted earlier when they were dragging out the body of the crewman who fell off the mast.

Hoes and mattocks, bound in bundles of ten. He grinned and told the others, who got the idea at once, though one of the crewmen stepped forward, scowling.

'That is valuable cargo,' he said in Greek. 'What will we live on if you destroy it?'

Drust looked him up and down, from his bare, calloused feet to the thatch of unruly black hair and beard. His name was Kalistokos, Kisa declared, and he was the mate of the vessel — captain now that Atakan was dead, he supposed.

'You will not live at all unless we escape,' Drust pointed out. 'Besides – two-fifths of this is ours, under the deal we made with Atakan. Be assured of three-fifths and work to earn it.'

Kalistokos spoke to the others – in some local form of Persian, Kisa reported later – and clearly did not know Kisa understood, since he used terms Kisa would not repeat regarding Drust and the others. But it seemed they would obey, though they did not like it.

The ship nudged up to the narrow part, sliding into the shingle until it ground to a halt, and robed men fled, leaving the smouldering remains of the timbers. Drust ordered them dirt-smothered, to see if any could be rescued. Then he put men on either side, shields up, while the others began the laborious task of pitching out the cargo to lighten the load and started hauling the vessel up and over to the sea on the far side.

At which point they all found out that the timber fires had not been lit just to burn the hauling logs. And that the fire-starers had not run out of arrows.

The boats slid in like skimming insects and a shower of fireflies, bright even in the morning sun, showered down like hot rain. One slapped the timbers of the ship and Kag, roaring annoyance, tried to pull it out, snapped it, and then found sense and smothered it with his ripped and stained red cloak.

'Fuck you all,' he roared, beating the sparks out of his cloak and glaring like a routed boar. Men laughed, but there was little humour in it, and Praeclarum was set to scoop water and watch for more such arrows.

The hauling took time. Arrows flew – two good shots landed in the flaked sail and Praeclarum had a hard task putting the flames out. 'God-cursed little fire fucks,' Sib rasped, the sweat rolling off him. 'Don't they ever give up?'

Drust eyed the man in the boat offshore, the one wearing some necklace that sparkled and flashed. That and the hand-waving, points and shouts marked him as leader, and if these fire-starers had been on land, he'd have been the one they rushed. Kill him and all is done, Drust thought, but no one's god was Poseidon or Neptune or anything like it, so running on water was out. Neither did they have a bow, nor even a decent throwing javelin.

The leader sent men to pluck stones from the ridgeline and now the slingers got back to work – one of the ship's crew went down like a felled ox when one hit him low on the back of the neck. When he came round, he could not use his right arm and Kalistokos cursed at the loss of one more crewman. Later, a burning arrow killed him.

Then the boat stuck on the downward path, sliding off the unwieldy rollers and burying its fat nose in rocks and crushed shells. Men groaned and cowered as arrows flew, for it would be a hard struggle to get it back on the wooden road to the sea, even without folk throwing fire and missiles at them.

'Wait until night,' Kag advised. 'It will be cooler and they won't be able to see.'

Drust looked at the high sun and then at the determined heat-wavering figures. They had hauled their own little boats across and were now on the far side, on the Ocean; he knew they were not about to give up, even after the ship had been put back in the water. They would chase us all the way to Hades, he growled to Kag, who hawked and spat and scrubbed his head furiously – but could only agree.

'Give them back,' Praeclarum said, and there was a moment when everyone wanted to roar at her. Instead they fell silent.

Drust thought about it for a moment, sighed, straightened and held out a fist to Kag, who knew what had to be done but scowled and growled as he handed over the bag.

Holding both hands high, one empty, one with the bag, Drust sucked in a scorch of breath and stepped out, away from the whale of a ship and his men, out onto the ridge towards the man with the glittering necklace, who sat offshore in his boat.

Drust stood for a long moment, arms out where they could be seen; the world held its breath and every part of him shrieked and cringed from what it expected to be struck with.

Then he tipped the bag up and the blue stones tumbled to the ground, sparkling and glowing in the noon sun. He turned and walked back, feeling his spine itch and crawl at the expected shower of unseen arrows.

There was a long moment, then a shout from the leader of the fire-starers; a boat scudded in and men scampered along the shore. They reached the eyes and gathered them up; there was a strange series of yipping cries and then the men scampered away again.

In less than an hour, there was not a boat to be seen, and eventually Quintus straightened and grunted as his knees cracked.

He glowered round at everyone. Then at Drust.

'This has been a bad day for the Brothers of the Sands,' he declared. 'This is what happens when you defy the gods, even those of others. We have been beaten by a ragged-arse bunch of inbred goat-fuckers and no treasure is ours.'

He stuck out one hand, palm down. One by one the others came, Praeclarum and Stercorinus no longer embarrassed that they had no knuckle tattoos to show their old slavery; they had the marks on them, all the same. The ship's crew watched, sullen and anxious at what would happen now with these strange Romans; they knew they were locked in a wooden cage with wolves.

Kag, with one last glare in the direction of the folk who had just forced riches from his fist, turned a baleful eye on the canted ship.

'Fortuna, loveliest of ladies,' he declared, spitting on his palms, 'help us get this log in the water.'

Chapter Eight

The tree was a twisted torture, a bent and wrinkled crone all knobbed with old galls and mostly bare of leaves, so that it seemed to claw out of the ground. It crouched malevolently in the middle of a festering marsh, studded with tussocks and pools, pinging with insects.

The Zonius River – the Golden River – flowed out into the Hyrcanian Ocean here and the distant green, steep-gorged line of it marked the good land round the Wall from the drab dust of the north. Much like all the other golden objects we have been led to, Drust thought, its shine is less bright than promised and much like every map he had ever known, it was not the only name this river had. Sarnois was another and Atrak yet a third.

The surviving crew of the ship had been reluctant to come too close – their new leader, a Persian called Mazarbak, pleaded the draught and the possibility of grounding, but Kisa said it was because they feared this place.

'It's supposed to be a trade place,' Sib argued. 'I have seen this before on the fringes of lands – look, there are the remains of old signals that there are folk wanting to buy and sell.'

He was right – there were weathered scraps of faded cloth and other items hanging from the tortured branches and Mazarbak confirmed that trade had been carried out here, circumventing the Red Serpent taxes and bribes.

'Not lately. Not for some time,' he added, squinting at the shoreline. 'The Tschol have seen to that.'

The Tschol, Kisa explained, was a large name for a lot of peoples of the Land of No Return – the Red Hawk tribe, the White Stallions, the Bones of the Earth and others. The names made people hunch in their necks and peer warily left and right. This was the land of wolves, of giant tigers and creatures that were, perhaps, even worse – so bad they needed to be kept behind a Wall.

'Ha,' said Kag when this was slithered out. 'We have been over such a Wall – remember? And the worst beasts we found when we got there were…?'

'Ourselves,' Sib muttered, and Kag smacked his hands together like a lawyer making a fine moment in a speech; others winced at the noise.

'None of these folk sound friendly,' Sib added. 'And where is Manius? Or Dog?'

All Kisa had been told was 'follow the river'. Mazarbak and the remaining crew had been grateful that their ship wasn't burned to the waterline and promised to return in thirty days and wait two. If no one came, they could sail away. If there were people waiting, they would carry them to safety and receive gold in reward. They had seen the gold – Drust had dug it out of a secret place while ransacking Atakan's sleeping place.

They watched the ship slide into haze, slapping insects and wondering what they ate when the Brothers of the Sands were not around. Then they sorted out what gear they had, which wasn't much. Atakan had provided hard leather breastplates and helmets, they had their own worn weapons, some food and a riverful of water.

'All in all,' Quintus declared, grinning, 'we aren't so badly off.'

'You are a man of simple tastes,' Praeclarum answered, slapping something to a bloody smear on her upper arm.

Ugo stood looking at the tree – Stercorinus prowled it as if it was a live enemy. Bones hung from the branches, a belt with a rusted buckle, skeins of dead flower-chains. It dripped with dusty old skins – a lion, Drust saw, touching the dry-rotted thing with wonder. There was a knife long rusted to shards, and newer bits too – a lump of amber on a cord, a horse amulet, the intricately carved bone handle of a broken knife. They knew god-places when they saw them and moved quietly here, hushed and reverent; the affair of the blue stones had shaken them, though none would admit it.

'I saw such trees as these when I was toddling,' Kag said, squinting up at the clawed branches. 'Along the Arda river. Once I saw a carved horse, maybe put there by one of the tribals, and I took it. My da made me put it back; he knew it was wrong and an insult to the gods and the locals.'

'Smart man, your da,' Praeclarum answered. 'What was he?'

'Legionary. 13th,' Kag answered, short and hard, with a look that told Praeclarum he wanted no more talk on it.

The line of the river was a burst of eye-watering green after the soulless grey-blue of the sea and the endless dusted tan of the land. It was mountainous here and covered with trees, the river slid and snaked over rocks – further up towards the hills, Drust knew, it would dance and spray.

This side of the ocean was the land the Greeks called Hyrcania, Kisa told them. 'Varkana, the land of wolves,' he added, his unease flowing from him like heat. 'Even the Great Iskandr walked softly and eventually built the Wall they call the Red Serpent to keep these people away from decent folk.'

'Well, how far do we have to go?' Ugo asked, looking at the green-choked gorge up ahead.

'Not as far as the Great Iskandr,' Kisa declared and Kag laughed.

'He fell off the edge of the world, no doubt.'

'He was poisoned,' Kisa corrected sternly. 'By his own.'

'That's the East for you,' Quintus said, hefting a pack and adjusting it for comfort on his shoulder. 'The further to the east you go, the more you meet the secret dagger and poison rather than a decent *harena* fight.'

'A little trust goes a long way,' Kag added and the others echoed him, the rut of his sayings well worn now.

'The less you trust, the further you get.'

'Speaking of which,' Drust said and drew out a scroll from inside his tunic, the seal on it broken. Everyone saw Kisa's face drain.

'This also came from Atakan's squirrel-hole,' Drust said. 'I want it read out now so that we all know where we stand. It is written in Latin and none of you reads well enough to get it all, so listen.'

He cleared his throat.

> *To Lucius Julius Aurelius Sulpicius Severus Uranius Antoninus, Decurio —*
> *Greetings from Kisa Shem-Tov.*
>
> *First Hour of Creation Day, 978 anno Urbis conditae, at the port of Kesht on the Hyrcanian Ocean — may the God of my fathers render this country desolate, though He will not have much to do.*
>
> *Thusly has God taken pity on me and delivered me to safety after such adversity as would take more rolls of papyrus than I possess to detail. Which rolls, Your Honour, are running low. Also, if these folk are going on it may be impossible to ensure safe delivery of these messages — already I am not certain if these sons of pigs I am entrusting epistles to will obey the writ*

of the Emperor. As you know, I was not supposed to come this far but have been forced to it and so carry out your instructions to relay all of interest regarding these amphitheatre performers.

Well, it fell to me to overhear the one who calls himself Drust and the abomination of womanhood named Praeclarum speaking close in the dark, where they thought no one could hear, while we waited for the tide to take the ship from the port.

They spoke of Drust's lost comrades, this Manius and this Dog, and were sure this in itself was not the reason for the journey, while the fetching of tigers was a laughable ruse. Your Honour will remember me bringing this up at the time and though the Shayk swallowed it, these so-called Brothers never have. I have not been taken into Your Honour's confidence regarding the true reason for the journey, which is placing me at some risk – these people, particularly the leader, this Drust, have threatened harm to my person unless I tell them all I know.

This Drust noted that good men were already wavering and that Fortuna seemed to have deserted them, but they had good hopes for a new enterprise, one which we are about to sail on. It is, Your Honour, little more than a pirate raid, and nothing to do with the business at hand, while putting us all in danger.

Then the woman said that their Brotherhood was stronger than any chains and no matter that rescuing two of their own was not the real reason they had been sent, it was real for everyone here. This seemed to please Drust, for he held her hand a while.

I do not know what they will think when they arrive at the Place of the God Tree, where they are to seek out their missing comrades — it is a dangerous land and I remind Your Honour of the risks I am taking in this enterprise and look to have Your Honour's consideration for it.

Signed by my hand,

Kisa Shem-Tov, Your Honour's servant and vigilant Watcher.

There was no silence, just the opposite — the loud hiss of Kag's dagger coming out of its sheath.

'Abomination?' growled Praeclarum. 'And I did *not* hold his hand. I mean, I did, but not…'

'Do not hurt me!'

Kisa's squeal cut them all off, save for Kag, who was growling incoherently, his blade at the little man's throat. Drust knew that one small movement would set life flowing out that could never be put back and he said so.

'Did you forget what was said when we left Singara?' he asked. 'The part about being in this together?'

From somewhere deep came a flare of little-used courage, a fire that burned hot, but very briefly. 'I am no ex-slave, no brother to any of you. I am a *frumentarius* and should not be here — yet you dragged me along,' Kisa spat. 'At least now you know I work for the State.'

'You work for Uranius,' Drust corrected, 'which is not necessarily the same thing.'

'How many of those have you sent?' Quintus demanded and everyone saw the part they had missed.

'Three. One from Singara, two from Kerch.'

Kag dragged his head back with a wolf growl. 'You fuck. You flap-sandalled *Stupidus*…'

'Ease,' Drust said sharply, seeing blood spurt. Kag gave a last grunt of disgust and hurled the little man from him into the dust, where he lay a moment, then got slowly to his feet and began patting himself off. Blood slid greasily down his neck and started to dry in the heat.

'Now we know how the Persians got on our trail,' Drust pointed out and Kisa blanched; it was clear he hadn't thought of it. Then everyone saw the sick flicker in his eyes at the knowledge he had killed Darab and the others.

'You too if you had been there,' Sib added with a sneer. 'Still – after how they beat you, it was a good, cold revenge, eh?'

'I did not know that,' Kisa answered shakily. 'I did not want...'

'If you are leaving tracks,' Kag muttered, looking round as if to see silver-faced helmets and galloping men, 'you are being followed.'

'We should kill him here,' Sib said flatly. 'Leave him at this god-tree as an offering to any who will help us now. Let the trouser-wearers find him when they follow his nice directions.'

Drust pointed down the river and told him to go and make sure of the trail ahead; he did not like the hate in Sib's voice and did not want it slathering everyone with a poison that would make them do something rash.

He pitied the sailors of the ship now; if they went back to Kerch, they'd find Persians waiting and would tell all they knew. There would be no one waiting in thirty days and a strong possibility that messages would be sent along the Red Serpent, spilling men after them. They might risk the tribes of the Land of No Return to get us, Drust thought. And if so – why are we so worthy of it?

'We should wait and ambush them,' Ugo declared when Drust pointed all this out. 'Then we will find out why they hunt us.'

Praeclarum laid a hand on the big man's thick forearm. 'There will be a lot of them and even if we win and keep one alive, all he will tell us is that his commander ordered it.'

Ugo admitted that with a nod. 'Some of us will die in a fight like that,' he added.

'Not me,' Stercorinus answered. 'This is not the place I am fated to die.'

'If your god speaks the truth,' Quintus added. 'I am no priest, but I know how gods work and the truth is something like forge-iron to them – they like to beat it into new shapes. This blue-stone business proves it – we should never have had such trouble over raiding them. Let's hope Rome's gods are more powerful than the ones in this land, else we are fucked.'

They hefted packs and moved on, slapping the insects until they had got to where a wind, hot and fetid as the breath of a dragon, blew the stingers away. They could stop and rest in the shade of cool trees that hissed, watching the sunlight dance on water.

Sib came in, loping silent and clutching something caught up in the bag of his cloak. He brought them out one by one and tossed them to individuals.

'I have found the gold of the Golden River,' he declared with a bitter smile.

They stared at the knobbly yellow fruit and knew them at once. '*Etrogim*,' Drust said, turning it over and then putting it to Praeclarum's nose for her to smell. She did and smiled.

'Too bitter to eat,' Sib said. 'Mostly rind and what little flesh there is has a weak, dry flavour – but it is good in cooking and for sweetening the breath, in small doses. Worth a fortune in the City, but not for that – when one has drunk deadly poison, a brew of this upsets the stomach and brings up the venom.'

'You can see how that might be useful up on the Palatine,' Quintus laughed.

Praeclarum cut one and sucked, thinking mainly of the breath sweetening – the taste made her gag and spit and it burned her gums. Everyone laughed.

'This is what they trade,' Kisa added, desperate to be helpful, to be useful and not be left for dead in this place. 'The tribes along here. There is a city, so I am told, though I do not know where. It is, I had heard, at the mercy of raiders from the north of here and may have been abandoned long since.'

'So you say,' Sib replied viciously.

'I do say,' Kisa spat back in a spasm that surprised everyone, as was the reverence in which he turned the knobbed yellow fruit in his hands. 'This is holy to us, so we know it well. On the fifteenth day of Tishrei is *Chag HaAsif*, and this is one of the four species used in ceremony.'

'You worship this yellow fruit?' demanded Stercorinus. 'And scorn me for my god?'

'Did you see any sign of the people who grow this?' Drust interrupted, but Sib shook his head.

'This is wild.'

'It came from orchards,' Kisa said firmly. 'My home is across the water from here and this is where we went to trade for *etrogim*.'

'With whom?' Kag demanded, but Kisa shook his head.

'I was too young to know. Anyone who would sell. We brought them good weave and decent pelts in exchange.'

Sib took water and went out again, gnawing on bread. They did not have much of that, or anything else, but when the shadows grew they dipped into the trees at a point where they could get down to the water and made camp.

They risked a fire for it, hoping that being down from the plain would hide the light of it and also because they could make the gruel they knew well. Hot porridge, laced with whatever they could scavenge, braided them together and Praeclarum went from one to the other with her oils and unguents. They were almost out of farro grain, wine was a distant memory, but worst of all the oil was running out so they had none to spare for keeping leather from drying out and going brittle, or rubbing on chafes and bruises.

'Where does it hurt?'

Inevitably, the answers were all the same – feet, legs, back. Ribs on the right side – that was Ugo, a legacy of being smacked by the biggest beast anyone had ever seen, a bull. A neck – that was Kag. Everyone had pain, deep bone aches and fiery twinges, a legacy of a life spent in hard training and muscle-racking spasms of frantic fighting. Of hard knocks and bone-breaks and, though Drust did not like to admit it, the age that fed on it year on year. Kisa's beaten face had faded and returned to a semblance of normal; Drust's ribs still twinged.

'How do you feel?' Praeclarum would ask and inevitably the weary answer she'd get back would be the same one, every time. I feel like Milo. Eventually, of course, she asked.

Only the old ones remembered Milo, Drust told her. He owned a *taberna* called the Inn of the Brutii. It was a plaster-peeling dump with a painted sign on the wall of two toga-clad men with blond curls, each holding up the hand of the other and surmounted by laurel wreaths. The brothers Marcus and Decimus Brutus, who had wanted to give their father the greatest funeral Rome had ever seen and had, so the legend went, invented the idea of fighting in the ring.

Opposite it was a painting of a beautiful and clearly high-born woman riding the cock of an appreciative gladiator and looking lovingly at him while she did it. She looked like a dutiful wife and the myth in that was as true as the one about the brothers Brutii.

The Brutii was always full of charioteers and gladiators, a lot of them past their best – Milo was a former *primus palus*, the best of the best. He had spent twenty years in the sands, had had his name on cups and dishes and scrawled on walls – whenever he fought, crowds doubled and he had made it to the *rudis*, the wooden sword that said he was free.

What had he got out of it? A scabby *taberna* in the wolf's den of Subura, one leg that dragged, a right eye that never stopped weeping and no teeth. The high-porridge diet, when training stopped, had bloated him, the unworked muscle had added to it and the added weight seized his overstrained joints so that he moved like a cripple. Drust and the others went there to see themselves in years to come, same way they went to the boxer on the Quirinal.

Now, Drust told Praeclarum, it comes nearer and nearer each day.

He got up, feeling stiffer than before after remembrance of Milo, and climbed up to the edge of the trees, to where the sun was a half-*aureus* on the edge of the world, a semi-circle of Jupiter's genius, gazing balefully over the green scrub and gnarled trees until they dribbled out where the water didn't reach. Stercorinus was a little way away, his sword stuck in the ground and the shadow of it long, like a sundial. Perhaps he prayed or perhaps he measured time, Drust did not know, but the latter was an exercise in futility – the desert made its own time and they lived in it now as if nothing else existed.

He wondered where Manius and Dog were and fought sleep, his head nodding, until he woke with a start to feel the heat, see the shadow. He did not need to see her face to know it was Praeclarum.

'Are you hurt?'

'No more than usual,' he answered, trying to be light.

'You were muttering,' she said, and Drust was appalled at the idea of speaking aloud with no control over what he said. He did not dare ask, but she provided the answer.

'Manius, you said. And Dog. You have told me about them and I am here chasing them, but I am no closer to realising why you do it. What makes these two worth all this effort?'

Drust hesitated and she thought it was reluctance but it wasn't. She was here, after all, and deserved at least to have an idea of why they were seeking two lost comrades.

'Manius is a *mavro* from the far desert south of Lepcis Magna,' he said. 'He is… strange. His face is partly burned from another time, when we used Quintus's carefully gathered naphtha balls to defeat an enemy. Sib did that to Manius and no one was sure then that he had not done so deliberately – he believed Manius was some sort of dark demon from the desert. In the end, though, Manius saved us all and Sib has been trying to atone since. I would not mention any of this to him, all the same.'

Praeclarum was silent.

'Manius is tall, dark, lean and an expert with a bow,' Drust went on and she knew he was speaking to himself almost as much as her. 'He was taken when we were escaping from under the Flavian and we thought him dead – but he got sent to the mines, the gods know where. Dog got him freed when Elagabalus became Emperor – Dog worshipped that boy and the Sun God he claimed to be. He got favoured and became a priest.'

'Manius?'

'Dog.' Drust shifted, looked at her and smiled, the last blood of the dying sun staining his face. 'I never thought Dog believed in anything, but he and that boy dragged us into trouble once before – and here we are again. Kag is right, all the same.'

He told her what he remembered of Kag's philosophy on why they persisted in this enterprise.

'You are closer to Kag than the others,' she said and he jerked at her insight, knowing it was true. 'His father was a legionary, he says – didn't that make him a citizen?'

'In those days such marriages were not official,' Drust answered. 'He might have ended up a decent auxiliary given time – but the Red Flux took both ma and pa and that was it for him. He was taken as a slave.'

He looked at her. 'Never ask him.'

She nodded, changed the subject.

'What is Dog like?' she asked. 'Everything I know comes down to a man with a face like Charon, who is sought by everyone here and cursed for it.'

What is he like, Drust wondered. A savage killer, ravaged by old grief and resentments. A man who could skin-mark his face with a skull in order to try and save the boy who would become Elagabalus the Emperor and his mother. A man whose leg Drust had once broken and everyone else kicked to ruin because he had crossed their master, Servillius Structus. A man who could take heads, children among them, because the Army paid bounty on them. A man who had saved Drust's life at least once.

She waited. He answered, 'He is as mad as a helmet of boiling frogs.'

He was surprised when she laughed. 'He will fit in well with this life we have, then.'

She was right, he thought. There is life here among us, charged with the stink and sound of death, carried like a strain of plague, a life lived in a ring of sand, on long camel trains and wagon convoys, on brief, bloody spasms of fights for water or shelter or just to keep what they owned, or even just for the delight of those who would pay to see it. It was a life that fed on itself, raped the ground it travelled and sat apart from the rest of the world, which needed it and despised it in equal measure.

They sat. She leaned a little and he felt the heat and fell towards it like a man putting hands out to a fire. They sat shoulder to shoulder until it grew cold, but neither of them noticed anything but the warmth they leached, one from the other. It was all that Drust needed and so much more.

—

They found the grave the next day, nestled under the twisted trees of a feeder stream which came down through the flat plain, flowing faster as it neared the main river it was joining. It was steep-banked and choked with green, so crossing it was awkward and dangerous.

Sib found the easiest way and everyone noted how churned it was by unshod horses. On both sides were the marks of old fires, the withered detritus of past gatherings.

'The folk who came here did so to make noise and drink,' Ugo said, looking round.

'Worship,' Stercorinus added, pointing to where offerings hung on the short, gnarled trees – a faded strip of coloured cloth, an amulet on a leather thong made brittle by age and heat. They made it safely across but the only joy in it was the moment they could splash water on their faces. Then, sorting themselves out on the other side, Kag found the grave.

It was a pile of stones lifted from the river and laid over a shallow scoop; they found this because they dug it up, no one wanting to admit that they feared the worst.

'It's been made like this because they had no good tools for digging with,' Kag pointed out, rolling a stone away and wiping his forehead with a sleeve. 'People in a hurry, perhaps. Hiding, too.'

'We should move away from here,' Stercorinus said, cradling his sword and looking one way, then the other.

'Is there no mark for it?' Praeclarum asked and this made them look, squinting at the stones until they found one with a flattened side. *D.M. Vix ann XXII.* Latin – Drust's heart lurched and he could see it was the same for the others, but the epitaph gave nothing much away – a dedication to the Manes, the fact that whoever was in it had lived twenty-two years. But it was in Latin, by someone who could write.

'Too young to be Manius or Dog, and if they buried it they were not the ones who marked it,' Quintus said as they finally rolled the stones and shifted the dirt clear to reveal a skeletal figure, dead for some time by anyone's reckoning.

'Roman, that is clear,' Stercorinus said, squatting with the inscribed stone, turning it over and over in his hands.

'Romans made the stone,' Kag corrected. 'They came when the riders who are normally here had left. It seems to me they recovered this body from what had been done to it. Might be anyone in the grave.'

'Might be Dog,' Quintus mused. 'It was always hard to tell how old he was, what with having no head hair and that face.'

'Well, it looks like Dog's face,' Ugo said and that made folk laugh. Then Sib appeared from where he had been scouting, limping a little from old wounds that had started to nag anew. He glanced in the grave and gave a grunt of relief while he wiped his sweat-streamed face.

'Not Dog or Manius, then.'

'How do you know?'

'Looks like Dog,' Ugo repeated, but no one laughed this time and Sib glanced from face to face with an expression of quizzical amusement.

'Because it is a woman,' he declared and pointed. 'Look at the pelvis.'

They looked but no one was sure, not even Praeclarum, and Kag clapped Quintus on one shoulder.

'Thought you might have known that, at least.'

'Not my type,' Quintus fired back. 'Too skinny.'

Sib was ferreting in the pack he had left behind and came up with a pot, smearing the contents on the back of one hand and an elbow.

'Hornets,' he explained. 'There's a nest further up, in a tree. Got too close. Bastards sting like spearmen.'

Kag took over scouting while Sib ate and everyone poked about the grave, eventually coming up with a necklace of blue stones. Quintus held it up.

'This some of those fire-starer stones?' he asked. 'Like whores wear?'

Ugo spat. 'They are not, but do not remind me of that. My knees will never be the same from those stairs.'

'You should have saved them and joined us jumping off the cliff,' Drust pointed out bitterly.

The best explanation they came up with for the dead woman was that she was some whore or a slave, taken by raiders and badly used.

'A Roman woman,' Praeclarum growled, 'used for some foul rite.'

Who had buried her was most of the mystery and eventually they settled on it being traders. This was one of the many Silk Road ways, so it was possible – and the only explanation of how a Roman woman came to be buried with a Roman epitaph, however brief.

They gathered themselves, getting ready to move out again away from the stream a little way to where the scrub was less dense and allowed easier walking. They kept the river on their right like a smoke of green and would dip into it when night came.

Then Kag came up, loping fast, kicking up dust spurts. He pointed behind him as he slid to a stop, panting from the run – everyone saw the dust cloud.

'Storm?' Praeclarum suggested, but Kag shook his head, getting his breath back. Then they heard the howls and yips; Drust's flesh crawled.

'Wolves?' Kag demanded. 'Some size of pack to make that much dust.'

'This is the land of wolves,' Stercorinus reminded them and Ugo hefted his axe.

'Not wolves. I know wolves.'

'He's right,' Kag finally managed. 'Riders. Maybe twenty or so.'

'Make for the trees,' Drust ordered at once. 'Stay quiet and hidden.'

They filtered down the gorge and crouched by the river, listening to it slide among the stones. It was wide and slow this close to the ocean, which let them move out into the quiet eddies. After a while, Sib slithered down to join them.

'They are making fires,' he reported, which made every heart fall. 'About twenty of them. Dressed like every goat-fucker you have ever seen – robes, Persian trousers, boots, bows, swords, little shields. Not our silver-faced pursuers, though – these look like bags of dung from the north, on ponies the size of dogs.'

'They will be in for the night,' Kag growled, wiping his face and flicking away a black ball of sweat-grease and insects. 'By which time we will be stripped to the bone and every insect won't have to eat again for a year.'

'Can we fight them?' demanded Stercorinus and Praeclarum looked sourly at him.

'I take it your god did not report this as the place you would die. If you want, charge up the bank and take them on – I will be interested to see if your god is as fickle as all the others I have made offerings to.'

Stercorinus merely cradled his sword, smiled mildly and wiped insects from around his eyes, trailing his fingers in the water to clean them.

'They may come down for water,' Kisa said fearfully, but Sib gave him a scathing look.

'They have the smaller stream,' he pointed out.

'We can't stay here,' Quintus declared after a moment or two longer.

'If we move, they will see us,' Kag said. 'If that happens they can shoot us down, in or out of this gorge.' He wiped his mouth and added bitterly, 'Besides – we have left tracks all over the place up there. And if you leave tracks…'

They might just leave offerings, drink their drink and leave, Drust thought.

'Go and see if they unsaddle the horses,' he told Sib, spitting out something that had crawled onto his lips. Sib looked dark, like a dog just kicked, but he went. He was not away long.

'They have tethered the horses, but the saddles are on.'

That left their bows cased, together with the arrow quivers, on tethered mounts. In case they had to move off in a running hurry, he thought, so they were not masters of this place, only bold.

He sat back on his heels. 'Well – we can try and move off, quiet as you like, and hope we are not heard. Or that in the daylight they don't see the marks we left all over the same place and send scouts out to find us.'

'Or we can fight.'

'Never run in the ring,' Quintus said, grinning, but Kag was scowling.

'They have bows and will shoot us down.'

'If they didn't have bows,' Drust said thoughtfully, 'it would be more of a fight in our favour.' He looked at Ugo.

'You remember that tale of your old granda?' he asked and Ugo frowned, then brightened and nodded. He unfastened his faded red *dromedarii* cloak, inspected it with deft fingers, then did the same with Kag and then Praeclarum. Hers he beamed at.

'You are a lesson in neat,' he said and she scowled, seeing her cloak vanish. It was because it had the tears and frayed holes repaired when no one else had bothered, but the price of that was Ugo spreading it out and fetching a head-sized stone from the stream. Then he punched slits in the ends and wove in a piece of leather thonging from Kisa's sandal.

'Lead me to it,' he said to Sib and the pair of them slid out. Praeclarum looked from face to face until Quintus grinned, spat insects away, and said simply: 'Hornets.'

Kag made more of it. 'Ugo's granda fought Romans once and broke up a whole unit by throwing bees at them. Or so Ugo says.'

'He wouldn't have lived long to enjoy the honey of that moment,' Kisa added and Quintus agreed, smiling.

'Lived long enough to tell Ugo of it before our giant of the Germanies got snatched as a slave.'

'Get ready,' Drust said, trying to see how it would unfold. Sib would lead Ugo to the hornet nest and the big Frisian would fold it into the cloak, weighted with a stone because the nest was made of some papyrus-like substance and too light to throw.

Then he would creep as close as he dared, whirl it once or twice like a sling and let the whole cloak fly. Hundreds of angry, stinging hornets the length of a finger-joint would burst out among the horses, who would be driven mad and tear free of tethers – even hobbles would not stop them. Their riders would be hard put to do anything to control or soothe them, for they'd be too busy running from hornets themselves. And all the bows and arrows were on the mounts.

'Then we move out. East, along the river. Keep below the lip of the bank and we can sneak away,' Drust told everyone. And they waited for Sib and Ugo, who came back in a sweating, panting rush. Sib ran straight out, fell over a rock and came up blowing water. Ugo flailed his arms round his head, trotted out as far as his waist, then sank his length.

'Done and done,' he declared, surfacing and blowing like a whale. Drust flapped at an angry hornet and everyone began to move off, splashing as fast as they dared through the uneven shallows, ducking the angry buzzing.

It is working, Drust thought, and then the horse burst over the lip of the bank, driven mad and bucking, running blind and heading for the smell of water, which was always a refuge from stinging insects; Drust cursed, because he had overlooked that.

A leg snapped with a loud crack on the first plunge and it went rump over mane, crashing and squealing until the loud thumps of its head hitting rocks stopped its squealing and the great fountain splash of it hitting the river drowned all else. It kicked in spasms and moaned.

Kag hated to see horses hurt and was turning back to it when Sib moved, oil and silk. He had less emotion for horses, having had to clear up the wreck and ruin of race days, when mounts speared with chariot poles was the least of it.

'Horses is not idiots,' he would say morosely. 'Most of the cavalry's thinking is done by the horses, but they is idiot loyal and will do things they would not if left to their own. Like us,' he would add and grin.

Now he did a thing he would not normally do, just for the horse. He sloshed back to where it kicked weakly and opened the heart in its throat; the blood skeined away in swirls.

'Leave it,' Kag shouted. Sib left the dead beast, sloshing through the stained water just as another mount careered over the bank further down. Then the man arrived.

He was running and flailing and yelling with a seared breath, but the ground vanished from under his feet and crashed him down, rolling him over and over and into the water almost at Sib's feet. Sib paused, turned and knifed the man in the throat, though it was likely he never felt it; hornets droned and zipped.

'Leave it!'

It was good, screamed advice but too late. A second man staggered to the lip, teetered and slid down, waving at hornets – but he had seen the men and the dead horse and his dead mate. He skidded to the edge of the water and his sword came out. Sib floundered away from it and Drust cursed – another horse crashed over in a shrieking flail of hooves. More men appeared, some falling, some drawing swords.

Drust unshipped the shield from his back and drew out the *gladius*, obsessively sharpened down the final third to the point; the rasp had once grated on nerves, but now no one noticed it round the fire.

Sib had his own sword out, the dagger in his other hand, but he wore a head-covering and no helmet, had tunic, robes and trousers, all soaked and dragging – he was a dancer and a mover and he could not work that here, shackled to the knees by the drag of sodden trousers and over-robe.

Stercorinus lunged forward, leaped out of the water with a high shriek that stunned the man who had just arrived over the bank and down to the shallows. The curved blade sheared through the man's sword-arm just below the elbow and, even as the blood spurted, the back-blow scattered teeth and took the jaw off.

Sib parried and fell under the weight of the blow while his opponent sloshed towards him, as water-sodden to the knees as Sib himself. Drust arrived just as the desert warrior was raising the long, straight sword for a downward blow, and he struck, a flick like an adder tongue. He felt the tug of it, no more than that, but the man's throat spat a gout of blood and he shrieked and fell away.

Drust made for the shallows, anxious to find better footing; he heard Sib follow and by the time they got there Ugo was at the top of the bank, the great axe hissing. It had little edge left, was simply a great hammer that smacked a man in the side of the head, slamming a dent into the helmet and making his eyes bleed. 'Rome is Mother to us all,' he roared and plunged away out of sight.

Arse, Drust thought savagely. Who does he think he is – a centurion of Heavies? Then he realised that Ugo was trying to make it sound as if that was what was here, out of sight but arriving fast.

He slogged up the bank to the lip of the bank, saw Quintus and Kag moving like a cunning toy, sliding this way and that, perfect and deadly. They had done this before in the *harena* and the ones who ran at them had no chance.

Horses spilled right and left, throwing up dust and shrieking. Something like fire made Drust yelp and shake his shield arm – for a moment he thought he had been arrow-shot, then saw the exhausted hornet fall away and buzz the dust; he stepped on it with a vicious curse.

Men were down or running in a dirty haze. A horse bolted, bucking, slammed into Praeclarum as she tried to protect Kisa; they both went over and Drust darted to them.

'Take him back to cover,' he yelled. 'He's worse than useless in this. They'll use arrows in a moment more...'

The riders had worked it out and a few had got to bows and the arrows for them. Ugo moved into the haze, bawling out commands to invisible units; he hit a horse in the face as it kicked past him and the beast screamed and shied away, vanishing into the swirling dust.

'Back to cover,' Drust yelled, but his shout was choked to a rasp. Kag and Quintus arrived, backing off, shields up.

'Should get back to cover,' Kag panted, almost chidingly. Drust cursed him, then saw the arrow whick out of the cloud and hiss into the ground.

They backed off. Something struck Drust's shield, hard enough to stagger him and skew it sideways; a barbed point stuck a finger-length through it, and he thought, with a surge of fear, of what that would have done to his arm. These round shields are no good, he thought. Boiled leather and no boss, so the next shot could come straight through my knuckles.

A man lunged out, making Drust yelp and throw up the shield in a reflex; the slashing blow sheared into the rim and part-way down. For a moment they were locked, the man trying to tug his sword free, Drust trying to rid himself of the shield because the blade was touching his arm.

The man was a greybeard, pocked by scars of old sins and battle, his eyes bloodshot and the welt-marks of stings all over his forehead and down one side. He wrenched just as Drust managed to uncouple his fingers from the grip and the sudden release staggered them both backwards. There was a sudden wind on one side of Drust and then a dull sound, like mud thrown at a wall – the greybeard fell away with a look of surprise and an arrow in his neck.

A second man staggered out, confused and swinging madly. Sib, able to slide and move, gave him iron in the chest, the dagger in his eye, then threw back his head and howled like a manic pi-dog.

Another came and another behind him. We are fucked, Drust thought. He saw Praeclarum parry and duck and slice – the man facing her took an arrow and another slammed off her shield. They were coming from everywhere, it seemed, shooting one another in their panic…

Sib had caught the reins of a horse, vaulted into the saddle with the expert grace of long practice. He turned to say something and the arrow thundered into him, a drum-sound that drove all the breath out. He reeled and looked like he would fall, while Drust gaped.

Sib slid off the beast, gasping, his legs folding him into the dust; Drust made for him while the horse bolted off. The second arrow came right over Drust's shoulder, that same dark wind he had felt before. He was trying to shout out even as it hit.

There was a gout of blood, an explosion of teeth, and Sib went away into the haze, the arrow like a sapling growing out of his mouth.

Drust went after him, though it seemed Sib had vanished. He heard shouts, the screams of dying horses, and yet they seemed far away; he found himself kneeling by a body and only Sib's wet bubble of breathing and the pounding of his heart was loud, a bird flutter that roared like thunder.

Drust knelt, cradling the head, saw the smoke slide into the eyes and grasped and clawed in the slippery mud of gore, as if he could find the source of life and put it back.

'Manius,' Sib said, stretching out one bloodied hand, and a figure appeared, knelt, took the fingers in a hard grip.

'Here, brother.'

Sib opened and closed his mouth a couple of times while Drust sat back, his strength ebbing with every last pulse of Sib's breathing, while Manius crouched and held his hand, and above them all, Dog-Dis grinned his skull-face.

Chapter Nine

The harshest truth of the moment was Sib. They brought him down to the scooped-out grave in the first stars of dark. Drust saw Kag's face and it came to him that he had shrunk and that they all were empty as withered wineskins.

Kag and Quintus lowered Sib as gently as they could into the shadow beside a gathered pile of stone that they would tomb up round him. The others seemed reluctant to either come or go, Drust was thinking, and not just the strangers, the ones who had come with Manius and Dog. Ugo and Praeclarum and himself stood around for a moment and gradually, one by one, those who had meant something to Sib moved closer to the body. Not so much to look, Drust saw, as to say something final, to him and to themselves.

Dog, his face made into a bloody parody of death by torchlight, lifted one hand, as if waving farewell, then let it fall limply to his side.

'Gods curse it,' he said, looked down for a few last moments and then turned and left.

Then Manius came up and looked down into the dead Sib's face, left unwrapped. He spoke directly to him, as though he were alive.

'May the gods above and below watch over you.'

Praeclarum squatted down and reached and took out Sib's hand, sat there for a long time holding the dead hand in her own and looking intently into the dead face, and she never uttered a sound all the time she sat there.

Finally, she put the hand down, reached up and gently folded the last of the cloth over the face. And then she got up and walked away down the road in the moonlight, all alone.

Kisa crouched and threw a handful of dust into the grave, a little hissing rattle of sound that seemed, somehow, louder than a drumbeat. The others, the strangers to them, stood politely and one or two helped stack the stones. Finally, Quintus placed the one with the flat side and an inscription that said Sib's name and then 'VI'. Those who knew that was the term for a fighter who had lost and died would know a gladiator lay there.

They sacrificed a horse, the one Ugo had mouth-smacked which made it easy to catch, and Drust tried to find Mars Ultor or Jupiter in the blood smell, but saw nothing to suggest any god watched. Saw nothing at all, heard only the anguish in men's voices, tasted only the stink of death. Ugo wailed, Stercorinus mumbled prayers, Praeclarum sobbed quietly where she thought no one would hear and yet, when Drust wept, it was not for Sib.

–

Later, in the firelit dark, Drust and Kag met Manius and Dog, though it was not anything like the way Drust had envisaged it.

'We arrived too late,' Dog admitted.

'Timely enough,' Kag replied, picking his teeth; they had eaten fried goat and greens, the sort of food they had not seen in a while. Grief made it taste of ashes, but they were gladiators and ate what they could when they could get it. There was wine, thin and harsh but still wine, a fire and a surround of more men than they felt comfortable with. The men Dog led, it turned out, were not his but caravan guards for a man called Yalgoz Bashto, or so it seemed when Manius said it.

'You will meet him tomorrow,' Dog added. Drust looked at him, trying to see past the ink-marked death to the face beneath and realising it was no less a mask. Dog's eyes, all the same, held something rarely seen, though Drust knew it — fear. He has walked into deeper water than he can handle, he thought, for all his bravado.

'Is this Bashto the reason we are here?' Kag demanded.

Dog made an ambivalent gesture and Kag spat in the fire. 'Do not start with us, Dog. Sib is under the ground and we have all had a hard time reaching here, all because of a message you sent by some madwoman. I will not suffer more of your lies.'

'Madwoman?' Manius interrupted, leaning forward. 'What happened to her? Is she alive?'

'Last we saw,' Drust answered, 'she dances for Shayk Amjot and eats poppy.'

Manius growled in the back of his throat. 'He was supposed to care better for her than that. She is Roman. She has a name…'

'If it is Julia you can sod off over there,' Kag growled. 'When you reach it, sod off further…'

Drust laid a quietening hand on Kag's arm, looking at Manius and seeing lines and frets that hadn't been there before. There was a scar too, which added nothing to the side with crumpled flesh and no ear. Manius saw him look and touched the place briefly, then managed a wan smile.

'Overseer whip,' he said, and now Kag saw what Drust was seeing.

'What happened?' he asked. Manius shook his head.

'Mines. I survived,' he answered and Dog cleared his throat and then spat it out.

'Her name was not Julia, it was Luculla. She was a slave but one who could read and write.'

'So we guessed,' Kag replied, still looking at Manius, who would not look back. 'We found a grave, too, of a woman. It had a Roman inscription on a stone which is why we dug it up. That and we thought it might be one of you.'

Manius wiped his face. 'You must show me that by and by. There were two Roman slaves, Luculla and Macra, and we sent them out – the one who made it must have stayed long enough to bury the other. That was brave. That was the dancer who eats poppy, though she was more than that once.'

'More than a clever slave who dances,' Drust said levelly. 'What would that be?'

'Handmaiden to a high-born of Rome,' Dog answered. 'A dresser of hair, applier of make-up...'

'Do not tell me this is all about women,' Kag said warningly. 'Not again, Dog. I knew it was not about tigers – but women?'

There was silence and then Dog laughed, though it had no mirth in it. 'Talking of women,' he said, 'I see the Brothers have a sister. She is no looker and I saw her fight, so I am supposing she was once of the *harena*.'

'We were all of the *harena* once,' Drust replied flatly. 'They call her Praeclarum.'

Dog's head tilted a little, playing shadows over the horror of it, making the skull grin. It was clear he had heard something extra in Drust's voice and Drust was angry that he had revealed it.

'Remarkable,' Dog said, rolling the name in his mouth. 'Now there is a name – what is the other one called? The lean one who looks like a desert pole-sitter who fell off his perch?'

Kag told him and both Dog and Manius chuckled. 'I would not say Little Shit to his face,' Manius added, 'when I am within the arc of that blade he carries.'

'There is also the Jew,' Drust pointed out. 'His name is…'

'Kisa Shem-Tov,' Dog finished. 'Yes, we know him. Surprised to see him here, all the same. I did not think he had that much sand in him.'

'I kicked him into it,' Drust said blankly. 'He works for Uranius — but I am guessing you knew that, and that you are not thinking you are here for what Shayk Amjot seeks. Enough of trying to put this talk on another path — what are we doing here?'

Dog agreed. 'We have some new faces too,' he added. 'You will meet them by and by. But I am heart-sorry for the loss of Sib. Do you remember the time he drove that donkey cart round the forum, made it seem like a four-in-hand in the Maximus?'

'Or the time he beat that big warrior beyond the Wall, using only saplings? Like a whip. Beat him bloody.'

Manius laughed softly at the memory.

'Or the time he and you walked round the *harena* in the lunchtime heat,' Kag said to Manius, soft as venom, 'and he threw little balls with tokens in them into the air for you to shoot open over the crowd?'

No one spoke while the air coiled; a rogue breeze flattened then fanned the fire.

'Used that to good effect with those naptha pots north of the Britannia Wall,' Kag went on, silken vicious, 'though he mistimed it.'

They saw Manius lift one hand to the shiny scars plating one side of his face, to the ear that was a lump of wasted gristle. Those clay pots of fire, even a cat-lick of it, were terrible.

'There was always the idea that he had timed it perfectly for what he intended,' Kag added.

'There was no proof of that,' Dog interrupted sharply. 'Manius bore him no malice. And speak no ill of a dead Brother, Kag.'

Manius uncoiled and moved softly off into the shadows. Silence fell, the ice of it seeming to dim the fire to dying embers. Eventually Dog shifted and spoke.

'They dragged him out of the undercroft of the Flavian,' he said flatly. 'You remember? He shoved Sib to safety and put himself in danger.'

'We thought him dead,' Kag muttered. Dog laughed. They all sat and remembered The Hood, Caracalla, Emperor of Rome and if you are measured by the stature of your enemies, Drust thought bitterly, then we were ranked indeed.

'The Hood was never going to make such an easy exit for one of us,' Dog went on. 'He sent Manius to the mines, all the way back to Britannia, to the gold mines at Luentinum, a wild place where all those Druids once came from. When Elagabalus took the purple I found Manius again and got him out – didn't expect him to be alive let alone fit. Seems he found a talent for repairing the hydraulic machines, which saved him from dying of the wet cough or under a pile of roof-rubble.

'Seven years he spent there. Never ask him about it,' he added, putting his hands on his knees and levering himself up. He wore good boots, Persian trousers, a decorated tunic and over-robe, a linen head-cover that reached to his shoulders, a fancy curved knife thrust into a cloth waistband.

He and Manius had done well, Drust thought, and said as much to Kag when they had walked alone into the shadows.

'So it would seem,' Kag answered. 'Manius deserves it, for sure. Seven years – longer by far for a man used to the open desert and the big night sky.'

He stopped and shook his head, half admiringly. 'And they still have told us nothing about why we are here.'

Drust had realised it long since, but he was dull with unease, with the nag of something that finally could not be contained. He vomited it up while Kag listened.

'The arrow, the one in the face; it came from behind me, over my shoulder, close enough to feel the wind.'

Kag blinked. 'He had two in him.'

'The one in his face, the one that…' Drust stopped, unable to go on.

Kag hawked and spat in the fire. 'He had one in his chest that was not likely to be removed without killing him. What are you saying?'

'That it came over my shoulder, from behind.'

'There was fighting everywhere.'

'Perhaps,' Drust echoed dully, then locked eyes with Kag. 'Or perhaps Manius had spent a long time brooding in the dark hours spent in that mine, or the time since. We left him behind in the undercroft of the Flavian, remember, and it cost him seven years in a dark hole.'

'He left himself behind,' Kag said sharply. 'It was bravely done and we all thought him dead at the time.'

'Better, perhaps, if he had been,' Drust said softly. 'Sib always said so. Said he should never be allowed into the world because he was a demon.'

'Sib was many good things, but he was hagged by gods and demons both,' Kag replied.

'He tried to kill Manius that day out beyond the Wall. Tried to kill him in a rain of fire…'

'No one knows that for sure,' Kag fired back. 'Only Sib and now no one at all.'

'Manius does,' Drust said, 'and now he has answered it.'

'No one knows that either,' Kag hissed, looking right and left as if someone might be listening. 'Gods above and below, Drust – do you hear what you are saying?'

'I hear it,' Drust said sharply, then sighed, feeling a crush on him, like he was buried under stones. Like he was Sib.

–

His mood was no better the next day and everyone saw it, was wary of it and left him alone, though Praeclarum kept shooting him assessing looks as they moved up the river. They had camels now, which made most of them groan, but Dog was anxious to put distance between themselves and the fight.

They followed a track slender as an old thread and strewn with grit until the night closed in, when they moved back to the river. The banks here were less steep, had more trees, and the river was narrower and musical over the stones. They hobbled and unpacked and lit fires.

'Ahead lies a small place called Umut,' Manius said and widened the grin. 'It means "hope", because that is all the folk there have to live on. Beyond that way is the *caravanserai*, which is seasonal.'

A brace of shadows closed in on the fire, one of them eating, tearing hunks from a loaf. Dog looked up at them and grinned.

'The big one is called Mouse. That is how his name sounds to us, because he comes from well up the Silk Road, east. He was also a fighter, a wrestler. He speaks decent Latin and better Greek, but cannot read nor write in any tongue. He eats everything, all the time.'

Mouse was as big as Ugo, who appraised him professionally, but a wrestler who was well out of training. He had a belly, decent breasts, big shoulders and arms with strength in them, enough to let Drust know he would have been formidable when at peak. His face, though, was all of the moment, for it was the Quirinal boxer in the flesh.

'I do not eat all the time,' he said in a slightly lilting voice, pitched too high for a man that size. 'I eat when hungry.'

'Which is all the time,' the other man said. 'Except when sleeping.'

This one was introduced as Mule, which was Army, because they carried so much on a march. Drust was certain that the man carried a *signaculum* in a leather pouch under the neck of his stained tunic and remembered the big Thracian commander, Maximinus, saying how that mark of a legionary was what deserters discarded only at the last. Under his Persian trousers, Drust was sure he would see legs scarred from a centurion's vine staff, but now the man had hair done in the Persian style, little braids fastened with beads and trinkets.

'So,' Dog said, 'you will be wanting to know why you are here.'

'You think?' Kag answered, scowling. 'What gave it away – all the questions about why the fuck we are here, perhaps?'

'Be nice to know what Sib got sixed for,' Ugo rumbled as Mouse squatted beside him and indicated the uneaten portion of his bowl.

'You want that?'

'It concerns the secret of Rome,' Dog said, and Drust looked meaningfully at Mouse and Mule and then Kisa. Dog smiled.

'All Brothers here,' he said and Drust acknowledged it.

'The secret of Rome?' Kag prompted.

'Where to get a decent hot pie at midnight,' Manius growled.

'Or a clean whore under the Flavian during Ludus,' Quintus added, grinning like a roasting grill.

'Or how to sit on the Hill and keep your laurels on your head and your head on your neck,' Drust offered. Dog smacked his palms and pointed at Drust as if he had made a killer point in a Senate debate.

'Close – you have not thrown the Dog.'

That had a few laughs, but mostly folk waited.

'It involves a woman,' Dog went on, and Kag flung up his hands with an expression of disgust.

'I fucking knew it. Gods above and below, Dis fuck me in the arse sideways with his hammer – a woman. It is always some woman with you – you are worse for it than Quintus and at least he fucks them, not sticks them on a pillar and bows.'

'Are you finished?' Dog asked mildly.

'Not hardly. I thought since the last one you worshipped got sixed along with her marvellous boy you'd have learned a lesson. It seems...'

Drust leaned forward, laid a hand on his forearm. He felt the tremble there and saw the anguish and rage in Kag's face. It wasn't about women, or Dog or Rome's secrets, he realised. It was about Sib and, perhaps, Manius.

Praeclarum appeared, scowling, and dumped her pack.

'They say these sand roaches have a thousand names for camels,' she spat. 'I hope none of them is "cunt" because I have decided that is the name of the one I am riding.'

'They do,' Mule answered sagely, pouring wine into a bowl and offering it to her. 'One for a beast which drinks once a day, another for one which drinks twice a day, and yet another for...'

'… one which drinks three times a day,' Kisa finished with a snort. 'I see where this camel is going.'

Mule shook his head with sorrow.

'You do not,' he answered. 'No camel drinks three times a day – but the best ones drink once every three days and there is a name for them.'

He stopped, frowning. 'I know them all, but there is no point in telling you – it would be like pouring into an overfull cup.'

Kisa scowled but it was only for show. Mouse chuckled and called Mule a useless fart but Drust saw that it was a worn rut of old friendship and heard Sib and himself – and others – echoing such scathe from the dark of the past. He felt tired and old.

'Is there a name for the man-beast that humps camels?' Praeclarum snarled. 'Is it the same as for the Army runaway who cared for them once, I wonder? Did you run off from that Palmyran lot in Dura?'

Quintus and Kag and Mouse made awed sounds of admiration, while Mule managed a grin and acknowledged the stroke from Praeclarum. Kag had had time to recover and Manius had seen it.

'Tomorrow you will meet Bashto,' he said. 'He is a good trader and most of the men here are his – the camels too. He is the one who knows Shayk Amjot and got us all in this.'

'In what?' Drust demanded. 'What is the secret of Rome?'

'The true name of the City,' Dog put in. 'Some say it is Hirpa. Some Evouia or Valentia, but they are all wrong. I have said those names and I am still alive, unlike Soranus, who died for violating the prohibition for saying it aloud in public.'

'Soranus?' demanded Drust.

'Quintus Valerius,' Kag put in, which made Kisa blink a little; but Kag knew some scholarly matters, courtesy of having been bodyguard to a young squit of the nobility and making sure he went to lessons. Kag had learned more.

'A poet in the time of Sulla,' Kisa interrupted and Kag nodded agreement.

'More to the point – a tribune of the people. They crucified him in Sicily, but I heard it was politics that got him nailed up. I always thought it was his bad verse.'

'The City's true name exists,' Dog said. 'Armed with it, enemies can capture it, or so it is believed.'

'The City has been captured before – did those sheep-shagging Gauls have the name, then?'

Quintus was grinning with his mouth only, but Dog merely tilted his head a little, unconcerned.

'Gauls sacked the City, all but the Hill, and then those defending the Capitoline came out from behind the walls and kicked their arse,' Kag said thoughtfully. 'So they did not conquer the City.'

It does not matter what we think, Drust saw. Such a belief would be a powerful tool for anyone looking to send men against the Empire, and he said as much.

'Uranius found this out and now wants us to rescue the word and return it to safety,' he added.

'Rescue the word? Is it imprisoned, then? Shackled in a grammarian, perhaps?'

Quintus laughed at his own joke, but no one followed, too fascinated by what Dog was about to say.

'The woman,' Kag said suddenly, and heads turned to him. Dog nodded admiringly.

'The very same. Empress of Rome is more proper, though.'

'Oh Bel-Shamun, you show me the way of it. I stand ready.'

He did not say much, but when he did it was always a show-stopper and all the heads turned to where Stercorinus stood like a stele at the edge of the fire. No one laughed and he said nothing else, so Dog told them the rest of it – the woman who knew the secret name of the City had been wife to Elagabalus. Twice. And her name was Julia.

When he said this, everyone who remembered the Severan Julias groaned. There had been a gaggle of them, all relatives of the Sun God boy Elagabalus, all priestesses of the religion in Emesa, and all deadly. Mother, aunts, grandmother – they were all regal and beautiful and poisonous. Now the one who was mother to the current Emperor Alexander was the most deadly of them all.

Kag said as much, almost desperately, but Dog just spread his hands.

'It's a name, that's all.'

'So is the secret one for the City,' Drust spat back. 'Yet here we are because of it – and one Brother less.'

He fell silent after that, feeling ruffled as a cat in a storm. He knew of this new Julia – Julia Aquilia Severa, daughter of Quintus Aquilius who had been twice consul under Caracalla; the 'Severa' *praenomen* had been given to her when she married Elagabalus. He had divorced his first wife to do it.

It was just one of Elagabalus's scandals – Julia Aquilia was a Vestal and, by tradition, should have been buried alive for breaking her vows of chastity and virginity. Worse than that, the boy-emperor symbolically married Vesta the goddess at the same time; he was full of shit like that, Drust remembered, even when he was nine and being rescued by us from the Land of Darkness beyond the Walls of the north.

In the end, his grandmother Julia Maesa, the one who had engineered him into the purple cloak, got it all revoked and made him marry a sensible choice. Not long after, he divorced that wife and went back to living with Julia the Vestal, presumably no longer virgin.

'The grandmother got rid of her at the same time she got her grandson and his mother assassinated,' Dog ended and Kag blew out through pursed lips.

'Then your sometime Empress would be dead too. They wouldn't have missed her.'

'I was her guard,' Dog said simply and Quintus flung back his head and laughed like a howl of a wolf.

'You let her live.'

'I did as I was told – it is the worst curse of the gods to kill a Vestal save by burying her alive in the Temple, and that would have taken too long for grandma, who feared people might agitate over it. She arranged for the Vestal Empress to go to Emesa and be sold as a slave.'

'So where is she now?' Drust asked, feeling a sick slide of apprehension even as he said it.

'The city – well, that's what they call it here – of Asaak. A good camel ride from the *caravanserai* we will reach tomorrow.'

'She is a slave?' Praeclarum asked and Dog looked at her; Drust was pleased to see she didn't wince under that Dis gaze.

'She is no slave in Asaak,' he said, 'but our new Emperor Alexander wants her back.'

'Is he next one up on the mare?' Ugo growled. Dog spat warningly in the fire.

'She is an Empress and a Vestal. All of those daughters of Vesta know the secret name of the City – but they stay cloistered, so it is never a problem.'

'Now it is? What does our boy-emperor fear? The Parthians are beaten into the ground.'

Dog shook his head sombrely. 'They are fighting each other – but the old king is dead and this new one, the Sasan, calls himself *shahanshah*, King of Kings, in the old way of the Persians. When he finishes cleaning out the house, he will turn on Rome.'

'So young Alexander sent Uranius and Uranius sent you,' Drust said.

'More or less. Uranius can't trust anyone out East, but the Emperor trusts me. I helped kill his rival, after all.'

Drust stared. The boy Dog had gone wide-eyed years before over the golden priest of the Sun God – and his mother Julia Soaemias. They had all spent a long, hard time rescuing that pair because of Dog, and Drust remembered the mother, an elegant sway of perfume and sharp intelligence. She had not deserved to be dragged by the heels through a Praetorian camp – but he had not known Dog had been involved.

Neither had anyone else from the old Brothers; Kag just stared and shook his head, Quintus spat in the fire. Ugo lifted his hands up and then let them fall as if they weighed too much.

'So you have tracked her down. You have the men – why are we here?'

'We had the men,' Dog admitted, 'but they ran off. Camels died. Raiders. Sickness.'

'So you called us.'

'We met this Bashto before we were too weak to be unimpressive. He knows we want a captive Roman woman, but not why, and he wants the head of the ruler of that city. Seems the ruler taxed too heavily, Bashto argued and now his trains are banned from trading. We tried once but only managed to release two of Julia Severa's slaves – the one in the grave and the one Shayk Amjot treats so badly. It was them we sent with the message.'

'Jupiter's cock, Dog,' Kag said wearily. 'You are tiresome in the way you arrange your life.'

Dog spread his hands in supplication. 'I need you because you are unknown – all Bashto's men are known, as is Mule, Mouse and others. My face is... obvious. But you can get in and out with the Empress and the head of *Farnah-vant*.'

'It means "full of splendour" in the Persian tongue,' Kisa said softly.

'Don't give a fuck for it,' Kag snarled. 'Don't want any part of it. What's in it for us, Dog? You are always doing this – we got nothing from the last Atellan farce you put us through. Unless you count exile as a gift.'

'You got citizenship,' Dog fired back. 'A copper plate to say so.'

'You sold all of our copper plates for a horse,' Ugo pointed out. 'Besides – everyone got made a citizen not long afterwards, by decree of Caracalla.'

Drust held up a hand and waited for the quiet. 'We are here. One of us lies in a tomb. If we rescue this Empress and get her to safety, then riches will follow, sure as rain follows cloud.'

'Exactly,' Dog beamed.

'As ever with these affairs,' Stercorinus said into the silence that followed, 'it's how the stroke is done, not the death that follows.'

Chapter Ten

They bumped darkly up to what Manius announced would be Umut and on the way the Brothers variously conspired to walk with Drust for a while. They got little out of it, for Drust had no more insights than they already had.

Stercorinus was not one who made his way to Drust; instead, he rode his camel like he walked – upright and cradling his sword, staring at nothing. Praeclarum, the only one Drust welcomed when he walked, pointed out how the Little Shit had changed.

'He is like a dark pool now,' she said. 'You cannot see into it and hesitate at the edge, wondering what lurks there. I think he heard his god speak.'

Drust was forced to agree, but he was more concerned about her, for she had been struck hard by Sib's death. Now she dismissed it with a slight wave and a lying shrug.

'I am well enough. I have no teeth, my hair is a mess and I do not know whether to grow it or shave it back. It needs washing, either way. And I feel hollow, nothing more.'

He did not know why he did it, but Drust laid a hand on her shoulder and when he looked at her, eye to eye, he saw them widen, felt... something. Looked away. They walked, hardly daring to breathe, feeling trembled and lifted and strange, and would not have wanted to be anywhere else at that moment.

It was not a mood destined to last; it vanished an hour later, shredded away by the familiar stink on the wind and the raucous quarrelling of carrion birds. Drust did not need to utter a word to get the Brothers falling into a half-crouched huddle, weapons up and shields ready. Dog's own borrowed men did the same.

They waited and watched, while Mule hissed orders to shepherd the groaning camels safely into the lee of the warriors; slow as prowling cats they came up to where the dust swirled in hissing little circles round the strewn dead. The ugly-necked buzzards spat at each other and tore red gobbets.

Drust looked at Dog and was pleased to see that he knew, at once, what was signalled with just eyes; not all of it is worn out, he thought. He took Manius and Ugo and six or seven others and started to move towards the weathered mud-walled buildings. Drust found himself shoulder to shoulder with Kag on one side and Mule on the other, with Praeclarum not far off. He could not see Stercorinus nor Kisa.

'Move out a way,' Kag said to Mule. 'This is not the Army. We need fighting space.'

Mule grinned savagely back at him and nodded so his hair-trinkets rattled – Drust had learned that they were fingerbones from the ones he had killed, or so he had claimed to anyone who would listen.

'Is there a name for a camel that drinks less than once a day?' Praeclarum called out, and Drust knew she did it to throw dust on the fire forming between Mule and Kag. Ahead, a buzzard flapped off a corpse and hopped lethargically, too gorged to fly.

'No,' Mule said eventually, moving away from Drust and Kag, 'but there is one for a camel that drinks only a little water at a time. And one for a female camel which smells water but will not drink it.'

'So there are different words for a female camel that drinks once a day and a male camel that drinks once a day?' demanded Praeclarum. Drust saw Dog kneel by the corpse, examine it and move on, stepping cat-light and swinging from side to side. The day sweated.

'Including one for a female camel alone in a herd of males,' Mule replied, cheerful now.

'You have not told us any of these words for camels,' Stercorinus growled out, appearing suddenly on the other side of Drust and walking casually, as if he was strolling. Mule admitted this was true, for he had forgotten most of them.

'I do not know much,' Stercorinus snarled, while Drust wondered where the anger came from, 'but I know the name for one who talks always about camels. No Teeth, he is called, for it seems to me the likely outcome of annoying many folk with his camel-talk.'

'Ho – hold your lip on the jests about teeth,' Praeclarum added, which made everyone laugh and then unstick their top lips from their own teeth, trying not to show their nervousness to anyone else.

Drust moved forward to where Dog stood while men lashed out and kicked carrion birds off the dead. There was a good score of them, women and children among them.

'What happened here?' he asked. Manius rinsed his mouth with some hard-won spit and gobbed it into the dust, then read the marks of it as if tracing letters on papyrus.

'They were slaughtered like hogs,' he answered and jerked his beard at the one who lay at their feet. 'This oldster was stabbed lying down. Several times – he held up his hands to ward off the blows, for you can see a spear went through the palm of one. He was spear-hit in the neck, chest and the groin about three or four hours ago and he has not improved since.'

Mule came up blinking sweat and sorrow from his eyes, for he knew the man and most of the others. All villagers, he told them, rounded up and killed.

'The *caravanserai* is just beyond here,' he added bitterly, 'but no one came to their aid. Bashto would have heard the screams, but he did not send help.'

—

There had never been a chance of Bashto risking anything for the people of a mean place called Hope, as Drust saw later, when he was ushered into the dim of the fat tent he occupied. It was sparse and cool and the usual reek of a compound of men and camels had been chased off with a fragrance, hot and strange.

Men moved with a purpose over a coloured weave of square carpets laid on the ground, round a pile of cushions on which sat a man in loose trousers, red slippers and patterned, coloured robes. There was a great fat winding of linen round his head, with a fan of it sticking out of the top; a blissful smile wreathed out of black beard streaked with silver.

The smile was because of the cup he held under his nose, whose fragrance filled the room and which he inhaled. He looked up as Drust came in with Kag and Dog.

'This is Lotus Blossom *chay*,' the turbaned man said with relish in good Greek. 'Brought all the way from the lands of the Wei.'

He held up one hand and between thumb and forefinger was a small, round ball of what seemed to Drust to be dried grass. He had seen stranger, more innocent sights that turned out to be able to spin you through Elysium once you had swallowed them.

'*Chay*,' the man declaimed. 'Lotus Blossom. I have Jade Ball and Black Ring as well and each one is worth a fortune. It is this, as well as *riso* and silk that Farnah-vant wants to strip me of. May the Holy Fire scorch his fetid balls.'

The man laid down his cup and waved; slaves brought three more cups and set them down, then filled them. The man signalled expansively for them to drink, and Drust did when he saw the turbaned man's eyes seemed clear enough and he appeared to be in his right mind.

It was hot and the fragrance was strong but the taste, as Kag said later, was similar to *caldarium* water that had been given a severe beating. Neither of them could see that this was worth much in trade with Rome or anywhere West – but silk and *riso*, a little white grain prized as medicine, would fetch high prices in the City.

'Forgive me,' the man said suddenly, unfolding himself from the floor and bowing. 'I am Bashto. You need not bother with more, because it is unpronounceable in your tongue – I do not think you even have the letters for it.'

Kag said his name, short and barked. Drust did the same.

Bashto nodded and smiled out of his black-bearded face, sipped his perfumed hot water, and revealed his sorrow for the villagers of Umut. He was the perfect figure of a concerned uncle and it was all a lie, Drust saw.

'Raiders,' he said finally to Dog. 'I do not think they were from Farnah-vant, but I will not stay here very much longer just in case he has found me. What must be done must be done swiftly now.'

There wasn't much else, though Drust and Kag wanted answers they did not get. In the end, they were ushered out and none the wiser.

'It is just his way,' Dog said, shrugging. 'He is more ruffled than he allows by the presence of these raiders – but the country all round here is stiff with followers of the old Parthian king, supporters of the new usurper, and those riders from the Grass Sea in the north who are taking advantage.'

He paused and looked from Drust to Kag and added, 'We do not want to be where these silver-faces you spoke of appear.'

–

In the quiet dark where fires bloomed, surrounded by the high mud walls of a compound, men chaffered and laughed, feeling safe. Drust did not. Kisa was no better and said so.

'This Bashto sat drinking his heated water and ignoring all the people being killed,' he pointed out. 'I do not trust him.'

Coming from him, this announcement made for some genuine laughter that made him pull in his neck and sit, sullen and scowling and silent.

They sat round fires made from dried camel dung and twisted wood and spoke of women and drink after that, swallowing locally made wine made from fermented dates and raisins. Drust sat and listened, watching Praeclarum who was sitting with Stercorinus, the pair of them talking, head to head and with urgency. He felt an unreasoning rush of resentment.

A silent shadow came quietly and invited Drust to follow him. He knew it was a slave come from Bashto and, when he rose, Kag cocked a quizzical head, but Drust signalled him to stay. Dog hissed warningly about guarding his tongue.

The trader was at the entrance to his fine tent, sitting on cushions in loose trousers and an over-robe against the night chill. He held bronze curve of metal, staring at the stars and lifting it up to eye level now and then.

'Tishtrya,' he said dreamily. 'Queen of the skies. The Greeks call her Seirios. She has smiled on Persia since the time of Keyumars, the first man and king.'

Then he spread his arms wide and declaimed in Greek: *'For Zeus it was who set the signs in heaven, and marked out the constellations and for the year devised what stars chiefly should give to*

men right signs of the seasons, to the end that all things might grow
unfailingly. Wherefore him do men ever worship first and last. Hail,
O Father, mighty marvel, mighty blessing unto men. Hail to thee and
to the Elder Race! Hail, ye Muses, right kindly, every one! But for
me, too, in answer to my prayer direct all my lay, even as is meet, to
tell the stars.'

He stopped. 'You understand Greek?'

'Enough,' Drust answered.

'You have read Aratus of Soli? The *Phaenomena*?'

'If it was not on a wall in Rome, then no, I missed it.'

Bashto pulled his guttering torch closer, bent and made a
note. 'It is written,' he declared expansively. 'Everything we
learn, we write and keep for others to read.'

'That I know well enough – tithes, taxes, bills of lading...'

'Wayfinders,' Bashto answered, smiling broadly. 'Isidore of
Charax and his *Stations*.'

Drust had never heard of the man, nor his stations, but he
did not think he would be long ignorant. He was right.

'Did you know he was born in the city now ruled by the
diseased prick Farnah-vant?' Bashto said and shook his head
sorrowfully. 'The man who laid out the ways from Antioch to
the Pandyas.'

He peered at the sky, squinting over his strange device, then
sighed.

'Mind you – he did the distances in "ropes". How long is a
"rope" in the name of Holy Fire?'

'Long enough for what you need,' Drust replied and Bashto
chuckled and nodded.

'You may as well measure the depth of a woman's part as the
length of one of Isidore's ropes.'

'I know the answer to that,' Drust said flatly. 'Deep enough to lose your house, your slaves, your money and, finally, your mind.'

Bashto laughed.

'Is this woman you wish returned one of those with such a depth?' he asked, clapping his hands softly to bring another shadow with cups. More of the *chay* stuff, Drust saw; he wished for a decent wine.

'I ask because I am aware that some of your kind,' Bashto went on carelessly, 'keep such folk to read and write for you. Some clever slaves can read and write and are useful to those who do not.'

'She is not a slave,' Drust answered, stung by this reference to perceived ignorance and suddenly aware that this trader was mostly right. I call myself a trader, Drust thought, but I can barely master the lading, the lists, all the clerk work. This Bashto would be effortless at it.

'Then why travel all this way to rescue her?'

'Friendship. Besides – she is a citizen of Rome and Rome honours that.'

Bashto sipped appreciatively, smacking his lips. He does not know who or what this Julia is, Drust thought, for all his tallies and scribbling. He knows she is important enough to have brought desperate men at great expense to pluck her from the city.

'Ah,' Bashto said knowingly. 'Cicero's *civis romanus sum*. But this is not the Empire.'

Drust said nothing and eventually Bashto sipped and smiled and made marks on his papyrus.

'This Dog claims you and your friends can kill my enemy and rescue this woman, so I have agreed to help – the enemy of my enemy is my friend, after all. I am simply wondering why she is worth such attention.'

'Are you writing of what we say?' Drust asked and Bashto paused, blinked a little, and then laughed, shaking his head.

'I am writing about the star,' he said. 'In a wider sense, I am also making a writing of all that has happened to Persia since the time of the first man to the coming of Sekandar – the Great Iskandr. Six thousand years, which will be lost to memory if I do not write it down.'

'The gods will know,' Drust answered, for something to say.

'Which ones?' Bashto countered. 'There are so many. The Greek ones, of course. The tribes north of here worship rocks and stones and I myself was born to people who think the sky itself is god. Of course, I am more enlightened now.'

'Now you are what – a fire worshipper in the Persian way?'

Bashto paused, frowning, then clapped his hands to summon a man. There was an exchange of whispers, the man left and returned with a cloth-wrapped bundle which Bashto took and unwrapped.

It was a small figure, made of jade, smooth and deep green as a summer sea. It looked as if a portion of the water had been shaped into a sitting man holding a drum – then Drust realised it was not a drum, but a bowl held in the crook of the man's impossibly positioned legs – no one, he thought, can sit comfortably like that, not even Berber women. Above it, a smooth, bland-smiling face seemed to be lifted a little, as if contemplating the sky, and one hand was turned so that the fingers were uppermost, the forefinger and thumb making a tiny circle.

'It is a representation of Buddha with his offering bowl,' Bashto said. 'It is carved from jade dug out somewhere far to the east, which is also where this Buddha was born. He was a prince, I believe, but became a wandering holy man and a teacher. His teachings are now followed by so many people that I suppose he has become a god to them.'

'Do you follow this god?' Drust asked, and Bashto smiled indulgently, as you would to a child; Drust did not care for it.

'He is not a god, just a man.'

Drust drank *chay* and thought while Bashto lectured.

'This Buddha person taught many things, mainly about how to give up the matters of the world – power, riches, the lusts of the body, the appetites. He sat under a tree and lived on what folk placed in his bowl. Eventually, he went out of his body – you understand?'

'He died?' Drust asked.

'No. He just left his earthly body for a time and then returned to it.'

'Like the Christian god.'

Bashto frowned. 'I have heard something similar about the Christ… perhaps he did it for the same reason, to gain more in the life that comes after this one, you understand?'

'Well, if the Christ did that, then Romans helped him with nails and a couple of bits of wood. I know of such matters,' Drust spat back, annoyed. 'When we die we go to Elysium or Tartarus and reap the rewards of what we did in life.'

Bashto smiled.

'*Thus shall ye think of this fleeting world: A star at dawn, a bubble in a stream; a flash of lightning in a summer cloud; a flickering lamp, a phantom, and a dream.* This Buddha wrote that, according to a strange book that came all the way down the Silk Road from the far east and the Land of No Return,' he added, then took a deep breath. 'But you have not told me about this slave woman.'

Drust heard laughter from the fires and wanted suddenly to be away with them. There were too many matters whirling here and he wanted to sit with the others and try and sort them out amid the comfort of familiar banter. One thing he was certain of, all the same, and he leaned forward so that Bashto listened expectantly.

'The enemy of my enemy,' he said darkly, 'is my enemy's enemy. No more.'

He got up and moved off, back to the flicker of fires. A flash of lightning in a summer cloud; a flickering lamp, a phantom, and a dream.

Chapter Eleven

They came up to the city of Asaak across a bleakness of gritty dust, pallid scrub and the tortured remnants of strangled trees. Not even birds seemed to want to challenge the sky in such a brooding place.

The city flourished, all the same, on a feeder stream of the main river and bright with its gold – the orchards of *etrogim* that had been made on the other sides splashed brightly out of the tan wastes. But the main wealth of the place was that it squatted on the trade routes and sucked the juice from them.

'He's not a tyrant, nor a monster,' Dog said when they assembled at the fringe of fields, carefully hidden from any eyes. That surprised Drust; they had just been tasked to kill Farnah-vant, ruler of the city, and it seemed strange to hear Dog making excuses. He said as much and Dog shrugged.

'Bashto wants him dead and proof that it is done, but all that will happen afterwards is that someone else will fill the hole he leaves. Tithes and taxes won't change – Farnah-vant is like Servillius Structus when all is said and done.'

Manius laughed quietly from the shadows at the mention of that name, but Drust knew what Dog meant; when the old man died – peacefully in his bed, which he hadn't deserved – no one inherited what he had built. His organisation fell apart in petty squabbles and fighting until another strong hand beat everyone to submission.

'Have you told Bashto this?'

'Bashto is a poet,' Manius declared darkly. 'A dreamer with a head full of the old times, when Persia was great and before Iskandr came to ruin it all. He looks at the Red Serpent and wails about how the world will never see the likes of it again. Oh Persia, where are thy heroes now?'

He laughed. Dog laughed. Drust felt acutely aware of all the Persians lurking in the undergrowth round them and wondered how many spoke good enough Latin to understand.

'No matter what I think, or you, or anyone else – the price for Bashto's help in this is the death of Farnah-vant,' Dog said. 'When you have the Empress, move fast back to here. Then we will head for home.'

Drust was none too sure of how this would be done, though he and the others had asked it, along with other questions. The Empress had been imprisoned as a slave for at least four years and, since Farnah-vant dealt in slaves among other commodities, it was something to note that she was still with him.

Dog had made it clear that Bashto was to be avoided once they had the Vestal Empress and no one doubted the implied treachery in that. Yet it seemed strange as a two-headed calf that folk would take this secret name of Rome seriously.

'That's because you are not Roman,' Praeclarum told them when they had brought this up. They started to argue, then realised it was true. They were citizens, had lived inside the Empire – inside the City itself – for most of their lives, but they were still not Roman.

Nor was it clear how exactly they would get back over the Red Serpent and away to safety, though Dog hinted he had a way. For now, though, there was only the subterfuge of getting into the city – four camels, three of them laden with bales of silk, though if any guard dug too deep they would find the core of it was cheap felted wool.

For a moment they all stood together, then Dog thrust out his hand, palm down. Manius did the same and, for a moment, Drust hesitated, and Manius's eyes flickered though his face remained stone. Then Drust thrust his own hand in and one by one everyone did the same – Ugo, Kag, Dog, all of them.

'Brothers of the sand, brothers of the ring.'

'Fortuna smile on you,' Dog said as they broke apart. 'Remember – watchers will be here for when you get back. If you take longer than thirty days, though, I will consider you dead.'

'Consider coming to find out,' Kag declared sourly, then looked at Manius. 'When this is done, Brother, we need to talk.'

'Sib's death was none of my doing,' Manius answered quietly. 'But if you need such a talk I will be waiting.'

They moved out of the shelter of the trees, kicking reluctant camels and feeling the heat of the men at their back. Wondering if they would meet again.

'I will meet Manius again,' Kag said, smacking a camel viciously enough on the rump for it to moan and trot.

'You think he did it?' Drust asked and Kag frowned.

'That we will speak about,' he said and Praeclarum arrived at his other side.

'Both arrows were the same,' she said and Kag scowled at her.

'This is none of your concern. Men are speaking here and you are ill equipped.'

Praeclarum's lip curled. 'Am I part of this or not? Is my risk the same? Was Sib not a friend – recent, I will allow you that, but a friend?'

'How do you know about the arrows?' Drust asked and Praeclarum's gaze was flat and hard.

'Who cleaned him up and helped wrap him for the grave? I did. Ugo too, so you can ask him and neither of us was *Stupidus*. We examined the arrows and they were the same – grey or speckled brown feathers, no markings on the shaft. Same as every other shaft we found.'

'Manius used the same,' Kag argued.

'Everyone did,' Drust pointed out, yanking the camel away from grazing.

Kag sighed and rubbed his face. He did not want it to be true, yet he could not rid himself of the nag and neither could Drust or any of the others.

'There is more,' Praeclarum said, 'and it concerns Stercorinus.'

Kag spat in the dust. 'He is more god-hagged than ever. He says nothing and sits alone and prays when he thinks no one can hear or see him.'

'His death is upon him,' Praeclarum answered, 'or so he thinks. His gods told him he would die under the eye of an empress, listening to the cry of eagles.'

There was silence while they sought out Stercorinus with their eyes, squinting through the haze to where he stalked, as seeming solid as ever, cradling his sword.

'Is there more?' Kag asked bitterly.

'Does there need to be? Would it help?' Praeclarum countered, which was so like Stercorinus that Kag laughed, choked in the dust and had to stop.

Quintus came up. 'The gates can be seen. Get ready.'

–

They called it a city, and for this part of the world it was, Drust thought – but the truth was that Asaak was the least part of a district in Antioch. If you dropped it in Rome it would vanish entirely, like a drip in the sea.

They had been guided to the *caravanserai* just outside the walls where dealers had swarmed them, looking to snap up bales of silk before these new arrivals could find others to haggle with. Drust resisted them, paid to stable the camels and store the bales; he wanted no one unpacking them and discovering the truth.

They spent the night in the *caravanserai* and everyone's unease about what they were doing, about Manius, about Dog, was salted with food and drink – and women.

Three girls, with their hair in some impossible fastening and their faces painted in amazing masks, leaned over the railing of a balcony that ran round the second floor of the *taberna*. They smiled and beckoned and smelled of flowers; if they were bothered by the look of the Brothers they did not show it.

Shame, however, made the men douse themselves and comb the raggles and worst of the nits out of their hair – then they came back and sat, scrubbed and damp and astounded. Praeclarum did the same, smiling at the others watching the women drift back and forth.

They ate lamb and bread, spiced in the way Persians do, enough to make Drust's eyes water. They drank decent wine for a change and folk were laughing by then so that his splutters only added to the moment. They clapped him on the back and passed him more drink.

They spoke among themselves and with the women and the others in the *caravanserai*, switching seamlessly between three tongues. Two of the girls returned, wearing elaborate costumes in eye-watering colours, and the third tapped a drum while the pair danced.

They had their left hands on one hip and bent like reeds in a high wind while they twirled, the long, flowing skirts turning, the bells at wrists and ankles jingling. They all sat entranced until the girls pulled down their tops to reveal small, round breasts, and slippered towards the roars of approval, while hard-eyed men watched from the sidelines to make sure no quarrels started.

Praeclarum smiled and stared straight ahead. It would have been polite to ask her to leave, but Drust did not want to ask her to leave. In the end, she rose up and left of her own accord, despite the chaffering from Ugo, who had the drummer woman on his lap, and Quintus, who had the other two on either arm.

Kag slid to Drust's side, head to head so he could talk above the din without shouting; Drust saw Kisa look at them, then pretend he had not.

'Stercorinus has gone to find a temple he has heard of,' Kag said. 'I set him to finding out what he could about where this Farnah-vant lairs – and where his slaves are kept.'

'Is he the one for it?' Drust asked. 'I hear he is god-hagged by prophesies of his death. Is there a temple to his god here?'

'The temple is not to his god – perhaps he is looking to change, see if he can avoid this prophecy. Mind you, it is one of those fire-worshipper temples, so that's no good thing for us. Perhaps you should question Praeclarum more on it – last thing we need is a Stercorinus rolling his eyes and drooling.'

A bench went over and Quintus was glaring at someone who was blatantly annoyed at his monopoly on the girls, but Ugo stood up and the man backed away. This will not end well, Drust said and Kag nodded agreement.

'Best we put a stop to it.'

'Get them out of here,' Drust instructed. 'We have rooms to go to.'

'They will take the girls,' Kag warned and Drust pointed to the man who ran the *taberna*. Kag grinned and went off. Salt it with silver, Drust thought. It was always the way...

He went to her in the dark, fumbling up the stairs to where she had a room of her own, away from those who would quarrel and try to tup her. The room was dark and he heard her turn in the bed, so he paused, frozen.

'Who is that there?'

He leaned his back on the door, closing it.

'Me. Drust.'

There was a rustling as she got up and then a soft chip–chip and sparks flew.

'I need to know more about Stercorinus,' he said, and the soft flare of flame on candle stub brought her into view, no more than an arm length away. 'Kag sent him out to ask about Farnah-vant and slaves and anything else that might be useful. I am wondering if he is sound.'

'Liar.'

She held the candle higher and the flame made her face golden, her eyes flicker with small lights. Her laugh was low and hoarse.

Drust tried for words and failed. He knew she was right and he fought to deny it, but he wasn't ready for this. Neither was she. She did not move away when he went closer, so near he could smell the clean of her and see the flush on her skin. When he kissed her, he felt her lips, soft as pulp and her breath smelled of citron. Her head was a deep fuzz of new growth.

She set the candle down and went to the truckle bed and climbed on it, tucking her feet up; she looked like the girl she had once been and Drust's mouth was dry.

'Quintus says it is always a bad idea, this,' she said and laughed nervously.

'It is for Quintus,' he said. 'Yet you are here, looking like a bride.'

'And you are here, with your mouth open and the eyes of someone needing his colt watered.'

Drust flushed. She laughed softly and held out her arms.

–

They moved in a group and only got a few looks from those who wondered at sun-slapped grim men dressed like wanderers from the Grass Sea beyond the Red Serpent, and yet so clearly Roman. Yet it was the *bāzār* of Asaak and folk were used to stranger sights; they parted briefly, then fell back in behind the group, a wake of noisy crowd who were only interested in profit.

In one section wooden stalls were piled high with skeins of wool and thread, glowing with all the colours of the rainbow. Next to it, brushes and brooms hung like broken branches and baskets in all shapes and sizes dangled from the awning rims like garish mushrooms.

There were bales of fabric everywhere in shrieking colours and patterns, and folk who argued, crumpling the cloth with their hands to test texture.

There was a stir among the throng around the craftsmen, where Ugo and the others were headed, past the rope-makers to the leather and metal workers banging great sheets of brass, copper or iron. They were making them into pans, pots and cauldrons; Drust looked round, smelling the forge metal and disappointed that all they did with it was tinsmithing.

The stir rippled like a pool from unseen fish and they all saw the horseman, armoured in a coat of splint-metal, his helmet off so that everyone saw his savage glare. Behind him came men in leather and on foot, holding panting dogs on chains, and in the middle a woman stumbled and fell, staggered up and was dragged on, fastened to the crupper of the uncaring rider.

The Brothers backed off a little way, into the raw cotton and combed wool piled in bales. The young men beating the wool with long thin whips stopped to stare unsmiling at the procession; the wisps fell round them like a memory of snow.

'No Empress, that,' Ugo offered.

'A good eye you have, giant of the Germanies,' replied Kag laconically, 'but the man beating her with a stick is a better sign that she is a slave of no account.'

The whack of the stick on the woman was loud and sent her spinning, only to be dragged a little way until she scrabbled back to unsteady legs. She was fine featured under the dirt and bruising, and Drust stepped forward.

'Greetings to you, Mistress, in the name of the gods above and below.'

Her head came up, wobbling on the stick of her neck. She knows Latin, Drust thought triumphantly, then turned to see the others watching. He reached up and took the bridle of the armoured rider's horse.

'Hold up,' he said. The rider snarled and Drust felt Kag and Ugo close in. The moment hung like a bad cloak on a shaky peg.

'That is a poor way to treat a woman,' Drust declared in Persian and the man looked down astonished – as if a monkey had spoken to him, Drust thought; he tried not to boil up.

'Step aside. She is no woman, but a slave bound for Farnah-vant.'

'A slave, eh? Then it is a poor way to display trade goods. If I buy, I expect them in good condition.'

The rider jerked at his reins, but Drust's grip was stronger. The rider scowled. The woman's eyes had lost some dullness.

'She is not for sale, even if you rag-arses could afford her. Now stand aside.'

He raised the little whip he carried and heard the growl from too many throats just before he saw what made it; the whip lowered and he blustered instead.

'She is bound for Farnah-vant and her fate is sealed. So stand aside, dogs, or face the same.'

Drust let go the bridle of the horse, smiled at the rider as he jerked savagely, making the horse squeal and toss its head. The man sneered his way past and the cavalcade followed on; the woman turned red, hopeless eyes briefly on them, then was swept on into the crowd.

'What was that?' demanded Kisa, appalled at the stares from all round. The others knew more and waited, looked steadily at Drust.

'That was Fortuna,' Drust said. 'Follow the goddess.'

'Looked like one of those girls from last night,' Quintus declared. 'All of them, in fact.'

'You should know – you had all of them.'

'It has been a time,' Quintus admitted, grinning.

They went on, shouldering through the stink of the meat stalls and men carrying bloody carcasses on their shoulders, stripping flesh from heads of sheep and smiling-proud of their agile hands.

They moved round porters carrying heavy loads, ducked past shrieking demands to consider wares of all kinds, gasped through the swirling throat-catch of spices piled on trays, a rich flood of colour and scent that made everyone stare as if their heads were on stalks.

'Look,' Praeclarum said once, pointing. 'That is where those women get the stuff they put on their hands.'

'Tell Quintus,' Kag advised. 'He thinks they have given him a rash on his nethers.'

They laughed and moved past the bright red dye that women used on the palms of their hands, for no reason anyone could understand. The stalls drifted to threadbare, then shifted into other buildings. Here were two-floored *tabernae* for travellers, others were *caravanserai* compounds for the favoured.

One of these was a fortress which brought everyone up short, watching the rider, the men, the dogs and the staggering woman swallowed by the shadowed door. This one had four floors at the front, a gatehouse tower of intimidating solidity. The other sides, two floors high, formed a courtyard. If it ran true to the way others were built, Drust thought, then the other buildings were used as stables and storage on the ground, while the floors above were used as living quarters.

It was fitted with huge wooden gates, decorated façades and high-hooped entrances, and the top floors had large, arched windows with shutters and latticed coverings for when the weather got too warm. But this was a giant of a place.

'It is hot now,' Kag said when the high openings were pointed out, 'and the nights are warm – those shutters will be open. An agile person could be up those walls and in easily enough.'

'Let me know when you find one,' Drust said scornfully. 'What would such an ape do when he got up there and inside – open those big heavy doors to let in the rampaging army of a handful of men? I know enough about these places to know there will be many guards all over the place – many slaves too. We could spend hours trying to find her.'

'Fortuna will favour us,' Quintus pointed out. 'That slave speaks Latin and I am betting sure she knows where to find this Empress.'

'Perhaps she was the Empress,' Kisa offered and they fell to debating the point, eventually deciding that the woman was one of the others, like the one in the grave and the one who had escaped back to Shayk Amjot.

'Handmaidens,' Praeclarum said scornfully. 'To a woman much prized, who has been here for four years at least and may not want to leave at all, let alone quietly.'

'That is a good point, well made,' Kag agreed, then grinned again. 'It comes to me that if anyone could get in those shutters it would be a remarkable woman like yourself.'

She took him by the arm and hustled him right up into the lee of the walls, then slapped his palm against it. He stroked, looked up and then nodded grudgingly.

'Smooth as the arse of last night's whore,' he admitted. 'I had no trouble climbing that but I doubt anyone would scale this.'

'Besides,' Quintus offered, 'our Praeclarum must be exhausted after all the sleeping she did last night. We saved you a place by the fire, but you never came down?'

'I did not want to witness you rutting,' she answered, and Drust looked left and right, anywhere but directly at her.

'Well, we can hardly go through the door,' he said, to change the subject.

'A double fist will fell any enemy if it be delivered without warning,' Ugo rumbled and then shrugged. 'I have done so many a time.'

'Not here, I think,' Kag replied, thrusting a beggar out of the way with a disgusted snort, and never breaking the stride of his speech as he berated the man. 'Go and fight someone, or find work, you bitch-licking tick. Become a slave if you must – but begging? Have you no pride?'

'I have traded only a little,' Kisa said and they stopped to listen to him, frowning. 'I have seen you at the work of it and know you to be skilled. I have watched long hundreds of goods in trains up and down camel trails all over Syria, and in the end realised that folk trade only the one thing – do you know what it is?'

One thing? There was a moment of pause, then Drust answered. 'Desire.'

'Just so,' Kisa said admiringly. 'Traders have what people want and everyone's desire is different, so you have to find it if you are a trader. That takes many forms, so you also have to keep a note of it or trust to memory. In there will be bills of lading, lists and more that will tell us where to find the woman we saw, and she will tell us where to find the woman we want. Since this is the biggest building of its kind in the city, there also will be Farnah-vant.'

'None of which gets us inside,' Drust replied, bringing them back to the main problem.

Stercorinus stopped so suddenly that folk collided with his back and cursed, hopping to prevent knocking him over. He simply nodded down the street and they all saw it, a set of double doors set down a ramp. A side entrance into the fortress, open to reveal barrels and bales and sweating slaves and watching guards.

'If we get in quick and quiet,' Kag said softly in Drust's ear, 'we can pluck her out like snicking meat from a whelk with a little knife.'

It was, as Ugo said while they ate their evening meal in the insect-pinged torchlight, a bloody big whelk and a piss-poor knife.

'Who here is skilled in sneaking?' he demanded and waited.

'Quintus,' Kag said. No one argued.

'Which of us who can sneak cannot read?' Quintus said and slapped his chest.

'Who can read and sneaks like two camels fucking?' Kag added and slapped Kisa on the chest; the little Jew acknowledged the laughter.

'I will go,' said Praeclarum. Quintus ruffled her bristling hair, which made her smile. Once, Drust thought, she'd have taken off his hand – the thought made him warm inside, a feeling he suddenly realised he had not had since Sib died.

'We should all go,' he said suddenly and then faltered when he felt the eyes; he could not say it was because he liked the glow of brotherhood. Kag, however, nodded and sucked barley porridge off his spoon. He had not shaved nor had his hair cropped because, though they wished for it, they could not look like Romans.

'It's sound enough – but we should leave Ugo behind with Kisa.'

Drust knew why he did it. They all did – especially Kisa, who tried to look sorrowed about it while hiding his relief. But Drust did not want it, not now. There had to be a gesture, if nothing else, to the ring of palms.

'We will all go. Even big Ugo can wait in the street and thump those we miss.'

Ugo lifted a hand, turning as if to an amphitheatre crowd in victory, but Kag scowled.

'The Jew will raise the alarm first chance he gets.'

'Why would he?' demanded Stercorinus mildly, as usual surprising everyone from the shadows. 'He will then die with the rest of us.'

Kag had no answer; Kisa looked sick and stared at the floor.

'So,' Drust said, 'we all know what we are doing? We find the lists and ladings, whatever is written that will lead us to the slave woman we saw. We get her to tell us where the Empress is kept and where we can find Farnah-vant. We free the one and take the head of the other.'

'Be sure to get it the right way round,' Kag added, and the laughs were as soft as the padding of wolves setting out on a hunt.

Chapter Twelve

They came down the night-washed street hugging the shadows and sweating in dark hoods, even if they were only loops of faded red cloaks. Kisa led the way, while Drust brought up the rear, and in the moonlight and empty of people, the street seemed larger, Farnah-vant's citadel bigger than ever.

Voices shrank them into the shadows, and Praeclarum slunk off a little way and peered round the corner. When she returned, she had a thoughtful look.

'It is the entrance we saw. There are slaves moving off into the building. They have been unloading goods from a camel-string.'

Kisa raised his head slightly and sniffed like a dog finding a new arse. 'Smell that? *Achaemenis*, which is added to wine to make it stronger.'

Kag sniffed, found nothing but camel shit and scowled when he reported it. 'How do you know the smell of this… stuff?'

'*Achaemenis*,' Kisa repeated patiently and stared Kag in the eye. 'We use it too, as *frumentarii*. You feed the right amount in a couple of cups of wine and a prisoner will tell you anything you want to know.'

'Kag does that after a bowl or two of bad Kos,' Ugo rumbled, but Kisa never took his eyes from Kag.

'If you get the measure wrong, though, there is only death in it,' he said.

'No matter to us if these Persians like their wine strong. It means the doors are open for us,' Quintus flung in. 'Move, brothers.'

'What will you do?' Stercorinus asked drily. 'Rush in and slaughter everyone?'

'It would be a fine matter,' Kisa said, white-faced with terror in the moonlight, 'if this was achieved with no killing at all, which will raise alarm and we will never escape. Also, rushing in is likely to cause the same.'

'Did you miss the part about cutting the head off the ruler here?' Quintus pointed out and Kisa's face flamed, visible even in the dim.

'Apart from that one,' he muttered.

'Then we must be quick,' Drust said and laid out a plan which left Kisa trying to work spit up into his dry mouth at what he had to do. Which was simple enough. Once the slaves had gone, dragging the grumbling beasts with them to where they could enter the compound and stables, Kisa walked up to the open door, kicked it hard, and tried to smile when the truculent face appeared.

'We... ah... missed a camel,' he said to it and Kag rolled his eyes. Drust could almost hear the squeak of the guard's brows as he frowned.

'We... ah, um... lost it,' Kisa went on, his voice growing high with desperation, '... and found it again – but it fell. Snapped a... er... um... leg. The skins are leaking.'

'Leaking?'

'One is, like a poor dam,' Kisa agreed, and the man licked his lips at the possibilities and stepped out into the street.

'If it is not emptied, it will be lost – bring your helmet and we will fill that first. We might need help,' Kisa suggested and the man grunted that there was only him, so that would have to do. And he stepped out, pulling off his helmet and eager with the anticipation of free drink.

Which is when Ugo slid out behind him and felled him with a single smashing blow to the back of the neck; the crack of it was like a branch breaking and loud enough for Kisa to crouch and whimper.

Kag clapped Kisa on one shoulder. 'Not bad. Too many ums and ers and ahs, but not bad. We could get you in a Plautus, perhaps as the clever slave who wins his freedom.'

Kisa swallowed hard and said nothing as the others came up, but his expression made it clear what he thought. Kag simply grinned back.

'Hurry,' said Kisa, his shadow dancing in the flickering lantern light of the cellar. 'Why do you wait?'

'Kag is thinking whether it is best to leave this man alive behind us, or slit his throat.' Praeclarum answered and Kisa looked alarmed.

'No deaths would be preferable. If we kill anyone, they will not spare us if caught.'

'*Stupidus*,' Kag declared scornfully. 'That is clearly the Atellan role for you. You can carry the head of Farnah-vant because you are bound to have an astounding excuse for having it.'

Drust bent by the guard, queasy about doing it but determined to take it on himself, as leader. Instead, he found no pulse; Ugo nodded and beamed.

'Thought it was a good blow.'

The cellar was large and vaulted, lit only by the pale yellow of a horn-panel lantern where the solitary guard had made a nest for himself. The rest of the place was a series of alleys between bales, boxes, barrels of pungent spice and ranks of *amphorae*, stacked like the army on parade.

'Wine, silk and…' Kag said, stopping to sniff. 'What *is* that smell?'

It was oil, but not the aromatic one from olives they knew so well; this was black, sticky and pungent.

'The black pitch we were told of,' Kisa said, looking round uneasily. 'The stuff that burns in the eternal flames of these fire worshippers.'

Quintus had found stairs and they went up them like prowling cats, latched open the door at the top and moved into another vaulted room.

Cloth-wrapped meat hung from skewers, together with bunches of herbs; there was an extra warmth here that made more sweat break on them; most of it came from a large clay hump where embers glowed. That and the copper wink of pans and pots and cauldrons told where food was cooked, and Kag confirmed it with a snake hiss in Drust's ear.

'Kitchen,' he said, 'watch for the cook.'

'Too hot,' Kisa said. 'He and his helpers will be on the roof, where it is cool.'

They moved out of it into a bigger room, full of trestles and benches they recognised at once from their own communal eating days. There were stairs in one corner and fat double doors at the far end, which Quintus whispered led to the courtyard beyond, for sure.

Where would they keep slaves? Drust did not want to go out into that courtyard – there will be sentries, he thought. He went up the stairs, hugging the shadows like a cloak, and found himself in a small square with a shuttered window on one side; passages led off to the left and ahead, with arched doorways blocked by no more than fringed silk and beaded hangings.

They heard snoring from one, balked at going in, and moved on, dripping sweat. They peered into another and saw nothing in the darkness, save some bulk that looked like barrels and moved towards them. The room was full of them and there was that same sharp, pungent smell which no one liked.

'So much of this black oil,' Kag hissed in Drust's ear. 'Some fire ceremony perhaps?'

'You don't waste this on the gods,' Quintus muttered. 'This is for selling to those who want to make *naptha*.'

If anyone knew that, it would be Quintus, who had used the stuff before.

Ugo came up, a great looming shadow who moved surprisingly lightly when he needed to. 'There are rooms, lots of them,' he growled and his bass rumble made everyone wince.

'Important folk sleep here,' Kisa said, so close to Drust's ear that his breath scorched the lobe. 'Rooms to themselves alone. Up higher is where the tally-places are – cool, so the scribblers can work in some comfort. That will tell us where the slaves are kept.'

They went higher, into another passageway, and saw more shuttered windows; here was where I would have come in if I had been able to climb, Drust thought.

He moved to an arched doorway – with a proper door in it this time – and opened it; the creak made him wince. His eyes were dark-visioned now and he saw the blue-dim clearly, saw the woman tied by outstretched arms to rings set in the wall, the rich carpet, the small table, the bed and the snoring man. It was the woman from the market, the one who had been whipped.

The woman saw Drust as he saw her, so he put one finger to his lips and slid forward, Kag at his heels. For a moment, as Drust looked down at the bearded figure – the rider whose bridle he had seized – he considered a simple blow behind the ear. Then he saw the shackled woman's wound-stripes, her battered face, her bruised nakedness, the blood on her thighs. He raised the *gladius* and looked at her with silent question.

Her nod was a tremble of vehemence and Kag grinned and clapped one hand over the man's mouth, holding it long enough for his bemused, horrified eyes to open. Drust let him see Kag's wolf-savage smile, the dagger, the blazing gaze of the wall-shackled woman. Just at the point he started to struggle, Drust slit his throat, a simple gesture, a tug that parted the flesh like rind on cheese. He held him while the blood vomited and the man kicked and gug-gug-gugged, trying to tear away.

When he was silent and still, Drust moved to the woman and cut her down; she sagged against him for a moment, whimpering, then levered herself up, hawked and spat on the dead man in the bed.

'You kill is good,' she said in Latin. Her accent, Drust realised with a sudden pang of unease, was thick, making the Latin sound awkward. 'I pull a deep inside not me. His eyes turned seeing me. I wanted to send him to the stone village – pah!'

She spat again. Kag looked at Drust, bewildered, but took her by the wrist and pulled her off the bed; like a camel train they left the room, desperate to find the others. They were in a smaller room, trying to spark up a lantern.

'Is this her? The Empress?' Kisa asked, and Kag laughed softly.

'You tell us, scholar. She speaks Latin like she chews cloth.'

Kisa glanced at Drust, saw the bloody knife. Said 'Aaaah,' in a high, thin voice.

'Who did you kill?' Quintus wanted to know. 'Are there any others?'

'No, just the one in the marketplace who brought this one in.'

Kisa whined. 'In the name of the true God, tell me it was not that one. He is called Zavan, right hand of Farnah-vant.'

'Zavan? You found this out and said nothing?' Kag demanded, making Kisa step back.

'Zavan,' the woman said and snarled out words in her strange way. 'He is planted horseshoes – pig. Dog. Rough uncle. Fit to the *Dis*...'

'She speaks like that all the time,' Drust said to a bemused Quintus. 'It is Latin, but makes no sense.'

'She is Persian, at least in part,' Kisa answered and then rattled off some long phrase in a tongue no one knew. The woman replied.

'She is called Robab, though that is the name for a stringed instrument for playing music...'

'Not interesting,' Drust hissed and Kisa stopped, took a breath. He was trembling and nervous and spoke more when he was like that.

'She is from the Oxus, some Bactrian tribe, because that tongue is native to her. That bit about "planted horseshoes" is how you say, "kicked his last"? "Stone village" is a cemetery. She calls him "rough uncle", which is a bandit, I think. She is talking her own language, but in Latin.'

'How does she know Latin?' Drust demanded, and Kisa spat and popped out the words, had them fired back.

'She was handmaiden to Farnah-vant's woman – presumably one to replace the two who ran off. I am guessing that her mistress is the Empress we seek, but you have to wonder why all her handmaidens take to their heels.'

'Where is she?'

Kisa asked, the woman answered, and he turned, squinting and frowning.

'Up a level.'

Made sense, Drust thought, it being safer and cooler. Kisa wiped his streaming face.

'They call the Empress "Anahita" here, which is the name of a Persian goddess, a virgin sometimes regarded as the consort of Mithra, god of light.'

Light flared and Praeclarum arrived, thrusting her torch into the proceedings.

'Linguistically,' she said drily, looking at the shivering woman, 'I agree this one is an interest. But she is naked and it would be better for everyone if she was not.'

Quintus chuckled, took off his cloak and wrapped it round the woman's shoulders; she clutched it to herself and stood, shaking. A thought came to Drust and made him icy sick.

'Ask her if this Anahita is a slave, or free to come and go.'

Kisa rattled it off and everyone else exchanged glances. Then Kisa licked his lips.

'She is mistress of the city,' he answered miserably. 'Consort to Farnah-vant and beloved by him. This girl was her hand-maiden and broke a mirror, so was beaten and about to be sold back up the Silk Road to the Land of No Return. So she tried to run.'

He looked from one to the other. 'You saw her fate.'

'So – our once-Empress is no slave willing to be freed,' Kag said bitterly. 'Instead, we have a Sabine to be lifted.'

'We cannot stand here all night,' Praeclarum hissed, and that made everyone look left and right and realise they were standing in the middle of an enemy fortress, with guards likely to arrive at any minute.

'Move,' Drust said softly. 'Look for more stairs, go up, kill this Farnah-vant, grab the Empress – and do it as quietly as we can.'

'Good plan,' Quintus began, then stopped, his mouth open; there was a sound like running mice that made Drust whirl in time to see the heels of the slave disappear down the tiled corridor. He ripped out a hissed curse and went after her.

There was the flicker of a figure and he went through the arch after it, skidding a little and losing a sandal. He hopped for a second or two and then he saw stairs up and down, just as Kag and the others galloped up.

'She might be making for the cellar and out into the street,' Quintus gasped out. 'Hoping to escape…'

The shrieks let him know how wrong he was. It was wild and high Persian, loud as an alarm-iron from above and Kisa gave a little whimper.

'She is calling for guards, screaming of murder.'

Treacherous little bitch-tick, Drust thought, but he could see the sense in it for her, even as he went up the stairs, having to elbow past Ugo to be first. Zavan had been murdered by men out to kill Farnah-vant and her former mistress and unlikely to escape or be spared afterwards. Better for her, Drust thought, to make it clear where her allegiance lay.

When he hit the top step he saw the pale, wild stare flung over one shoulder as she fought the tangle of a curtained arch; Drust thundered after her, ripped through the thin cotton, hit the polished planks beyond and felt his one sandal catch and tear, propelling him forward until it slithered his legs out from under him.

He gave a yelp as he thundered to the floor and skidded into a table, which careened madly off and hit another; the lamp on it flew off and smashed on a wall – and someone grunted a query, woke in a panicked flurry of movement.

Drust cursed himself back to his feet, saw the sudden mad flicker of running flame as the oil caught. Beyond it, red-dyed by the sudden soft whuff of blossoming fire, a figure rose sleepily into a growing horror he had only seconds to contemplate. Drust fumbled for the *gladius*, dropped when he fell – found nothing. The woman was screaming, turning this way and that, and then suddenly darted past and out the door. Drust let her go, busy scrabbling fiercely for the dropped sword.

Other shadows loomed – this was where the guards slept and Drust had another fierce moment of raking the floor for the *gladius* when a new, bigger shadow loomed over him and a blade snicked into the firelight.

Ugo stepped over Drust, beat the man he had stabbed to the ground with his left hand and then kicked him hard enough to shift him backwards; two more half awake men, wild with fear, fell over him.

A stumble of guards were heading out of the burning room and two more tackled Ugo, who had to wrestle with them. One careered past and came at Drust, who had managed to find his eating knife by the time the man flung himself like a panther.

They locked, sweating and reeling, fetid breath mingling and the flames scorching them both. Drust's fingers clawed for the heart in the throat and then he drove the little blade in and ripped it across as if wiping a mouth, scattering little ruby red drops. A gout of blood splashed his eyes, blinding with its hot scour, and he spun away, trying to clear his sight and cursing roundly. The man was gasping sprays of blood, struggling to stay on his feet and finally collapsing at the door, where he tried to claw himself out.

Kag booted him in the head and then ran him through the back, just to be sure.

'Get up and finish it. We have problems here.'

By the time Drust was on his knees, the place was running with oiled fire and it was dripping through the gaps in the floor; the man lying in the middle of it drummed his heels and waved his arms as if trying to swim to the surface of a deep pool and take a breath. Ugo grabbed Drust's arm and hauled him all the way to his feet, thrusting his big face close.

'Got sense? Good. Then move – my arse is burning.'

Drust ducked out of the room, looked down the corridor and saw the whole gods-rotted moment of it. Kisa was locked in a panting struggle with the dark figure of the slave, who had lost her cloak. Quintus lay on the floor groaning, and Praeclarum crouched and danced back and forth against two guards.

They had hard leather armour and metal helmets in the Persian style, covering almost all the head save for the face and with a ridged crest. They had shields and even spears – well, they were guarding the boss, after all, so they had to look the part.

Thing about spears is, Drust thought, smearing more blood out of his eyes, they are useless in a narrow place like a corridor unless you just stand and poke them. Praeclarum was showing them why that was a bad idea, but then the door behind them opened and a new figure appeared.

He was naked to the waist, which was that of a dancer and how it supported the broad chest above it was a mystery Drust had no time to worry about. He had a too-handsome face with a well-groomed beard and a fistful of curved sword like the one Stercorinus waved impotently behind all of them.

'Kill them,' this new man commanded, but he only had one guard left to listen – Praeclarum, with a wicked scream, had leaped into a forward roll and come up to stab the other in the groin. His shrieks drowned everything out, including the slave girl, but hers were cut short when the half-naked man sliced her jaw off.

It was meant, Drust supposed, to remove the head in a casual display of strength and skill, but it fell well wide of the mark. It was also a stroke on someone who might just as well have been a block of cheese or a piece of furniture; with only the briefest of moments to contemplate how her plan had failed, the slave girl from the Oxus crumpled in a bloody heap.

'I will gut you like cod if you fight me,' the man bellowed and Drust supposed this was Farnah-vant himself. Ugo shouldered forward, grabbed the spear a guard thrust at him and pulled hard, so that the owner stumbled forward. The guard should have let it go, but was stubborn and died in an instant of blood and agony that didn't even give him time to realise what a fool he had been.

Farnah-vant crashed forward and blades sang like broken bells as Praeclarum and Ugo struggled to match him.

'He's good,' said a voice in Drust's ear and he turned to see Kag gazing admiringly.

'Oh – perhaps we should give him the contest then? Move him up the rankings also?'

Kag scowled and shrugged – then was flung sideways as Stercorinus bludgeoned his way through. There was a moment when he hovered behind Ugo and Praeclarum, looking for an opening – then he took Praeclarum by the collar of her tunic and yanked her backwards, leaping into the hole she made.

There was a moment of blistering speed and high, sharp rings, then Ugo lurched backwards and stood, panting. He turned, bewildered, to the rest of them.

'I can't get into it – too fast for me. Need an axe and can't swing one here even if I had it.'

Drust caught Praeclarum by the wrist when he saw her suck in a breath, as if about to dive into a pool.

'Leave them – get into the room and fetch the Empress. Kag – go with her. Quintus, find us a way out of here – we don't have long.'

The corridor was filling with smoke and the reek of blood, the stink of fear. There was another clashing ring of blades and then a grunt, no more. Drust shifted closer, stepping over the body of the slave girl, feeling the blood slick against his naked soles; something crunched under his instep and when he looked down he saw part of her jaw.

He could not see through the smoke now, but Praeclarum and Kag loomed, the latter dragging a woman by one wrist. She was shouting at them to let her go, calling for help – then she saw Stercorinus appear and she screamed, her free hand going up to her mouth.

He strolled out of the smoke, which swirled round him like a cloak. The curved sword was over one shoulder, dripping slow greasy pits and pats, and in the other hand was a bloody, raggle-necked head that had once been too-handsome with a beard. Now it was slack-mouthed and trailed blood and gleet. He looked at the woman who stared back, a tic starting under one eye.

'Anyone hear eagles?' he demanded. 'I was listening for them all the time I fought this one. He is brave and skilled, so I thought this might be the time...'

'Out,' said Drust, and the woman struggled and fought and shrieked until Praeclarum turned and slapped her once forward, once back, rattling her head. She started to fall and Ugo snatched her up over one shoulder.

'That will part pay for the handmaidens,' Praeclarum scowled. Drust stared at the sprawled corpse of Farnah-vant, the raggled neck spilling a viscous pool. He had ruled here for a long time and ruled well if all they had heard was true. Fine and handsome and as unlike Bashto as shit to shining sun – and now he was nothing at all at the hands of a mad Palmyran with bad hair and a strange sword.

They went down through the smoke, cringing from the flames which spouted from the room and the one below it. There were shouts and the screams of maddened beasts, but they made it all the way to what they thought was the bottom, staggering out into clear air, where they wiped streaming eyes and coughed.

By the time they realised they had taken a wrong turn and come out into the central courtyard, it was too late to go back. For a moment they stood in confusion, surrounded by running people and horses and camels, too panicked to notice them. So far...

'How do we get out?' Kisa yelled, his voice rising with fear.

'This way,' Drust said, though he had no more of an idea than anyone else. Four or five steps convinced him of how wrong he was and, just as he was about to turn and tell everyone to run the other way, a dragon bellowed and Drust watched in fascination as the whole of the main fortress heaved, the plank floors splintering upward as if driven by a fearsome breath. Then light and heat and that same scorching breath slammed into them all like a fist.

There was a long moment, an era, of floating, of a whirl of strange images – wood and shattered mud-brick tumbling in mid-air, a rain of firefly embers, the woman with her mouth open and arms flailing as if she was trying to fly.

Something hit Drust like a horse-kick, drove all the air out and rolled him over and over. He saw flames and a dark shape

– Dis, he thought dazedly, but the pain let him know he wasn't dead.

He tried to look round, but the head on his shoulders didn't seem to be his own and would not work. When he got it wobbling, he saw blurred, double images of folk running one way, camels another, and fires everywhere. Jupiter, he thought dully. Jupiter threw a firebolt…

Someone coughed and heaved up out of the rubble and dust next to him and it took him a long moment to realise it was the Empress, looking like something coming out of a tomb. In another second, Kisa unearthed himself nearby with a series of gasps like a breaching whale.

'Others,' he said, but Drust was lunging at the woman as she tried to run, grabbing her by a torn sleeve and clutching her like a lover.

Kisa looked up and began to stumble away from them both, while Kag turned at the little man's yelling and stopped tugging Ugo to his feet.

'Run,' said a voice, and Drust realised it was Praeclarum, but he was trying to hold onto the woman, who struggled and cursed, though the sounds seemed to Drust to come from a long way off. He did not even recognise the fingers clutching the woman, nor the hand, nor the arm they were all attached to; he could not have willed them loose if he'd tried. They staggered together in rubble and ruin.

Then he saw her look of horror – upwards, at the sky – followed it and saw the entire remaining wall of Farnah-vant's fortress seem to waver, to rock slightly, as if all the screams bounced it. That's why Kisa was running, Drust realised.

It fell in one solid piece like a collapsing cliff. The Empress gave a great cry and tried to spring away, but he held her locked with both arms and saw her reach one beseeching hand as if to claw into the dark and be plucked to safety – then the shadow of the falling wall blotted out everything else.

Drust heard Praeclarum scream, but a great roaring rush of sound and dust beat it away, scattered all sound, all sense.

Drust was still standing – or at least he thought he was. No pain – perhaps that was the last gift of the gods. They drive the life from you instantly and you feel nothing, don't even know you are lying flat and pulped. Perhaps this is my shade, he thought, perhaps this was how a shade felt, standing bewildered like the man he had once been and no more substantial than the clouding dust, waiting to fade finally from the world of men…

Then he felt every bruise and ache and cut. Felt her, clutched close, shaking and crying. She moved, her face lifted, a bewildered patina of sweat, dust and tears. The haze billowed and Drust was suddenly aware of Kag on one side, coughing and snotting, Ugo on another, slapping Quintus awake. Kisa crawled out from a pile of dust and rubble like a spider.

The Empress and Drust stood upright, perfectly framed by the arched window whose flimsy lattice had been splintered out. The rest of the massive wall lay in cracked lumps around them.

'Jupiter,' Drust managed to croak, and Praeclarum came up, blinking into his face. She elbowed the weeping Empress to one side, took his filthy face in both hands and kissed him with trembling, dirt-covered lips.

Kag staggered wearily upright, weaving. 'You are the favoured cock of Fortuna,' he said, looking at the perfect framing. Then he shook his head and stumbled on.

Drust could not deny it, but all of the moment was kissing Praeclarum.

That stopped when Stercorinus lurched up, pasted with sweat and dust, his sword in one hand and the head still in the other. His clothes – those that weren't ripped off – were tattered and blackened.

'This way,' he said hoarsely and pointed with the sword. 'There is a way out to the street.'

Ugo hauled up the Empress, who was lolling and mumbling, while Quintus paused, snatched up a swathe of cloth from the ground and slapped out the embers. 'Wrap that head,' he growled, and Stercorinus saw the sense in it.

They moved over the shattered compound, littered with mewling camels and mules, crawling, running people. The ground was pocked with broken bales, burning debris and shattered pieces of mud brick; no one bothered with them, one more stumbling group in a crowd of mayhem.

'What happened?' Kisa wanted to know, half falling and hauled up by Praeclarum.

'Hubris,' Kag declared savagely. 'All that *naptha* pitch in one place…'

The burning oil from the fire I started, Drust remembered, dripping through the gaps in the floorboards…

They came out into streets where people ran in confusion and fought through them to the market. The traders had all taken their goods in for the night, but those with homes above the shops were out, shouting worriedly to each other.

The woman started to stir on Ugo's shoulder and Drust looked at Kag, who stepped sideways and grabbed an awning – without missing a stride he tore it free from the lashings, ignoring the annoyed shouts of the owner.

Praeclarum walked with him and used her knife to cut strips off, using one to gag the Empress. Then, in a last flick of expertise, Ugo dropped the woman onto the spread awning and she was wrapped and trussed and back on his shoulder with only a few strides broken.

They got to the gates out of the city and leading to the *caravanserai* — only one guard was left, looking uneasy and gawping at the flame-dyed carnage. He waved his spear and said 'curfew' in Persian.

A deep coughing thump reverberated out and a blob of fire shot into the sky, trailing a fiery tail. The guard gawped.

'Tell it to that,' Kisa said and elbowed past him. Kag, beaming, followed and the guard stepped aside, bewildered and afraid. If he saw the awning bundle at all, he wisely fastened his lip on it.

Inside, they went to their quarters while people huddled and asked what was happening and whether it would be safer to pack up and leave — fire was something they did not like.

They ignored them and gathered what gear they had, realising now how tattered and bloody they looked. Quintus started for the camels, lugging a saddle, but Drust stopped him.

'No time. Leave now and run.'

'They will be occupied with that inferno for hours,' Kisa argued, but Kag hefted a bundle and slapped him on one shoulder.

'We have their ruler's head and his concubine.'

That was enough; they ran.

They had made it to a place where the burning city was a red glow before they heard the shuffling thump of camel pads. The enemy made good time, Drust thought bitterly. Went straight to the *caravanserai*, asking about a handful of strange folk in tatters... and now here they are.

'Form,' he called out and they did so, in pairs as they would in the *harena*. The padding came closer; Ugo dropped the woman at his feet, where she wriggled and let out muffled curses — he ignored her and hefted his axe. They all waited.

'Ho,' said a voice and then a pale camel loomed out of the darkness, three more behind it. The rider unwound his face-veil and grinned his death grin.

'Your faces,' Dog said and laughed. Then Manius came up, leading more camels, with Mouse and Mule behind with yet more, some of them laden with packs. This is not where we were supposed to meet, Drust thought, feeling chilled.

'Climb up and let us go,' Dog said, 'before those bitch-ticks of Bashto find us. He has only gone and sent word to the Red Serpent to send soldiers.'

'Why?' Drust wanted to know as the camel laboriously knelt. Dog laughed and looked at the red glow.

'That,' he said. 'I am thinking he saw his prize vanish in smoke. Did you get the woman?'

Ugo unwrapped her and made the mistake of unfastening the gag; he bound her up again when the vitriol burst out.

'Well,' Dog said, 'Bashto wanted the woman and the death of Farnah-vant – and an intact city with all that lovely Greek Fire ready to sell to the Persians of Ardashir.'

'And we were not about to be considered in it,' Drust added as the camel lurched upright.

'Well, luckily for you, I foresaw this and have a plan.'

Kag cursed him and spat. Stercorinus lifted the bundle. 'Is this not necessary now?'

'It is not,' Dog answered, and almost before he had finished, the wrapped head had been flicked away like an unwanted apple core; the woman listened to it bounce and made hoarse, incoherent noises.

'What is this plan?' Kisa wanted to know and at least three heads turned scornfully to him.

'Run if you want to live.'

Chapter Thirteen

The land was usually green but the weather had changed and withered it to rust and iron grey. Manius had scouted several roads and all of them led up into a great tangle of high ground, ragged as a wolf's jaw.

They rode hard across this dusted, cold land, looked up at the iron teeth of those mountains – big to the south and east of them, bigger still to the north – and cursed their camels carefully, for they needed the beasts and the favour of Fortuna if they were to get away.

That's if Dog was right, Drust thought and looked at him yet again; he seemed unreasonably cheerful about their prospects and nudged his beast closer when he saw Drust staring.

'Look,' he said. 'There is a way through the mountain. I have it on good authority and no one else knows of it. If we get the Empress back to Rome, to Uranius, we will get the reward.'

'Good authority?' demanded Drust, and the woman, hands tied and ungagged, gave a short, vicious bark of laughter.

'Some whore told him,' she spat. 'You will all die.'

'The woman,' Dog replied flatly, bludgeoning the Empress with his death-face. 'The one you were sure was a spy and handed over to those bow-legged horse-cocksuckers from the Grass Sea. The one I found later and buried – but she had already told me all that was needed.'

Drust gawped from him to the woman. 'You said her friend had buried her, the one who now dances and eats poppy.'

Dog shrugged. Kag said nothing, his face stony.

'Look,' the woman began, and Drust gave Dog one last glare and fought his camel closer to her. She was not young, he saw, every line etched with dust and blackened filth, her uncombed hair free of artifice that kept the grey at bay, her lips unpainted.

'Do not bother pleading,' Drust said and tested the thongs that fastened her at wrist and ankle. 'You will not be released save by death and your man is not coming for you.'

'Persia will, all the same,' Dog interrupted. 'You won't be any better off with them, for all they will promise you.'

Kag was on his usual fret – if you are leaving tracks, you are being followed. He was less worried about the mountains ahead than the road behind, and each time Drust turned, he found Mule plodding his camel stolidly back from another lookout.

'See them?' Kag always asked and Mule would shake his head. Then he'd wait until everyone had passed, stay there for a long time before turning and shuffling after them at a trot that must be killing the beast, since it killed them all to watch.

In the end, they had to get off – all but the woman – and walk.

'I can feel them,' Kag would say every so often and then saved his breath. He needed it, for each step was an effort of pain. Quintus, though, was grinning his big wide grin.

'My balls are heavy, my shield is light, my *spatha* swings from left to right. Left, right, left…'

They laughed and kept the rhythm like the legionaries who chanted it from one end of the Empire to the other, until the breath left them and it fell apart in gasps and limping.

Mule got on his camel and rode back down the trail until he was small, then stopped, leaped up onto the hump and stood, shading his eyes with one hand, looking for dust. Kag saw this feat when he turned his head to blink dust from his eyes and pointed it out to the others admiringly. Ugo spat and eyed the camel next to him with a bloodshot orb.

'If he tried it with this flat-footed spitter,' he offered, 'he would fall off at once. This is as bad-tempered as my old ma – but her armpits were hairier.'

Mule rode back and walked his grumbling camel alongside Manius, glancing only briefly at the laughing men; Drust knew he was wary of the men he had not known until recently, and it was the same for them. We are former slaves and gladiators, yet we are not so low as a deserter from the army, Drust thought.

'Dust,' he growled and they all simply nodded and plodded on.

They filed across a scrub-studded plain, heading towards the tall ground which loomed ever higher, forming into formidable steeps.

'We are looking for a big tower,' Dog told everyone. 'They call it Iron Blade and it is an outwork of the Red Serpent, which ends at these mountains. Those who built it judged that no one would be able to cross them, but they stuck watchtowers up just to be sure.'

They were not manned, he said, not since the garrisons were all withdrawn by the Parthians to fight the usurper Ardashir – but since he had beaten them and killed the king and now called himself King of Kings, it might be that his soldiers were returning to man the Red Serpent and the outwork towers.

They camped near the remains of a building, the mud-brick melted almost back into the landscape. There were some twisted trees, the wood tortured into uneasy shapes, and so they had fires, ate barley porridge, and wondered how close the pursuers were and if they would come all the way up to the mountains.

'What do we do if this Iron Blade is held against us?' Kag wanted to know.

'Avoid it. It isn't the way out – that lies north and east of it a little. After Iron Blade we are climbing and will find a valley. There lies the way out. Don't get too attached to your camels, for we will have to leave them eventually.'

'I will eat mine,' Mouse declared sullenly and Ugo grinned across at him; they were united in their hatred of the beasts.

There was no camel to eat, just barley, roots and flatbread ugly with grit from poor milling, but there was wine still, though there was no sign of water and that was a worry.

Drust watched them, brooding on yet another enterprise gone to rot – yet they laughed and ate and only now and then peered up at the spangled blue of the sky, so clear and bright that the jagged peaks of the distant north mountains seemed to move towards them.

It made everyone hunch in their necks and shift closer to the fire. Praeclarum slid closer to Drust and sat for a while, then looked sideways at him.

'You have a face like two miles of bad road – why so?'

'We have dust and rocks, hardly any coin, weapons, food or water, but bruises and cuts and sores. Nothing much else to show for this endeavour. Is that not enough?'

Praeclarum's hard nut of a fist smacked his shoulder, but she was smiling.

'Should I worry? Would it help?'

Drust laughed, despite himself.

'We are alive,' she added, 'we have the Vestal Empress we came for, the two friends you sought and a way out.'

She was right and he found himself smiling back at her.

'Tell me again why she is important,' she asked softly as they slid closer, leaching warmth, listening to Kisa yet again trying to get the Empress to confirm what everyone believed – that there was a secret name for the City and that she knew it.

'You should tell all,' he said once more, 'so we know we did not come all this way for nothing.'

The Empress adjusted the tattered remains of her dress, which had been night attire only, and huddled into the only other clothing she had, the awning they'd wrapped her in.

'I am not here to make you feel better,' she said.

'Tscha!' Kisa growled. 'You can benefit here too, you know.'

'I will benefit only when you are taken and beheaded,' she replied, glaring. 'The goddess will see to it. Daughter of Saturn and Ops, sister of Jupiter Best and Greatest, Neptune, Pluto, Juno and Ceres…'

Kag laughed. 'Lady Julia, you are so removed from the gods of Rome you could not see them with the eyes of Mercurius. That's what happens when you give up your Vestal vows for the cock of a boy-emperor.'

'Ho – no need for insults,' Stercorinus said, which made everyone stop and stare. The Empress seized her chance to leap in.

'It seems the gods have abandoned you, not me,' she declared with a wry twist of grin. 'You will be caught and killed and I will be free.'

Dog leaned closer to her and she drew back a little, despite her best efforts; not many can stay firm under the stare of that face, Drust thought.

'The only freedom you will find if the Persians get you is the one that takes you to face the walls of Rome and call out the secret name of the City at the head of an army. You will either find perfumes and riches or hot irons – either way, this Ardashir will get the flame he desires to put fire in his men. And Romans will revile you.'

'It will be perfumes and riches,' Praeclarum added. 'Her nature already tells us what she is.'

'Abomination,' the woman spat back. 'Everyone can see what your nature is. You call me a whore – does everyone else know you fuck the leader?'

Drust felt himself burn and itch, but Kag grinned.

'Of course we know, and we say Fortuna's kiss to them.'

Drust, however, watched Dog's face and thought that there was something in his look that said he did not believe Drust was leader. They had had this grate between them before.

'There are too many gods here,' Quintus offered and Ugo agreed that with a grudging nod.

'You were a fire worshipper back in Rome,' he rumbled at the woman. 'And then became a bigger one when you married the boy-emperor. Then you came here, to be concubine to a silly little city governor in a place of Persian fire worshippers.'

He turned and stared round them all with his big, broad, ingenuous face. 'Maybe those people who hunted us for the blue stone eyes are still chasing us.'

Dog and the others had heard the tale and laughed at it, mostly – especially the bit where Drust and others had gone off the cliff. They were not laughing now, Drust saw.

'It would not be strange,' Mule noted bitterly, 'for they did not seem to want to give up, according to what I heard. Perhaps, once they stuck their eyes back, they thought of continuing the chase.'

'There are too many chasers,' Drust offered. 'And gods.'

Mouse looked at the Empress's bowl. 'Will you be finishing that?' he asked.

'Leave the bowl at least,' Kag growled drily.

There is no point running in the *harena*, Drust thought, since you only arrive back where you started and get killed tired.

'Maybe we should fight,' he said, and Kag agreed to it almost at once with a loud 'Ha!' of approval.

'We could get in this Iron Blade if it is unmanned. Defend it.'

'We'd be trapped,' Dog pointed out. 'With little food and water. They need only wait.'

There was enough hard truth in that to shut everyone down for a while, until the Empress started in about how it would be better for them all to surrender. Ugo squinted and scowled.

'There is no old ma's remedy for what is going to happen. So let it happen,' he said, 'and fight like brothers all the way out the Death Gate.'

Drust did not know what was worse – the idea of them having to run on, or this resignation that they were all sixed already.

He fell asleep aware of Praeclarum breathing beside him, of her body warmth. The memory of her held close made him stir inside and, at the same time, filled him with dread. He did not know what to do on this path or where it would lead.

In the morning, as they moved off, Drust looked them over as they collected their gear and their camels, these people he had travelled and fought with, it seemed forever. Even Kisa and the new men, Mule and Mouse.

Kag was solid as ever, ragged and stained and filthy, his hair and beard wild. Next to him, Quintus grinned and chaffered with the woman – we keep calling her Empress, Drust thought, and there must be something in that.

Praeclarum fussed with her festoon of bags, full of herbs and foul-tasting potions and with bits of charcoal she had filched to give to Kisa when he fretted over not having something to write with. He still did, but had no one to give the results to.

The eye-frets on her face were scored with dust like the ruts of a bad road and her smile was as toothless as ever when she opened her mouth. Her eyes still smiled when she looked at Drust, and now and then one or other would thrust a strip of wound-linen at her with the offhand gesture that said it meant nothing when, in fact, they had ripped it off the hem of their already tattered rags.

Dog, silent as ever, stood hipshot, with a shield resting against his knees, stroking his face with a knife which had to be razor sharp because it took off beard stubble with only a lick of his wine ration to help. It was not vanity so much as a desire to keep his death-face a clean weapon to hurl at people when he needed to. He and Manius, Mule and Mouse are the best armed of us all, Drust realised.

Manius was lean but the muscle was going stringy, Drust saw. Seven years in a gold mine would do that, even if you were a water engineer. He was squatting like a desert raider, knees up round his ears, peering up the way ahead as if something lurked there. Perhaps it does, Drust thought. Of us all, he can feel the enemy – perhaps he is the *jnoun* Sib thought after all.

Mule mocked Mouse for his eating, the fingerbones woven into his beard clicking and rattling, every one from a supposed dead enemy; in his pack, Drust knew, was a box with at least one festering finger which he would boil the flesh off when he could.

Mouse chewed bread as if his life depended on keeping his jaws moving. He was still a man-mountain, taller than Ugo – though Drust would never say it aloud – but soft in the belly, which grew no less.

Kisa squatted, sullen and watchful, while Stercorinus fastened up the girth of a camel saddle ready for the Empress;

his sword was stuck within arm's reach and his face, it seemed to Drust, was grimmer and older than ever before.

Everyone was, he thought. Hard and grey-grim these men, and he became aware suddenly of what he looked like, mirrored in their faces. A medium-sized man striding down the slope of his life, a face that had never been one to grace commemorative cups and with the harsh lines of life and age outlined in dust and the bruises and cuts still unhealed.

Hunched under the grey-streaked tangle of unwashed, uncut hair, with Dis and Mars Ultor sitting on each shoulder crushing me groundward, he thought. He straightened almost at once, but knew he would fall into it again.

The Empress looked at him, ice-chip eyes and her awning pulled round her like a robe, trying to look imperial and haughty. She was smiling but did not do it for any pleasant reasons.

'We will get there, if that's where we have to go,' Dog said, glancing up at the brooding peaks.

'Not if what you hold to be true is truth,' the Empress interrupted blandly. 'You are slaves and gladiators following a man with the face of Dis. More doomed would be hard to find.'

'Dog does not lead here,' Drust declared, looking steadily at the man. 'He simply knows the way. And the one who is most doomed, lady, is the one who betrayed her vows, her family and her own heart.'

She blinked and looked away, which made Drust savage with triumph at having inflicted a stroke. Then she recovered and turned, stone-faced.

'Firstly,' she answered, 'you will have to deal with them.'

They all followed her pointed finger, to where the distant dust bloomed like a foul flower.

'Kick your camels,' Kag bellowed, 'if you want to avoid the pain of dying for a little longer.'

Chapter Fourteen

In the light that spilled wearily into their faces the land seemed red-brown and cracked, littered with scree and dusted lightly with green to show that water was here somewhere. There were trees too, all tortured and bent and rattling spindly limbs as if shivering in a sudden chill; the whole place was a bad memory of lush.

They were stopped in the lee of a wall, another huddle of melted stone and old archways, but welcome because it was something that made the great roll of wind-sucked land seem less like the worst sea they had ever sailed on. They were heading uphill now and had been for some time, and the camels were suffering from no food, no water and the harshness under their pads.

'How far have we come?' demanded Ugo, in between sucking in air. Manius looked back down the long bleak trail of scarred scree.

'Not far enough,' he said and that was all the truth. The dust was still behind them and it seemed to Drust as if it was bigger than ever. Also, he had noted that they were going more east than north because of the slope.

'There must be hundreds of them,' Kisa said tremulously. 'Look at the dust they are kicking up.'

Manius looked at Kag, who looked at Drust and all knew, all the ones who had lived in the sands, ate it, slept in it, been scoured by it.

'Storm,' Quintus said.

Manius nodded, then added sadly, 'Sib would have spotted it earlier than this.'

Drust wanted to believe him, but Kag exchanged a look that said he didn't believe the sorrow in Manius's voice. Not that it mattered, for Mule had leaped up on the back of his camel and perched there; Kag shook his head with disbelief and admiration.

'There is still the dust of riders,' he called out and then slid easily down onto the beast, which rumbled and moaned about it all.

No one spoke much, simply shouldered into the whining wind and moved off again, covering faces against the whip of cold dust. After a long time of this, Drust was gasping and almost on his knees and no one else was much better – no one was riding.

Then, like a death knell, one of the pack camels groaned, stumbled and fell to its knees. Quintus went to it and both Ugo and Mouse tried to haul it up, but it was blowing hard, the neck snaked; if it hadn't been for the packs, it would have fallen sideways.

'It will take some time to sort this out,' Manius said to Drust. 'I can take the fittest of the beasts we have left and back trail a little, see if I can spot anything.'

Drust nodded and set Mouse and Ugo to unpacking the dying camel and seeing what could be rescued. Mouse wanted to butcher the beast and get a little meat from it, but that seemed a pointless waste of strength. In the end, they left it alone folded and forlorn and moaning about it.

Dog had moved a little way upslope and came back grinning. 'I am sure that tower is just up ahead,' he said and Drust went

264

with him to see. It seemed to him that it might have been as Dog said, or no more than a pinnacle of rock.

'Well, we will find it before the day is out,' Dog declared firmly.

'We had better. A day is about all we have that won't have blades and blood in it.'

'Worried about your little *gladiatrix*?' Dog asked lightly. He was grinning, and for a moment Drust hackled up, and Dog saw it, putting up placating hands.

'This is why you should never have women in a School,' he said. 'It is the one thing Quintus and I agreed on.'

'This is not a School,' Drust answered sullenly, feeling ridiculous for saying so. Dog laughed and went off down to the others, speaking over his shoulder.

'You were always soft for women. Love, like the poets have it. Had no place when we were all slaves, and no matter what copper plaques we have that say different, we are still the scum of Subura to anyone in the Empire.'

'Fine words coming from you,' Drust answered bitterly, catching up with him. 'You loved that boy who became Emperor – and his ma. Dragged us all through the shit over that and here you are doing it again.'

Dog stopped and turned. 'I dragged that boy and his ma through a Praetorian camp by their heels to execution,' he said. 'Don't confuse what I do for love, Drust.'

–

The wind was starting to moan and swirl, but the stink of blood wouldn't be blown away. A figure wavered into view, hazed by rising dust, and they all squinted into the nag of wind, red-eyed and weeping, cracked lips bursting blood with snarls. Manius appeared, leading his plodding camel.

'There are at least two hundred horses coming,' he said. 'Half of them are those fast little fuckers Bashto had, marmots with robes and trousers, but they can shoot you full of arrows.'

'The rest?'

Manius blew snot out of one nostril. 'Horsed bows, with iron hats and ring-metal coats.'

'Persians,' Kag said and spat. 'Bashto is bought and sold.'

'We are bought and sold,' Drust corrected, 'but not yet delivered.'

'Then we must find a place to make a stand,' Kisa declared, looking round desperately.

'You are doomed,' the Empress said through a curling lip. 'The gods have forsaken you, Drust. It seems a pity that everyone else had to be woven into that.'

There was a sharp, flat sound and the woman staggered sideways, holding her cheek in disbelief. Praeclarum took her by her awning cloak and propelled her to a camel.

'You are a woman of a certain type,' she said, 'whose heart is on a wheel, never settling for one matter when another will roll around to take its place.'

Mouse laughed. He was sitting on a rock and looked, suddenly, more like the Boxer on the Quirinal than ever. They all saw it and wondered what it meant.

'Move,' Dog said. 'The tower we needed to find is not far ahead. Besides – this storm will help us.'

It did not seem so to anyone as they stumbled on, the wind tearing at what remained of their clothes, catching their legs, hurling grit in their faces. Mule lost his camel, which bucked and kicked and tore free; he took two or three steps after it, but it became a shadow in the moaning haze and then vanished.

'Riders are coming.'

They lumbered into a shambling run and stumbled into a new and strange landscape of buttress and wind-melted walls, only realising it when they were forced down a snake-knot of tracks.

'Walls and houses,' Quintus yelled to be heard above the wind. 'Look – this was a town once.'

Now they peered in wonder, seeing the remains of doorways, the collapsed litter of clay walls. There was nothing of it higher than waist height and most of that was choked and drifted with dust, beaten shapeless by the wind and shoved into huge, deep drifts of scree. Town was too big a name for it but it was undoubtedly a place where people had lived, laughed, loved and traded – and died.

Kisa stopped by what seemed like a pillar, scoured to the shape of a rotting tooth. 'Look,' he yelled above the wind. 'A statue.'

'The sand eats everything,' Ugo shouted, 'this day or the next... keep moving.'

'It has something,' Kisa said, kneeling and peering. 'Wait. Wait...'

Ugo took the little man by the collar and dragged him until he kicked on to his feet. 'That was important,' he yelled. 'I saw the word *Roxana*... that was the Great Alexander's queen.'

'*They* are important,' Ugo growled, whirling him briefly to face back towards where the shadowy shapes, eldritch in the swirling haze, were getting closer and closer. Kisa yelped and hurried after Ugo without argument.

Dog cursed and stopped. 'I am running here,' he said with disgust and, balked in the act of passing him, Drust knew what he meant. You never run in the *harena*...

He stood, panting, then looked up the steepening slope at a looming shape. 'If we both saw it true, then that is the Iron Blade,' he gasped.

'Fuck their mothers in the arse,' Dog growled. 'I am running from goat riders.'

He turned, hauling out both his swords, savaging everyone with a grimace and a snarling cry. Drust went on a few steps, then stopped, panting, bent over with his hands on his knees. From somewhere came the hoarse cry, 'Rome is mother to us all!'

An answer swirled on the wind: 'The *harena* is our country!'

Drust took a step away from Dog, the wind dancing dust with a rising moan of glee, but could not take another and knew what he had to do. When Dog roared out 'Pairs', Drust howled back and turned into the fetid breath of Dis. The wind shrieked happily through the funnel of old streets.

The riders came out of the dust, which was now swirling in yellow clouds. They saw their enemy too late, checked and milled, horses dancing as they dragged out their little bows – one shot off a shaft, but the wind dragged it sideways and it vanished into the yellow fog.

Dog gave a hoarse shout and rushed at them; with a curse, Kag followed. There was a brief flurry of clatter and grunt, then some huge shadow leered out of the dust and Drust slashed wildly, then smashed into it with his battered shield.

The pony screamed at the cut, tossed its head away from the battering, rearing and lashing out; a hoof clattered off Drust's shield and sent him spinning – by the time he got back to his feet, spitting dust, the horse was gone.

A bundle of wind-whipped clothes lay nearby, moving weakly, and Drust shuffled to it; a pale face with eyes slitted in pain and a straggle of wisped moustache looked desperately up, but there was no mercy in Drust and he bladed it with a crucifixion of iron – one stroke down, a second across the eyes. The man's face opened like a bloody flower.

Another shape drifted out of the swirling dust, but it was Dog with his swords resting against his shoulders, limping back and as unconcerned as if he was off for a day's fishing. He glanced at the dead man and grinned a bloody mile at Drust, who had to blink and focus – the wind was a thunder that had got inside his head.

Then Dog scowled at the shapes who came staggering up – Quintus, Manius, Mouse and the others, all wild and matted with sweat and dust and blood.

'Too late, you poor swords – Drust and I have done with them,' Dog declared.

'Bravely done,' growled Ugo and pointed with his long axe. 'Then those will be the harmless shades of the folk who once lived here.'

They looked back and saw the smoked shadows of more horsemen.

'Oh fuck,' Kag said wearily.

They turned and ran, heading for the huge dark shape that fingered into the hidden sky. The world was ochre and howling and Kisa screamed out that it was a tower, a real tower. In the lee of it, they stood at the splintered gates, which Dog said was a good sign that no one was home.

They stumbled inside to find a courtyard and some surrounding buildings, all marked with the char of old fires and fallen roofs, long abandoned. Ugo and Mouse started to try and shift the doors, but they were canted and useless. Camels milled and groaned, then sought shelter from the scouring sand-wind inside the broken houses; there was a second floor on the largest one and perhaps there had been one after that, but some of the

269

planks of it had fallen to the ground and the stone curve of staircase was choked with spilled timbers.

'The entrance is narrow,' Kag yelled, 'and this wind will send arrows everywhere but a target. Fortuna smiles yet, brothers.'

'There is water here too,' Mouse roared out, spitting dust. 'I know this because I have pissed myself.'

They laughed like baying, and crouched down while Kisa and Mule unloaded the bales from their last pack beast and tethered the others to make sure they wouldn't bolt.

Voices shouted. Stercorinus raised his curved sword in both hands and spoke, a sing-song chant no one understood – but they knew prayers when they heard them. Drust slithered to where Kisa huddled, trembling.

'Look after the Empress,' he ordered and handed him a knife. 'Make sure she does not run.'

A horseman plunged under the door arch just as Drust turned back. Ugo banged hard into the rider with his shoulder, staggering the horse, then he slashed him from the saddle with a savage axe swipe and ploughed on, cutting and slashing so that the enemy horsemen scattered away from him. These are Bashto's men, Drust thought. No armour or balls for a stand-up fight. They like to ride around in circles and turn you into a hedgepig.

'No eagles can fly in this.'

Stercorinus followed up his scream by leaping over the dead rider and the kicking horse, sped past Ugo at the gate and vanished into the wind and dust, swallowed from sight and then sound. There was a moment when only the wind moaned and the dust hissed across their bodies. Then more horsemen burst out of the murk, moving as if half blind, scarcely more than stepping over spilled bodies and stones the dust-wind hid. These were big men on big horses, all ring-coats and conical, studded helmets, shields and cased bows – and long, straight *spathae*, the slashing sword.

It was a madness of half seen images, a panting whirl of confusion as the horsemen tried to force a way through the archway. Drust stabbed and ducked and once he fell and rolled. He crashed through a thicket of drunken stones that straggled along the top of the slope the tower stood on, his breath harsh in his ears, and only realised that he had left the shelter of the tower when he saw riders loom and vanish.

On his left, Ugo and Quintus stood side by side, Ugo roaring out defiance each time he scythed that great axe. Kag and Dog flitted like dark shadows, the one half crouched and raking along the girths and bellies of horses with his *gladius*, the other stabbing the fallen with both swords, making sure. Manius had given up his bow and was working his arm like a launderer at a washboard as he pounced on the dazed fallen. There was blood all round his mouth and Drust, half dazed, felt an icy stab of fear that Sib might have been right all along.

Ugo blasted the legs out from under a horse with a stroke, spilling the rider off it, so that he rolled towards Drust's feet and moved weakly, groaning and flapping an arm. Drust moved towards him on legs like timber beams; by the time he reached him the man was on his back, struggling to rise, but weighed down by the long ring-coat and stunned so that his arms and legs waved like a tipped-over beetle. His helmet had a face-veil of brass rings that flew up like gold teeth when Drust's *gladius* lanced into his neck, opening a bloody gape that made him scream. The next stroke was a blur in the haze and choked off screams to a gurgle as the apple was hacked from his throat. Drust kicked the body away with his boot, then fell over and sat.

'Off your arse,' shouted a voice, and Praeclarum sped out of the shrieking dust, her call enough of a warning for Drust to block the snake-tongue stab of a spear – the rider lunged past into the dust-mist. Praeclarum snarled after him and Drust wiped his burst, dry mouth with the back of one hand.

'This is no good,' Praeclarum yelled. 'We must get back into the tower.'

Stercorinus came running past gasping, hurdled a dead man and then a still-kicking, screaming horse; a rider followed and the long lance skewered Stercorinus with a thump that lifted him off his feet, shrieking. The rider shouted and then started to shake and jerk the lance, trying to free it, while Stercorinus flopped like a child's straw doll.

Drust struggled up, but Praeclarum was quicker and sprang forward just as the lance came loose. She knocked the spear point away with her scarred little shield, then bulled in, slashing sideways left and right, cutting at the horse's eyes. It screamed and danced away; the rider dropped the lance to cling on, and suddenly the world slowed to a strange, flickering honeyed light. The inside of Drust's head was colder than steel.

Armour rattled – Drust heard it, knew that it was the rider who had fastened it badly, could even see the loose leather shoulder pieces as the man fell. It will be his ruin, he thought, seeing the gap such carelessness had made.

The rider was off the horse and his movements seemed slow... so slow. Drust had time to pluck up the dropped lance, time to pick the spot as if he was lacing a helmet thong. The man jerked and screamed as the lance point went in, right under the badly fastened shoulder piece, though it made no sound to Drust, and the dying man looked like a cod opening and closing its mouth as if trying to breathe. Drust laughed with delight.

There were others, and he moved steadily through whirling dust and dancing shadows, slapping away a man's spear, chopping at his knee so that he reeled away, clinging desperately to the plunging horse.

Another fallen rider scrambled up, tried to dodge and duck away from Drust as he strode forward on ground he owned. The fleeing man tripped, fell and took the lance so hard through his leather and rings that the shaft snapped. A high wailing scream burst from his mouth, then cut off abruptly as Drust beat the last life from him with the broken shaft, raising and thudding it down like a hammer on an anvil, until it was frayed and blood-clotted and the thunder of it drowned out even the mad wind...

He found himself slumped against a stone, blinking back into his head while the wind shrieked and danced dust everywhere.

'Form. Form.'

It was a call with a long-ingrained response and Drust was up on legs like twisted trees before he even knew it, but he weaved and staggered and could not take a single step until, suddenly, Praeclarum was there, one hand under his elbow.

'This way.'

They moved to the sound of a hoarse voice – Kag bawling out so that people would come to him. Quintus was next to him, big Ugo with his axe all bloody, Mouse standing with his head bent, hands on thighs, puking; he stopped long enough to moan that he had lost his camel haunch. One by one the others came, crouched like bloodied dogs, fresh from a ruck. I should be doing that, Drust thought, but he was too gasping to do more.

'Where is Stercorinus?' demanded Kag, and Drust shook his head.

'We saw him skewered,' Praeclarum added.

'Dog?'

273

No one knew. They clustered, panting and squinting into the dust, then moved wearily back into the tower, stepping over bodies, pricking them to make sure. Ugo battered the life out of a horse, whose screams were high and thin and still drowned by the wind. They crouched like they'd been whipped and Drust tried to make sense of what had happened, that strange light, the feeling inside his head… what he had done.

'I killed four,' Kag said dully.

'Three,' Quintus declared. 'And Mouse took two, I saw. Beat them to pulp with bare fists.'

'We all killed,' Drust managed to growl, slumping down and feeling sick, 'but it is like picking leaves from a tree – there are always more when you look.'

'We need Mars Ultor or Fortuna,' Kag declared with a snort of disgust as he inspected the bloody lips of a wound on Ugo's arm. Mule came up with a bucket and a ladle; the water was brackish but tasted like Falernian. Drust saw there was not a mark on Mule and that he probably had not left the tower.

Kisa came up, round-eyed and blinking; the Empress was with him, looking with horror at the bloody carnage.

'Black you are,' she hissed at Drust. 'Black-browed, black-hearted and black with the blood of innocent slain…'

Mule jerked her to silence with a tug and Drust suddenly realised he had tied her hands and tethered her to Kisa. When he saw Drust looking, he grinned like a feral cat.

Manius was looking up and round, though what he hoped to see escaped Drust entirely, for the world was the colour of dirty honey and seemed to lurch and sway and spin if you looked too long upwards. The shriek of wind was rising.

A figure walked in under the archway and everyone spun round, weapons up – but it was Stercorinus, slathered in blood so that only his eyes showed.

'You were dead,' Praeclarum stuttered hoarsely, and the man looked at her as if from a long, long way away.

'That was a surprise,' he said and offered a bloody grin. 'No eagles, though.' He walked on, cradling the sword until he found a place to sit. Someone gave him water and Praeclarum brought more and knelt, sponging him; he did not acknowledge it was happening.

'Don't waste that,' growled a voice, and suddenly Dog was there, swords dangling loosely from either hand, his death-face dripping with mud and sweat and blood.

'He's not dead,' Praeclarum snapped back, 'but he isn't unhurt either. Needs cleaning – that lance went right through and probably had all sorts of shit on it.'

Dog simply took up the pitcher she had brought and drank deeply, then handed it back.

'They are coming again!' bellowed Manius and had to burst his throat to be heard above the risen wind now; the sand stung and lashed. A rider lurched out of a haze which had turned sickly yellow like the eyes of a mad wolf. He came so fast that Ugo had no time to swing, was hit by the shoulder of the beast and flung sideways – the horseman plunged on towards Dog, who had just stuck his swords into the ground to drink. He stepped back and flung his arms out.

'Come ahead,' he roared.

The wind caught his words with an exultant shriek, whirled them up and away into oblivion; the horseman clattered up, stabbing his lance at the disarmed Dog, and people yelled and scattered. There was a growling sound, a great puff of shrouding dust.

When it cleared, Dog, horse and rider had all vanished.

Chapter Fifteen

The wind seemed to take a deep breath and then screamed like a burning cat – Drust felt his feet slide and fought for balance as the stinging scour of grit turned into a vicious rake of stones. He could not hide from it, could not walk in it, could not even crawl in it…

Something gripped his ankle and pulled. A voice bawled meaningless words, whipped away by the mad wind, then he felt his feet go out from under him and there was a moment of gibbering panic, when he thought the little hook-men of Dis Pater were hauling him down and down, to meet the hammer…

There was a moment of weightlessness, a strange sensation of floating – then he landed with a thump that drove the air from his lungs.

Gasping, he rolled over and crawled up, hearing the wind and seeing billowing dust like smoke, but as if it was far away. He bumped into something soft and recoiled from it, feeling a sticky wetness.

'Horse,' said a voice and then sparks flew. Dog blew life into the charcoal cloth, fed it to something on a stick – a torch – and light flared, turning the swirl of zephyred dust to a dance of gold. Drust looked up, stunned, at where the world howled; we are down in a hole in the ground, he thought dazedly…

'Horse broke its neck falling,' Dog declared with a wondrous regret. 'That was Mars Ultor, right there. Crushed the breath out of the rider – that was Fortuna. I called on them and they answered.'

'Where… are we?'

'Cellar,' Dog declared, and now Drust could see the long space, the trestle table, the ancient boxes and barrels and webbed sconces with old torches. The rotted stone floor of the courtyard had given way under the weight of those above – the horse and rider had finally broken it…

Dog walked to where other torches were sconced on walls, touching one after another into life. The light grew brilliant and danced flickering shadows in the wind, lighting up a table set with dishes and cups and bench seats. Above, the wind fingered the fallen-in roof and howled frustration and dust at not being able to do more.

Drust felt weak and trembling at what had happened to him; he had felt a lick of it once or twice before, but nothing like that, like being possessed by Hercules or even Mars Ultor himself. Something slithered from above and a body crashed down, followed by another, as one by one the others came down the hole. Last to arrive was Mule, who threw Kisa in and then dragged the Empress after him, like a cat on a string.

'Just in time,' he growled, looking up. 'I have seen that stuff before and it is not pleasant – it is now taking the sand and using it to scour everything. It will flay anyone not in shelter. That's how all the mud walls look as if they've been melted in a forge.'

Ugo made the horn sign against evil and Kisa, wiping blood from his lacerated face, whimpered unintelligible prayers. Mouse slipped on his way down the rubble heap and growled in disgust at landing in the dead horse's last voidings.

'Why me? Out of all of you, why is it me who falls in shite?'

277

'Better luck in falling than him,' Dog pointed out, nodding to the dead horseman trapped under the beast; his head was facing back over his own shoulders with an expression of agonised astonishment.

'How long will it last?'

The voice was hoarse but still haughty, as the Empress tested the strength of a bench and risked it, perching like a bird.

'An hour or two. A day – the gods above and below know,' Mule replied. 'Last time I was in one was up near Palmyra; it lasted a week.'

'Then we will all be dead,' she replied. 'Of starvation and lack of water.'

Mouse looked amazed. 'There is an entire horse here – and back there, unless I am mistaken, is a well. Maybe there is even wine – that lasts forever if the amphora is plugged sensibly with wax.'

'Well – the horse will last you for a day,' Quintus spat back, grinning. 'The rest of us will wait – and then eat you.'

'Here is your escape and reward,' the Empress persisted with a sneer, though her voice shook. 'No glory here.'

There was no answer to it, for it was so completely what everyone had been thinking that they were stunned to silence.

'Well,' Drust said. 'It seems the bad cess of your life has trapped us all here.'

He walked two paces forward and she leaned back despite herself. Drust stopped, looking into the deep brown of her eyes; they were flecked with gold, he saw. She had never been a beauty but she was Julia Aquilia, daughter of a consul and once an Empress of Rome. He felt a crushing weariness.

'I never meant you harm, lady.'

'I will see you killed,' she said softly, her eyes level and hard.

There was a loud crack and a crunch; they scattered away like water from a plunging stone. Another followed, and another. There was a pause while the dust swirled, and then a man yelled, staggering blindly.

'Welcome to our hall,' Ugo growled and struck him in the face so that he fell back; the iron stink of blood washed out, and suddenly everyone was moving.

There were only two enemy left and one of them went down under Mouse's blows, the big man snarling like a rabid dog as he did it. The last backed up against the far wall, a curved sword in one hand and a sneer on his sweat-streaked, dust-grimed face.

Kag lurched at him and the man expertly blocked his strike; the counter almost took Kag's arm off and the man grabbed the Empress by one arm, sheared through the tether and dragged her back, further down the dim room.

He was cased in splint armour but had lost his fancy helmet in the fall; Ugo leaned on his axe and picked it up and studied it with an expert gaze. It was silvered and bronzed and had a veil of metal rings, hinged metal lappets and a noseguard with a stylised Ahura-Mazda, the wings spreading out like eyebrows.

'There's fancy,' he said and tossed it casually to one side with a clatter.

'Come forward,' Dog said softly. 'There is no escape that way – we have looked and the stairway is blocked.'

'I am Borzin,' the man said defiantly. '*Stor bezashk* of the Aswaran. If you value this woman, throw down your weapons.'

'No,' Drust said. 'I do not care for that plan, so here is another. We will wait and kill every one of your men who stumbles down that hole in the roof. There will not be many, for this is a storm I have heard of – you will know better what it does. It will last for days and anyone not down here is dead.'

'Most of those down here are already dead,' Borzin snarled back. 'The rest will be when they come at me. I can last as long as you, Roman – and more men will come to find me. Messengers have been sent...'

Kag shook his head. 'No one will find you. Your messengers will die.'

'He sounds important,' Mule argued. 'Maybe they will come looking for him.'

'He is a *Stor bezashk* of the Aswaran,' Kisa offered. 'Which is an animal doctor for the fancy horse units.'

'A horse doctor?' Quintus demanded and flung back his head to laugh. The Persian growled angrily, but did nothing rash, which Drust found disappointing; the man was backed up into a narrow place and he clutched the woman close to him like a shield. He was also between the well and everyone else.

'It is a title, no more,' Kisa explained. 'He commands this unit.'

'He commands fuck all,' Dog said.

'Wait,' said the Empress, looking desperately from one to the other. 'Think. It may need all of us to get out of here.'

That brought everyone up short and they looked at the hole in the roof, which Drust now had to admit was easier falling down than climbing up; even standing on Mouse's shoulders, he thought, I could not reach the crumbled lip.

'True,' said Stercorinus. 'The more you kill, the harder it gets.'

He was whey-faced and slumped, slathered still with blood and sand and cradling the blade; Praeclarum was tearing strips off her own tunic to bind one side of him with, but each new one flushed with scarlet eventually.

'Have you a plan, woman?' Dog demanded, looking at the Empress.

She nodded eagerly and pointed to the table.

'Take that and lay it up as a ramp. Then we can get out whenever we like – though I would wait until the storm is over.'

'Then do it.'

'We could use your strength, Persian,' Drust said, looking at the heft of the table. 'Also, we will have to move the bales on it...'

'You are treacherous,' Borzin snarled, though everyone saw him wipe his dry mouth. 'You have two of the biggest men I have seen.'

Drust shrugged; Dog laughed. Then Mouse and Ugo and Kag worked swiftly, lifting the mouldered bundles and bales while others watched Borzin carefully. A bale withered away in Mouse's hand, spilling the blackened contents, and Manius pounced like a striking serpent, rubbed one of the objects on his filthy sleeve and then held it up, turning it this way and that.

'Silver,' he said and they all peered. It was a small bowl, beautifully chased with dancing figures.

'A votive object,' Kisa noted expertly.

'Silver gilt,' Kag declared with disgust, taking the chance to pick one up. 'Cheap stuff.'

'Tawdry,' the Empress agreed. 'Like all your dreams of riches.'

'Enough on that,' Quintus spat, and the Empress smiled a sneer at him, then turned to Drust.

'This is all of your life and beyond,' she went on. 'Even the Elysian Fields will be a patch of waste ground in Pluto for you. Do as this Borzin says – throw down your weapons and surrender.'

'You think that favours you, woman?' Dog answered dryly. 'What do you think the Persians will do with you? You are no better with them than the Empire.'

'The Empire sold me,' she spat back bitterly. 'My husband's mother – the one you dragged by the heels – sold me to prevent him living with me ever again. That's how I ended up in the hands of Farnah-vant.'

'You didn't seem to mind those hands much,' Praeclarum declared, straightening from Stercorinus. 'You went to him with handmaidens, slaves like yourself. You tried to kill them all – one is buried in a shallow grave and one is poppy-mad in the clutch of Shayk Amjot. What did they do – get in the way? Remind you that you were a Roman and a Vestal, which would be inconvenient? You are the abomination here, lady. You defile the name of Empress and even of woman.'

'Slave,' she answered viciously. 'A foul little slave, no matter what these others try to make you. All of you are slaves, born and bred, and nothing will ever change that. They want me back and sent you – think on that.'

'You think on it,' Dog said. 'They don't want you back to feed sweetcakes and good wine in the bosom of your loving family. They will pay to put you in a hole where you can explain to Vesta why you did what you did.'

She did not answer and they sweated in the wind-tossed dust to crack the front legs off the table and raise it up with everyone working at it. Slowly, slowly, it wavered up until, at last, the stumps of the broken-off legs hooked into the hole's rim; dust sifted down like a waterfall and Drust wondered how solid the rim was. The table was now a steep and smooth incline; above it the wind mourned for the ones it could not reach.

After that, they stripped the bodies of anything useful, which was just about everything. Praeclarum caught Drust's eye when he looked at Stercorinus, and they moved quietly away from the others, head to head.

'His god lied,' she said flatly, and Drust felt the weight of it; he hadn't known the man long but they had already shared more than two lifetimes, it seemed. He thought of Sib and did not want to lose yet another.

'Does he say so?'

She shook her head. 'All he will say is that part of it was being watched by a powerful woman, a queen or greater. With eagles crying above. The spear took him by surprise.'

'He is not dead yet,' he said, but Praeclarum persisted.

'If I fed him the soup,' she whispered, 'you would smell it in half-a-candle.'

There was nothing more to be said, but Kag knew as soon as Drust looked at him and nodded imperceptibly. Everyone shared out what they had taken from the dead, according to their needs, and Dog looked across at Borzin, still crouched in the half-dark with the woman held by one arm.

'Come out and fight, horse doctor,' he said. 'I want the rest of that fancy armour.'

Borzin said nothing and everyone sank into themselves, listening to the wind rising to an eldritch howl, watching the dust and grit swirl into the hole and then get scooped out again.

Then suddenly Mouse gave a bellow, and they all turned in time to see the woman leap up onto the table-ramp, scrabbling for purchase – and getting it. Behind her, a bewildered Borzin leaped up, his blade ready – but he dared not come closer. She was almost at the lip when Mule grabbed the trailing edge of her tattered skirts and hauled her up short.

The others sprang to help; the Empress lashed out a foot and took Mule full in the face, so that he sprang blood and fell back with a yelp, thumping into the dead horse and rolling away;

his loud howls drowned the final rat-scrabble of the Empress clawing out of the hole.

Then she was gone, leaving only curses. Mule staggered up, holding his bloody nose with one hand. Quintus roared out a curse, and Kag flung his new helmet down in frustration.

Then there was a sudden flurry that brought all heads round in time to see Borzin, curved sword drawn and a feral snarl on his lips. He had lost the protection of the woman and now there was only one option for him – fight his way out.

'I'll have that war hat back, slave,' he said to Kag, who turned a cold, hard glare on him. His growl was deep in the back of his throat, but Dog laid a hand across his chest. Kisa was yelping and whimpering like a kicked pup until Praeclarum slapped him hard once or twice; eventually he shook himself, then fell on his knees and moaned.

'Mine,' Dog said.

Borzin came forward, his red-rimmed eyes narrow as an angry boar and the curved sword flicking this way and that, like the taunting tongue of a hunting snake. He had no way out other than up the same ramp and too many enemies to make that feasible, so Drust was struck by his courage. He is more than the title 'horse doctor' would suggest, he thought…

Borzin struck and Dog parried it, the blades rang like bells and sparks flew; there was hardly room for dancing and ducking, so it gave the advantage to the man with the armour. He crouched and came in like a boar, low and hard, with that single curved tooth slashing up. Dog blocked two more blows and then Borzin hooked the *gladius* out of his hand; everyone watched it spiral off.

No one had seen such a thing before and hands went to mouths, throats clogged. Dog was the only one unconcerned, his death-face grinning in savage triumph as if he had already won. He reached down and flicked out the knife from his boot as Borzin slashed, missing and hitting one of the mouldy bales, old dust flying. He did it again and again, slashing and howling while Dog grinned his skull-grin and did not seem to move much — but each sway, every lean made the curved sword cut air.

Once Kag started forward and Dog snarled at him, never taking his eyes off the Persian.

'Stay back, or I will cut your heart out.'

Then he turned back to Borzin, who stood like a sacrifice bull, heaving in breath, the sword wavering in his grip and his head swinging from side to side.

'This is the ring, horse doctor,' he said, twisting his skull into a leering grin. 'This is the *harena*, our place, the place of Dis and Mars Ultor. We and the gods live here and heathen fucks like you have no place in it other than to kneel and receive the iron.'

This is no more a fighting ring than I can fart gold, Drust wanted to shout, but the air was thick with strangeness, the shadows danced and grunted, the wind shrieked like a crowd demanding blood.

The end came swiftly, it seemed, after so long a fight. Borzin was big and armoured thickly, a weight that made him launch himself, feeling his strength wane. He snarled out a flurry of blows, and Dog made one shoulder dip, took one step and flicked out his arm.

Borzin felt it go in, under the armour, into the armpit. He was still staring disbelief when Dog plucked the curved sword from Stercorinus's weak grasp and brought it down like a scythe of light.

It was a poor stroke. It should have taken Borzin in the forehead, splitting his head down through his face. Instead, it missed, carved his ear, smashed his shoulder blade and went on through the splinted metal and leather slantwise down his chest, where it stuck. His screaming fall bent it almost double and Dog let it go.

There was a moment of ragged breathing and moaning wind, then Dog moved unsteadily to sit. Drust felt as light as the corpses in the corner.

'Good stroke,' Stercorinus growled hoarsely, 'but it is polite to ask before you borrow. Give me my sword back.'

Outside, the wind screeched laughter like the Fates gone mad.

Chapter Sixteen

They crawled out on the second day, trembling and fetid, to find the world altered beyond all recognition – moved from here to there and back again. The old streets they had come up were gone, buried under dust – yet others had been exposed, new walls melted by the rake of a wind which had picked up fist-sized rocks. They shuffled down them, exclaiming when they saw a splintered horse leg and a human arm, though the very armour on it was frayed and the hand flayed to ruin.

Kag found a camel alive, standing near where it had allowed itself to be buried and shielded from the wind and stones. That made him shout and beam with delight, as if he had found his own da in the ruins. It even had the pack, lopsided but intact, and they fell on the water and food.

'This is why the folk of this place prize such beasts,' Mule declared proudly, as if he had raised it himself.

'Does it have a name?' Quintus demanded sarcastically. 'If it does – is it the one camel-name you remember?'

Mule frowned over it for a while, then brightened.

'It does have a name. Fortuna's Blessed.'

He went off laughing and the camel trailed behind him like an obedient dog. Manius shook his shaggy head and watched it admiringly.

'Horses die, men die – but that hairy hunchback simply buries its snout in the sand and lets such winds blow until they crack their throats.'

Horses had died, that was clear, Drust saw. Men, too – they found some of them half buried and dragged them up, stripping off their ring-coats and taking their weapons. It was a grisly task – some of them had no faces and their equipment seemed to have been ravaged by some clawed beasts. But they still managed to get themselves better equipment than before – and were sure that not one of the pursuing warriors had survived.

'There was a long hundred of them at least,' Mouse marvelled and shook his head. 'The wrath of Fei-lan is fierce.'

It took some time to find out that Fei-lan was a god of wind from further east than anyone had heard of, and through all the talk Kag nodded absently and stared across the ravaged waste. Finally, he looked at Drust. If you are leaving tracks, Drust thought...

People moved back and forth, awed and searching for anything that might be useful. Drust listened with only half an ear, searching for signs of the Empress, with Praeclarum at his side. Perhaps, like the camel, she had burrowed into the ground, he thought. He could not believe she had gone far.

The wind had been the wrath of Aquilo, or Boreas, or Jupiter, or Mars Ultor, that was certain, but now it was as if it had never been. Drust looked at the peaks around him, sharply cut against the cloud-wisped blue sky on a diamond-bright day, a day like clean linen.

The horizon was far away and Drust recalled how this was only a few footsteps into the fabled trade routes east, the ones that trailed great caravans of rich spice, fine silks, jade, gold. It was hard to believe; there seemed no road at all, only the merest thread shrouded with new dust. He squinted, looking for the spice trains, the dancers and pilgrims, the jugglers and travellers. There was nothing but an endless ochre dusted thinly with green stretching east and west, lonely and bare as a carcass picked by crows.

'What do we do now?' Kisa asked plaintively and Kag blew out his cheeks.

'Be mannered, be efficient, salute frequently and have a plan to kill everyone we meet.'

Drust turned from the weak laughter to ask Dog which peak they were heading for – and saw the figure, stumbling this way and that, falling over and getting up again, reeling with no direction. There was a strange mewling that unnerved everyone, even when they saw where it came from.

'Jupiter's cock…' Quintus cried out and everyone saw the figure stumble and turn, head to one side to listen, tilted slightly to the sky.

The skin was flayed from one side of her face, the beautiful eyes were now gaping pits, and her lips were scoured off so that she opened and closed her mouth like a fish. The only sounds that came out were meaningless whines, croaks and rasps, for the flaying wind had stolen even her voice, so all you could hear in her throat was the blood. She huddled in darkness, her mind a bowl scoured out. She was querulous and afraid and tears of blood tracked through the layered dust.

'The Empress Julia Aquilia,' Dog said, and no one cared for the cruel leer in his voice. 'No relation to any of the other Severan Julias save by marriage and a shared viciousness. No friend of the gods of Rome, who have decided to stop her mouth on the secret name of the City.'

'Friends,' Drust said softly, ignoring Dog. She knew his voice, shrank away from it and moaned, flapping her hands; the fingers on her left hand were bloody stumps with bone showing like new splintered wood. Dog stood and watched as they captured her as they would an abandoned dog, wrapping her up like a child.

'Should leave her,' Mouse said. 'She cannot speak the secret word of the City now, can she?'

Praeclarum looked knives at him. 'She can write,' she answered simply, and left Mouse frowning.

They went on, upwards still to where the air was cool and you could taste wet in it. Above, the peak brooded down on them like an accusation.

'White Tiger Mountain,' Dog said on one of their rest halts – frequent now because of the Empress and Stercorinus, who no longer walked upright cradling his sword; he crept in a hunch, one arm across his body as if to keep people from seeing the wound, the sword trailed behind him, scouring a groove, bumping over stones.

Praeclarum had bound the Empress's eyes out of kindness, but she had a face like half a skull made of tight dried flesh – Manius looked her over on one rest stop and gave a mirthless laugh.

'She looks like she was made from bits of Dog and me,' he growled, but only Dog laughed. The Empress made sounds, was eyeless and incoherent, and Praeclarum had cropped her head because there were parts on it where the hair had been scoured to bloody scalp. She went where she was bid, without demurring, ate what was thrust in her hand, and it seemed to Drust that all her hate and hubris had been scraped out of her, by whose god he did not know. Everyone saw the terrible price for it, all the same; everything that had made her was gone.

At one halt, Dog doubted she could remember the secret name of the City, let alone write it out if tasked.

'You want to cut her throat, then?' Kag answered, chewing and drinking sour wine. 'I mean – we still get the reward if she is dead, right?'

Dog said nothing, which told everything, so Kag spat out grit from the bread and swilled the wine round his mouth. 'There's your answer then. We carry her if necessary.'

'Where to?' Drust demanded of Dog, who looked up at the peak in answer; Drust had had enough of that.

'Not good enough. If you die, I need to know how to get everyone else to safety.'

Dog looked at him and grinned. 'If I die it will be too late for safety.'

'This is not the time to test me, Dog,' Drust answered levelly, and eventually Dog shrugged.

'There is a temple,' he said, scratching in the dust. 'Somewhere up ahead. We enter it from here and come out on the other side of the mountain. It is the only way through the mountains here – and the only way to avoid the Red Serpent, which lies to the west and ends at these mountains, which are as good a barrier as the Wall itself.'

'A temple,' Quintus repeated. 'To what gods?'

'Does it matter?' Dog answered. 'Are we going to make offerings?'

'It might be advisable,' Mouse put in. 'Can't have too much holy help – are you done with that bread?'

'The only muscle you have left is in your jaw,' Dog growled at him and threw the bread. Mouse caught it and looked aggrieved, but he ate it.

'Where is this temple?' Drust demanded, and Dog waved airily.

'Up there somewhere.'

'That's it?' Kag spat back. 'Up there? That's all you have?'

'It's a temple,' Dog growled, half rising. 'What more do you need? How many fucking temples do you think there are up there?'

'One less than what we need,' said Kag, getting to his feet. 'I do not like having been dragged here, having had to do what had to be done, just to be told the arse who said he knew the way is a face-fucked *Stupidus*.'

Dog's growl was incoherent and he was springing when Drust rose up and banged him in a short, sharp shoulder charge; Dog went sideways and sprawled in the dust, his fancy new helmet spilling and rolling. He got up, pig-eyed, to find Drust pointing a *gladius* at him.

'Like I said, Dog. Don't test me.'

Dog got up, snatched his helmet and shook the grit out of it, then put it back on. By that time he had found a grin as well.

'The temple will be there when we find it,' he said.

Two days later, they still hadn't found it, and Manius had loped back in from their back trail to announce that he had seen riders. Kag flung up his hands.

'Don't these fucks give up?'

'It is the blue-stone people all over again,' Ugo growled, then looked at Dog. 'Tell me this temple has nothing to do with blue stones or fire-starers, Dog.'

'All I know of it,' Dog answered, 'is that it has a door on this side and a door on the other side.'

All I know is, Drust thought wearily, that there is no sign of as much as a single stone of it.

–

Drust lay in the dust and peered through the scrub. It was the last hillock on the flat before the trail wound down behind him to the gorge and the wooden bridge that crossed it; the hill was no more than a nub beaten down by the wind and the hissing scythes of dust.

There were grander cousins soaring all round, their flanks treacherous with scree and seemingly the bones of the world, stripped down to the colour of old cream – yet, between them, a tumble of eager water spilled and danced. This was a blasted place and now Drust knew why it was called the Land of No Return.

The river had come from the north, down from the White Tiger, then turned west and scoured a way across their path. It was a good arrow-shot wide and deep enough to hide a Subura tenement, the steep slopes dazzling with a green that hid the ankle-breaking rocks and crevices. Kisa said it went on west to spill out onto the plain at the foot of the Wall, where engineers had made a ditch of it, all the way to the Hyrcanian Ocean.

The same engineers, he said – the Divine Iskandr's men, perhaps – had made the fortress here, which was now no more than a litter of broken walls that had guarded a stone bridge, long since tumbled into the gorge.

There was a wooden one now, an affair of crude, twisted beams and split planks that didn't look much younger. It was the only way to cross the river without travelling east and then north to where it was more easily fordable – or there was another bridge.

They had staggered up the trail and over the bridge, driven by the promise that this was the last best hope of fighting off their pursuers; the hard pull of it had all but ended Stercorinus – Mule and Mouse had to take an arm each and haul him. Praeclarum did the same for the Empress and had tethered her to one wrist to lead her like a goat. At the last, the Empress had lost her strength and Ugo carried her. On the far side of the bridge, they took time to hang their heads and pant, take in water, sort out weapons.

And cut the bridge – Drust screwed his head round to where the rhythmic thud of the axe bounced. He did not like the idea of big Ugo making a mistake and cutting through the last of the supports before he and Mule got back across.

Mule squinted and muttered quietly in his ear. 'A hundred. More, perhaps.'

Drust cursed. They were all better served with weapons and armour than they'd ever been – even decent robes and boots – but none of that would help them against a hundred Persian horsemen, all bows and longswords and, no doubt, orders that would get them flayed if they came back empty-handed.

A hundred men, Drust thought. More, perhaps – someone really wants us dead as much as they want the Empress. It will be for making that fortress burn as much as for the Empress fastened to Praeclarum. He wondered who would pay more – and ruthlessly quelled that thought. Handing her to the new Persians of Ardashir, King of Kings, would mean they'd never be able to go home.

'Time,' Mule said suddenly, and Drust jerked away from thinking, slithered backwards below the crest until he could stand, then levered himself up. Muscles screamed and he even felt the catch of pain in his ribs from where the legionary had slapped him in the *harena* at Dura. So long ago, he thought, that it seems almost a dream. A flash of lightning in a summer cloud; a flickering lamp, a phantom and a dream, he thought, and remembered Bashto.

They trotted back across the bridge, doubled-up awkwardly on the camel Mule called Blessed and would not give up. The bridge seemed disappointingly solid and Drust said as much to Ugo when he slid off the camel's back.

The big German could not answer for trying to breathe and was thumbing the edge of his axe mournfully. 'This business will ruin the edge,' he muttered.

'It has to have an edge to be ruined,' Kag answered, and Mouse offered to take over, but Ugo would not place the weapon in any hands but his own.

Everyone had something to do, with steel or leather. Stercorinus sat on a stone with his battered sword across his knees. He was covered in dust like everyone else, but that did not account for all the grey in his face – nor all the grim, Drust thought.

Ugo honed the edge of his long axe with a whetstone the length of his finger and fastened round his neck like an amulet; there was little of it left. Then he rolled his neck muscles and struck chips from the wood, squinted at the cut like a bird with a snail; Drust wanted to tell him to hurry, that they were close, but the tension was braided enough.

Manius and Quintus had bows and a double handful of shafts culled from the dead at Iron Blade. Quintus had not shot in a long time and Kag was curious to see if he still could – no one doubted the skill of Manius, and yet again Drust watched the lean *mavro* from the deep desert of Numidia and wondered if he had shot Sib.

Kag and Praeclarum offered sharp comments and nudging laughs which the two bowmen ignored; it was all whistling at fear, after all, and even the blind Empress sensed it, gibing against her tether and whimpering like a kitten.

'Can we hurry this?' Drust demanded, finally fretted too far and hearing Ugo stop yet again.

Ugo did not speak, just wiped the sweat from his face, took out the whetstone and grated it down the edge.

'Has to be just right and no more,' he pointed out.

'Just cut the last timbers and go,' Praeclarum persisted. 'Or are we fighting and dying here?'

'They will go east and maybe even have to go north a way,' Dog answered gently. 'Those horses are not the bow-nosed little ponies from the Grass Sea – they are heavy horses for iron men and so it will take them time. Yet, if we let them, they will be back hagging us in a day, perhaps two.'

'You know of another crossing then?' Kisa asked querulously.

'This river will grow narrower and scour less deep the further east and north you go. Eventually these Persians will find a place that will not risk too many hooves.'

'We will not hold the bridge long,' Kisa pointed, desperate with apprehension now, 'with two bows. They will stand back and shoot us to ruin, then ride down those who are left.'

Manius waved his curved bow and grinned darkly. 'They have to ride across the bridge to get to us – and it is a long shot to send an arrow from there to here with any accuracy. I look forward to seeing who can do it.'

Mouse patted the little Jew soothingly. 'Stand behind me, if you like. Is there anything left to eat?'

'It is a madness,' Kisa said pleadingly to Drust. 'There is no point to everyone dying. How do we snatch riches from that?'

'Matters are said to a man a thousand times a day. If he is not persuaded, then he is blameless.'

Stercorinus's voice was a harsh shadow of what it had been and everyone looked at him, knowing this was his moment. He got up with a grunt and Kag clasped him wrist to wrist. As if he was headed off to the next *taberna* down the street, Drust thought, and watched as Quintus and Mule carefully dressed him in helmet and studs and metal. In the end Stercorinus blew out his cream-pale cheeks and nodded.

He wore Dog's fancy helmet, carried a round shield, a solid affair of wood and leather and metal boss, marked with a scarred picture of a winged lion on the outer leather. He wore a ring-coat but the padding for it was a weight too far, so he had left it off. He walked stiffly and the sweat stood on him, while the eyes which rested briefly on Drust were bird-bright with fever.

Drust moved to him and stuck out his hand, palm down to show the knuckles. One by one they all came; Kisa crept closer, just starting to see what was happening here, but stayed beyond the circle of them.

'Brothers of the Sands,' Drust said. 'Forged in a ring.'

'Brothers of the Sands,' they echoed. 'Forged in a ring.'

Everyone growled agreement and Dog flung back his death-face to the blank sky and howled.

'I was born a slave, thrown away as a slave, rescued as a slave and used as a slave,' Stercorinus said hoarsely. 'The Temple of Bel made me an executioner for those found guilty of trans-gressions against the god and most of those were Christians.'

No one spoke, aware that this was a confession, a prayer, an epitaph. He bowed his head, looked at the curved sword. 'I killed a lot of Christians, until one day there were too many and my arm failed. I was told to take a hundred of them to Emesa, where the Romans wanted them, so I did, feeling proud to be in charge of men and camels so that I did not feel like a slave. Glad not to be judged for my lack of skill.

'When I got there, I saw the Christians were for the amphitheatre – the morning shows, which you know well. They took them and crucified them, upside down sometimes. A few they set on fire. The children they hung up by the heels so that starved wolves had to leap for their meal.'

He stopped again. 'I saw what I was then, a slave who killed slaves. I heard the god and I never returned to the Temple of

Bel. I did what I was told and offered myself to the *lanista* and he agreed, but after three fights he sold me. To you. And you made me free.'

He looked round them all; no one spoke. 'You asked me what god spoke to me, telling me where I would die. I do not know. I think it may have been Bel, or the god of the Christians. He told me I would find my death under the eyes of a powerful woman, listening to the call of eagles.'

He looked round at the high place, then smiled, turned and walked unsteadily off, limping out into the middle of the bridge towards a large pale stone placed there by Manius.

'What is he doing?' Kisa demanded, as Stercorinus stopped two paces back from the stone – a marker showing the range of archers shooting from the far side of the bridge; Drust hoped Manius had judged it right.

'What is he doing?' demanded Kisa in a higher pitch and no one bothered to answer him, for it was clear enough and you would think such a clever man would see it.

He was dying and making the death a good one, like Horatius One-Eye. They waited in a silence broken only by the steady thunk-chunk of Ugo's axe. When it stopped, the silence was broken once more, by the high, shrill cry of a hunting bird; they all looked up and then at each other while the black crucifix shape hung high up in the clear sky. It might have been an eagle, Drust thought, and his flesh goosed and chilled.

The riders came up, all dust-shroud and muted jingle, stopping when they saw a lone man in the middle of the bridge and then trotting forward a little, unshipping their little curved bows. Drust did not want to watch but could not look away as Stercorinus set his shield and crouched low behind it.

'We should run,' Kisa began, and Kag slapped him hard enough to make him jump.

'Quiet. A Brother of the Sand is sixing here.'

The leading rider moved another few paces and there was a flicker at the edge of Drust's vision as Quintus nocked, drew and released, all in the one breath. It hit the horse in the neck and sent it squealing and kicking. The rider went flying then hit the ground with a thump and a puff of dust. He did not get up for a long time.

'By the balls of Mars Ultor,' Kag said with wonder and admiration. One or two of the enemy, straining, shot arrows, but they were at the limit of their range and they plunked harmlessly short, or spiralled into the gorge. A lot of them shot at Stercorinus, but the shafts fell short an arm's length from the pale stone.

'Well marked, Manius,' Mouse said, nodding.

The riders milled, then one rode out and pulled his helmet off; they saw it was Bashto and Mule yelled out to him. Bashto raised one hand.

'There is no need to die here,' he shouted back, his voice a thin thread on the wind. 'Give up the woman. Let us discuss surrender.'

His voice was floated and faint. Drust looked at Manius and nodded, saw the dark smoke of the eyes and the feral gleam of his teeth.

'We do not have the food or water to take you all prisoner,' he shouted back. 'And this woman is a citizen of Rome. Go back home and do what you always do – fight each other.'

Even from a distance Drust could see Bashto's suffused face.

'These tribes here all hate each other,' he bellowed. 'But they say down with the Romans anyhow. Clear out, double quick, they say. And if Ardashir does not make you, his son Shapur will, or whoever comes after that. If it takes fifty times fifty hundred years they shall get rid of you all, all driven out of the desert and beyond. And then, yes, they will get back to fighting each other.'

'Do a Sib on him,' Drust said viciously and Manius winced at that, just as he shot. The arrow whipped out; Bashto screamed and fell off the horse, which bolted, but men ran to help him up and he rose, holding one cheek.

Manius turned a slow head, a stare that promised slower death. Drust kept his face in it, but it was like thrusting it too close to a fire.

'I should have asked Quintus,' he said eventually, and Manius swept the roasting stare away and stalked off.

'Are you trying to make an enemy of him?' Kag hissed in his ear. Drust wanted to tell him it was too late for all that, but was sure Kag knew it.

The riders got to the moment of charging, but slowly. First they tried darting runs to shoot arrows, galloping up, releasing a shaft and wheeling round to speed away, but everyone knew that was a trick for lighter men, not ones wearing all that armour and with horses whose fronts were covered in leather leaves and metal studs.

The first of those who did it, though, took everyone by surprise; released two arrows and then had to rein in and wheel away, unscathed, or plunge on to the bridge itself, where turning would be harder. One arrow hissed past Stercorinus, the second staggered him when it slammed into his shield.

The second one to attempt it had two arrows in his horse before he had released even one of his own, and Quintus claimed he had hit first; Manius said nothing, just nocked another shaft. It did not matter much since both arrows felled the horse in mid-run, pitching the rider between its ears so that he rolled over and over in a ball of dust before vanishing into the gorge with a despairing shriek.

'Get Stercorinus back,' Kisa said suddenly. 'There is no reason for him to die here.'

'Save his god,' Kag answered.

'He is dead already,' Drust added gently. 'The poison-fever is in him, so here he makes a good death and gives some time for others to escape.'

'A warrior in the *harena* knows this,' Dog growled. Kisa fell silent, gnawing a knuckle.

The Empress heard his voice and, like every time he spoke, it drove fear into her so that she started to keen. Drust was sure the noises were growing stronger and that perhaps her throat was beginning to work again. Whether she could order the sounds in her head was another matter.

He jerked his chin at Praeclarum, who took her tether and moved her away; the others began to move too, slowly, deliberately, shields slung and chivvying Blessed the camel with loud voices.

The riders saw them move up the trail – as they were supposed to – and there was a moment of dancing dust and argument. Drust turned once and saw Bashto, wearing a spiked helmet with bright blue cloth round it, pointing and yelling, though he could not hear the words.

He didn't need to hear what Bashto shouted. What was it Kag had said? A man with a head full of old times, when Persia was great and before Iskandr came to ruin it. That was Bashto's truth, right there. Then he realised it hadn't been Kag who had said it, but Manius.

The riders obeyed Bashto eagerly, lurching forward, banging one another to be first onto the bridge, which was made to take loaded camels. You could get two of them side by side, if they did not mind their big feet being crushed; horses managed it well enough, even with fat stirrups and metal men on them.

Quintus ran back, Manius close behind him, both nocking arrows. Out on the bridge, Stercorinus set himself behind his shield.

An arrow from Manius slammed into a rider and rocked him in the saddle, but his studded leather was too strong for it. Quintus shot a horse in the chest, but the armour there was tough too, though the horse balked and stopped, then reared.

The rider flew off, hit the railings with a splintering crash and went over with a falling shriek. The horse kicked and screamed, trying to turn, tangled the feet of the one next to it and sent it stumbling into the other side of the bridge. There was a crack and Drust thought the railings had broken completely, but a second arrow took the horse in the muzzle and it simply sank to its knees and trembled, blowing blood and making a thin, high wailing sound. It started to struggle to rise and could not.

The rider, caught like a fly in a web, panicked and started to scramble off, but Stercorinus moved forward, stepped daintily between the flailing legs of the dying horse and slashed him once, twice, and then split his skull.

'Ho,' said Kag softly, 'give that man the palm.'

'The bridge is blocked,' Kisa screamed, moving backwards and forwards. 'Stercorinus can escape. He does not have to die here if someone goes and tells him.'

No one answered and Drust felt Praeclarum's eyes. The inevitability of it all was like the falling wall in Asaak.

The riders only paused a moment to hear new, screamed orders, then flung themselves from their mounts. There was a long hundred of them at least, and even when some were left to hold the horses, there were enough to crowd onto the bridge and advance, shields up, long lances now long spears. The commander had ordered the rest of his force to wait, mounted, for Stercorinus to be killed and the horses butchered out of the way.

Stercorinus battered sword on shield, an invitation to fight and a small sound that bounced round the gorge. Now is when Bashto will feel unease, Drust thought. When he will wonder why one man stands there and yet no one he is buying time for is moving to escape, as it had seemed they were doing. The act which had launched men onto the bridge...

The first of the enemy reached the horses and scrambled over them; someone ended the dying animal's screams and Drust was almost sorry that man would die. They stumbled on the trailing hems of their long coats, slit for riding, and the first ones got close enough to start stabbing at Stercorinus, who fended them off with the shield and slashed wild ruin into their long shafts. One splintered and broke and Kag cheered.

There were more and more enemy crowding forward like water in the neck of a corked bottle, and Stercorinus, staggering and slashing, was almost at the end of what little strength he'd had, having to step back pace by reluctant pace.

Now, Drust thought, as Bashto imperiously waved his horsemen onto the bridge, walking casually up behind the mass of men on foot, all blocked by that one small figure.

Now.

Now.

NOW.

There was a crack and a lurch that stopped all breathing, that seemed to suck all sound. Into it, bright as triumph, came the single, high-pierced shriek of the circling bird; no one now doubted it was an eagle.

Bashto got to it too late. Drust saw his mouth open with horror, trying to form words, orders, sense, when there was another crack, a slight hissing rumble. The half-axed supports collapsed under the weight, the bridge fell in a long tumble of timbers, a whirl of arms and legs and despairing shrieks.

Dust swaddled where the bridge had been, drifting slowly away in a sift of grey to reveal a few timbers on either side, splintered white as new bone. Below, the river sucked up the blood of scattered dead; the dust settled on them like a shroud.

On the far side, a knot of horsemen who had not been involved danced to control their frantic mounts.

'Mark Stercorinus as six,' said Drust wearily, turning away.

Chapter Seventeen

'It will be Iskandr,' Kag said with relish, studying the half-buried little statue. 'Look – that's an old Greek helm he has there. I bet he had a sword or a spear in the other hand, before it broke – or was stole away from him.'

Kisa frowned at it and ran one hand through the wet of his hair.

'Why is he holding a torch in his one hand?'

'Ah,' said Quintus, curdling his brow. 'You would need such a light if you were going to a dark place. Like a temple.'

'Small lad, Iskandr then?' Mule asked pensively. 'With three heads?'

There was a movement off to one side and everyone tensed, weapons up; Manius slid out like a tendril of the mist and moved through the dripping ranks to Drust's side, where he took a knee and wiped his face.

'A dwelling, small, with smoke coming from it. No dog, one cart. Some chickens.'

Drust thought and blinked rain from his eyelids. It had been a blessing, that rain, and they had revelled in it – Quintus and Ugo had stripped naked and danced in it like *bacchae*, to the cheers and laughing of the others. Even the Empress raised her bandaged, ruined face to it as if it was balm.

That was good for a day, but it wasn't a downpour, just a sifting, fine as baby hair, out of a mist that clung to everything and did not want to stop. In the end, they started to curse the drip and soak of it.

They were higher in the mountains now, awed by the strange tints and colours – emerald green, grey, ochre, pink – heading up a valley green with juniper and thick with wild grapes, pears and hawthorns, which made the green part feel more like Apulia. Dog was beaming at the statue, for all that it was bird-slimed, pocked with age and might have been anything; beyond it would be more stones, he said, making it clear where the temple would be.

'Who wants to live up here?' demanded Kag, and Mule wiped rain from his face and spat.

'People who skulk and hunt,' he growled – he was aggrieved because Blessed was dead, killed by an arrow fired from the higher rocks. It had unnerved everyone and no one could be sure whether it had been aimed at the beast or just missed another target. Manius swore he had seen the shooter scampering off and that he had nicked him with a shot of his own; he went off to track the blood, but the rain had made that hope fade quickly.

'Let's go,' Mule urged. 'I want that bowman.'

Privately, Drust thought the camel's death the best blessing it would get; its pads were cutting up on the poor ground and there was altogether too much wet for it. All it meant to him and the others was that, yet again, they had to carry what they could and abandon the rest.

Not to Mule, all the same. He was steaming with the heat of his revenge.

Which is, at least, one way to keep a foot travelling in front of the other, Drust thought. The truth was in the weary stumbling, the savage glares folk gave Dog, the way Drust could not look Manius in the eye. All the old breed, he saw, are shackled by their Brotherhood, but the chains of it were straining. He remembered them after the failed assault on the fire temple, how they had snarled at each other like a frustrated dog pack for a day – then braided back together.

'Well,' Kag grunted, shaking drips off the noseguard of his helmet, 'a place with a roof is surely better than sitting in the rain telling lies about this boy and his lost spear.'

Manius uncoiled, glanced at the statue and grunted.

'That boy has tits,' he said casually. 'You should read the scratchings under the vines at the feet, Jew. Might tell you who it is.'

He went sliding off into the rain, leaving everyone squinting – the Greek tunic and hunting boots had thrown them and the misshapen head had been ravaged so that most of it was missing. Kisa went to work, grubbing in the muddy earth, scraping it out, pulling up clinging vines.

'She Who Works Her Will,' he read out in Greek. 'Crone, Maiden and Mother.'

The Empress gave a low moan, which made everyone else jerk. 'She Who Works Her Will. Hekáte,' she said in a voice like a broken file on a rough rock. 'Diana Trivia…'

Like nails on a slate… Drust felt the wind rush through his head. Crone, Maiden and Mother… He peered, wiping rainwater from his face, seeing now that there had once been three faces, not one.

'She speaks,' Kag said softly, pointedly.

'Is this Hekáte not a guardian of the crossroads?' Quintus asked lightly, and Dog agreed.

'Huntress, Queen, Moon, that's Diana…'

'Goddess of the night, of ghosts and dangerous oracles,' Kisa said. 'Of divination from the dead – *necromantia*, as Origen of Alexandria has it…'

Almost at each word the Empress moaned and growled and shook her head, which wasn't pleasant.

'Bind your mouth,' Ugo growled at Kisa.

'I preferred it when she was mute,' Mouse added, but Kisa gave a half-smile and glanced from one to the other.

'Not only can she speak, but her mind is not scraped clean after all.'

'Which makes her worthwhile again,' Dog flung in cheerfully and hefted his swords. 'Onwards, brothers…'

There were mutters about him and the Empress and the rain – and then the vicious insects which appeared when the rain stopped and heat came back,; the wet earth steamed with a feral breath, adding to their discontent and Drust felt their eyes, felt the dark looks they shot him. Gods-cursed, he fancied them saying, and all of us caught up in it.

Suck it down, he snarled silently back at them. Swallow it like bitter wine, for you die if you do and die if you don't…

'Are you well?' Praeclarum asked, falling in beside him. 'You have a face like that dead camel.'

He laughed despite himself and was lifted by it and her. They went on up the valley, following the others. They saw nothing save some little sheep, nub-horned like goats and thick with fleeces that made them look like bracken haystacks that had learned to walk.

The villa was a tumble of stones and timbers in the rough shape of four walls, the roof turfed and allowed to grow out as shaggy as the sheep. There was a sagging outbuilding or two, chickens and no dog, as Manius had said, but he had omitted the slow curve of the shallow stream – and what was in it.

'Dead sheep,' Mouse declared when Quintus cried out with delight and pointed. No one who had the stink in the back of their throat could disagree, but Quintus turned on him and spat with disgust.

'You would miss riches in a treasure room,' he growled back, and then everyone peered and saw the fleeces, just under the shallow run of the stream, pegged out. Everyone frowned at Quintus's delight.

'Not a dead sheep, then,' Dog said wryly, 'but a sodden skin.'

'Gold,' Kisa said, and Quintus clapped his hands together and pointed as if he had made a killing point in a Senate debate.

'They do this across the ocean, where I come from,' Kisa went on, as Quintus splashed into the water to wrench one free. 'My people were famed for it, so much so that Apollonius Rhodius told of a band of Greeks led by King Jason who came to the land to steal the wealth they made.'

Quintus dragged the dripping thing back and heaved it onto the bank where it leaked and smelled. Then they looked more closely at the sharp glints of light which caught the eye. It was gold – at least some of it – caught as grains in the fat-rich fleece as it washed down from the mountains above. Now they saw six or seven such fleeces pegged out and went splashing after them, shouting out.

'These sheep farmers herd gold too,' Quintus declared triumphantly. 'Now you know why they live up here.'

'Beware the dog,' Drust called out and men cursed, spun round with their weapons ready and found only a hard stare. With a cold-water shock they realised they had let their guard down, and the thought of what might have come at them brought them back to sense.

Dog toed the fleece soggily to one side. 'Hardly riches,' he pointed out, scattering droplets as he waved one hand at the villa. 'If they harvest gold with fleeces here, then it is not enough to afford a decent door.'

The others laughed shame-facedly. Then the sagging door moved back on its poor leather hinges and figures came out — a woman, a girl and a boy.

The woman was in a patched and stained dress, the girl and boy held close to her. She had never been pretty, Drust thought, so age and care had less trouble to ravage her face and turn her hair to raggles of grey. Her eyes were rheumed, but defiant even in fear.

'We have found the Crone,' Mule grunted which raised a laugh. Quintus shouted out to search harder and uncover the Maiden, but Drust glared at them and they fell silent. Then he sent them right and left to search anyway, but for any menfolk that were hiding. The woman watched them, spilling out incomprehensible words to which Drust replied in Greek, but got no response and turned to find Kisa. The boy stared at him with naked hatred.

There was a clatter and a crash and the woman yelped, one hand flying to her throat. Mule and Praeclarum appeared, dragging someone up to Drust; Mule pitched him to the ground. A man, bearded and exhausted, with a bloody cloth round his leg.

'Hiding under fodder,' Praeclarum declared and Mule kicked out at the fallen man. The woman flung herself forward, but Praeclarum caught and held her while she babbled. Drust knew pleading no matter the language and thought the man was her son, or her husband.

'Or both,' Kag added in Greek at the end of this, and others laughed.

The man growled and spat. 'She is my ma, rot you...'

He saw Kag's slow smile and clicked his teeth together at having given himself away, but it was too late for that, as Drust told him.

'You shot at us, that is clear,' he added, squinting at the cloth. 'That's the arrow you had in return.'

'You killed Blessed,' Mule roared out and lashed out with his foot, only to have Dog take him by the collar and haul him back, hard enough to pitch him on his back. Mule sprang up, face a mask of snarl, but Dog simply stood and looked at him; Mule muttered and folded his arms sullenly.

Manius knelt by the man and unpeeled the cloth as gently as he could while the woman and girl whimpered; the boy, Drust thought, was pale, with lips like a thin wire and eyes trying to be hard and failing under wetness.

'There you are,' Manius said when the cloth was off and everyone saw the ragged hole and the clotted blood. 'Went in only a little way, but it cracked the shin.'

'I was running,' the man said through grimaces 'I thought you were raiders.'

'You did well to get all the way home with that, then,' Kag offered admiringly, and Mule flung up both arms in frustration.

'Suck his cock, why don't you?'

Kag looked levelly at him. 'I know you miss that beast and can only presume that you fucked it nightly while the rest of us were asleep. But if you speak like that to me again I will make you a second mouth.'

Dog laughed, a nasty sound, but whether it was at Kag or Mule was hard to tell. Probably both, Drust thought.

'There are more important matters,' Mouse said seriously. 'Is there food here?'

Everyone else groaned; the man twisted a grin onto his pain-ravaged face.

'Look at us closely. We are trying something different to eating.'

Mouse scowled while Drust squatted by the man. 'Name,' he said and the man hesitated, then his shoulder slumped a little; his mother and sister were wailing now.

'Bahar.'

'A father? Brothers?'

He shook his head, which was only to be expected, but if he had any male relatives around, Drust was sure they were nowhere helpful.

'We seek a temple – you know of it? Where it can be found?'

His mother had stopped wailing as soon as the word 'temple' was mentioned and Dog did not miss it either. Bahar's head wobbled slightly as he hovered on the edge of losing all sense.

'No one goes there,' he managed. 'The ghost...'

He was gone into oblivion and the woman and children wailed, thinking he was dead, so Dog kicked him so that the pain brought him round with a scream.

'Where?' he demanded, looking at the woman this time. She stared defiantly back at him and made a warding sign.

'Tie him by the ankles,' Dog said, 'and haul him up.'

'Leave him,' Drust snapped, and Dog turned. Perhaps he had a mild stare – it was hard to tell with that face – but his voice was flat and level.

'We need to know.'

It took time to find a bast line good enough for the task, and all the time Bahar's mother and little sister pleaded and cried, while the boy clenched himself like a knot and made no sound. Until Bahar screamed. It was a heart-scrape that sound, which was only to be expected, Drust thought, when you are hauled up by a broken leg. He clenched his fists until the knuckles creaked and felt sick with the knowledge that he should never have allowed this.

'This is not right,' Praeclarum said, and Drust felt ripped open by it – he knew she was right and he knew Dog was right and he said so. Dog asked the question; the woman had subsided, melted into sobbing and clutching the little girl, who had exhausted all her own screams. The Empress seemed to catch what was flung out from all this and started to moan and make hoarse noises which might have been screams once.

In the end, Bahar put them on the trail, but he had thrown up twice and passed out four times – he was tough, as Kag pointed out admiringly.

'If you like him so much you can take him down,' Drust harshed back, made bitter by it all and still slathered with the loss of Sib and what Manius had to do with it, the sickness of the rage that had taken him over, and the way Dog kept pushing him. 'Get Mouse to help, since he is only poking about looking for coin or food.'

Mouse started guiltily since that was exactly what he was doing, but Kag scowled, paused, then shook his head and loosened the rope so that the man fell badly, on his wounded leg. He shrieked at the pain and then went limp; that was when the boy broke.

He made his first sound, a harsh growling scream, and ran for Dog, hauling out a little knife from his boot. He had courage but his timing was off; Dog sidestepped neatly and whicked out one banging stroke with the *gladius*, slamming the boy straight in the kidneys in midstep; the woman shrieked.

'Fortuna's arse,' Kag said bitterly. 'That was poorly done.'

Praeclarum and Kisa sprang to the boy and began to help, while Mouse held the mother from doing something rash and adding to the bad cess of the moment. The others looked at the ground and shook their heads, but Dog simply wiped his blade on the grass.

'Kits breed rats,' he said coldly, and there was silence for a moment, broken only by the mewling woman.

'In the back?' Kisa said, scrambling up. 'You could not kill a boy from the front, to his face? Truly, that face marks you.'

Dog turned, and his look when it crashed on Kisa was a grue of ice.

'Anyone who knows me will tell you I am tender to children,' he answered levelly, 'and do not like them to see their death. But I will stick this in your face, little Jew, should you give me more cause.'

'Easy,' Kag said warningly, and then Praeclarum rose up and said wearily that the boy was dead. She looked at Drust, who felt the weight of it all, felt the disappointment in her shoot through him from heel to crown.

Kisa turned and walked away in silence. Kag drew in a breath and looked sorrowfully at Drust, who had had enough of being blamed for this.

'Find a spade,' he growled, 'and bury the boy.'

'What will we do with the woman?' Mouse demanded loudly. 'And the girl?'

It was such a loaded question that Drust's head thundered but he did not turn from looking at the dead boy when he spoke.

'Eat them or fuck them, Mouse. I have no preference.'

–

They came on the great wheel of stone not long afterwards, wide as outstretched arms, thick as a handspan.

'Just as the man said,' Kisa said, wiping his streaming face. It was raining, a light mirr that at least helped wash the sweat and stinging insects away. He did not look at Dog when he said it, but everyone else did; Drust did not like it. The moment at the farmstead had stained them all, it seemed.

It was just as Bahar had told them – great tumbles of stone like slices from a tree, all parts of tall pillars once. Now that they saw them they also saw the faint outlines of flagged floors under a nap of green and tangle.

Half crouched and wary as kicked dogs, they went on, weapons unashamedly gripped in fists and their backbones curled with a sweat that had nothing to do with the fetid heat of this strange mountain.

The fallen pillars had once been thick as a forest and were now scattered down like windblown trees, the last stumps forming an avenue leading up to the wall of rock they had been heading towards for some time. Grey-green and grim, it now towered over them, while the avenue of mossy stumps led to root-tangled steps and then up to a pillared portico, set right into the rock face.

'Is this the place?' whispered Mule and Kag snorted.

'Does it look like a fitting place for ghosts?

He spoke normally, unfazed by the hush that seemed to have fallen over everyone else, but it boomed loud and folk winced. Quintus put his uncaring foot on a tilted statue of a woman, right on the carved jut of her breasts, and squinted at the steps and the entrance. He grinned, bright as sunlight, and Praeclarum offered a toothless reply; it went some way to banishing the memory of Bahar's 'ghost'.

'We will need torches,' Drust said. 'We can build a fire in the shelter of that pillared place.'

They moved off, leaving Drust staring at the statue, this one holding a torch in either hand. She had three faces this time, two in profile and one staring, fixing him with a sightless glare; and, peculiarly, seemed to have one foot bare and the other with

315

a lace-shoe which had once been bronze but was now green. Drust felt his flesh ruche to gooseskin; there was altogether too much of the gods around, and the Empress was now sitting and rocking, making baby sounds.

Fires were lit and smoke shrouded the dim, though the talk was muted and folk looked to their ties and straps and edges as the day dimmed to blue twilight. They bound up torches with what rags they could scavenge from old serks and hems, and Drust moved among them, offering small comment and praise. Kisa did nothing but drink; they had found skins of a thin, vinegary wine and the little Jew had been pouring it down his throat since they had left the farm.

By the time pots had been scoured of the last gruel, the fires were red blossoms in a bowl of night and Drust sat at the edge of matters, his head whirling like a mad chariot race. He was grateful when a shadow shifted out of the dark, became Praeclarum and hunkered beside him; someone laughed from the fire, a nasty sound, and Drust suspected it was Mule.

'Do we go in?' she asked, and Drust looked at the black maw of the entrance.

'Wait until light.'

'It will be dark inside anyway.'

'Let us have this peace and sleep,' he answered. 'That was a bad business.'

Praeclarum leaned against him and he hesitated a moment, then put an arm round her.

Across the way Mule looked at the two-headed shadow and spat in the fire.

'No sleep for them,' he growled. Kag said nothing.

Mouse, scraping his spoon raw on the inside of an empty pot, looked up bitterly.

'Eat them or fuck them,' he said and shook his head. 'That was no way to speak.'

Dog grinned across at him, his skull-face leaping with bloody firelight. 'Which did you do?' he demanded, but no one laughed and Mouse shot him a sorrowed glare.

The night grew chill, tendrilled with witch-hair mist and threaded with screeches from owls. Or the mysterious ghost, Kisa slurred, which made Quintus tell him to fasten his teeth on that.

The little Jew shifted up unsteadily and those who watched him could see he was not happy with matters. Not that that was any help to anyone. He stood up, bowed slightly, nearly fell and recovered himself.

'I am sorry for your losses, in every way,' he declared, speaking slow and solemn, so he would not fall over the words. 'I would like to help, but I am not the sort to halt such terrible matters, as we all knew at the start of this enterprise. Now you are fucked and I am fucked for being part of it, and Uranius is fucked for having thought of it, and the Empress is fucked because people will not believe she has no power.'

He pouted like a baby.

'We are all fucked. This is what happens when you outrage God. Now I am going to get drunk.'

He started to reach for the slack wineskin, stumbled and almost fell. 'More drunk,' he corrected.

Kag and Dog laughed and watched the little man until he fell asleep, mumbling. They waited another suitably polite interval and then moved to where Drust and Praeclarum shared the same blanket.

The frantic gasping and clutching had been done, the fever ebbed and, for Drust, the best part of the affair was now being shredded to mist by the pair's arrival. Praeclarum shared

317

that view, scowling while Kag held up his hands in placating apology; Dog said nothing, simply squatted and seared them with his face.

'The other side,' Dog said simply, and Drust got on one elbow, feeling the night chill his skin. 'It may not be entirely free of threat.'

'You said no one knew of this mousehole.'

Dog made an ambivalent side-to-side head movement. 'That Bahar did. And his ma.'

'Possibly the boy,' Praeclarum added, soft as bitter aloes, 'but he is no threat now.'

'None,' Dog answered. 'Might have been better if we had finished the business and left those who follow us in the dark.'

'Are there still those who follow us?' she demanded and Kag laughed.

'You leave tracks...' he said.

'What of the other side?' Drust interrupted and Dog nodded.

'Just saying. If people here knew, perhaps people there do as well. And that is the side where the garrison of the Red Serpent – if there is such a thing now – might be more easily found.'

'So,' Drust concluded, 'what you are saying is that your escape hole is no escape.'

'What *we* are saying,' Kag answered, 'is that it is a long way back to Dura.'

'Even there,' Dog said simply, 'we might not be safe. Shayk Amjot will know the truth by now, and even to get there we will have to avoid all the trouser-wearers this side of the Euphrates. We have no mounts and no supplies.'

'So there is no hope?' Praeclarum exploded. 'Is that what you came to tell us?'

'There is always hope,' Kag answered smiling. 'I came in the hope of seeing your tits – no offence.'

'Now you know the true measure of hope,' Praeclarum said, gathering the blanket round her, but she smiled all the same. Drust neither smiled nor spoke and the silence stretched. Finally he turned out one hand like a beggar and made an impatient glare.

'Right,' Kag said, looking at Dog, who grinned.

'There is a camel trail a day down the other side of the mountain,' he explained. 'It is the one that comes from the Oxus down to Zadracarta, the Yellow City, and is well known for fat caravans. We can sell ourselves to a train as guards.'

'If they don't kill us on sight,' Drust pointed out. 'And Zadracarta is right behind the Wall,' he added, remembering Kisa's droning on the subject. 'It is a base for the Persian soldiers.'

Kag nodded, beaming. 'They will not think to look for us there if they are not waiting outside the mousehole.'

It was yet another tenuous plan, more a thread of hope than anything else, but it was all they had. As Praeclarum said when they had left, Kag had more chance of seeing her naked.

Morning took an age to drag itself over the horizon. Their battered pots were cleaned and stowed, fires kicked out, torches gripped in fists, and when Drust eventually moved to the middle of them, they shot sideways glares at him, like a pack of feral dogs.

They looked like a long walk of bad road, he thought, scored by lines of weariness and bruise-eyed from lack of sleep; he would not look any different.

He stretched out his hand, knuckles up, and one by one they added their own, broken-nailed and grimed. They said the words, looked in each other's eyes and felt the burn of it, that glow that told them they were still Brothers of the Sand. Drust took a torch from Manius and led the way inside, *gladius* ready and the flame held high.

The inside smelled of old stone dust and bad air – and taint, harsh as old piss. Everyone smelled it and Manius tasted it with flicks of his tongue, like an adder, then spat.

'Not right,' he said.

'Now there is a surprise,' Kag growled. 'It smells like every bad camp I have ever been in where the shitter is anywhere you squat.'

Which was true enough for folk to laugh a little and be eased. Yet Manius prowled, looking this way and that as they came into an open area where the floor was solid with old stones and the curve of the walls covered in faded paint. A solitary statue stood sentry, with what seemed an inscription on the base.

Kisa, who had spent his time being whey-faced sick, was now prodded towards them, Kag holding a torch so he could see better. 'Read it out, scholar,' he growled.

The writing, if that's what it was, seemed a meaningless procession of figures to everyone but Kisa, who started to mumble until Mule called attention to the statue itself; the Empress, tethered to him, was on her knees before it, but whether that was because she was crazy or because she was worshipping was not clear. Either was an unnerving thought.

What was clear was that the statue stood at the exact point where the floor stones crossed, leading to three identical dark ways.

'Your three-headed wife, little Jew,' Kag declared, and his echoing voice made folk wince. Kisa waved one hand and the noise of him being sick in the dark grated on everyone.

It was the same statue as outside, only taller and with all three faces intact, stone stares as haughty as the Empress's had once been; now she whimpered and mumbled and had to be jerked upright by Mule.

The torches in the statue's hands could be lit, Drust saw, save that they were withered, but a face stared blankly down each path; it was not hard to work out what was meant here, but no one cared for it, Kisa least of all.

'The smell is wrong in here,' he muttered.

'Stop puking,' Kag advised. 'Anything useful to tell us?'

The little Jew looked down the dark ways and frowned, swallowing bile. 'I think this might be a labyrinth.'

The moment hung on the shaky hook of this for a moment while everyone raked their head for what they knew of labyrinths. All knew of the Cretan one, simply because every other mosaic floor of a fashionable Roman atrium was based on the design of it. No one wanted to think of the monster which had lurked in it.

Ugo knew more. 'A Spiral Dance.'

'A what?' demanded Mule sourly.

'A Spiral Dance,' he repeated, 'with Máni in the middle.'

'The Moon Goddess,' Kisa muttered and Ugo nodded sombrely.

'You choose the right way, you get to the centre and the goddess will grant your request.'

'That's a dark way,' Mouse declared in a harsh whisper, 'no matter the path.'

'The light at the end of it,' Dog answered carelessly, echoingly loud, 'is the shine of a way out.'

'Or the eye of a giant fucking *draco*,' Mule grunted.

'There is no such beast,' Quintus told him, grinning. 'If there was, we'd have netted it for the Flavian long since.'

'Attilius Regulus killed one,' Kisa declared suddenly. 'During the fight against Carthage at Bagrada River, a dragon attacked his army, or so he claimed. The battle took many soldiers to kill this dragon – many soldiers were taken by the dragon's vicious mouth and many others were crushed by its tail. Its hide was too thick for their weapons to get through so they started using the siege weapons to crush it with heavy stones. When it was dead, they skinned the creature and sent it back to the Roman Senate. When the Senate measured the skin, it was one hundred and twenty feet in length. The hide was on display in Rome for a hundred years.'

'I never heard of such,' Quintus said, scowling suspiciously.

'Is this the same Regulus who got his arse kicked by Carthaginians and was taken prisoner?' Drust fired back drily. 'If so, I fancy the dragon story was better than telling the Senate he had lost an army to bad generalship.'

Mule laughed and Quintus joined in. No one else did and the feral stink of the place now began working on everyone's worst fears.

Chapter Eighteen

In a while, everyone knew it was the wrong way, but they were lost by then.

Worse than that, they were, as Kisa had known, in a labyrinth whose walls were narrow and lined with panels of Greek marble where they hadn't fallen off to show the cut stone beneath. The floor might have been flagged, but was covered in marble dust, fine as flour and sparkling like a sun-kissed sea in the light of the torches.

Which were failing. When they did, they would be in total darkness – in a wyrm circle as Ugo kept calling it. It did not help that he then explained how 'wyrm' was what they called a dragon in his land. It raised hackles on all necks, for each path was a tunnel and the tension – and air – was thick in the place.

Round a corner, then another, with Drust ordering different people to take the lead, which was at least fair if not welcome. Manius had better eyes and ears and nose than any other – though the last, he claimed, was leading him closer to the smell he did not like.

He edged around a corner, the others shuffling through the ice-stone dust like a breeze through fallen leaves. There was a sudden curse from him and he stopped.

'Something moved under my foot,' he said, and folk drew back, then crouched even closer and tighter as they heard a rasp and grind. Kag growled, was reaching out a hand to grip

Manius by the shoulder when there was a last slap of sound and dust puffed from the roof.

Then Dis opened and the dead fell on them.

Manius gave a shriek and bolted, barging through the men behind, who were at once panicked and scuttled off, shoving those behind them into moving. Drust, cursing and bellowing at them, was slammed into one wall; an elbow drove air from him and someone crushed his instep. They bellowed like stampeding cattle and vanished around the corner they had come from.

Drust, whooping in air, managed to haul out his sword and almost poke Dog, who returned with a disgusted scowl twisting the skull on his face – and a desiccated horror in a helmet held up in one hand.

'The dead,' he growled, holding it up for everyone to see. 'For frightening children and the weak-minded.'

It was a long-dead skull in a helmet so rotted the leather had fallen away and left only some of the metal bands and the rim. It was now set jauntily on the leering head so that it seemed like Dog's face had come to life and been plucked off into his hand.

He flung it at the feet of the others, who were crouched and panting like dogs. Mule was missing, and the Empress was huddled, but mercifully silent; Praeclarum gently raised her up, soothing her with pats.

'This is your walking dead man,' Dog declared scornfully, 'who was not walking at all, but fixed to the roof by ties, only one of which was left. He once had a spear, but it had fallen off into the dust and the whole silly trap was set to frighten and no more.'

'No matter how big the giant,' Ugo declared, drawing himself up scornfully, 'it always has to fit through the door.'

'As if you were not leading the fleeing,' Dog scathed.

'I would not have run,' Ugo declared, glaring at Praeclarum, 'if she had not.'

'I only ran because he did,' she answered accusingly, pointing at Manius. 'He came past me faster than Mouse looking for sausage.'

'I was not looking for sausage,' Mouse began angrily. 'What is this matter of everyone speaking of my appetite? It is no more than an ordinary healthy man…'

'Where is Mule?' Drust demanded and they looked at each other.

'He ran off,' Kisa offered, and Drust scorched him with a look.

'I can work that part out – did anyone see where?'

'He must have taken that turn to the left,' Praeclarum offered. 'Just before this… thing… fell off the roof.'

It made sense, but was no help. Wherever he was, Mule was lost and in the dark.

'We should call for him,' Ugo suggested, frowning, but Kisa whimpered at that.

'And wake the dragon?'

'There is no dragon,' Drust spat and everyone looked at the floor or each other, shuffling.

'So you say,' Mouse muttered. 'Perhaps we should go back.'

'Back where? Do you know the way? And do what when we get there? Perhaps we can walk back to that farm and ask the man we shot and whose son we killed for shelter and food?'

'No point,' Manius answered and his black-smoked look told it all. Drust felt the icy shiver of him, heard the thunder in his head. He looked at Kag, who indicated he had not known, but when he looked at Dog, he knew who had whispered in Manius's ear.

Dog shrugged. 'The dead do not speak,' he said, and Drust felt the drum noise rising, moved forward a step so that Kag had to catch his arm. Those who watched Dog were amazed to see the man draw his skull-face back a little and take a single step backwards. They had never seen that look before on him and it took a while for them to work out that it was fear.

Just then the last torch not in the hand of Drust went out. He shouldered to the front, and after a brief pause they followed him, clinging to the light. As he passed Dog, Kag stopped and squinted at him.

'You will push our Drust too far one day,' he said simply, and for once Dog had no answer, was still trying to work out what he had seen in Drust's eyes, in his very face. To work out what it had done to him.

Not long afterwards, they had stopped to rest and suck water, for the place was hot and the feeling of being closed in made it warmer still; everyone eyed the dull flicker of Drust's torch and tried not to think about what matters would be like when it went out.

In the last blood-glow of it, they saw a shadow ahead and this time they gripped hilts and handles and braced, trying to work up spit as they edged forward. The shadow did not move, though folk heard growls and mutters.

'Dis,' Quintus declared portentously. 'I can smell it.'

The shadow suddenly ran at them, roaring and bellowing, so that the sound bounced round the walls and buzzed all their ears. Manius drew back to the rear but his elbow was thumped hard by Drust and the arrow spanged off the wall and whicked down the narrow way.

'Hold!' he bellowed and there was a moment of confusion and a brief clash of blade on shield, then folk broke apart panting, and everyone saw Mule, who was laughing with mad relief – everyone was, banging shields and helmets together with the ecstasy of finding him and not some beast-enemies.

'I almost had your head from your shoulders, Mule,' Ugo roared; Mule glared at him.

'You may have dreamed of it,' he growled back, and folk went off into more wolf-snarl laughing.

'That was too close,' Manius said, blowing out his cheeks; Drust fixed him with a stare the archer did not like.

'We don't need more Sibs,' he said, and Manius's face twisted into a snarl that Kag stepped into and held until Manius stalked off to find his arrow.

'How did you get in front of us?' Quintus demanded, and Mule blinked and then shrugged.

'I lost you when the monster came...'

'Dog killed that,' Praeclarum interrupted and everyone laughed.

'Well,' Mule went on, clearly confused by the easy dismissal of the undead, 'I went on the way we thought was most likely and came to another of those Sister carvings. There were three more ways leading off and I went for the sword-hand.'

'Can you find it again, this carving?' demanded Drust, and Mule frowned, then nodded and pointed back the way he had come up.

'Down there and to the left.'

They reached it just as the torch faded and died. Manius was already crouched at it, having found his arrow in the dark, and everyone took note of that, especially those who had always thought there was something unearthly about the man. It took long moments of harsh breathing and slow walking down the corridor for everyone else to get their wits and dark-sense into play, but when they did they all saw the carving, the same three-faced woman as before, no more than a dim shadow in the dark.

'Hekátē,' Praeclarum said, peering at it.

'She Who Works Her Will. Hekátē,' said the Empress, her voice a rasp of hoarse, cracked like an old bell. In the blue-black, her voice seemed sucked away.

'That way,' Drust said, pointing, and Dog snorted derisively.

'The last choosing you made has had us walking to nowhere for some time,' he growled.

'I choose that way,' Drust said, 'because it seems lighter.'

Dog blinked and stared – everyone squinted.

'Now that Drust points it out,' Mouse muttered, 'it does seem less dark in that direction.'

Kag settled it by moving off and everyone followed; Drust found Kag in his eyeline, just as the last man went past, leaving them in the dark.

'The missing is found,' he said, 'which is Fortuna's blessing. It may be that she smiles on us now.'

'There is cheer,' Drust answered scathingly. 'The coda of the dice-player – I am happy for you.'

Kag only laughed, but he was proved wrong not long after, when Manius stopped dead in his dust-shuffle and announced that something had moved under his foot.

'Fuck Fortuna in her arse,' Kag declared savagely. 'You have good eyes and a better nose, but your feet betray you – you would do well to cut the pair off.'

Drust moved to where Manius stood, half bent and frozen still; he peered, but it was too dim to see his own feet clearly let alone anyone else's. To everyone's astonishment, Kisa got down on his hands and knees and gently started brushing the dust away. The others crouched and listened, waiting for the grind and rasp, but there was nothing.

'It is another old trap-frightener,' Kisa declared assuredly. 'Broken, no doubt.'

Manius shifted his foot one step and there was a crack; Manius flung himself flat and was so crouched he was halfway to the ground before he started; others flung up shields and there was yelling.

Nothing happened. Then the roof leaked some dust and a desiccated animal fell to the floor.

'Gods above and below,' Kag said, rolling the object with his foot. 'This is a dead fucking wolf. Fixed to the roof with a swinging cradle. Look – the metal of the cradle is rotted with age.'

Dog toed the dried snarl of the beast and nodded. 'There is a spear through it. If it had worked as it should, the spear would have gone through someone, as if the beast had attacked.'

They all saw that it was true and Kisa looked fearfully around. 'This is not the easy way, then. You would not be coming in here just to ask the seer who you would marry.'

There would be an easy way – but, as Kisa pointed out, they had missed that, and now had to watch every step.

'Especially you,' Kag said to Manius.

Drust put Mouse in front and they crept on, though most were now unconvinced that the way Drust had picked was any lighter. A little later, Manius stopped again, and Kag ripped out a curse that would have stripped the gilt off a forum statue.

'Again with your feet?' Kisa demanded and then looked at where Mouse was, ahead of the others. 'The fattest man we have managed not to set off a trigger, but you follow him and do.'

'Do not move, Manius,' Mouse snarled. 'At least until I am well away from you – and I am not fat, you little worm.'

'Something went click a little,' Manius admitted and then stepped away, looking around. Nothing happened. Then Praeclarum squinted and pointed. There was nothing anyone could see but the myriad points of sparkle from the dust... Drust grunted when he realised it.

'The dust,' he said and everyone saw it now – the dust, that dark shuffle through which they had moved, breathing in the harshness of it, was now sparkling again. Reflecting light. Already it was thinner here, enough for folk to see the flagged stones once more.

'You were right after all,' Kag announced cheerfully. 'This way is lighter. Probably a fleece of gold shining in the dark.'

'Don't sound so surprised,' Drust said, aggrieved. 'I am right a lot of the time.'

No one spoke in defence of it and Mouse broke the moment.

'I do see the shine of gold,' he said. 'A fleece, for sure.'

'A dragon's arse,' Mule declared. 'For sure.'

'If it shows me its arse,' Ugo growled, hefting his axe, 'then it is not a dragon. It is a good sheath and a pair of shoes. Perhaps a hat...'

That made them laugh, and Mouse shouted out that he could see more light – a pile of gold, for sure. He shuffled into a trot.

'Wait,' Drust called out, and Kag lunged to grab Mouse but might as well have caught hold of a downhill cart.

'Watch your feet...' Quintus yelled.

The crack had an inevitability that made Drust's belly sink to his boot soles. The floor panel Manius had activated was supposed to work when someone stood on it, but age had caused one half to drop and the other half to stick. Mouse stopped too late, teetering. Then he tried to jump, landed hard on the other panel, and they all saw him vanish with a despairing shriek.

There was a moment of horrified stares and whipped-dog fear, then they braided themselves together, crept cautiously to the edge of the black pit. Without light they could see nothing.

'Mouse,' Drust called, his voice rasped with the dust in his throat.

'We have to get him out,' Praeclarum said, but then she saw Drust's face.

'We have no rope,' Kag said.

'No way of seeing how deep the pit is,' Quintus added, 'or what is at the bottom.'

'Spikes,' said a voice, thin as a vagrant wind.

'Mouse,' Mule yelled. 'Mouse… wait, we can get you out…'

'No point,' came the bleak reply. 'I am rammed through and through and leaking out here.' There was nothing left but the last of his strength and the final rasp of his voice, wavering and weak; they could all smell the blood now – he had been a big man so there was a lot of it.

'Anything left to say?' Dog asked him, looking for a message for someone somewhere.

There was a choke that Drust took for an attempt at speech, so he bent closer with Dog. He realised, when the words came, that the choke had been laughter.

'Tell Drust – eat me or fuck me,' came the last moth-wing hiss. 'I have… no… preference…'

–

They sat until they were sure he was dead and then started to move, helping one another across the dark gap. Drust levered himself up on legs that felt like wooden timbers and led the way, away from the iron reek of Mouse's blood, stumbling onto the smooth flags and on towards the light. They came out into it like wary wolves, moving in crouched half-circles.

There was a great open space, a seeming circle with the light falling from a shaft in a roof no one could see clearly. It was sharp and golden, that light, enough to bring tears to scoured eyes and make people squint. The centre of the Spiral Dance, Drust thought and looked round, as if the goddess would suddenly appear.

The light fell directly on an altar, a great slab of marble stained with ominous dark marks of old bloodletting. There was no sign of worship now – whatever oracle had once pronounced here was dead and gone and all that was left was a pungent reek; the golden glow of riches was simply the distant sun.

Now everyone peered and sniffed and spat out the last of the cloying, dusty passages, then fell to wondering what was happening and where they were.

They moved cautiously out into the far, dark reaches of the circular chamber, widening like slow ripples from the ice-stone altar. There were torches, some fallen, some still in sconces on the rough walls, and they lit a couple of fresh ones, exchanging soft words of relief, exultant now that they seemed safe. One by one they filtered back to report what they had found, which was much the same – fallen statues, smashed pots, old must smells, a heap of bracken and a scatter of old bones.

'This is wild pig,' Manius said, holding up a skull. 'There are the bones of some big horned beast here, too. Mountain goat, I think.'

'There is something different here,' Drust declared uneasily – then Praeclarum let out a cry and dipped. When she turned, she held a small white bundle of fur, cooing to it. It was still blind, looking for heat, and Praeclarum nestled it inside her tunic, beaming her gummed smile to everyone.

'It's a kitten,' she declared, then saw the horrified faces. 'What?'

'Here's another,' Kisa said, darting across the floor to where something crawled. He held it up, a bundle of white fur that mewled out little piping snarls.

'Fuck me with Jupiter's cock,' Kag growled, and did not need to say more to those who had hunted beasts for a living.

'Out,' Dog snarled. 'Get out of here – run.'

The shape came out of the corridor where it had prowled, attracted away from the kittens by the smell of Mouse dying. Frustrated by not being able to reach the rich blood smells, she had come back, following the strange new scents that unnerved her – now she heard the panicked, angry mewling of her offspring.

Drust saw the huge, white shape of it, the stripes barely darker than the rest. Big as a small horse, he thought wildly, white as a walking shade. The idea of meeting it in those tight, dark corridors almost made him cry out.

Kisa stood with the mewling cub, fixed and frozen, watching the huge beast seem to shrink, belly low to the ground. The shoulder blades went up like moving knives and it padded sideways, silent, showing fangs longer than their hands, and the eyes, cold and green, were locked on the man who held her cub.

The Hyrcanian tiger, Drust thought. A rare white one – we ignored the very name of this mountain. We forgot about the ghost we had been warned about, forgot all about tigers entirely...

Slow and silent, the tiger drew its hind legs up into a crouch. It swayed slightly, gaining balance, and the muscles on it quivered. It tilted the massive head to one side and jaws opened wider, revealing the yellowed length of those fangs.

Drust had seen all this before, watching from safety as lions and tigers and leopards stalked the sands, fixed on the *venator* who was equally fixed on them. They would roar, a belching blast of sound designed to paralyse; then they would pounce. This was not the safety of inside looking out…

'Put the cub down,' Kag said desperately to Kisa. 'Gently. Then step back from it slowly. Do not run. Do. Not. Fucking. Run.'

He ran.

Two steps was all he got before the huge ghostly cat lunged, one paw clipping his heels so that he sprawled and rolled. They all knew such hunting cats, had watched them in amphitheatres the length and width of the Empire – knew that the next move would be a massive, crushing pounce, a bite to the throat or neck, a disembowelling rake with the rear claws.

Ugo was there, swinging his big axe and roaring; the beast reared back, snarled soundlessly and gave the big Frisian time to grab Kisa by the slack of his tunic and back up, dragging him.

The cat crouched and again the jaws widened, but no sound came other than a slight, high rumble. Drust realised it had no voice, was some strange mute, pale version of what should be.

The beast moved swiftly to the cub, picked it up in massive jaws and swung round, loping away. Drust saw the smooth speed, the bunched muscles, and let out a breath he hadn't realised he'd been holding in.

'Out,' he yelled, and they scrambled, heading for the narrow entrance to a rough-hewn corridor. The darkness should have warned them all, but panic drove away sense and they came up short, crowding against a solid wooden door.

'The way out for the oracles and priests,' Kisa gasped through rattling teeth and shivers. 'They would not want anyone wandering in this way…'

'There must be a lock,' Mule said from the back, his voice rising as he shouted.

'I think I can open it,' Quintus said, bending and squinting. 'Hold that torch closer, Dog – mind my fucking hair, you arse...'

There was a lifetime of sweating, crammed together at the bottom of a dead-end, breathing each other's fetid air while Quintus mused and picked. 'Think it is rusted... if we have some oil...'

'It's coming back,' Mule howled. Dog cursed and shouldered his way through the pack to the rear, sword determinedly up; when Drust risked a look, he saw the pale wraith pad one way, stop and then pad back. Dog moved to it, waving the torch, and it backed away, shaking its head while the eyes seemed to glow.

We are trapped, he thought, bunched like sheep in a pen...

'Bring back the torch,' Quintus protested. 'I need the light...'

'Out of the way,' Ugo said. 'I will show you how to pick locks.'

Drust fought his panic, fought for breath. He heard Dog muttering something – prayers to the gods, no doubt. Drust had tried to be a follower of Stoic once, had tried to believe there were no gods, that the world, the universe was governed by a Divine Reason which the Stoics called Logos, Zeus or God.

Yet each time my life is versus steel or fangs, he thought, I summon every god I know at the top of my voice...

The smell of smoke drifted to them, making heads turn to see a flare of flame. Dog came back, his grinning skull seeming to glow in the dim light, and Drust realised he had set fire to the bracken nest; the piping wails of cubs floated to them.

335

Ugo put a shoulder to the door, drew back and rushed it. There was a crack. He did it again and the lintel broke. A third time burst him through and everyone scrabbled after him, out into cold, rainwashed air and a light that scoured their eyes to tears.

'There is also that way of lock-picking,' Quintus growled sullenly, but Ugo merely grunted. Smoke billowed out, sucked by the new flue they had made.

'Move,' Kag warned. 'She will shift her cubs to safety and then maybe come after us.'

'She will stay with her kits,' Dog argued, but no one rightly knew what such a beast would do. They had seen Hyrcanian cats before, but they were golden with dark stripes, not ghostly grey with faded markings. Not ones which made no sound, even when snarling.

They stumbled away from the entrance, sliding on weed-covered steps which curved down a steep green pass between tan and pink hills that seemed to stretch on until their blurred eyesight failed. When the stair curved round, still heading down, exhaustion drove them to a halt, panting and gasping; for the last few hundred steps Ugo had been helping Praeclarum carry the Empress, who was now slumped at their feet. Mule, hands on thighs, kept lifting his head and looking back up the trail, which Kag noted.

'If you are leaving tracks,' he said.

'Shut up,' Drust snapped. He was jangling like temple bells at the thought of being stalked by the ghost-cat and did not need Kag's wisdom right at this moment.

'Pray,' Ugo suggested, seeing Drust's distress. 'Mars Thingsus has never failed me yet.'

'There is only one god,' Kisa muttered.

'It is convenient that there be gods,' Kag said, smiling, 'and as it is convenient, let us believe there are.'

'Ovidius Naso,' Dog said as he passed them, heading downwards and picking his steps carefully. 'I never liked him nor his verses – neither did the Divine Augustus, who banished him.'

'For conspiracy,' Kag shot back, 'not for poetry. He was part of a plot.'

'He only knew of it because he was fucking the chief plotter's wife,' Dog answered, 'who was also Augustus's granddaughter.'

He stopped and turned, grinning his horror of a face at Kag. 'See? Not the only one who knows the finer things. I wonder what gods Ovid prayed to when he realised he should have told his pillow-talk instead of waiting?'

'Probably the same ones we are about to beg abjectly to,' Praeclarum declared, 'for help against those.'

They all stopped and stared at the line of warriors stretched implacably across the path. Armed, armoured in long ring-coats cut for riding, with shields and spears and bows; they all had blank, silver faces save for one, who was cloaked in a white that seemed to dazzle. He stepped forward, his ornate helmet held in the crook of one arm, his black-bearded face smiling with triumph. His oiled ringlets tinkled with small silver bells when he shook his head with mock amusement.

'Well,' he said in Persian, 'what is this that comes from the mountain? I was told to expect a woman of high birth – which one of the pair of whores would that be?'

Kag spat at Dog's feet. 'No one knows of this mousehole, you said. It is a secret way through the Red Serpent Wall, you said.'

Dog shrugged and his swords came out; the men on the path closed ranks at the front and the ones behind unshipped bows. Drust stepped forward.

'You can't fight this,' he said. Dog looked at him and his laugh had neither warmth nor mirth in it.

'This is what happens when you get cunt-struck. You can't save your woman by throwing down your blade.'

Praeclarum shouldered him aside so roughly that Dog staggered and would have fallen if Drust had not caught and steadied him.

'You can't save even yourself by behaving like a fat cock,' she growled on her way past, striding towards the Persians. 'When I do what I do, spring up off this path, high as you can get. Do not hesitate.'

She strode on towards the black-bearded Persian, her arms wide to show she was unarmed.

'What the fuck is she doing?' demanded Dog.

Drust had no idea, but something clicked behind them, and Mule spun, appalled that he had forgotten to keep watch; the sound that came from him was a long, slow whimper as the stone, dislodged by a massive paw, tinked and rolled down towards him. He looked back up to a ledge where there was another opening into the temple, too high for mere mortals.

The huge beast looked even more ghostly in daylight.

Chapter Nineteen

It came padding out of the mountain, extended claws clicking, big head swinging left and right as it prowled the ledge, back and forth, back and forth. Afraid, Drust thought wildly, of a gauntlet of men madly scrambling to the illusion of higher ground. Like the cats released into the Flavian to tear the *noxii* to pieces but who were cowed by the blast of noise and people and shrank to the edges, cowering.

It dropped to the ground, a near-silent affair of fluid muscle, then stopped belly-flat. Drust saw the silver-faced men flinching and drawing back, the ones behind trying to get their bows up; the commander stared, his mouth a circle of horror, and Drust knew the faces behind the masks were the same.

Praeclarum turned, dragging something from inside her tunic, and Kag said, 'Oh fuck,' very softly as she held up the last cub, the one she had plucked from the floor and put under her tunic and leathers for the warmth. Now Drust knew why the tiger had followed them.

Awake and chilled and roughly shaken, the cub made a little piping snarl of resentment that the mother heard, which made her hindquarters twitch and her tail whisk and her ears go flat.

'No...'

Drust heard the voice but could not equate it with himself, was starting forward when Kag and Dog grabbed him, pinning him despite his flailing struggles. Then there was a blast of cold air, or so it seemed, and Drust saw a monstrous pale shape flying

339

in mid-air, a shattering of images as if seen in the shards of a broken, slow-moving mirror.

The huge paws, big as eating bowls. A mouth curled back in a completely silent snarl, the fangs as long as curved daggers. Praeclarum, tossing the cub casually at the Persian commander and flopping like a dead weight to the ground.

The commander shrieked and fumbled, his reflex catch failing as the cub squirmed. He batted it once, twice, while someone behind him got off an arrow at the tiger as it landed in a skidding spray of grit and stones, right in front of Praeclarum.

There was a pause; Drust saw Manius at full draw, the arrow quivering in his grip. 'Shoot!' he screamed, but Manius simply held the pose.

Then the commander gave up with the cub, turned and started to elbow back through the ranks behind, which started them doing the same; the cub fell, unseen and screaming in a high, thin wail.

The mother sprang over Praeclarum into the middle of the running panic of men; screams got loud and Drust saw men flying everywhere, bits of scales scattering like leaves, helmets rolling and tumbling. The cat was never still now; the commander was grabbed by the neck and shaken viciously sideways until his head tore loose in a spray of blood. Talons raked and punched.

In a moment, there was no one left save those who could not run; one of the silver-masks was crawling, his legs raked to bloody frets of sinew and bone from the rear talons of the beast, which casually closed massive jaws on his face until it crunched. When it turned, the silver mask was fixed to one fang, crumpled like cloth; she shook it free, to tinkle softly on the stones like a knell.

'Shoot,' Drust whimpered, but Kag slapped a hand over his mouth and Manius held the draw, though it quivered violently now.

The cat snuffled in the gore, pawed over a body; someone else was screaming in pain, but the tiger did not seem to care – it found the cub, lifted it gently in those massive, blood-soaked jaws and padded soggily back to Praeclarum. No one moved. No one breathed.

The tiger nosed her limp body with its bloody muzzle, still with the cub in its jaws – then it stepped over her and loped silently past everyone, gave one mighty, easy leap and vanished back into the mountain.

Suddenly released with everyone's breath, Drust staggered and slid down to where Praeclarum was lying, skidding to a halt and, now that he was there, unable to touch her, to do anything.

Her head turned. One eye opened. She grinned gums at him and sat up.

'Woo,' she said. 'Ma's breath stinks a bit, let me tell you…'

She got no further, the words crushed out of her by Drust's arms, so that she had to gasp at him to leave off. When he did, she flung her own round him and they laughed, shaky and high, while the rest closed in on them.

'Clever,' Dog said admiringly. 'How did you know?'

'I worked with cats,' she answered, climbing to her feet and looking down at the bloodstains on her tunic. 'You can starve them for days, but they won't even attack all those who sit passive, wailing or praying. We had to convince them to get up and run, because it's what makes cats hunt. If they didn't run about, we told the *noxii*, there would be worse fates in store for them.'

Ugo, stepping carefully in the welter of bodies, paused and raised his axe, then brought it down with a casual, dull clang; the screaming stopped.

Mule crouched in the path, staring back up at the mountain stairs, to where they curled round out of sight and into the lair. Drust had an idea he would be doing that in his dreams for the rest of his life.

'Six dead,' Kag called out, stepping carefully over bodies. 'There were twenty at least.'

'They won't stop running until tomorrow,' Kisa declared vehemently, shaking his head and staring wide-eyed at the headless body of the commander, the neck raggled with bloody flesh.

'Ring-coats cut for riding,' Quintus pointed out. 'Somewhere there are horses.'

'They may not run,' Kag declared, and Drust nodded, squeezed Praeclarum one more time and drew out his sword. He felt big and filled.

'Finish them,' he snarled. Dog laughed, then started the hard work of worrying one of the scaled coats off a dead man.

'There's a lot of coin in all this,' Kag said, looking round. 'We may have done ourselves some good after all.'

'Watch the real prize,' Drust muttered, feeling his omnipotence draining away; he was surprised when Praeclarum laid a hand on his shoulder, sensing it. Then he felt the warm glow of it anew and waved to Mule to bring the Empress down towards them, away from any possible return of the beast; it was not an idea to make Mule easier in his mind.

'Shame about that cub,' Praeclarum muttered. 'Would have been a good prize.'

'Not weaned,' Manius said as they began to trot downslope. 'Would have died.'

'A bit of intestine as a teat and goat's milk,' she argued, but Manius's laugh was a scoff of scorn.

'You'd try and feed a Hyrcanian tiger on goat's milk?'

'It would die,' Quintus declared flatly. 'Trust in those who have captured every beast known. Help me with this...'

They stripped the dead, who marbled softly in the chill air sighing round the rocks and stones. Ahead was a long, gentle scree-slide around a corner and down into the ochre and tan and fuzzed green of a rolling plain.

'Can we move?' Mule demanded, looking anxiously back the way they had come.

'Do not fret,' Manius said, his dark face gleamed with sweat where he had been hauling the boots off someone whose legs had been savaged by claws. 'The beast will die soon.'

Praeclarum looked at him and Manius shrugged. 'I saw an arrow – one of those silver-faces got lucky. In the belly, though the shaft snapped off and only left a nub end. It will fester, though.'

Drust saw her glance up at the lair and straighten thoughtfully.

'Don't think of it.'

She bridled for a moment, then shrugged ruefully. 'Shame to think all those cubs will die.'

'All things die,' Dog said, shaking himself in the new coat, so that he rattled and shushed. He grinned his death-grin and looked from arm to arm admiringly. 'That's the truth that is, right there.'

'Truth is salt,' Kag growled, hefting scales over his shoulder. 'Everyone loves the taste and it is so valuable you can use it like coin. But too much makes you sick up a dog.'

'You should wear that,' Mule pointed out, cheered by the idea of the beast being dead. Quintus grinned.

'Too big for him and too heavy. But it's too much coin for him to leave behind.'

They chose new helmets, unfastening the ruined face masks, though Dog had one which worked; when it was raised he looked like a strange-beaked bird.

'Keep it down,' Kag advised laconically.

'I am crushed,' came the muffled reply from under it. 'A man of lesser character might take offence.'

'What character?

Manius looked at Drust, who nodded permission for him to lope off down the slope. Drust watched him go, wondering if he had really shot Sib. At least he had held his hand from shooting the beast, which would have put Praeclarum in danger, for sure. So he was not as viciously dark as Sib had thought and Drust too, for a while. Dark enough, all the same...

Mule had re-tethered the Empress to him and Kisa was kneeling beside her, still trembling from the beast. So big, he said aloud. So... powerful. He looked up as Drust approached, his face pallid as a worm.

'Tigers were never in it,' he said shakily, and Drust acknowledged the attempt at humour with a smile, then moved to kneel by the woman. The Empress, he corrected. Here was a woman who had been born into the upper ranks, who had dedicated herself to a goddess, the very soul of the City – and who had sold it for an Emperor. She heard the voices, felt the heat of Drust, and the blind face turned, seeking him. Like a cub to the teat, he thought, a flower to the rain.

She was nothing like as loveable. She was tattered and filthy, one hand a claw stripped to the bone and, despite washing and unguents, still unhealed and unhealthy looking. Her face was scoured on one side and across the forehead and the bridge of her nose; it wept in sympathy with the ruin under the strip of cloth across her eyes; fluids stained with blood leaked from under it. All her arrogance was gone, all her fire, all her courage.

'Can you hear me?'

She moaned, which was answer and yet not the one he sought.

Mule fumbled in his trousers, found what he was looking for and pissed with grateful grunts.

'In the name of all the gods you worship,' Kisa said. 'Have some respect.'

'She can't see,' he replied sourly.

'She can hear – and smell,' Praeclarum spat back, coming up unheard and tearing the leather leash from him. 'Why don't you go with the rest and leave her to me?'

Mule shrugged, tucked himself away and moved off, swaggering more than was necessary.

'Get that seen to,' she shouted after him. 'Whatever it is makes it smell like that.'

'Fuck you,' he called back and the others laughed.

'No cure for being a cunt,' Dog said loudly from under the silver mask. He guddled in gore for a moment – the headless commander, Drust saw – and came up with a wooden tube.

'This is something for you,' he said, waving it at Kisa. 'Have fun.'

Drust took it, wiped it down his tunic and then did the same with his fingers.

'What do you do for fun?' Kisa demanded sourly and Dog turned the blank silver face towards him; Kisa did not know which was worse, that or the one beneath.

'I sharpen my blades.'

Drust pulled out the scroll within the tube, unrolled it and saw at once that it was Pahlavi, which he did not read. He handed it to Kisa, who squinted at it; Drust saw his face grow pale.

'What?' he demanded.

'It is from Shayk Amjot to one Xosrov – could this be the one with no head? No matter. These are Parthians from the old regime, serving the ruler of Gorgan. That's the area along this side of the Red Serpent,' Kisa said, raising his head from the letter. 'It means…'

'It means that some commander has just seen his king die and a new one break everything apart,' Drust answered. 'So he has seized what he could.'

Kisa nodded soberly and bent back to the letter, peering and following his finger. 'Not quite. The House of Ispabuhdan has ruled here since the time of Darius and now looks to find a way to offer allegiance to the new *shahanshah*, Ardashir, and Shayk Amjot is offering his services. This letter was being taken to Gorgan, but the Shayk asked the commander to make his way to the White Tiger Mountain and wait for any sign of a party of barbarians with a high-born Roman woman. This commander is instructed to take the woman alive and…'

He stopped and Drust heard the letter rustle in his shaking hand. When he met Kisa's gaze it was stricken, set in a face drained of colour.

'Me,' Kisa managed. 'He instructs these Parthians to make sure I am taken alive.'

'The rest of us die, of course,' Kag put in, hearing this. 'You are spared that at least.'

They were laughing the way wolves might, and Kisa was amazed at how little fear they showed. He said as much and Quintus clapped him on one shoulder.

'We gave ourselves to Mars and Dis long since,' he said with his big, wide grin. 'Every day since is a gift from them.'

'And everything in it is the blessing of Fortuna,' Kag added and flung his arms wide, staring up at the sky.

'Goddess, I salute you,' he bellowed. 'Fortuna, you doubtful, fickle, vicious cunt – sometimes you kiss me and allow me a squeeze of your tits.'

He turned, tossing a purse in his hand. The coin he pulled from it was gold and Persian.

'You bastard,' Mule declared moodily. 'What have I done that she spurns me?'

'You pull out your cock too carelessly,' Quintus declared, his grin wide. 'It is a failing.'

'I would not worry, Mule,' Dog said cheerfully into the harsh laughter that followed. 'Fortuna is the goddess of bastards and the desperately broken; she will never be faithful, for her heart is on a wheel.'

They took what they could wear and carry, but found no more purses of gold – to Mule's annoyance. Praeclarum and the Empress sat together and Praeclarum stroked what was left of the Empress's ruined scalp. Kisa sat with the letter clutched so tight it appeared through his fingers.

'What will become of her?' Praeclarum asked Drust, who thought hard for an answer that was not a lie. In the end, he opted for harsh truth.

'She will be given back to the goddess she betrayed,' he said and she winced; everyone knew the punishment for a Vestal who broke her vows.

'Walled up? For obeying the Emperor?'

'She knew what she was about,' Drust replied, and Kisa slackened his grip on the letter, smoothed out the crumples and rolled it into some semblance of neatness and carefully slotted it back in the case.

'They will not,' he said, and Drust saw he wasn't trying to balm Praeclarum. 'Her father is rich and powerful enough not to have that happen. She might be a fallen Vestal – she is also an Empress.'

'She knows too much,' Kag said harshly. 'Whether it is all bollocks or not. They will six her.'

'Then why should we bring her back?' Praeclarum demanded. Kag squatted by them both, turning up the blind face of the Empress by her chin.

'Because the Palace on the Hill wants to know she is captured and then dead and no threat to Rome or advantage to Parthia. Or whatever is replacing it. And they will pay us for that, which is what this is all about.'

He let the woman loose and her head slumped; she mumbled.

'Not tigers,' he grinned and levered himself to his feet just as Manius loped back in and squatted for a moment to get his wind back. Then he waved his unstrung bow back the way he had come.

'Twenty-one,' Manius said. 'They have a camp, horses tethered and hobbled – tents too. They have been here a while.'

'Twenty-one,' Kisa exclaimed in shock.

'With bows,' Kag added, and Drust knew it was not just to make the little Jew wobble on his rock seat.

'We have a bow,' Quintus declared and Manius made a little side-to-side head gesture. He fumbled in his tunic and came up with a small triangle of green which he studied. Drust knew it was the strange concoction he chewed, a mix of leaves from his own lands and a resin from farther east which made him spit like he passed blood.

'This is the last of it,' he said and popped it in his mouth. The others tightened straps and sorted buckles; Ugo started to put an edge on his axe, a sour grate of rhythmic sound.

They sat, saying nothing, while the wind hissed and curled, cold and yet with no promise of rain in it.

The calm, Drust thought, before men murder one another.

'The Gate of Life is open,' he said and they moved off into the mourning wind, leaving beast and blood and all the lives that once had been.

-

An arrow slapped the air over their heads and Manius leaped sideways, drew and shot, then nocked another. Drust hefted his shield and crouched, but Dog lumbered past, his filched armour making a rhythmic shush.

'Don't stop,' he said, muffled under the mask, 'or they will shoot us down. Make a fist of it.'

He was right and Drust resented him for it – but he made the fist, a five-knuckle wedge of men. Kag and Ugo, who carried armour they could not wear, threw the coats to one side while Manius nocked and shot.

Arrows flew back. Drust saw Praeclarum, frighteningly naked it seemed to him, bound after Dog with Mule at her back, then remembered the prize they had. He turned, found Kisa and the Empress.

'Watch her,' he ordered, and the little Jew nodded so furiously it seemed his head would come off, relieved that he did not have to go further.

Drust took a breath, then another. He saw Manius shoot his last arrow, lay the bow carefully down and haul out two *sicarii*, the curved daggers he preferred. He grinned at Drust, his teeth bloody from his chewing-drug and his eyes glittering.

349

'I did not kill Sib,' he said, his voice trailing after him like a dark cloud as he leaped forward. Drust heard the clatters and shouts, cursed the whole business and ran in to find Praeclarum, which seemed the only important part of the entire affair. Yet he also cursed her fearlessness, pulled down the silver mask on his face and followed her.

The enemy, who were leaderless since the attack by the tiger, were now being attacked by horrors out of the mountain who seemed to have command of the great white beast. They had seen their commander's head torn off, had witnessed their comrades clawed and chewed. There was nothing left but the desperation of rats with nowhere left to go.

The man was just opening his mouth to scream when Drust rammed the *gladius* through the side of his cheek, then wrenched it free in a spume of blood in time to block a blow from a longsword; the bell-ring of it seemed to buzz his head under his helmet.

The second blow he ducked, shrugging so that it screeched off the scale armour, harmlessly vanishing over his shoulder. Someone grabbed at him and Drust smashed the man's nose with the pommel of the sword, rammed it into the blood-soaked beard, then stuck the point into his throat. Did it again. And again...

They were everywhere, flitting like shrieking shadows back and forth across the holes of his face mask. His world was lurching figures and flashing blades, screams and bellows that drowned his ears. He blocked and chopped and staggered and had no idea whether he was effective or flailing like a tiro. He saw shards of it – a blow which stripped little armoured leaves off like a blizzard of dull-iron snow. Another which spurted up dust from in between the scales, as if he was beating a carpet.

A blow made his helmet ring, dropped him to his knees. Another slammed into the face mask and skewed it off the hinge, so that he could see nothing at all. In desperation he wrenched it up, gasping at the sudden flood of noise and light.

The man who had smacked him had a young face, streaked with blood and sweat and burning with feverish fear. He had his longsword up for a third blow when he arched, screamed so loud Drust thought his head would burst; Manius tore both daggers from the man's neck and kicked him sideways, grinning with his mouth all wet and his eyes black as pits.

Praeclarum appeared, flitting like a wraith, slipping one way, dropping a shoulder to let a sword hiss with frustration over it. She stabbed and cut and vanished into the shroud of dust and misted blood.

Drust got to his feet, lurched forward a step or two, then tried to haul the lopsided ruin of face mask off the helmet, but couldn't do it. He fumbled at the buckle under his chin, almost cutting his nose off with his own sword, then gave up when he saw men come at him again.

It became a charnel house of hacking, stabbing, screaming. This is what we are, Drust thought dully with the part of him still outside the cave of his head. This is everything we are, for all we try and pretend to be more, to be better.

He lost the *gladius* in a face – always the face, the armour won't let you shove a point in – when the owner of it jerked and writhed, tearing the hilt from Drust's fist. He looked like Kag, and for a moment Drust stopped in his tracks, panicked that he had killed his best friend. Then he pounced on a discarded longsword, broken off a third of the way along and now a shard of steel with a vicious needle point.

There was a horse. Suddenly, out of the confused morass, there was a horse. They are trying to escape, Drust thought –

he may even have yelled it – but the idea of that roared through him like a fire. No one gets away. If they do, we will have them back at us again and again and again…

The horseman was in his element. This is what they were, these silly silver-masked fighters. They shot arrows until men fled, then rode them down, slicing them from the saddle with their longswords. They only ever put those masks down over their faces when they have no fighting to do, he thought…

The horse itself was a weapon – Manius was caught by the spinning hind end and sent flying. Mule tried to dart in and was caught by a rearing hoof, a smack right in the face; Drust saw him go down and then lost sight of him.

'Kill it,' someone yelled, and Ugo stepped up and axed the horse in the neck, chopping part-way through so that it squealed once and the head flopped. The man riding it had a face like something from an Atellan farce as the beast collapsed under him; he shrieked as it ground his leg in a spasm of dying, then Ugo carefully avoided the flailing hooves and brought the axe down on his middle.

There were no figures left. Drust looked, head swinging like a tired bull, but all he saw was Brothers – Dog, moving like a vengeance of steel from body to moaning crawler, his swords rising and stabbing. Kag and Quintus were bent, hands on knees, gasping for breath. Manius was moving in unsteady circles, seemed to be laughing maniacally – then he found his bow and took it up as if it was a child.

Praeclarum loomed. She was bloody and holding herself tilted, so that Drust's heart leaped like a trapped bird at the frightening possibilities.

'Cut my chest,' she said and showed him where the leather was neatly slashed and bloodied. 'Not that I had much to begin with, so that was rude.'

Dog laughed, hearing this. They all did. Laughed like wolves howl, for the kills, for having survived it and, in the end, for having recovered horses and supplies and even gold.

'They got paid in advance for capturing an Empress and killing us,' Kag declared, holding up a purse. 'I don't mind kissing the head of this new Sasan king.'

He did so, then flung the coin away from him, which astonished everyone else. 'To Fortuna,' he declared, and Dog, follower of the Sun God, paused from looting a corpse.

'Every whore needs paying,' he said boldly – but Drust saw him touch his Sun God amulet.

'Mule will be delighted,' Quintus said, then realised why he wasn't.

Fortuna had taken her price already. It lay in a heap with its head smashed in by a steel-shod hoof. Mule's mother would not know him, Drust thought, but he said nothing.

No one was untouched and they spent a long while binding and stitching before they even got down to dragging Mule into a shallow scoop of grave, piling rocks over him.

They stood for a moment, a small ragged band, bruised and bloodied and still with a long way to go. No one now had doubts they would make it, all the same.

Kisa came up, helping the stumbling Empress, who squatted like some pleb in a hut when she stopped moving. Kisa looked round at the carnage, at the grave, and then at everyone else until he had worked out who had died. He nodded, as if it had fulfilled some prophecy only he had known about.

'Where were you?' Dog demanded harshly. Kisa blinked back at him, then looked at Drust.

'I was told to guard the woman. With my life.'

Dog laughed. Drust laid a hand on Kisa's shoulder, but was looking at Dog when he spoke.

'So you did. Look at the prize, brothers. This is what we came all this way for – well, this and Manius and Dog, who begged for help.'

Dog dropped his eyes and then acknowledged the truth with a flap of one hand. Drust felt through his very pores the shifting change of the moment. When Praeclarum came and leaned against him, so that he put one arm round her, no one sniggered or made a ribald comment.

They had faced down the possibility of the last taste of wine, the last feeling of blood surging in their veins, and remembered the strength of it and that it was in the others, which made their own strength greater still.

They knew each other and the last days had been an urgency, like lust, to know each other as they had before; it was impossible but they had managed it and nothing would be the same ever again because of it.

'That's the way,' Drust said, pointing to the far horizon. They climbed on their plundered horses and rode away from the Red Serpent.

Rome – Six Months Later

The wedding party came down from the High Footpath on the Quirinal, a trail of well-dressed, happy people that those watching smiled at – briefly. Then they realised that they were all bruisers, men nicked and pocked and blotched – one had his face covered and even the most charitable of the passers-by muttered about leprosy.

The others in the wedding party were clearly gladiators, but it was hard to tell who was slave and who master. The groom, they decided, because he was the least offensive, but his wife had a simply stunning smile under her demure head-covering – until people realised it was false, a cunning contrivance made from pearls. Expensive, certainly, but still…

'So that's where your money went,' Quintus joked when they'd met at the feast. Praeclarum, beaming, had told him she could not eat with it, but it improved her bridal looks no end and everyone agreed with that. The Vestal Empress had been a richer prize than anyone had realised, but no one knew who had done the paying – the boy-emperor, her family, the College of Pontiffs? Perhaps even the Vestal priestesses themselves – Drust would not discount that one.

Dog kept his face covered, no one got so drunk they couldn't climb up the Quirinal to rub the fingers of old Theogenes, and most of them still retained a semblance of the decent clothes they had bought to make them presentable in Rome.

'What next, now that you are a married man?' Kag asked tentatively as they made their way back down into the Wolf's Den, where a clothing slip that revealed they carried lethal hidden blades would not bring a wrath of Vigiles. 'Chestnut farm in Abruzzo? Freight hauling for Papus the potter?'

'Can you see Praeclarum picking chestnuts?'

Kag laughed, then stroked his neatly trimmed beard. 'Well, the money we got for an Empress won't last much longer.'

Drust did not want to think of it, not because of the money but because of the Empress who had earned it for them. She had been in Rome for twenty-one days, with no word on her fate.

'I had Kisa set up a meeting with Audens,' Drust said quietly.

'At the Ludus Magnus? Is he still alive?'

Drust nodded. Not only was Cascus Minicius Audens alive, but he was looking for experienced beast-hunters to go north, up to the border walls in Raetia and Pannonia and beyond.

'In search of what?'

'Wolves, bears, anything we can get for the Flavian,' Drust retorted blankly. 'Death goes on…'

He turned as Praeclarum came up; she had lost her smile and he knew she had overheard.

'I meant to tell you…' he began, but she waved it away.

'Oh, I know of that – Kisa told me long since. Good idea.'

'Then why do you have your teeth in a pouch?' Kag asked. 'I like it when you smile.'

She looked out towards the roofs and the buildings, as if she could pierce the walls with her eyes.

'They blew horns on the Campus Sceleratus an hour ago,' Praeclarum said and turned blank eyes on him. 'Just as we said our vows.'

The Campus Sceleratus – the Evil Field – had a pit with a ladder down into it. The Empress would have been led down then left with some water and a loaf; the horn sounded when she was sealed in.

Now life would go on above as if she still lived. Her family could claim she had last been seen alive and with food and water. No blood was spilled, but the goddess was appeased and justice done, while the State had sealed the lips of a traitoress.

Kag muttered a prayer and Praeclarum held Drust by the hand as they turned into the dim tunnel of ramshackle tenements that was the Wolf's Den, where Dog unpeeled his head-covering and made sure the hilt of his *gladius* was now clearly seen.

They swaggered into the smoked, noisy dim, fearing nothing but the memory of a ravaged blind woman sitting in the dark waiting to die.

It would follow them like a silent, white wraith, padding all the way to the dark forests of Rhaetia and beyond the Wall.

Author's Note

In AD 224, the year this novel is set, the Emperor Alexander
Severus (or Severus Alexander, depending on your historical
preference) was seventeen years old and into his second year
as sole ruler of the largest empire on the planet at the time.
He was the heir to his cousin, the nineteen-year-old Emperor
Elagabalus, who had been murdered along with his mother Julia
Soaemias by his own guards.

Elagabalus and his cousin Alexander were both grandsons
of the influential and powerful Julia Maesa, one of the coterie
of Julias surrounding the throne. Julia Maesa had arranged for
Alexander to claim the throne and made sure Elagabalus and
his mother died.

Two years later, Alexander's reign seemed prosperous – the
Roman successes against the Parthians had weakened their old
adversaries to the point where civil war had broken out and
this very year the House of Sasan inflicted a crushing defeat
on the Parthian king, killing him in the field. But Ardashir still
had a great deal to do before the rule of the House of Sasan
was secure and the Sasanian dynasty took over the old Parthian
Empire. It was time the Romans could use to their advantage.

Except they didn't. The Roman military was becoming
increasingly undisciplined – desertions were rising, dissent and
revolts growing. There were clashes between the people of
Rome and the Praetorian Guard, leading to the death of two
commanders, Julius Flavianus and Gerinius Chrestus – both

killed on the orders of the Praetorian Prefect, Ulpian. The Praetorian Guard reacted, pursuing and killing Ulpian – who was a lawyer, not a soldier – in the imperial palace, in front of the boy-emperor. His assassin, Marcus Aurelius Epagothus, was 'rewarded' with the governorship of Egypt (Alexander and his mother were 'persuaded' to make the appointment), but he too would later be assassinated.

It is into this feverish hotbed that Drust and company arrive, looking – at first sight – to rescue two of their own from beyond the Red Serpent, a huge defensive wall across a geographic narrowing between the Caspian Sea and the mountains of north-eastern Iran.

It is one of the most ambitious and sophisticated frontier walls ever built and archaeologists and historians are still arguing as to whether it was constructed by the Achmaenid Persians, Alexander the Great or the Sasanids. The truth is probably all three, though the last rebuilt and re-faced a lot of it using thousands and thousands of locally made bricks, whose firing turned them the colour of old blood – hence its name, the Red Serpent. It is 195 km (121 miles) long and 6 - 10 m (20 - 33 ft) wide, with more than 30 forts spaced at intervals of between 10 and 50 km (6.2 and 31.1 miles). It is surpassed only by the Great Wall of China as the longest defensive wall in existence.

Elagabalus, that ill-fated boy rumoured to be the son of the equally ill-fated Caracalla, really did marry a Vestal – and, after being forced to divorce her, went back to living with her once he had been 'properly' remarried. This was one of the many scandals which astounded conventional Rome – some historians want us to believe that Rome was outraged by the fact that the Severan dynasty was darker-skinned than any previous and would like us to believe in a Roman racism. Too many histories make mention of 'the first black Emperor of Rome'.

The truth is more that the Severans came from North Africa, bringing that slightly exotic lick of Africa that had little to do with skin colour and everything to do with culture. That was coupled with Severan marriage into the Bassiani family from Emesa, Syria, an even more exotic family of eastern priests of the Temple of the Sun.

There is no record of what happened to Julia Aquilia (later Severa), the Vestal virgin who became an Empress. Some sources state that she was forced into the marriage. It is claimed by some historians, however, that many stories about Elagabalus have been exaggerated by his enemies, and so there is no certainty about what actually happened. Elagabalus also had relationships with men, and the historian Cassius Dio claims that Elagabalus had a more stable relationship with his chariot driver Hierocles than with any of his wives.

There really is a secret name for Rome – legend has it that Romulus shrouded the true name of the city he founded in mystery so that its enemies would be unable to bring curses upon it, and 'Roma' is simply a construction to enable public discourse. Consequently, it is a great sacrilege to speak the real name of Rome – and, yes, Valerius Soranus was crucified in Sicily allegedly for blabbing it. I have no idea if the Vestals knew the secret name, but the Pontifex Maximus, the Chief Priest of Rome, reportedly did.

Less than a dozen years after the events here, Alexander Severus would suffer the same fate as his cousin, plunging the world into what historians call 'The Crisis of Empire', fifty years of rebellion, barbarian invasions and military breakdown. There were some twenty-six claimants to the title of emperor in that time, mostly generals who assumed imperial power over all or part of the Empire. These included a certain Uranius, whose history is clouded, and Maximinus Thrax, whose history is not.

The giant soldier became Emperor in AD 235 and ruled for three years until murdered and beheaded by the soldiers of his own 2nd Parthica legion.

This is the atmosphere, the trickle-down of plot and politics, through which move the lowly, down-at-heel Brothers of the Sands, socially reviled as ex-gladiators and ex-slaves. Their attempts to make a sestertius by whatever means possible while staying alive to enjoy it is what most of the rest of the Roman world were trying to do while Emperors and generals squabbled.

Their story is worth hearing, in the flickering shadows made by a guttering lamp in a ramshackle tenement in Subura – but failing that, read it anyway.

Acknowledgements

The people without whom…

Kate, my long-suffering wife, the bedrock, lodestar and frequently abandoned woman who puts up with me living in some strange century with stranger people for protracted periods. If it is a lonely life being an author, it is worse still to be an author's wife.

James Gill of United Agents, a loyal and determined friend who has been instrumental in getting what I write to the right people for more years than I like to remember.

The good and professional people at Canelo – Kit, Michael and others. You know who you are.

The loyal fans of my writing out there. More power to you and I hope you enjoy this new direction.

Glossary

Mainly of gladiator and related terms you will find throughout the book. Most of them are easy to grasp without constant reference to this – but I know people love lists.

Atellan

Atellanae Fabulae or *Fabulae Atellanae*, also known as the Oscan Games, were masked improvised farces, short pieces usually put on after longer pantomimes. The origin of the Atellan Farce is uncertain but they are similar to other forms of ancient theatre, such as the South Italian Phlyakes, the plays of Plautusd and Terrence, and Roman mime. The farces were written in the Campanian dialect of Oscan and in later Roman versions, only the ridiculous characters read their lines in Oscan, while the others read in Latin.

Authentēs

A Greek term (αὐθέντης) – a bit of fawning with added barb. It can mean an absolute ruler, an autocrat, but also is applied to the perpetrator of any act, especially those who commit murder by their own hand.

Dis Manibus

A standard phrase of dedication to the Manes, the spirits of the dead. Effectively they are being warned that there's another one on the way. In the gladiatorial amphitheatre it was an actual person, also known as Charun, the Roman form of Charon, the Greek demi-god who ferried the dead across the Styx. Pluto, the Roman god of the underworld, was also used. A man traditionally masked as someone from the underworld, accompanied by other masked helpers, would stab the fallen to make sure they were dead and, if not, use a traditional hammer to finish them off. Then others would hook the body by the heels and drag if off through the Gate of Death. Those who had survived left the way they had entered, through the Gate of Life.

Dromedarii

Camel-mounted cavalry. *Dromedarii* were first raised by Trajan and used as border scouts in the desert provinces of the Eastern Empire to take the place of light cavalry in scorching desert conditions. Usually attached to a *cohors equitata*, between thirty-two and thirty-six dromedarii troopers are listed in the rosters of *Cohors XX Palmyrenorum Equitata* at Dura-Europos in the early third century.

Dura-Europos

Already famous by the time the Romans took it in AD 165, this became a vital fortress in the chain of defences designed to secure Mesopotamia – the same function it served for the Seleucids, successors of Alexander the Great, when they founded the city in 303 BC. It was, I have always imagined, the model for Mos Eisley in Star Wars – 'a wretched hive of scum and villainy' – though it was also one of the most multi-cultural. In the early 200s, the famed house-church and synagogue were built. There was also a Mithraeum, a Temple of Bel and a Temple of Adonis.

Flavian

Now better known as the Coliseum, it was originally known as the Flavian Amphitheatre since it was built by the Flavian dynasty. Commissioned in AD 72 by Emperor Vespasian, it was completed by his son Titus in AD 80, with later improvements by Domitian. Located just east of the Forum, it was built to a practical design, with its 80 arched entrances allowing easy access for 55,000 spectators, who were seated according to rank. The Coliseum is huge, an ellipse 188 m long and 156 m wide. Originally 240 masts were attached to stone corbels on the fourth level to provide shade on hot days. It was called the Coliseum because of a massive statue of Nero which stood nearby – later remodelled into the god Helios or Sol, and at times the heads of succeeding emperors.

Fortuna

A goddess who was the personification of luck in Roman times and, naturally, one much worshipped by gladiators. She was usually depicted with a *rota fortunae* (a Wheel of Fortune) and a Horn of Plenty, and could be represented as veiled and blind, as in modern depictions of Justice. The first temple dedicated to Fortuna was attributed to the Etruscan Servius Tullius, while the second is known to have been built in 293 BC as the fulfilment of a Roman promise made during later Etruscan wars – which is also the same time as gladiatorial contests are thought to have been created.

Harena

Literally, 'sand'. Possibly Etruscan, which was believed to be the origin of gladiatorial contests.

Hyrcanian tiger

The big cat was already a rarity in the late Roman era, but it survived until final sightings in the 1970s. It was once as widespread as the area east of the Caspian Sea, from Turkey and Iran through Central Asia into the Takla Makan desert of Xinjiang, China. It was one of the largest living felines and ranked among the biggest that ever existed.

Ludus

The gladiator 'school'. It's estimated that there were more than a hundred gladiator schools throughout the Empire. New gladiators were formed into troupes called *familia gladiatorium*, which were under the overall control of a manager (*lanista*) who recruited, arranged for training and made the decisions of where and when the gladiators fought. There were gladiator schools near all the major cities around Rome, and one which has stayed in history is that of Batiatus in Capua, where Spartacus was trained. But the most famous gladiator schools of all were those in Rome: the Great Gladiatorial Training School (*Ludus Magnus*), which was connected to the Flavian Amphitheatre by a tunnel; the Bestiaries School (*Ludus Matutinus*), which specialised in training those who fought, handled and trained the exotic wild beasts; the Gallic School (*Ludus Gallicus*), smallest of the schools, which specialised in training heavily armoured fighters; and the Dacian School (*Ludus Dacicus*), which trained lightly armoured fighters in the use of the *sicari* dagger, a short curved weapon.

Ludum venatorium (venatio)

In the animal hunts, *venatores* were skilled men usually pitted against carnivorous beasts; *bestiarii* were animal handlers and killers of less skill and finesse. Literary accounts and inscriptions often stress the numbers of animals killed. As in gladiatorial combat, men condemned to fight or perform in such games could sometimes win their freedom. By the third century the games had degenerated into vicious spectacle, with such crowd-pleasers as children hung up by the heels to see which of the starving dogs could leap high enough to get a bite, foxes let loose with their tails on fire, and worse.

Mavro

A Greek word meaning 'black' or 'dark'. When applied to people, it is simply a statement of fact – it is neither derogatory nor insensitive. However, in the third century, the Severan dynasty who hailed from North Africa were considered strange and exotic, not for their skin-tone, but for their cultural heritage, exacerbated by marriage into an even more exotic Syrian family of sun worshippers. 'Mavro' gained a note of disdain as a result.

Missio

A gladiator who acknowledged defeat could request the *munerarius* to stop the fight and send him alive (*missus*) from the arena. If he had not fallen he could be 'sent away standing' (*stans missus*). The Exhibitor took the crowd's response into consideration in deciding whether to let the loser live or order the victor to kill him.

Munus (plural munera)

Meaning 'the show', the term also has a connotation of 'duty'. It usually lasted for three or more days and, under special circumstances, for weeks or months. Provincial games rarely lasted more than two days, but Titus's games in Rome for the inauguration of the completed Flavian in AD 80 lasted 100 days. The classic Italian *munus plena* included *venations* in the morning, various noontime activities (*meridiani*), and gladiatorial duels in the afternoon.

Munerarius (Exhibitor)

The giver of the games. It could be a member of the nobler orders of Rome who put on the show privately (a rarity post-Republic) or in his official capacity as a magistrate or priest, but it was more likely the State organising games whose dates and functions were set in the Roman calendar. Outside Rome, *munerarii* were generally municipal and provincial priests of the imperial cult, or local governors.

Omnes ad stercus

Not strictly a gladiatorial term, but certainly used by them and liberally scrawled on walls all over Rome. Best translation is 'it's all shit', but 'we're in the shit' can also be used, depending on context. It is not, as internet translations coyly have it, 'get lost' or 'go to hell'.

Pompa

The parade that signalled the start of a gladiatorial *munus*; it included the *munerarius*, usually in some outlandish costume and carriage, the gladiators, musicians, a palm-bearer, and various other officials and personnel, such as a sign-bearer whose placard gave the crowd information about events, particpants and other matters, including the Emperor's response to petitions.

Palmyra

Documents mention the city in the second millennium BC, and by the third century it was the pre-eminent trade point for caravans travelling up and down the Silk Road and a city-state not dominated by Rome. The city's social structure was tribal, and its inhabitants spoke Palmyrene, a dialect of Aramaic, using Greek for diplomacy and commerce. It reached the apex of its power in the 260s, when the Palmyrene King Odaenathus defeated Sasanid Emperor Shapur. The king was succeeded by his wife, Queen Zenobia, acting as regent for their son. She rebelled against Rome and established the Palmyrene Empire.

Pollice verso

'With thumb turned'. Much debated signal, though most assume the thumb is turned down if a gladiator is to die. There are accounts of it being passed across the throat, turned to the heart, and so on.

Pugnare ad digitum

To 'fight to the finger'. Combat took place until the referee stopped the fight or the defeated gladiator raised his finger (or his hand or whole arm) to signal the *munerarius* to stop the fight.

Recipere ferrum

To receive the iron. A defeated gladiator who was refused *missio* was expected to kneel and courageously accept death. His victorious opponent would stab him or cut his throat. The referee made sure it was done properly and swiftly.

Sine missione

Without *missio*, a fight with no possibility of a reprieve for the loser. Rare.

Six

Number tagged against a fighter's name in the Ludus he was part of when he had died. Origin unknown – but to be 'sixed' means you are a dead man.

Stantes missi

A draw, with both 'sent away standing'. Both gladiators walked away, neither having won nor lost.

The Ludi

Games in general, and festivals involving games. Games could be private, public or extraordinary – since gladiators were so expensive to train and keep, they fought three or four times a year and, unless the giver of the Games – the *Munerius* – paid for it, there was no fight to the death. Contests were, in fact, one-on-one and regulated by a referee, usually a former gladiator. Criminals and prisoners could be damned to fight in the arena, with the hope of a reprieve if they survived a certain number of years. These men were trained in a specialised form of combat. Others, untrained, were expected to die within a short time. There were also volunteer gladiators, ones who either enlisted voluntarily as free or freed men, or who re-enlisted after winning their freedom. Even equites and, more rarely, senators sometimes enlisted. The word 'gladiator' simply means 'swordsman'.

The Mountain Jews

The Mountain Jews, or Jews of the Caucasus, have inhabited the region since the fifth century AD. Being the descendants of the Persian Jews of Iran, their migration from Persia proper to the Caucasus took place in the time this book is set, but it is believed that they had arrived in Persia, from Ancient Israel, as early as the eighth century BC.

The City of Sharp-Nosed Fish

A translation of Oxyrhynchos, which was a town south of Cairo now ennobled by its waste paper. The total lack of rain in this part of Egypt had preserved the papyrus beneath the sand, as nowhere else in the Roman Empire. This is where you hear the voices of the workers and traders set against the great events in the rise and fall of the Roman Empire and the coming of Christianity. If you never read anything else about Roman history, find *City of the Sharp-Nosed Fish* by Peter Parsons.

The Gladiators

Eques

A gladiator who fought on horseback, like a Roman knight, against other mounted fighters. An *eques* carried a spear, but also used a sword, so he could dismount to duel with an opponent. His helmet often displayed two feathers on either side of the dome (with no crest).

Essedarius

A chariot-fighter who probably dismounted to fight hand to hand.

Familia gladiatorium

A troupe of gladiators who lived and trained under one *lanista*.

Gallus

A Gaul, a type of heavily armed fighter named after the Romans' tribal enemy. The original *Galli* were probably war captives. This type of fighter died out in the Empire.

Hoplomachus

This gladiator was distinguished by his short, curved sword. Like a *Thrax*, he wore high leg guards.

Lanista

An owner, recruiter, trainer, and speculator in gladiators who sold or rented men to *munerarii*. In the Empire this job came under the jurisdiction of the Emperor.

Liberatio

The freeing of a gladiator who had served his time (a period of years varying according to when and how he was inducted).

Manica

Arm padding of wrapped cloth and leather.

Murmillo

A fighter apparently named after a Greek word for fish. He wore a crested helmet and carried a tall shield.

Retiarius

This was the most distinctive-looking gladiator, a bare-headed, unshielded fighter whose main protection was padding and a shoulder guard on his left arm. He used a net to ensnare his opponent and a long trident to impale him.

Rudiarius

A gladiator who had received a *rudis* – the wooden sword that marked him as retired and no longer a slave – was an experienced volunteer, especially worth watching. There was a hierarchy of experienced *rudiarii* within a *familia* of gladiators, and *rudiarii* could become trainers, helpers, and arbiters of fights, the referees. The most elite of the retired gladiators were dubbed *summa rudis*. The *summa rudis* officials wore white tunics with purple borders and served as technical experts to ensure that the gladiators fought bravely, skilfully, and according to the rules. They carried batons and whips with which they pointed out illegal movements. Ultimately the *summa rudis* officials could stop a game if a gladiator was going to be too seriously wounded, compel gladiators to fight on, or defer the decision to the Exhibitor. Retired gladiators who became *summa rudis* achieved fame and wealth in their second careers as officials of the combats.

Samnis

Like the *Gallus*, the *Samnis* (Samnite) was originally an enemy of the Romans, from Campania in the south. Captives taken in battle in the Republic undoubtedly provided the model for this type of heavily armed fighter.

Secutor

The 'follower' was paired with a *retiarius*. His armour was distinguished by a helmet with small eyeholes that would presumably impede the trident's prongs.

Thrax

The Thracian was another type of fighter equipped like a former enemy soldier (from Thrace in northern Greece). He fought with a small rectangular shield and his helmet bore a griffin crest.

Tiro

A gladiator fighting in his very first public combat.

Venator

Venatores were skilled spearmen, usually pitted against carnivorous beasts.

Veteranus

A veteran of one or more combats.

Fascia

A band of cloth or leather that protected the leg below the knee and provided padding beneath a greave.

Fascina (or *tridens*)

The long, three-pronged metal trident that was the hallmark of a *retiarius*.

Galea

The helmet worn by all gladiators except the *retiarius*. These were domed and often featured decorative crests and visors pierced with eyeholes.

Galerus

The distinctive metal shoulder guard of a *retiarius*. It curved up strongly from the shoulder, away from the neck, so that neck and head were protected but the fighter's head movements were not restricted.

Gladius

This was the straight stabbing sword of the gladiator after which he was named.

Ocrea

A metal leg guard that ran from the knee (or above) to the shin and protected mainly the front of the leg.

Parma

A round or square shield that was smaller and lighter than a *scutum*.

Pugio

A dagger, weapon of last resort of a *retiarius*.

Rudis

The wooden sword or staff symbolising a gladiator's *liberatio*.

Scutum

A large rectangular shield (curving inward so that it formed part of a cylinder) of the sort carried by a *murmillo*.

Subligaculum

A traditional loincloth worn by gladiators (the chest was almost always bare).

Brothers Of The Sands

Beasts Beyond The Wall
The Red Serpent
Beasts From The Dark